SHORTLISTED FOR THE 20

'This book will crawl under your s!
NRC Handelsblau

'Baram's most fascinating and moving book…A beautiful
and wonderful novel.' *Haaretz*

'Skilfully, Baram plunges into the world in between:
between life and death, childhood, adolescence and adulthood,
between being a child and being a father, love and hate, day
and night, intoxication and sobriety.' *Aargauer Zeitung*

'Baram is the best writer in his generation with no comparison.'
A. B. Yehoshua

'Baram's novels have the flair, emotional depth and wealth of
ideas of the great 19th-century Russian authors. A complex, deeply
felt but never sentimental bildungsroman…A wonderful tribute
to people dearest to him.' *De Tijd*

'A spectacular accomplishment by one of the most
wonderful Hebrew writers.' *Israel Today*

'The combination of honesty and lies, which the novel adapts
from the tragic pact between the two boys, allows the words
to accrue, to turn into pictures and scenes, into fine prose.'
Yedioth Ahronoth

'Virtuosic.' *Walla!*

'A rare book in Israel's literary landscape…Depicts the past in
the most profound way without a shred of romanticising.' *Maariv*

'One of the most beautiful bildungsroman books I have read.
A novel about a profound and moving friendship, about pain
and about life…Rush out to read it.' *Saloona*

Praise for Good People

'The novel is written with great talent, momentum and ingenuity…
It expands the borders of literature to reveal new landscapes.'
Amos Oz

'Quite possibly, Dostoyevsky would write like this if he
lived in Israel today.' *Frankfurter Allgemeine Zeitung*

'*Good People* is a masterful metaphysical novel written
by a true artist.' *Livres Hebdo*

'One of the most intriguing writers in Israeli literature today.'
Haaretz

'[Baram] asks what kind of people would choose to serve…empires
of falsehood with their eyes open and their minds sharp. Not
monsters or even cynics, he answers in a pacey, plot-heavy novel
of dramatic events and big ideas, but gifted storytellers fuelled
by ordinary motives of love, loyalty or ambition.' *Economist*

'Baram uses intense geographical plotting and is chillingly
eloquent…[*Good People*] is tremendous. I read it in two sittings
and I learned a lot. How does a man in his early 30s know
how to write like this?' *Australian*

'*Good People* is a richly textured panorama of German and
Russian life…This ample novel lives most memorably through
Baram's vignettes of people, dwellings, cities, landscapes and
the like that seem to lie, at times, at the periphery of its
central concerns.' *Sydney Morning Herald*

'Chillingly captures the terrors and tensions of life under Stalin and
Hitler. The chapters set in Russia are particularly effective, carrying
the suspense of a spy thriller. Nir Baram explores the frightening
speed and ease with which ordinary people become functionaries
in totalitarian societies.' *Times Literary Supplement*

NIR BARAM was born into a political family in Jerusalem in 1976. His grandfather and father were both ministers in Israeli Labor Party governments. He has worked as a journalist and an editor, and as an advocate for equal rights for Palestinians. He began publishing fiction when he was twenty-two, and is the author of five novels, including *The Remaker of Dreams* and *World Shadow*. His novels have been translated into more than ten languages and received critical acclaim around the world. He has been shortlisted several times for the Sapir Prize and in 2010 received the Prime Minister's Award for Hebrew Literature.

JESSICA COHEN is a British-Israeli-American translator. She shared the 2017 Man Booker International Prize for translating David Grossman's 2014 novel, *A Horse Walks into a Bar*.

NIR BARAM

AT NIGHT'S END

TRANSLATED FROM THE
HEBREW BY JESSICA COHEN

TEXT PUBLISHING MELBOURNE AUSTRALIA

textpublishing.com.au

The Text Publishing Company
Swann House, 22 William Street, Melbourne Victoria 3000, Australia

The Text Publishing Company (UK) Ltd
130 Wood Street, London EC2V 6DL, United Kingdom

First published as *Yekitzah* in Israel by Am Oved, 2018
Published by The Text Publishing Company, 2020

Book design by Text
Cover art by David Baker
Typeset by J&M Typesetting

Printed and bound in Australia by Griffin Press, part of Ovato, an accredited ISO/NZS 14001:2004 Environmental Management System printer.

ISBN: 9781922330178 (paperback)
ISBN: 9781925923612 (ebook)

A catalogue record for this book is available from the National Library of Australia.

In Memory of Uri

PART ONE

He rolled over on the wide bed, layers of sheets swaddling his shoulders, rib cage, knees and feet, until he imagined that he was unable to move a single muscle. When he wanted to touch his face, to recall how it felt, he could not disentangle his hands from the mess of snarled fabric. He looked at the sheer black curtains as if to find out whether it was day or night. He remembered seeing grains of light crawling along the floor, quivering golden stripes on the wall, flickers of sunlight, car headlamps, skyscraper lights. The bed was littered with pens, brochures, a bowl and two coffee cups, the sheets stained with ink spots, dribbles of pale-yellow soup, saliva, chocolate crumbs, and a few splotches that prompted memories of a blackish-purple sauce on some sort of meat. Occasionally, he would encounter his own smiling face in a brochure's old black-and-white photograph: his stern eyes looked straight at the camera, but his lips curled into a secretive smile that could be read as either sly or scornful. Catalog designers liked the commanding youth-fulness of that picture and, whenever he thought of sending a newer one, he always changed his mind; most people would not see him in real life anyway, and it was better for them to perceive him as the enviably fresh-faced man in monochrome. At times he felt that the photograph grounded him, attesting to the continual existence of his body when all other certainties had vanished.

He wasn't sure how long he'd been there, how many days he'd spent flitting between sleep and wakefulness through the disoriented twilight, seeing nothing lucid either in his dreams or his waking state. Nebulous figures and events burst into his consciousness every so often, shifting around in an all-encompassing white glare. He felt onsets of hunger, thirst and nausea, but they faded, as though a Ferris wheel of sensations were spinning before his eyes, and with each rotation a different impression glowed up high and then moved away, leaving behind a vanishing pallid trail.

The festival was over and all the guests—the writers, editors, journalists and publicists—had left the hotel, and probably the city. Yonatan always braced himself for the moment when the hubbub would dissipate, and tracked the stages of dissolution: first the people disappeared, then the posters in the square, the barricades, the lights, the volunteers with their courteous smiles. The cocktail bars and restaurants all emptied out, leaving behind a place that no longer existed. Sometimes he wondered why the other writers accepted the desertion with such equanimity, while he kept revisiting the sites where the festival had bustled, mourning the departed days. There were times when he tried to share his bereavement with other guests, but he was always misunderstood. They would reassure him that there would be other festivals in other cities, or this festival exactly a year from now, and they could not understand his sadness. He did acknowledge the passing of time, which must leave every event in the past, but a piece of him was also reluctantly left behind: something that had ended lived on in his mind.

He remembered one particular night, perhaps the last one before he crashed in the hotel room. He'd arrived at a party in someone's apartment and found four people he didn't know dancing in the living room. He stood watching them and they were beautiful. A pregnant woman put one hand on her belly as she danced, and with the other waved a plastic candle with a flickering orange-red flame. They all greeted him warmly but took no real interest. He drank some vodka and looked around for Carlos, who'd invited him to the party. He was surprised that no one asked who he was. He sat down on the cold floor. A breeze chilled his skin and he tightened his red wool scarf around his neck and stared at a string of colored lights hanging from the ceiling and a moth that fluttered around him. He might have dozed off: he remembered nothing else from the apartment.

Then he was in a crowded nightclub where local music blared, and like everyone else he bought a large bottle of tequila and stood on the dance floor taking sips. Other men and women occasionally wandered over and took a swig from his bottle, then passed it around, and a while later it would be handed back to him. He felt a dull pain in his knees and his back; it had been bothering him for the past year, along with a recurrent spasm in his ribs, and recently he'd become aware of the effort required to stand after lying down or sitting. Every day there were new aches and pains. Sometimes he imagined he was dispatching an eye into his body, where it saw his liver, heart, lungs, and kidneys the color of cigarette ash, and all his organs were writhing.

A black-haired young woman took his bottle and playfully ran her damp fingers over his forehead. Then she poured a little tequila into her palm and he closed his eyes and drank from her hand, and she put her wet finger on his tongue and he licked the tequila and tasted her skin, and then she smiled and pressed up against him and took her finger out of his mouth and slid it over his face, and he put his hand on her hip and they danced together and he smelled perfume, ketchup and sand, but when he opened his eyes she had vanished into the crowd with the bottle. He felt uplifted, perhaps finally roused from a slumber by the realization that he was fully there, taking in breaths, he hadn't crashed as he'd feared he might, he'd clung to life and could now see the possibilities alive in the people around him—their touch, the warmth of their bodies. Perhaps touch was what melted away loneliness and all the rest was meaningless, he mused; his eyes opened up to the women, to their faces and breasts and bare legs, to the sweat glistening on their smooth shoulders, to the lightness of their movements while they danced and twirled their hands in the air, caressed their hips, hugged their chests. He looked for the girl he had danced with— had he only imagined that she'd been barefoot?

He elbowed his way through the crowd, hurried to the bar, bought another big bottle, took a few sips and the bottle disappeared again. Then Carlos was standing next to him, and they went out into a courtyard where a group of people stood around a stall, gobbling hot dogs. He could smell mustard and ketchup, and Carlos was talking about an investigation into the disappearance of a group of students, which he was conducting for the government. Carlos held out a tiny bottle and a pen knife. Yonatan carefully tipped a bit of powder onto the silver blade and put it up to his nose, and he snorted it and poured a thicker line and snorted that one too, and when he gave the bottle back to Carlos he wished he'd done another line. Then it got even more crowded and he pushed his way around, losing sight of Carlos and the faces he remembered from the apartment.

A heavyset young woman with glasses hugged him—she looked familiar from an earlier moment that evening, or from the festival—and said she was really sorry. Then he remembered some lines he'd written when he was younger: "We studied death. Not the death that is not ours—we have no interest in that, we are not philosophers." It was a passage he repeated in every book he wrote, a talisman that protected him or reminded him of the genesis of things, and he knew that he had to wake up the person who had been dozing in his body for years. People around him always seemed to have a more clearly defined personality than his, conducting themselves according to procedures and obligations, constraints and rules, as though it were obvious to them what sort of people they were or at least what they could and could not achieve. Whereas he believed that there was nothing in his mind that either precluded or mandated anything. His breath grew heavy, his knees spasmed, and the mass of laughing faces melded into a giant grin. He was tempted, not for the first time, to believe in a conciliatory moment that would grace the future. A surge of emotion from the present to the future—never to the past.

Then he was lying on a couch in a long, narrow living room that looked like a train car, gazing at a bar full of bottles and all sorts of pictures that sprayed colors into his eyes until he shut them and heard someone yelling that he was cold and then he realized it was him. They covered him in a warm knitted blanket that felt like the orange one he had at home, and as soon as his skin was warmed he let his body drop to the floor, although he couldn't say why—perhaps he wanted to feel pain. Someone who sounded like Carlos said something in Spanish, and he hoped Carlos was there, and then someone answered, and they spoke about Yonatan tenderly, as though he should be pitied. A few minutes later he was in total darkness, with his head resting on the lap of the young woman with glasses. He could hear her heart beating when she caressed his neck and his face, and the way she touched his skin was deep and strong and he felt protected. She told him that she hadn't understood before, and her feelings might have been a little hurt, but now she understood everything: his best friend had died.

At the hotel, in another moment of non-sleep, he saw her hovering in mid-air at the Bolivian restaurant, where the three separate rooms had walls that curved and bulged to depict the continents—America, Europe and Asia. He was in the Asia room, with its strange angles and protrusions. It was during the festival, and they were sitting at a long table with one of the city's big magazine publishers, who was also a part-owner of the restaurant. He was in his mid-sixties, with a fuzzy white beard that he occasionally tugged at while looking gloomy and bored. His small blue eyes, with no trace of any eyebrows, appraised the other diners with a look reserved for coats in a clothing store. Everyone spoke in a hushed, horrified tone that could not conceal their elation at being let in on an exhilarating secret: a year ago, the publisher had been kidnapped and held hostage in a dank, dark cellar, where he'd subsisted on bread, vegetables, water and the occasional cockroach or worm. They said he'd been forced to eat his own shoelaces and scarf—monogrammed with his wife's name in gold thread—and that he'd begged his tormenters to season these items with salt. After a month, horribly thin, he was released for a ransom (some said a million dollars, others five million). Even now, they whispered, his face looked skeletal, and he'd been melancholy ever since, which explained why he was so gaunt and seemed to take no pleasure in anything. Perhaps it was in the damp cellars of the world that he had come to understand that all his achievements, all the things he coveted, were trivial ephemera. The guests also wondered whether it was even possible to comprehend a man who walks out of a cellar after a daily threat of a bullet in his head.

Yonatan wondered if all these questions really had anything to do with the man sitting opposite him, because the publisher actually seemed to be enjoying the evening and relishing his freedom to express his contempt for his fellow diners—writers and intellectuals foremost among them. He recalled that Carlos didn't believe the man had been kidnapped at all. At most, he might have been held for a few hours, and the rest was just an exotic urban legend which the Mexicans from the publishing conglomerates told foreigners so they could sell them lousy narcoculture novels.

Toward the end of the evening, the magazine publisher sized Yonatan up and asked what his novel was about. Yonatan looked straight at him and replied, "I'll send it to you," adding nothing about the plot or the characters or the themes. But if he had assumed the publisher would appreciate not being bored with those details, he was soon disillusioned, because the man was clearly disappointed in a response that did not allow him to mock the weak plot and flat characters, or point out books Yonatan had probably been imitating. The publisher tugged at his beard and told him that the truly dangerous artists are the ones who lack talent but have creativity. After that, he did not say another word to him. Yonatan wasn't sure if the girl with glasses had anything to do with his memory of the restaurant, or if that evening was blending in with other episodes from his few days in the city.

He started extricating his body from the sheets. He counted at least four of them, all crumpled and damp with sweat, and tossed them on the floor. He now discovered that he was still wearing his shiny black pants and plaid sweater and gray socks, and that his black shoes, caked with mud, were cradled between his feet. He took off his clothes and stepped into the shower. The hot water sprayed off his body and started to form puddles on the floor. He emptied onto his body all the little bottles provided by the hotel, nauseous from the mixture of scents, and rinsed off. The scalding water on the back of his neck felt comforting. He stepped out of the shower and gazed at the widening puddles, which had already wet the feet of the bed. He grabbed a few towels of various sizes and spread them out on the floor, then bundled up the bedsheets and mopped the water creeping toward the walls. He went over to the window and looked through the curtains at the night sky above the city, dotted with flickering lights. Then he put on some of his less wrinkled clothes, debated whether to shave off the past few days' stubble, decided not to and left the room.

A hotel employee smiled at him when he stepped out of the elevator, and the two women at the front desk looked at him expectantly. Yonatan strode past them, walked through the revolving door, hailed a cab, and gave the driver the name of the restaurant; he remembered it clearly because it was also the name of his editor and of the magazine publisher's wife.

"He knows literary people make fun of him, that they think it's vulgar to name a restaurant after his wife, but he doesn't give a fuck," Carlos had told him. Carlos, who translated American poetry into Spanish, loathed the publisher because he had once asked him to edit a new English-language edition of the magazine. "A millionaire calls you up and says you're going to be a big-time editor, but you have to come up with half a million bucks. I've never seen such a crook."

Yonatan remembered a bubble of light, but as he walked up the gravel path, with flowerbeds of purple and yellow circling a lemon tree on either side, the lights dimmed. He looked through the restaurant windows and saw that all the tables were empty. Two waitresses in suits and bowties were still moving around inside. He rapped on the locked glass door. One of the waitresses came over: he remembered her, but she looked older now, the skin under her eyes more ashen, and her faded blonde hair, which had been tied back, fell untidily over her shoulders. She asked who he wanted, and he gave the publisher's name. She asked if he knew him, and he said, yes, they'd had dinner here two or three days earlier.

She scrutinized him with a strange look and said the publisher had been in Buenos Aires and had only returned last night, and Yonatan mumbled that they must have met the week before. She squinted at him, and her face looked crude, as though she was not in control of her range of expressions. They stood facing each other silently, until he turned and walked out through the garden. On the side street, two men wearing leather jackets stared at him, and he lowered his gaze. He felt strangely unafraid, even though he was usually careful, avoiding alleyways at night. Perhaps he was too careful sometimes.

He circled the restaurant until he came up against a barricade and a dirt lot where a couple of black cars were parked. Two men in filthy aprons dragged enormous trash bags out and tossed them into a dumpster at the edge of the lot. Yonatan watched them repeat the process again and again; the fourth time, one of the bags hit the side of the dumpster and fell to the ground. The kitchen workers glanced at it and went back into the restaurant. A couple of minutes went by. Yonatan squeezed through the barricade, went over to the trash bag, and picked it up—it wasn't especially heavy but reeked of eggs and onions. He bent his knees, hoisted the bag in the air and hurled it into the dumpster. He stood there for a minute, satisfied with how high he'd managed to aim. He heard a noise from behind, and when he spun around he saw one of the workers staring at him from the restaurant doorway, cigarette in hand. Yonatan nodded at him and gave a friendly smile. The worker smoked his cigarette with great concentration and kept his eyes on him.

A light went on in the second-story window, and when he looked up he saw the top portion of a bookcase that almost touched the ceiling, lined with large books like the ones you might find in a museum or library. The kitchen worker crushed out his cigarette and came closer. For a second Yonatan considered running to the main street, but that seemed cowardly, and he wondered how many people had died under exactly such circumstances, afraid to seem spineless under a gaze that—at least in their mind's eye—was watching and judging them.

The man stopped a few feet away from Yonatan and gestured at the back door of the restaurant. They entered the kitchen, which was dimly lit and smaller than he'd expected. He made a left and then heard the man behind him, and when he turned back the man pointed to a black door, which he pushed open to reveal a narrow staircase covered with stained dark-red carpeting, like in cheap London hotels. He climbed up the stairs and his knees ached again. At the landing he was relieved to see a hallway, perhaps because its wood-paneling looked familiar. He ran his fingers over the walls, and the sensation reminded him of something that he couldn't quite place.

The hallway led to a room where the magazine publisher was stooped over an antique standing desk signing forms, briskly smoothing out each piece of paper first. On either side of the desk was a black leather couch, and a single bed covered with a wool blanket stood at the far end of the room. The walls were entirely lined with bookshelves. The top ones contained large old volumes with dusty blue-and-black covers, a few of which were engraved, but he couldn't make out the names of the books or the authors.

The publisher eyed Yonatan coolly and said nothing until eventually he put down his pen and looked up. "What are you doing here?" he asked.

"I wanted to see you."

"Not here, I mean in the city. Weren't you supposed to leave a couple of days ago?"

"Yes," Yonatan said.

"Yet here you still are, in our beautiful city."

"Yes."

"Is there a particular reason?"

"I didn't realize I'd stayed." Having clarified the understanding that had been squirming in the burrows of his consciousness since he woke up, he panicked. But this time he did not feel the burning sensation in his scalp that usually spread to the rest of his body. The panic had no physical symptoms—he simply knew that all this was alarming.

"You didn't realize you'd stayed," the man repeated, savoring every word.

"Yes. Not exactly."

"Where have you been hanging out?" asked the publisher as he twisted something with his right hand. He proceeded to unscrew his left forearm and toss it onto the black couch beside him, then pointed at the couch with his stump, inviting Yonatan to sit down. But Yonatan kept standing, motionless, staring back and forth from the prosthetic to the stump.

"I was in bed."

"For how many days?"

"I don't remember."

He was thirsty but too anxious to ask for water, so he swallowed his bitter saliva. He'd had trouble swallowing recently, the spit would get lodged in his throat, and he was worried there was something wrong.

"So why are you here, then?" the publisher asked, and sat down on the couch next to his false hand.

"I'm looking for someone," Yonatan said, speaking quickly, "I met her at a party in a nightclub near campus, a student party or something. You told me about the party when we were at your restaurant, and I told Carlos and his friends about it…"

"The past is yet to come," the magazine publisher said with a laugh.

"I don't get it."

"That's the name of the party," he muttered, "it's a series of parties, actually. So you met her, and then you lay in bed alone. Don't you know how to fuck?"

"That's not the point."

"That's not the point…" His tone turned grave, sharpened by a hostile note. "As you have seen, I am no longer interested in people, especially not authors and poets like you. You've all been engineered into professionalized types. The existentialist eccentrics of the seventies were boring, too—even more so—but at least you could spend a night star-gazing with them in silence, you know what I mean?"

Yonatan did not answer.

"Now everything has a purpose. Most nights I sleep here." He pointed his stump at the bookshelves to his right, used it to knock a pack of cigarettes onto the floor, and picked it up with his other hand. "I'm interested in the past, before everything got screwed up. At dinner you told me you were interested in the past, too, didn't you? 'The genesis of things,' or something like that."

"Not exactly. Not the genesis of things but the elasticity, when there are no boundaries or barriers. You wake up in the morning and your mind gallops between pictures of the past and the present, all in the same space and time. Like on the first day of a baby's life, when there's no past yet. There are people whose consciousness is like that, every event from every time screaming together."

"Maybe 'the genesis of things' is not a good name for it."

"Maybe not, but that's uninteresting."

"Uninteresting?"

"Your comment."

The publisher put his hand behind his head, perhaps to mask his surprise; he looked scolded. "Do you want to learn a lesson about time?" he asked, and pointed at a faded map of Mexico City with a few red squares marked on it. "You buy a place where there's nothing, a few old people in tin shacks, and then the artists come with all their entourages, and after the artists come the lawyers and the accountants and the rest of the faux-wealthy people, and then the bankers and all the really wealthy people and their fat kids, and then there's a war or an earthquake, and the whole thing starts over again."

"I see," said Yonatan.

"You want money," the publisher asserted.

"No."

"Don't lie," he snapped, "that's the thing about people like you writers: you're convinced that everyone else is as despicable as you are, and you think whoever doesn't admit that is fooling himself or the world."

"There is something to that," Yonatan admitted.

"So you really are looking for that woman. But why?"

"I told her something that I don't understand." He decided to finally articulate what he hadn't dared to before, not even to himself. He had somehow willed himself to obfuscate the reason why he was looking for the young woman with glasses. "She said that now she understood everything, that if my closest friend had died I must be feeling unspeakable pain." He paused, and a look of sour curiosity came over the publisher's face; he was probably still hoping to be disappointed. "But no one...I have to know exactly what I said to her, do you see?"

"No one...?" The publisher mimicked his pronunciation but could not hide the traces of his own accented English. "We're not talking about a mystery or anything cheap like that, are we?" He smiled and tugged on his beard.

And all at once everything seemed so logical, his sequence of actions made sense, as though mind and motion had finally merged. "But he hasn't died yet."

THE TOWERS
(LATE 1980S)

They grabbed Yoel in the thick of the wadi. He was wearing the white Sabbath clothes that his parents insisted on even though they did not go to temple or recite any of the blessings. Yoel vaguely recognized the kids—there were always a few who merged into a single face—from the towers on the hill that loomed at the end of their block and sometimes blacked out the sky. Yoel hadn't provoked them, he'd simply walked by humming "Purple Rain" to show how undaunted he was, but they knew, God knows how, that he craved their downfall. And now he was alone in the wadi, without Yonatan. When he realized the tower kids were going to jump him, he was surprised to discover that, more than being afraid, he was delighted to confirm that he and Yonatan hadn't been imagining their hostility for all those years. A shiver prickled his skin and a strange warmth spread through his skull.

They grabbed him and knocked him down, rolled him in the mud with their feet, rolled him over the stones, rolled him onto the thistles on either side of the path. They stepped on him and kicked his ribs and waist, one of them pressed his boot onto Yoel's neck until he screamed that he couldn't breathe. Only when they saw blood on his arm and trickling from his cheek did they let go and walk away, poking fun at his shouts, mimicking his whimpered threats. "How are you guys gonna kill us?" they laughed.

Yoel told Yonatan that he lay there listening to their voices grow farther away until it started to rain and everything around him went silent, and for the first time he considered the price he would pay at home when he showed up with his white clothes recolored reddish-brown by the wadi's dirt. He got up without bothering to shake the dust and mud off. Every so often he felt a sharp pain from the thorns that had pierced his skin. Odd how the pain was not constant, he mused, but came and went. He wanted to get out of the neighborhood, take the number 14 bus and go somewhere, maybe to the tennis center in Katamon, where they used to play for hours when they could get a free court. It was a wintery week, the days were cold and the nights even colder, yet still he imagined he could lie down on one of the courts and spend the night there. But he knew that in the end, after the blood on his face clotted, he would go home to his parents, and that every minute he wasted thinking about other places would only prolong the misery. They did not yet have that other place, the one they'd talked about for years, a place neither in the seemingly menacing neighborhood of Beit HaKerem nor fully outside of it. They had yet to create it by uniting their separate imaginations into a cohesive vision, still trying to each impose their dreams on the other.

They sat in the wadi, fifty yards from the two buildings they lived in, which faced each other at the end of the street. From atop a mound of dirt, they looked out at the rocky hill with a muddy path winding up to its peak, where the towers loomed. They liked that spot: from here they could observe the whole world, unseen by it.

Yoel played cards and talked about the animals that disappeared from the wadi in winter: squirrels, hyraxes, cats, foxes. Yonatan replied impatiently that he'd never seen anything there in summer either, except cats. Foxes? What was Yoel talking about? Next he'd be missing the springtime leopards. Yoel focused on his card game, but Yonatan hated these games Yoel made up, always full of arbitrary rules that made no sense. When he leaned over to pick up the apricot pit they used as a ball, Yonatan beat him to it and threw it away.

"Are you an idiot?" Yoel shouted and glared at him. "I was in the middle."

"Not anymore."

"Go to hell," said Yoel, "I'm going home."

"Is everything okay?" He grabbed Yoel by the shoulder. He was stronger, and they both knew it.

"Everything's fine."

"Fine how?"

Yoel ignored the question. He sat on the ground, smoothed out the creases in his button-down shirt, and started talking about Soviet rockets that shot into space and then fell back to Earth. He was currently investigating whether that was really possible; if the rockets flew through space at high speed, then they should return to an Earth that was already much older than them. His father was reading a book called *Perfect Spy* and he said everyone in the USSR and the US was a spy, the whole Cold War was only so that people could keep their salaries.

Yonatan commented that this was pretty much Yoel's father's explanation about everything. He asked Yoel again: Is everything okay? And Yoel nodded. Okay how? It had been a week since that Saturday, and Yoel hadn't said another word about how the kids from the towers had rolled him in mud and thistles. His patience wearing thin, Yonatan put his hand in a puddle, picked up a leaf and held it to his nose—he couldn't smell anything—then ran it over Yoel's coat collar. As expected, Yoel grimaced and pulled back.

"Look up," Yonatan said, pointing to the hilltop. "We can't get to the towers without them seeing us, right?" They had already discussed this many times: only one path led to the top of the hill, and whoever walked it was visible from anywhere around the towers.

"So we'll climb at night," Yoel said.

"Don't be dumb," he snapped, "we've talked about that: at night they're asleep at home, we don't even know exactly where they live. And, even if we find out, are we going to attack them at home? And their parents?" He was surprised at having to spell it all out again: this score could only be settled in daylight. "We have to find a way to get there during the day, you understand?"

He leaned over, happily inhaling the smell of fresh earth after the rain. His fingers pulled up wet weeds and he realized that he was tearing them into shreds. He put his muddy fingernails up to his nose and smelled, and when he looked up he saw Yoel watching him wide-eyed. He wondered if Yoel had guessed his idea, and now he knew that they both understood that something big had been put down between them, perhaps the thing they'd been looking for since they met.

A year, and another year, and they were in first grade and third grade and now already sixth grade, and still they were searching for their point of unity. Sometimes, when one of them had an idea that the other found boring, they wondered why they were friends at all, and what they had in common. But they were fully aware of the answer. Yonatan lived in number 7 and Yoel lived across the street in number 10. When they played soccer they kicked and pushed and badgered each other, at school they expressed no affection, and did not play together at recess. Their world existed at the bottom end of their street, the steepest one in the neighborhood. It existed between their two buildings and the wadi, the forest that abutted it to the west, and the military factory that was bordered on the east by the towers. Year after year they entertained all sorts of grandiose plans that led to moments of elation—had they finally found the brilliant idea that would unite them?—before they crashed into yet another failure.

But now perhaps something had changed. They must not talk about that idea yet, they weren't ready. If they talked it might dissipate. For now they had to shield it, get out of that place and not mention it at all.

They stood up and ran along the mud. The cold wind whipped at their skin, and they felt almost naked. Their eyes watered, and they could not see anything, but still they charged over the soft dirt to the two last buildings on the street, which they could find blindfolded. When they finally reached the dirt lot, out of breath, they parted ways without a word, and Yonatan climbed up the steps to the third floor.

To his relief the apartment was dark and silent, the windows and blinds shut. He stood in the entryway and looked at the round armchair by the phone, which in the dark always glowed in a strange brilliant black. On the kitchen table was a plastic bag containing blackened pieces of avocado and two half-pitas. He went onto the kitchen balcony and flung the bag onto the strip of earth behind the fence that separated his building from the ones on HaShachar Street.

Yonatan looked out at the building farthest to the left, most of which was hidden by trees. That was where his nanny Ahuva lived, and her home was the site of his earliest memories, apart from the first one: he was two and a half, with his back up against the hospital room door, while his grandmother, Sarah, lay in bed. She smiles at him, her hair is wrapped in a headscarf, thick blankets cover her body, and he, at least in his memory, sees her for the first time in his life. She reaches out to the nightstand and feels around for something, and another pair of hands, smooth and young, rummage in the drawer with her, and finally she holds out a square of chocolate for him. But he doesn't want to go any closer. Everyone urges him to come forward. The grin does not leave her face, but something goes crooked, perhaps in her lips. He was seven at her funeral, and a man in a black fedora who looked vaguely familiar walked past him, stood near a distant row of graves and said something. He asked his father what the man was saying, and his father said it was Grandpa Albert, who'd come from Haifa.

"That's Grandpa?" he wondered.

"Yes," his father replied. "He is saying that his heart is heavy today."

The idea still sat at the center of his consciousness like a massive boulder. He knew it had to be revitalized, enhanced, its plot rewritten.

It was clear to them both that this winter, something pivotal had to happen.

———

The older kids whose apartments were also at number 10 heard about the incident and declared that this could not be allowed to happen on their street: a whole gang beating up one kid in the wadi? Was there no decency in the world? There was only one way to settle the matter: the kids from the towers would send two representatives to the yard at Rivka's kindergarten, where all the kids from the block had gone, and they'd hold a fair fight in the sandbox. The tower kids had to be the same age as they were, roughly in sixth grade.

The older boys—Shimon, David Tzivony and Tomer Fainaru—found Yonatan and Yoel in the windowless basement of his building, sitting under the dusty ping-pong table—they had always been enchanted by legends of the long-ago days when their older brothers had played on it—surrounded by a sofa with ripped cushions, a BMX frame with its handlebars wrapped in yellow foam, a heap of dusty books in Russian, a garden hose, and various other bits of junk the neighbors had no interest in ever seeing again. They were conferring over the outline of the trench, which ran too close to the electric fence around the military factory. They sketched possible routes in a notebook, discussed every twist and turn, and carefully mapped the path on a large piece of white cardstock they'd bought. They were making good progress and every so often they lay down on an old mattress with their eyes shut, but they couldn't stop talking about the trench and their retaliation against the towers, and also about how Yoel's mother said that in a year or two she wanted to have a baby girl, after the two boys, and they were in a cheerful mood, and they raised their voices a lot and complimented each other on the things they said.

As soon as they saw the older boys they flipped over the cardstock, threw their coats on it, and stood up. All at once the basement felt cold. The boys consoled Yoel over the terrible incident in the wadi, and said that, if any gang of kids attacked him again, he should tell them. They asked about his injuries and his parents' reaction, and Yoel kept saying, "It's nothing." It was obvious that their gentleness was masking a threat, and Yonatan was surprised that Yoel failed to understand this, instead riding high on their attention, boasting about the scratches that had already faded on his arms and cheeks. When they got bored with Yoel they headed to the door. "So we'll have a talk with the towers. We'll explain the facts of life, as they say, and we'll let you know when it's happening," Shimon summed up. "We're thinking Friday afternoon," added David Tzivony, who always insisted on having the last word.

Yonatan's legs were shaking. He struggled to steady them and pressed his shoes against the floor. "We want to talk about it first," Yoel said, "we might not want to get back at them anymore."

Shimon and his friends looked at him, surprised that he was under the impression that anything was up to him. Yoel glanced at Yonatan, who gave an encouraging glance back, wanting to wink but afraid of getting caught. Neither of them wanted this battle, they'd always been afraid of fights that had no rules and ended in someone's surrender. They'd seen Shimon kicking Itai in the face, and David Tzivony riding Amir while he writhed and screamed, "I can't see, I can't see," a line that every boy on the block kept mimicking for months. These were not the loser kids from his class, who loathed him but were scared of him and would only fight him if they were sure someone in the crowd would break it up after a minute. Besides, they were working on a plan that was going to stun the kids from the towers.

The older boys' smiles were gone. "Talk as much as you want, as long as you show up for the fight on time," said Shimon, who was wearing his usual ironed jeans and a black belt with a shiny silver triangular buckle. Tomer Fainaru, who was known as Bentz because his head was rectangular like Bert's Israeli counterpart, and who always got mad when anyone hummed the *Sesame Street* theme song, took off his glasses, as he always did before issuing a threat. "We'll bust up whoever doesn't show up," he said. "And if no one shows up," David Tzivony added, "we'll kill you all."

There was a knock on the basement door. Yonatan knew it was the girls—no one else knocked on that door. There were rumors that at night girls and boys made out in the basement and even had sex, and Yoel swore he'd found a condom there once. Shimon opened the heavy white door, and to Yonatan's surprise he saw Tali with a girl he didn't know; she was wearing a wool coat over a colorful dress that fluttered above shiny red boots; no girl in his class had boots like those. "Get the hell out of here, Tali!" he yelled.

Shimon slapped him. "You don't swear at girls."

They didn't like Tali Meltzer. She'd lived at number 8 since her family had moved to the neighborhood from Haifa, when she was in second grade and they were in third, and she used to monitor them from her balcony that looked onto the wadi. Once she snitched to Yonatan's parents that they were throwing mud balls at people, and another time she squealed on him because he'd called her "a peeping whore," although she insisted she'd only been standing on the balcony, doing nothing. Her father was a therapist and her mother an architect, both friendly people who made a point of saying hello to everyone, and they spoke a clearly accentuated Hebrew. They talked to kids and grown-ups in the same tone, because in their view—which they took the trouble to elucidate for his parents—"the child's position must be respected."

No one had any doubt that the Meltzers were different from all the other residents on the block, and it was also clear that, having despaired of educating their neighbors, they had decided not to befriend them. Yonatan's father viewed the Meltzers as an annoyance, the way he viewed everyone on the street who insisted on voicing his opinion on any matter, while his mother secretly might have envied how they lived, and the polite, cheerful way they and their two children spoke. "Life is one big party, I see," she hissed when she spotted them loading bags and a surfboard into their car on a Saturday morning.

After their altercations with Tali, Mr. Meltzer asked to visit them for a meeting, and for Yoel and his parents to be invited as well. (Only Yoel's mother came, and she sat there saying nothing, pulling out bits of her short hair.) Mr. Meltzer sat with a straight back, asked Yonatan's parents how they were and what they did for a living, and after twenty minutes laid out his arguments: firstly, Tali came back from the wadi saying ugly words that he would not repeat, and even if she was saying them jokingly, these things did seep in; secondly, they shouted and horsed around between two and four in the afternoon, and now Tali didn't respect the siesta hours either; and thirdly, it seemed they were treating her disrespectfully and failed to appreciate her virtues—she was a smart girl with integrity and a good sense of humor.

"Well, we could see that as soon as you moved here," Yonatan's father pointed out, though he wouldn't have recognized Tali if he'd run into her. Yoel tapped Yonatan's black shoe with his white sneaker, and he tapped Yoel back. The two of them muffled a giggle when his father gave them a cautionary look.

"But we're not your daughter's friends," Yoel said finally.

Meltzer stared at him until Yoel looked down. He was a broad-shouldered man, with piercing if friendly brown eyes. His expression was always polite, and it was only his pale pink lips and sharp chin that disclosed anything malicious. He'd recently joined forces with two fathers who were pillars of the community to establish an "exercise club," whose members gathered every Saturday to run at the stadium on the Givat Ram campus. (One boy who was invited said they made their kids run ten thousand meters on the track, and it was a wonder no one had dropped dead yet. "They're total Nazis, they're animals," he whined.)

Meltzer sipped his tea and seemed surprised by Yoel's remark. Yonatan looked at him, then at Yoel, and it finally dawned on him how credulous Meltzer was. "If you're not her friends," Meltzer finally said in a dry tone, "then there's no reason for you not to cut off ties with her. Sometimes good children don't get along, it's disappointing but not a rare thing."

"But there's nothing to cut off," Yoel insisted, while his mother put her hand on his knee and he put his hand on top of hers.

Meltzer had apparently expected her to restrain her son; he didn't know that Yoel and his mother sometimes acted like friends, that she knew all the kids in class, and was the type of mother who would ask if two girls who weren't talking to each other had made up yet. He cleared his throat and, in a slightly comical tone, said that in the interest of fairness he would now say something in their defense—was that acceptable to them?

Yoel and Yonatan both nodded.

"Truly acceptable?" he insisted with a meaningful smile and looked back and forth between them, searching for signs of admiration or at the very least surprise.

"Go on, they said yes," Yonatan's father snapped, and Yoel's mother lit a cigarette.

Of course he would never put words in their mouths, Meltzer explained, but perhaps Tali did not respect their games? Was that a fair point?

Yonatan proudly replied that he didn't want to say bad things about Tali when she wasn't there, and Yoel quietly waved his mother's cigarette smoke away.

"So can we," Meltzer asked warmly, "agree in genuine friendship to cut off ties?"

They all nodded.

Yonatan's father said, "Thank you for a successful visit," and stood up abruptly, held out his hand, and walked Meltzer to the door, slapping his back but in fact shoving him out the door. Once he'd left, his father laughed. "If you're going to suck up to someone before giving them bad news, make sure they really will think it's bad news, otherwise you've wasted everyone's time."

His mother added: "Mr. Meltzer is outflanking you to reach a goal that's already been achieved," and all the adults laughed.

His parents ignored Meltzer's visit, perhaps because they found his behavior peculiar: it was acceptable on the block that if someone beat up your kid or insulted him more than was necessary, you didn't sit down in their living room for a friendly talk and expect to be served tea, but you yelled at his parents like Shimon's mother had yelled at his mother after Shaul, Yonatan's big brother, had strangled Shimon with a garden hose: "Aren't you ashamed? Your husband is a respectable man!" Or the way Yoel's father had threatened Bentz after he poured glue on his son's hair: "I'll wring your neck with my bare hands!"

"Do anything you want, as long as he doesn't come back here," his father told them after Meltzer had left. But the truth was that Tali had defeated them, and after the visit they ignored her completely. Even when she was bold enough to follow them into the wadi and ask what they were doing, they didn't curse or threaten her, but sat there doing nothing until she gave up.

"Well, hello, ladies!" Shimon greeted the two girls who walked into the basement with impressive synchronization. It was clear to everyone that only in the inaccessible kingdom of girls was such precision possible. Yonatan wondered if the uninhibited closeness he sometimes longed for (even to hug Yoel or someone else really tight), but was always careful to suppress, existed only in the girls' world.

Tali took off her wool hat and shook out her brown hair, and for the first time it occurred to him that she might be not ugly. She ignored him and the other boys and turned to Yoel, toward whom she was obliged to demonstrate loathing simply because he hated her, and asked if they were doing something in the wadi. She said they'd found a strange mound of earth, "and it's obviously you." Yoel just stared at the cobwebs clustered above the girls' heads.

"A mound of earth?" he snorted, hoping Yoel would keep quiet and let him speak. "Do you know how many people hang around in the wadi?"

"We almost tripped on your stupid mound," Tali grumbled without looking at him, "it's dangerous."

"Where's the mound?" asked one of the older boys without much interest.

"We'll be there whenever you say!" Yonatan shouted. "But we want it to be clear that there's no sticks and stones, and that Shimon will be umpire." He was pleased with that last part (he didn't really care who was umpire), which immediately created a stir among the big kids, who exchanged looks.

"Fine, you little fucker," Bentz said with a giggle, "you want Shimon, you get Shimon." He delivered a slap on the back to Shimon, who maintained a blank expression, like a man acknowledging the weight of responsibility he bore.

Before Tali could say anything else, her friend, who seemed bored with the recent exchange, started doing cartwheels like they do in the Olympics. Every time she stood on her hands her dress fell down to her white underwear dotted with orange teddy bears or pink hearts—he couldn't tell—and everyone saw it and they also saw her thighs, which were whiter than her tanned shins. The boys spent a moment yearning, then started complimenting her and asking how many times a week she did ballet and what kind of things she learned in class. She answered tersely in a deep, languid voice that enchanted them, and when they asked her not to stop she shrugged and did some more cartwheels.

The basement was silent, and he wondered if he and Yoel could leave yet, but the older kids were blocking the door. David Tzivony asked Tali's friend if she'd be willing to do her cartwheels without her underwear on, and she said okay and took off her underwear and folded it and wiped the dust off the edge of the ping-pong table with her hand and put it down there, and now he could see that they were pink teddy bears of various sizes. He heard Bentz breathing heavily and he looked at her hole, the likes of which he'd only seen in *Playboy* magazines at Bentz's—once, last summer, he was asked over there and immediately warned: "Here is just for looking; you jerk off at home"—and turned to Yoel, who gave him a furious glare because he'd agreed to the fight without consulting him.

The older boys whispered and David Tzivony left the basement. Tali, who was blushing, stood near the door, and, while the girl did more cartwheels, seized the chance and said she had to go home. She urged her friend to join her—her mother would make them pancakes, she said—and the girl said she probably should go. Shimon and Bentz said they were really enjoying her cartwheels, but she could do whatever she wanted. She flashed an indifferent smile, though her expression remained unaltered, and Tali snapped, "Well then?" and the girl said, "Soon," in a slightly sardonic tone while she stood on her hands, and everyone laughed, except for Tali, who walked out.

To his surprise, he was relieved they'd let her go. Yoel took advantage of the break and walked to the door. Bentz stopped him.

"Let him go," Shimon said.

"It's too cold outside," Bentz scoffed.

"Let him go, I said," Shimon grunted, and Bentz moved aside.

Yoel walked past them, resigning himself to the thump that landed on his back, and to Shimon's kick.

"Wait, one important thing we didn't tell you," Bentz called after him, his voice sounding more mature and serious.

"What?" Yoel turned back and his face looked gloomy. His arm was dangling behind him, as though he were dragging something with it.

"Tell your mamma we can't make it tonight, maybe we'll send the Arab gardener instead!" Bentz cawed, and by the end of the sentence he was roaring with laughter. Shimon laughed too, and they exchanged back-slaps and high fives. Yonatan wanted to laugh but he held back. The girl stared at them uncomprehendingly.

Yonatan was left alone with the kids and the girl and wondered why he didn't leave, since he wasn't all that excited about the cartwheels, and seeing the hole over and over again. He couldn't understand why it thrilled them. David Tzivony came back to the basement and shoved something rolled up in a rag into Shimon's hand. Shimon, who'd been humming a song, went over to the girl—it was obvious that he was the only one she liked—and coughed lightly, the way he did before he spoke to girls or adults. He asked if she wouldn't mind doing another few cartwheels but slower, or maybe even a handstand, and she said she wouldn't mind, and Shimon asked if she'd mind if they took a picture of her so they'd have a souvenir.

The girl didn't answer and the other kids stared at her, enchanted, as she stood on her hands again, and Tzivony whispered to the others, "Do you understand what's going on here?" Yonatan was overcome by an ominous feeling. He wanted to tell the girl that she should go home because it was late, but he knew the others would kill him if he interfered, and he also knew that he would not leave the room now: under no circumstances would he leave her alone with them.

Shimon glanced at his watch. "*The A-Team*'s starting," he exclaimed, and David Tzivony narrowed his eyes at him as if waking up. Shimon and Bentz turned to the door but David Tzivony didn't move.

"Wait," he said to Shimon, "aren't we going to do anything?" He pointed to the camera.

"No," Shimon declared. He walked over to Tzivony, put his free arm around his back and shoved him toward the door, but halfway through the motion he changed his mind and went back to the girl and told her she was very pretty, and that she would be a wonderful dancer or something like that, but no one was going to say anything about what had happened here, were they? She stared at Shimon with her green eyes, squinting. Yonatan was surprised to notice crowded freckles around her eyes, which reminded him that she was younger than he was, and her expression saddened him and he looked up at the cobwebs again.

Her response did not satisfy Shimon. He kept standing there looking at her, until he picked up the underwear from the ping-pong table, kneeled down in front of her and handed it to her. She took it and turned her back and put it on. Shimon waited for her to finish and straighten out her dress and then he headed for the door.

"Don't talk too much," Bentz told Yonatan and gave him a look.

They didn't shut the door behind them. He hoped the girl wouldn't hear them laughing in the hallway, and to his relief all he could hear were footsteps and hushed voices. The girl stood there for a moment longer. He wanted to talk to her but did not have the courage, and he stared at the clumps of dried mud on his shoes. He soon heard her footsteps in the hallway, then in the passage leading out to the yard. After that it was silent.

———

"Put your hands inside your sweater," Yoel told him. "Do you want them to freeze?"

The wind blew from the north and struck their faces every time they put their heads up. A few dark blocks of clouds hung above them, but they were not rainclouds. They had no time to waste: the fight with the towers was inevitable, and it would either happen in their world or in the other kids' world; it was up to them. They wore wool hats and ugly parkas—his was from Florida, where a friend of his mother lived and sent annual packages of hand-me-downs—and Yoel had red Liverpool gloves. In the wadi they saw only two thin boys in wool coats who ambled down the path toward their street, smoking. Yonatan thought they looked big and beautiful, and he envied their interesting lives.

They had a shovel they'd pilfered from the garden where they worked in agriculture class, and two flashlights, some large plastic bags, a little bottle of kerosene they'd found in the basement, a loaf of whole wheat bread, sliced cheese and a bottle of Coke. Yonatan did not mention what had happened the day before in the basement, assuming Yoel was regretting leaving him alone there. But Yoel said nothing and he wasn't about to let anything come between them now. He knew what was worrying Yoel: why were they digging instead of preparing for the imminent fight? He was afraid Yoel might ask this question, in the next hour or the next day, and that then everything would collapse, because the things Yonatan did alone existed only in an unsteady way until Yoel joined in. He once again felt obliged to glue the fragments together with the fervor of words—with storylines he would invent about the wonderful things that would happen when they finished—and to present Yoel with a complete picture.

The first twenty feet of the trench were dug in soft earth that felt good to crush between one's fingers, taking handfuls of it and kneading it into shapes, and they easily dug up the few little stones and twigs. They made fast progress, each taking turns holding the shovel while the other loaded the dirt into bags and rolled them over to a black heap of trash that someone had burned. Yoel said his hand hurt, and when he removed the gloves that now smelled like leaves, they both stared at a pinkish-white blister that had developed on one of his fingers.

It was disgusting, but Yonatan could not look away. "Don't worry, I always get those," he said, and remembered that Yoel usually knew when he was lying.

Yoel blew on the blister and a little smile emerged. Yonatan felt a surge of emotion toward him and remembered how lovely Yoel's smile was when the skin around his hazel eyes rounded into crescents that also laughed. Like the wholeness of a baby's smile. He offered to switch, but Yoel refused; he had dug less than Yonatan today.

Yoel shook out his brown, frizzy hair and it fell on his high, acne-dotted forehead. His eyes were small for his head, but when he opened them wide they looked large and beautiful, giving his face a mature look. Even though Yonatan was a couple of inches taller, with broader shoulders and a slightly chubby face, when people saw them together—perhaps because of Yoel's moustache fuzz, his deep voice and flawless articulation, and the pressed button-down shirts he wore to school, always tucked in—they said Yoel looked older, like a seventh or eighth grader. Yonatan's mother even said Yoel looked like "a little man."

From faraway they heard the soft rattle of an engine, and soon a deafening screech rolled down the wadi, and at the edge of their street they saw puffs of smoke. He assumed his father was driving downtown for a meeting, even though his mother disliked it when he arranged meetings on Saturdays. They were used to that noise. On winter mornings the residents of their block often sat in their cars trying to start their engines, pumping the gas pedals. Only in the past couple of years had people begun to part with their old cars and nonchalantly slide into new Mitsubishis or Subarus—white, silver or blue—whose engines started up in an instant. Yoel's father had already bought a light blue Mitsubishi, and there was talk of a new car in Yonatan's home, too. It was the clearest divide on the block now: between those who sailed away in their cars and those who did not. If the car you bought was too expensive, however, like a BMW, you were branded a show-off, or worse: a potential member of the flighty, uneducated, bourgeois business world of Tel Aviv, as his uncle used to remark at family get-togethers on Fridays.

They both knew Yoel's mother would come out onto their balcony any minute to call him home for dinner.

"This was a good day," Yonatan said to Yoel. "Right?"

"Yes," Yoel replied, "this was a very good day."

FINAL YEAR
(MID-1990S)

He tried the handle and found the door unlocked. For a moment he wondered if they were back, then he took a few steps and stood in the entryway. All the lights were on inside, and the blinds were drawn. The floor was strewn with clothes, books, dishes and glasses, Coke and Absolut Vodka bottles, pizza boxes, ashtrays overflowing with butts, and pieces of the white vase that had stood on the piano, one of which was stained with three drops of a blackish-purple liquid that appeared to be blood. He also saw muddy footprints, toilet paper rolls, LP and CD covers. He walked over the debris, tripping on a little heap every so often.

The house was icy. Searching for the kerosene heater in the mess, he heard a crack beneath his feet and looked down to see that he'd broken *Bruce Springsteen Live*. He took his clothes off and kicked them in a pile toward the washing machine on the little balcony. Shivering, he ran barefoot to the bathroom and wrapped a damp towel around his body. He hurried to his parents' room: the sheets and blankets were tangled up on the floor, and he turned on the space heater that sat on a stool next to his mother's side of the bed, picked up a blanket, lay down on the mattress and covered himself. He was still shaking, but the warm air slowly restored ease to his body, and he felt better.

In his mind's eye he saw two pictures: in the first he walked his parents downstairs with their suitcases, and in the second he took his father to the airport, alone. The two pictures were mismatched—when exactly had they left? He heard a whistle, which seemed to emerge from within him, and he felt terrified. The soul's responses are usually as familiar as the furniture in one's childhood room—even in moments of anxiety you roam through a recognizable set of contours—but this prolonged whistle, like a new and frightening stab to his stomach, was something he had never heard before. He hoped he was not really hearing anything, or, conversely, that the whistle was in fact a familiar sound that he would soon identify. It gradually faded, leaving behind only faint echoes, as though it had split off into dozens of whistle-shards. He took air in and out, and felt something peculiar and unrecognizable blazing inside him. If he were to sleep here, in the only apartment he'd known since he was a baby, if he were to fall asleep in his parents' bed with the heater blowing warm air on his body, perhaps things would go back to the way they were.

When he awoke at 9:45 a.m. he found a phone message from his aunt, who said she hoped he was "taking care of the house." Last week she'd turned up with her son, a college student five years older than Yonatan, and they'd scrubbed the whole place in preparation for his parents' return from New York. "I've never seen such a pigsty in my life," she'd scolded him, and the rest of the time she'd barely said a word. He'd sprawled on the black armchair in the living room, smoked a cigarette and watched them scurry back and forth carrying piles of trash, Diet Coke bottles full of butts, glasses and plates containing remnants of pizza, falafel streaked with tahini, and chicken bones. He'd heard the vacuum cleaner, the washing machine, and taps running, he'd heard his aunt and cousin humming along with Shlomo

Artzi on the radio, seen them mopping the floor, piling up more and more bags and cardboard boxes full of garbage.

Their accusatory silence did not touch him. This was not what they were blaming him for anyway—that while his mother hung at death's door in New York he had the audacity to make such a mess of the apartment. That did anger them, but his real crime—that his mother had cancer partly because of the torments he had put her through—was one they never voiced. Sometimes they said things like, "You have to be kind to her now," or "You'll need to behave differently from now on, you're almost eighteen," but they did not mention whatever he'd done to accelerate her disease. Yet whenever anyone spoke of his mother's illness, he knew that was what they believed.

He once shared his feelings with Yoel, who stared at him as though such a notion had never entered his mind. Yoel believed his mother loved Yonatan and their relationship was special even if things had grown complicated because of her illness. Yonatan had felt grateful because the surprise on Yoel's face melted away his fear that perhaps, deep down, Yoel believed, as they all did, that he was guilty. He wanted to say to him then, "You and me, we've been making up stories forever. Can we even still talk about this world?"

His aunt asked him to leave the living room so they could clean up the rat's nest he'd left there, and she couldn't resist asking: "What on earth would you have done if we hadn't come over?"

"Not a fucking thing," he replied cheerfully. "That's what." Out of the corner of his eye he could see her son debating whether or not to intervene.

Yonatan got up off the couch and edged along the hallway so he wouldn't get footprints on the wet floor, lay down on his bed and fell asleep. When he woke up he was fully clothed, wearing a coat and shoes. Someone had turned on the space heater in his room, and there was a message on the answering machine from his father informing him that they were staying in New York for another ten days. The doctors they'd pinned their hopes on had decided to start a new series of treatments. Yonatan wondered if his aunt already knew that all her hard work had been in vain.

He washed his face and hair and drove to school in the filthy white Daihatsu. He listened to "Girlfriend in a Coma" and felt like laughing. He pictured Lior, and was struck by an urge to go somewhere else, to drive to Lior's school and wait outside until she came out, the way he used to when they were together. Sometimes Tali came out with her and the three of them would get in the car and the girls would say, "Let's go to Ein Karem and take the old route to Tel Aviv," and they'd speed up, get lost, find new roads and listen to music, and in the afternoon they'd lie on the rooftop of Lior's apartment building and smoke cigarettes until evening fell.

He got to school at the end of first recess, walked past the smokers loitering outside and his classmates sitting on the benches above the radiators. They all seemed to be wearing black or blue sweaters and blue or gray jeans and speaking softly. Yoel had pronounced the smokers and bench-sitters "castrated puritans" and said he was willing to bet there wasn't a single kid in their class who really knew how to enjoy sex. He said all the girls liked to believe they were rule-breakers, gazing longingly at the scruffy guitar player from Jerusalem's punk band and insisting they'd love to give him a hand job, and that they sometimes went to a nightclub in Tel Aviv with black lipstick on and made out in the bathroom with gay DJs from the army radio station, but that in fact they were unimaginative puritans. Yoel also claimed that all the boys who went on aimless pub crawls downtown with the same people over and over again, or grew their hair long and bought earrings from a stand in Cats Square, and read *Zen and the Art of Motorcycle Maintenance* or the first eight pages of *The Hitchhiker's Guide to the Galaxy* to pay off their debt to existentialism, and talked about drugs they had no idea how to get hold of and finished off the evening over a slice of pizza before running home to jerk off to a gorgeous waitress from one of the trendy bars—that they were worse (Yonatan assumed this was not the right moment to tell Yoel that he'd recently fallen slightly in love with the black-haired waitress from Glasnost whose green eyes turned gray as the night wore on), and were so dumb that even now, midway through their senior year, they still hadn't grasped that they'd wasted their youth.

He looked around but Yoel wasn't there. That wasn't surprising, given that he'd recently befriended a different group of kids. A lot of kids at school sought out Yoel's company these days, boys and girls, and maybe that was why he'd been hinting that it was time to dismantle their kingdom. Yonatan had been feeling for a while that he was clinging on even as Yoel drifted away, and that, even if he didn't want it to be over, he had to acknowledge the cruel law they had enacted together as children: the minute one of them lost interest, the world they had created together would disappear. Betrayal had always hovered over all their joint enterprises.

They had spent the past two years—since the end of sophomore year—constructing the kingdom, laboring over all its cities and governments, appointing ministers, governors and landowners, all of whose names were borrowed from their classmates. They concocted its pivotal events. Their kingdom had no name, nor did it exist in a particular time. It had a seventeenth-century sensibility, with occasional forays into the future, as when they invented a laser bomb that could implant other people's fears into someone's mind. Its annals were written on notes they passed back and forth in class. Yoel was Warshovsky, the great rebel whose entire family had been murdered by the king's father. Warshovsky assembled an army of foreign soldiers, and after a bloody war in which the heir to the throne was killed, he formed an alliance with the king and became his Captain of the Guard. Yonatan was the king. Together they drew maps, too, detailing the towns and districts and battlefields. Every new episode began with a note:

"Problem: the wealthy Liptzin is demanding that we stop levying taxes on his lands. As Captain of the Guard it has come to my attention that other landowners may join his demand. He may have enlisted a small army. How should we handle him?"

"It's time to take care of Liptzin and his crooked iron hand. He's a little fucker playing at pirates. For too long we have idly sat back. Do you believe the army is prepared to take City No. One? Is that fucking loser of a governor with us?"

"You appointed that amateur!"

"Me? He's your brother."

"A distant brother. Not the same mother. You appointed him because you wanted his wife."

"Who told you that?"

"You did!"

"Warshovsky, I've been informed that Berkowitz has taken over District Seven. I'm extremely disappointed—you got all the aid you demanded. I fired that amateur Yaron Hemo as per your demand and we still lost our only district with a port."

"It was just a retreat into District Y."

"You're in District Y? Humans aren't supposed to be there. District Y is only for the dead we allowed to become undead."

"And the dead don't eat, right? So the land is enough for the soldiers to live on. Berkowitz's troops are spread out all over District Seven. Liptzin will join forces with her. I'm maneuvering them to stay there as long as possible, we've heard they're practically freezing to death, their supplies won't last more than two weeks: I'm slamming them with a nineteen-forty-two-style Eastern Front! It's a good thing that pair's greatest intellectual experience is watching sketch comedy on TV. Stop listening to all your amateur advisors. Go smell the flowers outside and leave the job to the professionals."

"You have one month to complete the mission."

"I don't take orders from you."

"But I'm the king!"

"You're a puppet king. The army is behind me."

In the tenth grade, when they'd started writing the kingdom's history, before Yoel became popular in school, Yonatan suspected they were projecting their desire to climb up the social ladder onto their fictional land, infusing it with their rage at the popular cliques, which they viewed with contempt yet secretly wanted to join. Girls and boys they disliked were hanged, thrown off water towers or castle ramparts, had their hands, feet or heads chopped off, were appointed minor ministers, or simply exiled. If a girl they hated showed kindness to one of them, he would start showering her with honorary titles, leaving the other to puzzle over the sudden change. The entire kingdom was quite possibly a macabre map of their relationships with other kids, which they themselves did not thoroughly understand.

They desperately tried to believe that they wanted to be outside the school society they looked down on—all those pathetic, dreary kids who read boring old-people's novels and dressed like their parents and couldn't even see how gray and stifling everything was—but the truth was that they themselves were pretty tame, a fact they were repeatedly disappointed to discover. There were days when they came home from school with their backpacks full of crumpled notes covered with tiny, crowded, White-Out-smeared handwriting alongside pencil-drawn maps.

The kingdom was a place that could absorb all their ideas, a domain that lived somewhere between history, which Yoel liked, and imagination—mostly Yonatan's. But lately events had begun to follow a hackneyed formula, with more wars and ceasefires, more uprisings and exiles, and Yoel seemed to be losing interest, cutting off plotlines with terse notes that left no room for response. He said everything was getting too dramatic, the game lacked humor and lightness. Yonatan did not believe he would have the courage to put an end to the whole story, until the day when Warshovsky announced that he was retiring to his estate, where he would live out the rest of his days in peace.

When Yonatan came home from school the next day, he lay down on his parents' bed and fell asleep. He woke up when the phone rang. It was evening, and he could hear the crickets chirping in the wadi. Without any small talk, his father asked him to write a letter to his mother: the weeks in New York were passing, and she was suffering terribly from her treatments, yet she still talked about Yonatan all the time and worried about him being at home on his own for so long. He did not entirely believe his father. His father said the treatments took place every morning and they spent their afternoons in the hotel, usually just the two of them (sometimes his older brother visited), watching their favorite old movies: *For Whom the Bell Tolls, The Best Years of Our Lives, The French Lieutenant's Woman, Gone with the Wind, The Last Picture Show, The Deer Hunter.*

"But are the treatments helping?" Yonatan asked.

"I hope so," said his father.

He hadn't been expecting this gruff tone, which amplified the doubts and sounded too natural, as though his father were discussing his mother's illness with another adult. Yonatan often protected himself inside a fortress of childhood, using its defensive walls to ward off bad news from the adult world—as well as its messengers. All he wanted to hear now were the lines they had always fed him, about how the situation was complicated, how her condition was discovered quite late, but of course the treatments would help. He always knew that there were details he avoided, content to skip over them as he did cracks in the sidewalk when he was a child. Didn't every game have its own rules, wasn't every arrangement based on certain laws?

On the rare occasions when he did gather up the courage to ask about his mother's illness directly, the answers had never deviated from the predictable formula: vaguely hopeful platitudes. But now his father had abandoned his old tone and the delicate language they'd cultivated together, which, while it did not refute the disease, did not plumb its depths either, using generalizations that spoke in code even when they did not hide a complicated truth—locked doors to nowhere. Sometimes his mother violated this unwritten agreement and told Yonatan that the day would come when he would "visit her grave and place flowers on it," but he put this down to the hardships of the illness, whose details she herself was loath to discuss.

His father coughed, and for an instant Yonatan imagined he could hear another voice, perhaps his mother's or just someone on the TV in their hotel room. He swallowed, and pictured his throat filling up with thick, congealing fluid; Yoel and he had a name for that: "ant porridge dancing in your throat."

"But the treatments are helping," Yonatan insisted in a hoarse voice. He knew he sounded like a fucking coward—*will help, are helping, should help*. Just like Lior with her constant "Is your mom okay?" refrain. He would have given anything for Lior to be there now and say something to him. His knees wouldn't stop moving, he couldn't steady them, and he leaned on the wall by the black telephone armchair.

"I really hope so."

For a moment Yonatan imagined he could see the world through his father's eyes and he remembered how they used to hug. But then he was overcome with anger: these were not the right answers, his father must understand that.

"I know it'll be okay," Yonatan insisted again and his voice cracked.

"Let's hope it will."

There was another silence, and Yonatan believed he had decoded his father's real request: "Write Mom a *farewell* letter." From the moment that notion glowed in his mind, he feared he would not be able to remove it. His gaze crossed the darkness of the living room, perhaps the darkness of the years they had shared, and he was now hurtling through a tunnel, where every so often pictures he did not have time to decipher flickered on the walls. Even when he had contemplated his mother's death, he'd mistrusted the pictures he saw, perhaps conjuring them up because he didn't really believe in them.

"I don't understand," he insisted, "what do you want me to write?" He chased down the words, struggling to grasp them and the answers they sought. He said nothing more, but they both understood, and the weight of the unsaid words—a vision of this home in a few years, if they were even still living there—settled between them. Still silent, their breaths mingled. They had never spoken on the phone for this long. His father was an impatient man, and Yonatan hoped he would hurry up and say, "We'll talk tomorrow." Instead, he seemed to cling to this moment, and Yonatan found that terrifying: had his father been so depleted in New York that he was turning to *him* for comfort? This was how everything collapsed, he thought: a whole world, furnished with hopes and habits, emptied out in an instant, leaving only the fear.

Then his father seemed to break the spell. "Just write her a nice letter, I'm not asking for much," he barked in the same voice he used when he affectionately scolded Yonatan for being mischievous, usually at the request of Yonatan's mother, even when he himself viewed the prank as the sort of thing boys were supposed to do so they could toughen up ahead of real rewards and punishments. The instruction sketched the familiar outline of life, and, even though he had forced it out of his father, Yonatan felt relieved.

"Are you taking care of the house?" his father asked.

"Of course."

"Really?"

"Really."

"Are you studying?"

"Of course."

"You're not doing anything, are you?"

"I'm doing lots of things."

"Are you studying for your finals?"

"We don't have finals. They don't do that anymore."

"Are you talking with the family?"

"What family?"

"All right," his father said.

"I'm going away on Friday," Yonatan said.

"Where to?"

"Tel Aviv. To visit Yaara."

His father paused; the idea of him going to see Yaara probably sounded odd, but either he was too exhausted to interrogate him, or, more likely, he simply didn't believe him.

"But let them know you're coming," his father said in a commanding tone, "and say hello from us to everyone there."

"All right, Dad."

He was sweating. He shut his eyes, and when he opened them the house was cloaked in a vivid darkness like the wadi at night. He was certain, now, that he would stick to his story, even if no one cared anymore: he was going to see Yaara. Where he would really go, he had no idea.

He wiped the sweat off his face with his sleeve, and noticed he was wearing the red shirt his mother had bought him on his first day of high school. He'd come home that day grumbling that the other kids had nice clothes while he was wearing old rags from Florida, and that maybe they didn't get this, but he wasn't going to keep wearing hand-me-downs like his older brother had. No clothes—no school. When he went into his room that evening he found two shirts on his bed, one red and one blue, with a folded piece of yellow paper next to them. He couldn't remember every word it said, only the last part: that one day he would grow up and be wiser, and then she would tell him everything, but for now there were too many things beyond his grasp, and when he found out about them he would regret his misdeeds, and she hoped it wouldn't be too late. "You will feel remorse," she wrote, "and I hope you remember our better times. I still don't understand when things went wrong."

After he read the letter he could feel invisible fingernails scratching his body, and flashes of pain climbed up from the pit of his stomach to his neck and down his back. He sat on the floor with the new notebook he'd bought for the first day of high school and started writing things he knew and things he didn't know: the two years his parents and Shaul had spent in New York before he was born, a time of which he knew almost nothing except the way their eyes glazed over when they talked about it, as though a miracle had occurred there that had melted away the pains of life, and for two whole years they had floated through the streets of that city marveling at its gift. The close relationship between Shaul and his mother, he knew, had formed during all the crises that had befallen the family before he was born, and he felt that the two of them, unlike him, lived in the shadow of those mythical events. His mother had said that one day she would tell him everything and he would understand, but she'd also claimed he would understand too late, after she died.

42

In his new notebook, he wrote what he'd heard about distant times. By the time she was twelve, his mother was in full charge of her household, after her father, Albert Mansur, a card-playing ladies' man, had picked up and moved to Haifa, where he sold shoes. Yonatan learned more details from his paternal grandmother, who told him with barely concealed glee that his mother's family was poor, that his other grandmother, Sarah, never stopped loving her wayward husband Albert ("a charming gentleman whom the Jewish community here in Jerusalem could not comprehend") to her dying day, and that after Albert left she lay in bed for months on end, her spirits uplifted only by the occasional visit from her estranged husband and by Rabbi Ovadia Yosef's sermons at the synagogue. His grandmother also told Yonatan that his twelve-year-old mother was the only person in her family who took care of her little brother and sister, as well as their mother and Albert's elderly parents.

His mother did not talk about her childhood, but she praised Grandma Sarah for her generosity, modesty and devotion to God, who, unfortunately, loved sinners and did not reward the righteous. Once, when his mother was lighting Shabbat candles, standing quietly before the flames with her eyes closed, Yonatan asked with a touch of disdain if she believed in God. She said she wasn't sure. He insisted on knowing why she lit candles if she had these doubts, and she replied that she did it for her mother, who had never sinned and had lived a life of hardship.

As he touched the fabric of the new shirts, he thought back to a recent evening when Kowerski's mother, a therapist with cropped hair, turned up at their home with her son, who was invited for a sleepover. The two mothers sat in the living room, chatted and laughed, and arranged to meet for coffee downtown. When Yonatan came home from school the next day, his mother observed, "Madam Psychologist wanted to see if we were good enough for her son to spend the night here." He was disappointed, having hoped his mother might finally befriend one of his classmates' mothers, but more than that he was surprised: it had never occurred to him that anyone could doubt that his family was respectable. Sometime later, when his mother's friend Dr. Sternberg came to visit and the two of them sat in the living room reading Tolstoy and Dostoevsky and Nietzsche and Leibowitz, and his mother wrote down Sternberg's explanations in her notebook, it dawned on him that only one of Sarah and Albert's four children had gone to university—Yitzhak, the youngest. He replayed the distasteful way his mother had articulated the words "Madam Psychologist," and was saddened by her weakness. The first plan that came to mind was to run to the shopping center and buy her flowers or a mug full of candy that said "Best Mom in the World," like he used to do when he upset her as a child. On the bureau in his parents' bedroom there still stood a few musical mugs and decorative bowls with notes attached: "To the dearest/best/most loved mom in the world, I won't ever do it again/I'm very sorry for what I said." But he was in high school now, the mugs looked silly, and he didn't know how to talk to her about such sensitive matters.

He reread the words his mother had written on the note beside the shirts—"I still don't understand when things went wrong." His mother had always spoken of the harmony of the early years, when he had been desperately attached to her and swore he would marry her when he grew up. The two of them used to walk the streets of Jerusalem together for hours, or spend time in her office at the postal service reading books he loved, like *Sasha and the Dreams* and *Sasha and the Imagination*, and in summer they would spread a sheet out on the balcony and sit down to play "True or False." It was his mother who ruled the story that bound together his earliest memories, even though many of them took place in the home of his nanny, Ahuva. One memory was so lucid that he never doubted it: he wakes up in the early morning, light fog, silver clouds showering rain, Ahuva and her husband are still asleep. He hops out of bed and runs to the living room, slides open the heavy glass door, and walks barefoot across the frozen mud in the yard. Dizzied by the smell of onions, he kneels down and touches a bright green stalk, and licks drops of rain off its tip.

The commonly accepted narrative in his family was that at some point the amity between him and his mother was disrupted. He searched his memory, not for the first time, for the moment when the fissure had occurred, grasping at the tail end of events that might testify to the time before and the time after, seeking to sketch a map of his interactions with his mother in the notebook. But when he wrote, he found that in fact he was reconstructing her map, hunting for memories that would burnish the good era and blacken the bad. She had instilled in him, at a very young age, her narrative of the two separate eras, the long period of unity until he had betrayed her. The betrayal was unrelated to anything he did—it was simply the child he became.

He looked over the lopsided letters, the exclamation marks, the wide columns adorning the text—he always doodled columns—and ripped the pages out of the notebook. He stepped onto the balcony, turned his body against the wind, crouched down and held a lighter to the pages, dropped them in an old dish and watched them burn. Then he put on his smart black pants and the new red shirt, which he tucked in, even though he hated doing that. He combed his mane into a sort of side-part, but his head was shaved down either side and it looked strange.

When he walked into the living room and his mother looked up, she grinned: "That shade of red looks so good on you," she said, getting up to come closer to him. They stood facing each other, she straightened his collar and smoothed out the wrinkles on his sleeves. He pushed her hands away in playful protestation and said, "Stop it," but the futility of his response irritated him—why couldn't he sometimes just let things go?—and as she turned away, he put his arm around her shoulders and told her that he liked the shirt. He could smell her cloyingly sweet perfume, a scent familiar from childhood. She leaned her cheek on his arm, and he took her hands and held them up and spun her around as if they were dancing. Her black eyes beamed at him and her movements felt somehow airy as he whirled her around again, then let her spin him, and she said he was the only one in the family who knew how to dance, and that he would grow up to be a ladies' man. "I should have already been one by now," he remarked with a smile that did not conceal his bitterness. "I'm fourteen."

She came to his room later, with a dish of sliced apples, and exclaimed, "You won't believe this!" She'd seen in the paper that they were showing *Gone with the Wind* at the neighborhood cinema that night.

"What time?" he asked.

"Ten p.m.," she replied mischievously, anticipating his surprise.

"But that means it'll end at two a.m.!" he said.

She was delighted. "So you'll get up late for school this one time. So what? But only if you want to go."

"Of course I do," he said, sad to think she could doubt his ability to recognize how rare this moment was.

Later that night, his mother put on her white pants and cream-colored poufy blouse, and she asked him, the way she used to when he was a child, if her outfit looked good or if she should change. She pulled on her coat with the gray fur-lined collar, and he did not change out of his black pants and new shirt. In the taxi to the cinema they avoided talking, knowing the occasion was both festive and fragile. They sat in the second row; there were only four other people at the movie. After about an hour he fell asleep, and when he woke up he saw his mother's head drooping, her eyes shut, a few tangled curls clinging to her forehead. Every time he imagined her without her curls, the weary, plucked figure terrified him, and he still hoped it would not happen. Her eyelids fluttered and her upper lip trembled. He moved his right hand over her head and gently held her shoulder, and with his left he clutched her hand, as though seeking to protect her while she glided through the worlds of sleep.

He woke her up at the midnight intermission and walked her, still sleepy, out into the cold night. She huddled in her coat, held his arm, he pressed his hand on hers and they both looked up at the clear, starry sky over the shopping center. Her mood seemed cheerful now, and she told him that, when she was more or less his age, she'd spent several months in hospital.

"Which one?"

"Bikur Holim."

"But that's a religious hospital," he pointed out, and regretted his inflammatory tone. He knew she'd gone to Evelina de Rothschild, a religious school for girls, and that her tuition was paid by her uncle Aziz. What sort of clothes had she worn as a child? He tried to picture her in an ankle-length skirt and button-down blouse like the ones he saw on the religious girls downtown, but the fragmentary images—the girls downtown, the hallways of Bikur Holim, his mother as a young girl—refused to cohere.

Ignoring his comment, she told him she'd had severe arthritis.

"That sounds awful," he said tenderly, "you must have gone crazy in there."

She laughed and said it was a wonderful time, perhaps the best of her life. "You should have seen my doctor, Dr. Zussman," she said, pronouncing his name in a caressing whisper. "He was a real Clark Gable. All the women in Jerusalem used to line up outside his office, wearing their prettiest dresses, with hats and scarves and high heels, like they'd stepped out of a magazine, just to have him diagnose their illnesses."

"Are you saying you were in love with your doctor?" he asked with a chuckle.

She looked at him, baffled by how obtuse he could be, perhaps remembering why she didn't confide in him anymore. Her laughter lines vanished and her expression grew even more distant. He could not translate the meaning of the strange glow in her eyes, a verve that seemed to signal that all the emotions churning inside him, like his yearning for some girl or other, had once electrified her too.

"He was in love with me," she said.

That conversation had taken place more than three years ago, two months after she was diagnosed. Now, time was once again severed: instead of the bad years and the good years, there was the time before and the time after.

———

"Is your mother okay?" Lior asked.

He'd hated the question since they'd first met shortly after his seventeenth birthday. It always seemed somehow dubious, anticipating the day when the answer would be no. He answered that his parents were in New York for his mother's treatment. Lior expressed no surprise or interest, only repeating, "But is she okay?" For a minute he considered teasing her: "Define okay." But he couldn't summon the necessary irony. "I told you not to ask me that," he hissed, and remembered that she said he'd first caught her attention when Tali, her classmate, told her about Yoel's friend who got into a fight with some other kid after beautifully discussing a Goethe poem in class (something about a father riding a horse at night while carrying his dying infant).

Lior had been amused by the drastic swing between tenderness and violence, even though she found it immature, like something out of a teen TV show. "But at least you're trying to do something interesting," she'd said. Later, after they'd been introduced by Tali, Lior said she sometimes saw something apologetic, maybe even shy, in his darting eyes that avoided direct contact, and in the way he grimaced, but that it was quickly replaced by aggression because that way he felt more protected. She said there was something unnatural about how he moved and responded, which made people feel uncomfortable around him, and that maybe if he really were a thug things would be simpler.

"At the end of the day we're all thugs, aren't we?" he retorted, not entirely sure what he meant, although the idea sounded reasonable.

When the phone rang he knew it was her. He'd been waiting for months to hear her voice, since that morning in his room when she could no longer bear the way he interrogated her—he kept going even though Yoel warned him it would end in disaster—and admitted that she didn't love him and maybe never had. His passion for her must have infected her; she had tried desperately to love him. It was clear that she was acknowledging the truth of her own words even as she said them. For an instant he even felt sorry for her, because of the sadness in her voice and her expression, and he knew she'd done everything to convince herself that she loved him. When he picked up the phone he also knew that for the last four days he hadn't talked to a living soul or left the house except to visit Ratzon Dahari, the neighbor downstairs, where he sometimes had dinner when his parents were away.

"Have you seen her recently?" Lior asked.

"Who?" he replied with fake innocence.

"Have you seen her or haven't you? Have you seen Yaara?"

"That's not your business anymore."

Lior said nothing, and then she said she'd been missing him lately. He took a deep breath and knew what he had to say even if the answer would doom him to more loneliness, and that if he said something else she might come over and they would lie in bed and he would be buried in her arms—she always said that no human creature could provide the octopus embrace he longed for—and his pain would subside. But there was no other way. "You're dead to me," he said. She gave a wounded gasp of surprise and waited another moment before hanging up, as if she were still hoping he would say, "Just kidding." If that had occurred to her, it meant she really did not understand anything.

He swallowed down bitter saliva and waited for his spirits to lift. "The defeat is crushing," he'd written to Yoel after Lior left that morning, in a note that was ostensibly about affairs of the kingdom. For months he waited for her to take a step that would somehow soften his defeat.

A memory from last September came crashing down on him: shortly after they met, he got his driver's license and went straight to Lior's. They drove for hours, listening to her Gladys Knight & the Pips tape, and of course he lied about knowing "Midnight Train to Georgia." A warm, dry wind caressed their faces and its taste mingled with the sharp smell of cigarette smoke in the car (he'd bought a pack of JPS Black to impress her), and every moment his body wasn't touching her he was overcome by a terrifying loneliness. When he held her hand, stroked her hair, or when she clung to him, the serenity he felt was intoxicating and everything around them—the blue sky, the trees on Aza Street, the gas station by the museum—looked perfectly made, as though he were finally seeing a world he had not stopped searching for all these years, a world in which he was loved.

He was saddened by the knowledge that she had been alive for a long time without him, that she had been molded by forces he did not know, that she had trusted other loves. When they stopped outside her house in the evening she put her hand on his cheek and asked, as if she understood everything, if he could learn to rely on her love when she was not with him. He said he would learn anything she wanted him to, and she laughed: "You're totally in love."

He considered various niggling responses that would cast doubt on what she'd said, but he just wanted to give in to it all, to accelerate the dizziness even more.

He had trouble tolerating the fullness of that memory and the sight of his fawning smile when he sat with her in the car—it filled his throat with a bitter taste. He imagined his fingers reaching into his mind to tear out the entire month of August, throbbing like a heart removed from a living body, and burying it in the wadi.

In the living room he lit a cigarette, and was aware that in the more bearable moments of pain he could summon up the pathos required to act the tormented version of himself, instead of sprawling out on the couch and waiting to be swallowed by sleep. In the liquor cabinet he looked for the vodka he and Yoel used to drink when they roamed the wadi at night, still in disbelief at being allowed to be there after all the evenings they'd spent watching the black void from their balconies and yearning for nocturnal adventures. They never drank together anymore. All he found was his parents' cheap cognac.

He walked out of the living room, heading for the mirror in his parents' bedroom, the only one he looked in anymore. There had been a day in the school bathroom when the light was harsh, and his reflection had disgusted him: his face was too wide, his skin red and inflamed, his eyes sunken and large, one darker than the other, his nose was big, and his long, greasy hair sprouted out as if someone had perched an umbrella on his head. His expression looked banal, the kind you dismiss as quickly as you smooth out a crease in your clothes. He had walked away from the sight in shock, and since that day, light had become problematic. He didn't even turn the light on when he showered. On sunny days he was careful not to get too close to shop windows, because the glaring light exposed all the little defects in his face; he cherished gray days with no trace of the sun, when he would dare to look at his reflection from afar. In his parents' room, he had a ritual: he drew the blinds, switched on only his father's desk lamp, with the beam aimed at the floor, and then stood before the wooden framed mirror with the folding wings. In that faint light he was even fond of his face.

Looking at his reflection, he imagined that he could see a space opening up in the center of his chest—now that he and Lior were frozen in that state, nothing could change between them. The lucidity of the picture frightened him. It was not the imagination whose colors, pictures and hallucinations he knew, but a different force that swirled inside him now, and it felt foreign. He wondered what Lior was wearing when she'd spoken with him. He knew all her outfits: black dress, red dress with black circles, blue wool skirt, T-shirts with numbers or lettering, untidy hair snaking playfully down her neck, a thin silver necklace—these were for cafés, restaurant dinners, smoking pot at the biology student's apartment next door. Flared jeans and a tank top with strappy heels—for pubs and music shows. Sweatpants, plain white T-shirt, hair tied back—popping out to return a video, buy cigarettes or beer, visit a girlfriend. Sometimes she came out in a dress, and he liked to look at her as she walked down the path to his car, a sort of single continuous motion, with a domineering expression in her eyes, expecting something to excite her. "She's not special enough for that look," Tali decreed, even though they went to school together and were supposedly good friends.

He imagined a version of himself standing at this mirror in a week or two; maybe some of the humiliation, the shock of betrayal, would have subsided a little. Perhaps the person who constantly replayed their days together would have hardened. While they'd been together, after all, he hadn't truly believed in the possibility of losing her: he had always bought into dreadful scenarios he did not think would come true, bought into them because he did not believe in them.

His fingers played with her shirt—in fact with all her shirts, now patched into one—aiming to caress her stomach. He touched his face, which was sweaty and hot, or perhaps it was his fingers that were hot. How could he have failed to understand that as soon as he redeemed his dignity and the anger began to subside, there would be nothing to protect him from the longing.

"Have you seen Yaara?" He heard a screech and realized he was listening to his own laughter—was he really laughing? He strained his eyes and saw no signs of laughter. She really didn't understand anything.

Yaara was the daughter of his parents' friends in Tel Aviv, and he'd known her and her older sister, Avigail, since childhood. She'd never shown any interest in him, preferring the bronzed, muscular boys who wore colorful bermuda shorts and surfed in the daytime and played guitar on the beach in the evenings, with their long, sun-bleached hair flying in the wind—in other words, beach boys. To her it was audacious of him, a pale-skinned Jerusalem boy, to sport bright surfers' clothes in the late eighties. Last Passover, after Yonatan's mother finished a round of treatments and regained her strength, the two families had stayed at a kibbutz hotel in the Galilee. Avigail was almost nineteen, with black hair and blue eyes, a rebellious type who was about to begin her military service after announcing she wanted "either an office job near home or a wedding." Yonatan had always been slightly afraid of her sharp tongue. Yaara, who was born a few weeks after him, was a thin blonde with dark chestnut eyes, a kind, generous girl whom everyone admired. His older brother once told him that when the parents got together they disparaged Yonatan and Avigail but talked of Yaara as a prodigy.

When he stepped out of the car into the blazing sun at the kibbutz, he saw the sisters leaning carelessly on their dad's car, their faces turned to the sky and light dancing on the frames of their dark sunglasses. Avigail wore a short black tank top with one shoulder strap falling down her arm, which was slightly red, and a thin blouse tied around her waist. Yaara had on an airy, knee-length, cream-colored dress with black polka dots. Her feet moved on the hot asphalt of the parking lot, and her toes, with their nails painted dark red, played with the silver strap of her high-heeled sandals. The lust that surged through his limbs stunned him. The girls' bodies savored the sun, which threw bright light on their skin while other parts remained in shadow. He had never been so close to such exciting girls.

He put on his sunglasses and waved hello. They didn't see him. His mother went over to them, and to his surprise they called out to her and gave her long hugs. Finally his mother drew their attention to Yonatan and his father, who asked clumsily, "Everything going well, girls?" Yonatan sneaked a glance at his father, who looked at the three women and then at the asphalt and back at them, and for the first time in his life it occurred to him that his father was also a man who could feel passion, and he was overcome by embarrassment. Fortunately his father went back to the car and began unloading their luggage.

As a young boy he'd been embarrassed around the sisters, but in the year and a half since he'd last seen them things had changed. He was not the chubby boy they used to know. He had woven together a personality from gestures and tones he borrowed from people he knew and from protagonists in books or TV series. Yoel said the two of them had a problem: they were capable of liking themselves only by means of the contempt they showed everyone else.

At dinner on the first night, Yaara expressed some interest in Yonatan, and they talked about a lot of things. After the meal they left the group and walked alone on the damp grass, passing through the dark areas and the milky-white pentagons cast on the kibbutz paths by lamps. They trampled leaves and twigs and moist earth under their shoes, and reached a small hill at the edge of the kibbutz that looked onto the darkness of the bare fields. Slightly out of breath, they climbed up, walked down the other side and wandered through the fields. When their feet sank into a muddy puddle, Yaara laughed, and countless images—him caressing her hair, holding her hand, kissing her neck—flickered before his eyes, enticing him to make them come true.

The stones beneath their feet became larger and Yaara tripped slightly. He caught her upper arm and her body turned, their legs pressed together. Her face was very close and he felt his lips burning. But she quickly turned away. Perhaps he'd lingered too long. He jokingly offered—still reconstructing the missed moment when his lips had fluttered over hers—to carry her so she would not fall again, and she replied, "You wish," but in a playful tone, as though if he tried he might convince her. But he was afraid she would reject him, so he just laughed in a somewhat creaky voice.

He had not yet entirely let go of her, but Yaara gently moved her hand, ran her fingers over his bicep as if by accident, and they walked arm in arm and said nothing more. He took pleasure in the silence but was afraid she'd be bored, so he blurted out something about his mother, and when they started talking he realized that Yaara knew a lot about the illness. At one point she paused before mentioning the name of a new doctor his parents were seeing, realizing that she might know things that were being kept from him.

It's no wonder she knew things: before his mother got ill, his parents used to go to Tel Aviv every Thursday, and his mother would meet his father at the end of the day at Yaara's family home. Yaara said they missed his mother, who hadn't visited recently because of the treatments, and she described how they used to sit in the yard and his mother would smoke a cigarette and drink red wine or a martini and cheer them up with her imitations of his father grumbling about being tired.

Every Thursday in recent months his mother went to the hospital for treatments. Early in the week she would be in a good mood, and sometimes she even played hooky and left the house, but by Tuesday her face would be tense and her posture hunched, and anyone who tried to get near her would be accused of nosiness or even malice. Yonatan was usually tasked with keeping away the nuisances. By Wednesday she hardly left her room and spoke to almost no one. On Thursday morning a friend or her sister would come to care for her, and he felt their home fill with their calming presence. His own presence in the home, and the very fact of his existence, were of no use to his mother. Unlike Shaul, who used to sit for hours on the stool in her room and exchange secrets with her, Yonatan would stand preening at the mirror. They made fun of how long he spent on his hair, like a girl, and discussed him as if he weren't there. Unlike Shaul, Yonatan told his mother almost nothing. Perhaps that was what she never forgave him for. He had disappointed her bitterly, and by the time she became ill she'd lost interest in him. And so he preferred it when other people, those who were really close to her, filled her room with noises and voices.

Most days, it was just the two of them at home. She lay alone in bed and he orbited around her. He would sit in his room or in the living room and hear her groaning or coughing or watching television and talking on the phone. Sometimes he went to the shops and bought her a baguette or crackers with butter, food for when the nausea passed, and sometimes in the afternoon they lay on her bed watching TV together. At the end of the week her door was shut, and he saw her friends or sister going in and out, carrying the blue basin she vomited in. On rare occasions she left her room, thin and shriveled, wearing a white robe and a headscarf, and he would follow her with his gaze, fighting off his recognition that the disease was relentlessly diminishing her body. He knew that her friends, just like her, believed he could do more for her, and that their reserved but friendly demeanor was hiding outrage.

He began telling Yaara about the atmosphere at home and how much his mother complained about him and talked about things she'd missed out on in life. He stopped after a while because he did not want to muddy Yaara's vivacious picture of his mother. But a look of sardonic pity had come over her face, as though she'd been listening to him politely but without real interest, and he realized that the picture he was painting of his mother made no impression on her: it was as though they were talking about two different women. Yaara walked a few steps away. "I'm bored with rebellious adolescents," she said. He was enchanted by the slight contempt with which she regarded him, and by the way she moved, which seemed infused with a knowing serenity. It was as though while everyone else tried out different identity pieces, tormenting themselves over trivialities, she walked the world with the complacency of those who have always been loved and who never try to make people like them. She accepted his jabs with equanimity, as if she understood that she was obliged to overlook the jealousy of flawed individuals.

He woke up early in the morning, sweating, with a fever and a sore throat. Everyone went hiking and he stayed in bed. He tossed back and forth between sleep and wakefulness, seeing multiple faces that peeked in to ask how he was—perhaps they were there or perhaps he dreamed them. As the hours went by he found it harder to tolerate the waiting. He knew that tomorrow she would leave and that, if nothing happened now, it would likely never happen.

She came when evening began to fall and a few faint stars were already flickering at the edge of the sky, above blue inlets slowly turning purple. She stood in the middle of the room, without turning on the light, and debated which of the two beds to sit on while his body teemed with anticipation. The only sound in the room was his wheezing breaths, and he tried to stifle them. Finally she sat on the edge of his bed, put her hand on the mattress near his waist, and her hair touched his shirt. Her silence buoyed him: she recognized the intimacy they had woven yesterday, and now she did not know how to act; their childhood customs were no longer valid. At last, perhaps because of his high fever and the closeness of her body, he said what was in his heart: he'd been waiting for her all day. His fingers stroked her blue-painted fingernails. She put her hand on the back of his hot hand, and the world at once widened, new paths emerged before his eyes, and he believed he had the power to follow them, to overcome obstacles and explore choices.

He smoothed his left hand over the back of her neck, and his fingers caressed her hair. Suddenly they heard a noise and listened together to the voices in the hallway. To his horror they were coming closer, and he heard his mother saying she hoped the chicken breast hadn't got too cold. Yaara's father said it tasted like a rubber shoe anyway, and they all laughed. Yaara stood up, but stayed close, and their fingers were still intertwined. The back of his hand, where her palm had touched, still bore an odd sensation of nakedness. He asked if she would come later, after dinner, and she said maybe.

When he awoke the next morning, still groggy from the pills he'd taken, they'd already left.

———

He couldn't remember when he'd first mentioned Yaara's name to Lior. It might have been a month after they'd met, when he realized that Lior's past haunted her (it always haunted him). She often reminisced about her two previous boyfriends, but he had no equivalent memories of his own. In the storyline he told Lior and later had no choice but to tell everyone, he and Yaara had kissed on the kibbutz, and since then they met every so often in Tel Aviv, and they'd done "a lot" but hadn't had sex.

Then there was the story he wrote in his notebook: Yaara's father had died of cancer when she was in tenth grade. He had left the family some money and property, but after his death she lost interest in people. Most nights she lay awake in bed and the years with her father descended on her, there was nowhere to hide, and maybe she didn't want to. She got lost in a medley of colors, streets, cities, pictures and years, unable to isolate any single detail. When he saw her at her father's funeral—which he described sparingly, as he'd never been to a cemetery in Tel Aviv—he was gripped by a strange certainty, perhaps because of his mother's illness, that they would soon become close. This was a detail he always made a point of mentioning in his stories: that even then, two years before they kissed on the kibbutz, Yaara had become a part of his world. It's not that he'd fallen in love with her, but it was a closeness determined by life-and-death forces.

Every time Yonatan met Yaara's father he felt he'd done him an injustice, or that perhaps he'd cursed him and hastened his real death. In one of his accounts of Yaara and her father's death and her insomnia, he realized he was using images he feared would come to be in his own life, ones that had plagued him since his mother had taken ill. It was mean, he felt dirty writing it, but the story had taken on a life of its own.

He brandished Yaara every time he thought Lior was losing interest or pining for her ex-boyfriends, and if she mentioned a memory to do with them, he waited a few days and invented one of his own. Then he added it to the notebook. When Lior was focused on him, Yaara would disappear, and if Lior asked about her he trivialized her importance or sent her back to an ex-boyfriend. He was surprised Lior didn't notice the pattern. His work was complete when Lior said she would prefer him not to talk to Yaara anymore, and of course he agreed: it wasn't particularly complicated to do.

On the morning of the break-up, Lior told him: "So are you going to be with Yaara now?" There was a note of irony in her voice, or perhaps he only imagined it, and he was struck by despair upon realizing that even if it were true, it wouldn't do any good now. Later he tormented himself by wondering if Yaara's existence had accelerated their breakup, and whether, had he swallowed his pride and given himself to Lior, she might have stayed with him. At the same time he remembered that Lior hadn't doubted his love—the intensity of his love had made her believe that she loved him.

After the breakup, he kicked the plotline up a notch: he and Yaara became very close, not exactly a couple, but he'd gone to visit his aunt in Tel Aviv a few times and—as he told everyone, especially Tali, who he knew would tell Lior—he'd seen Yaara there. In fact he said he was going to see her this coming Friday. Maybe Lior had called because she'd heard he was going.

He went over to the window and looked across the street at Yoel's room. Four crows circled, screeching at the colorful curtain that Tali had sewn for him, then perched on the tree in the yard. Beyond the wadi a storm was simmering. The quiet suburban night was disturbed by the whistling wind, which sometimes sounded like emergency sirens. The branches moved, and the crows took flight. Yoel's light was on, and he thought he detected movement. He really was going to have to go somewhere on Friday now, because if he stayed home— even if he parked the car on another street—Yoel would know. He probably knew anyway, and that was why he hardly ever asked about Yaara, but that didn't matter. They'd always both known: the minute you invent a story, you are obliged to defend it and see it through to the end.

MEXICO

Silver and diamonds glistened on necks and hands, reflected back from the lobby's windows, chandeliers and mirrors. Countless little crosses glimmered all around him. The hotel was full of teenagers: boys in tuxedos, girls in high heels and ball gowns that grazed the floor, with gold necklaces, tiaras, bracelets and rings. They delighted in their finery, constantly touching their clothes, smoothing out creases, floating past the ogling hotel guests without a glance except when they stopped to hand someone a star-encrusted iPhone and face him with all their youthful vigor, arranging themselves in two rows—one kneeling, one standing—composed of couples embracing or trios of boys leaping on each other's shoulders.

Yonatan had never seen such an extravagant high school prom. He walked out to the patio overlooking the swimming pool, in the center of which was a fountain lit up in changing colors. He mingled with the kids, listened to them, looked them over. He was the only hotel guest brave enough to stand out there. One girl shot him a look and said something in Spanish. No one else took any notice of him, but he did not feel like a complete stranger among them.

He bummed a cigarette from one of the boys, whose eyes radiated light green under thick brows as he raked his fingers through his light-brown mane. The boy smiled and slapped Yonatan's shoulder as he handed him a cigarette. Yonatan asked, in Spanish, how his evening was going, and the boy replied in English: "Prom night, you know," gave a thumbs-up and turned his back on him slowly, perhaps so as not to offend him.

He walked back inside to the lobby, where people were milling around, and crossed over to the great room. Just last week there'd been young festival workers all over this space, patiently dealing with authors who pestered them about interesting places to see in town, grumbled about events attended by no more than ten people, including their editors, gave press interviews, or boasted to pretty volunteers in short dresses about all the languages their books had been translated into and about their drunken escapades with famous American writers whose books they made a point of bashing. On the walls, which last week were covered by plastic bookshelves and posters with hackneyed quotes about the love of literature, there were now green signs emblazoned with the slogan, "2050: Green Mexico City," alongside pictures of solar panels, electric cars and wind turbines. The boys and girls from the prom had vanished, apparently into the ballroom. He went up to the restaurant floor, turned right and took another broad but poorly lit staircase up one more level, and was surprised to hear nineties music blaring from behind three heavy iron doors.

He stood outside the ballroom for a while. Every so often a young couple walked by, holding hands. Finally he went back down to the lobby, which had gone suddenly cold. He rubbed his arms and walked faster to warm up, looking around for the young woman with glasses. But she wasn't there. The magazine publisher had told him he'd found her and that she'd be waiting for him there at nine this evening. Why had he even believed him?

Yoel had met Itamar only in the middle of last summer. A few times Yonatan had asked him over, implying that they were starting to feel hurt and that Shira might bear a grudge, but at other times he'd said it wasn't urgent, Yoel could visit whenever he felt like it. Finally, one Friday at five, Yoel knocked on their door. He hugged Shira and then Yonatan. He did not charge into the living room the way he used to, but walked behind them as they led him to Itamar, who was lying in his playpen. Yoel approached as if performing a practiced move, jiggled the baby's hand, stroked his cheek, kissed his belly, put his face right up to him and exclaimed in a put-on voice, "What a cutie! You little rascal!"

Then he straightened up and stood there, holding onto the edge of the playpen, and stared wide-eyed at Itamar—it was obvious that he was not actually seeing him—with the same look that had begun to appear in his eyes over the last year or so. At first it had led everyone astray because he seemed so focused, until they realized that it meant he wasn't listening to anyone and couldn't see a thing. It was a look that sliced through everything he saw and dived into another realm. There were many nights when Yonatan lay next to Shira and imagined Yoel in his childhood bed at 10 HaGuy Street, staring up at the ceiling. What was he seeing? Was there any way to know? They had already learned that one cannot see the world through another person's eyes.

For a while they stood there silently, the three of them, waiting for something. Yonatan knew he should say something upbeat, but a pain was sharpening in his hips and his whole body felt weak. Yoel turned to them with a friendly face, cleared his throat as if trying to choose the correct tone, but said nothing. Shira talked about the baby's weight, and Yonatan could hear Yoel breathing next to him. He hoped Yoel wouldn't ask to pick Itamar up, and felt ashamed of how repelled he was by the idea, but in his mind's eye he saw Yoel running to the window with the baby.

Yoel was apparently trying to enlist the cheerfulness he could always fire up at will. "He looks like both of you," his voice creaked, and

Yonatan could no longer interrupt the motion that would put him between Yoel and Itamar. As he moved closer, Yoel turned and sat down on the couch, as if his efforts had drained all his strength. It wasn't possible that Yoel knew what was going through his mind, Yonatan thought with horror. But then a deeper dread burst into his consciousness: even if Yoel did know, he didn't care.

"What about a drink, kind sir? A little whiskey would be nice. But gimme something from your secret stash, you cheapskate," Yoel proclaimed. He drummed on the table with his hands. "The things and I, we are good friends. It's secret, top secret." Yonatan tried to remember which of Yoel's old characters he was doing, then remembered it was an impersonation of a poet they'd once met, a young woman who spoke in raptured whispers about poetry and love until Yoel told her he thought Arik Einstein's pop songs were pure poetry.

He went into the kitchen. He heard Yoel humming a song they used to like, until his voice spluttered into a fake cough and the living room went silent. Without turning on the light, he stood by the kitchen window: a group of boys in shorts and tank tops leaned against the front of the building, passing a beer around and gazing toward Ibn Gavirol Street.

Yonatan picked up plates and glasses and put them back down, moved the bottle of whiskey back and forth, making noise that would attest to some sort of action and hoping that meanwhile Shira would cheer up Yoel, that he'd hear sounds of laughter. He considered suggesting a poker game—he could "spice up the deal with a little cash," as Yoel used to say—they'd started gambling at age eleven, playing poker in the neighborhood, then Texas Hold'em, casinos in Jericho, casinos in London, betting on races or election results—but he remembered that Yoel was disgusted by gambling now, and even more so by money. He tilted his ear to the living room: Shira wasn't talking with Yoel, and he silently cursed her as he walked back.

He stood the whiskey bottle in the middle of the table with three glass snifters, and waited for Yoel to tell his customary anecdote about the girl who'd once accused Yonatan of keeping two kinds of whiskey at home—an expensive one for himself and a cheap one for guests. But Yoel did not follow the ritual. After the first sip, Yonatan reminded him of the story and a faint smile flashed across Yoel's face, but it vanished so quickly that Yonatan couldn't be sure he'd really seen it. Yoel gave a sideways look at Shira, who was holding the baby, and mused, "Cute. Looks a lot like both of you." It was the first time he'd heard Yoel use his normal voice all evening.

Yoel looked at his blue bag and they both knew he wanted to pull out one of their crumpled old school notebooks but was afraid of Yonatan's response. He'd threatened Yoel that if he saw those notebooks again he'd burn the lot of them.

"I can't believe I actually left you in the basement that day," Yoel said. "What a shit I was."

"Seriously. Such a shit."

"You could have left too."

"True, I could have."

"So how come you stayed?"

"I didn't want to leave Tali alone with them."

"Don't lie, she left before I did," Yoel said with a sullen look.

"I was afraid she'd come back."

"Well, at least I didn't leave you to die alone in the wadi," Yoel said with a grin.

"You know I lost you," Yonatan answered, trying in vain to sound light-hearted.

Shira looked at him. She was familiar with the casual way the two of them conjured up the past, but she was still surprised by how natural his voice sounded when he answered Yoel. She came closer to them, with Itamar in her arms, and he suspected she was eager to get Yoel out of there.

"Look at his eyes," he said to Yoel, "they're a copy of Shira's."

Yoel glanced at the baby. "Yeah, you're right," he conceded, and looked away and sipped his whiskey.

There was a tense silence. Yoel was obviously hoping Shira would leave them alone. "Look at those calves," Yonatan insisted, stroking Itamar, whose eyes were smiling. He was overcome by a desire to cradle the boy in his arms and bury his face in his neck. Yoel touched the baby's shins for a second and pulled his hand back. Yonatan couldn't understand why Yoel didn't want to caress the baby and kiss his cheeks, and he tried not to get angry. Yoel stood up, went over to his bag, found a cigarette, put it to his lips and said he was going out to smoke. "I'll come with you," Yonatan said.

The asphalt under their feet was warm, and a curl of blue smoke glowed in the headlights of a car. The treetops looked enormous and enchanted; he'd never noticed before how their branches met in a sort of arbor over the street. They walked arm in arm, pinching and tripping each other up, while Yoel grumbled about the summer: everyone was sweaty and stinky, the world was a sticky mess, everything you touched stuck to your body like a magnet and it was completely suffocating.

He smelled Yoel's sweat, saw his fingernails that had grown long and dark, the scabby wounds on the back of his hand, his sparse beard with little bald patches. They always used to walk arm in arm, and weren't even aware of doing it until Shira once took a picture of them because she liked it. In the first few years of their relationship, her eyes used to light up every time they got together with Yoel, and she usually stayed for a while, enjoying their word games and the way they hurled insults at each other and tried to win her over. She sensed the element in their friendship that ignited whenever they met and lifted Yonatan's spirits. She said every meeting was a celebration, and she was enchanted by their delight in each other. But over time her comments began to change. She said there was a sort of lava that erupted from them; it spurted out of their language and was oblivious to the people around them, who were only there to confirm the perfect unity between Yoel and Yonatan. Once, after she'd spent an evening with them, she said with a surprised laugh that all they talked about was the girls from Beit HaKerem and the boys from Beit HaKerem and the fights in Beit HaKerem.

Yonatan was used to touching Yoel, but now walking with him he realized he was maneuvering his body to diminish their contact without Yoel noticing. He felt crushed by something akin to orphanhood, because he knew that the atmosphere when they were together now depended on him alone. "Everyone grew up and we're the only ones still pretending," they always used to say, but even when Itamar was born Yonatan hadn't felt the same need to grow up urgently that he did now.

He put his arm around Yoel, pressed his head against his chest, and pinched his shoulder. "May you know of no sorrow!" he yelled, summoning one of their touchstone moments when the past was what they needed. A friend of theirs had died at only twenty-five, and when they visited the family during the shiva, a woman went up to one of the relatives and clutched his hand, saying, "May you know of no sorrow."

Yoel corrected her, "May you know no more sorrow."

The woman gave him an astonished look: "That's what I said," she mumbled.

"No," Yoel replied calmly, "you said something else."

It was usually Yoel who told that story, though, reconstructing every detail, where everyone had been sitting or standing, imitating all the characters, while Yonatan laughed and egged him on. But now Yoel only gave an indifferent snort of laughter, and Yonatan overcame his reluctance and pinched him, squeezing so hard that he lost sensation in his fingers. He waited for Yoel to wriggle out of his grip, but Yoel rested his head on Yonatan's chest and stared at the treetops around them.

He took two breaths, which shifted Yoel's head slightly, then pushed him off and stood facing him. He stuck two cigarettes between his lips, lit them and handed one to Yoel. Yoel had gained weight, his cheeks looked chubby, and his curly hair was full of gray and white. For years Yonatan had gathered signs, mourning the passing time with Yoel—in fact more so than Yoel, whose observations were mitigated by a layer of irony and dark humor, with quotes from Bartleby or

Lenin. But after Itamar was born, he began to accept these signs as the natural order of things, and the passage of time they'd always feared stopped haunting him. Or perhaps, as Yoel said, he'd simply given up.

"I know I shouldn't show you this because you'll flip out," Yoel said, "but let me show you, just take a look for ten minutes and tell me what you think, you know I'd do it for you."

"I've looked at those fucking notebooks a million times."

"Just once. Ten minutes, man."

"No."

"I've read every book you've written."

"It's not the same thing, and you know it," Yonatan retorted, surprised.

"Not everything in them is accurate, it should be noted."

His skin prickled, he looked at Yoel: all this was unfamiliar and ominous. Yoel rarely voiced any criticism of his novels. "I don't understand," he said.

"Certain events in the books might not have occurred exactly in the way you've written them. You've never been very careful about being faithful to the truth, if we're being honest." Yoel gave a sort of giggle. "It was always kind of cute."

"They are novels, you know." How pathetic his answer sounded.

Yoel gave him a long stare, and for a moment his face took on a more lucid expression, reminiscent of when they used to work together on something. "Come on, don't talk to me like I'm one of those sweaty students in your writing workshops. You write those things because they happened. Dystopia, utopia, historical fiction—I can always see what you're really writing about."

Yonatan could not think of a response that wouldn't seem affected. The old Yoel, not the one standing before him now, had always been able to change the mood but Yonatan didn't have it in him now to do a magic trick. Yoel must have sensed his paralysis. He perked up and put on a mask of laughter. "Honestly, it doesn't matter at all. You, from the ashes of our childhood, you produce miracles." He looked around at the people on Rabin Square, then called out, "See how they applaud you!"

A few people gave them puzzled looks. Their familiar hyperbolic tone always emerged in tense moments. Yoel used it especially, attacking Yonatan with jabs and hints and then taking them back or at least denying their severity. It was strange that Yonatan preferred that tone, even though he knew that what Yoel had said before, which he hadn't completely understood, was what mattered. "Everyone knows you are a venerable leader," he told Yoel, completing the ritual. He looked at his watch and wondered if the baby was asleep yet. Sometimes they still called him 'the baby.'

"Just look at the notebook one more time, old sport," Yoel pleaded. "Be a real friend for once."

"I've already told you, I'm done with those notebooks," he snapped.

"It doesn't matter anyway, you're not going to improve me," Yoel said in a creaky voice. "I'm beyond help. So take a look, it'll help a little."

"I swear things will get better."

"People are pushed to their deaths while they polish their silver and read the newspaper."

"That's the only quote you remember."

"I like that line."

"You'll like other lines too."

"I'm going to die really soon."

In perfect synchrony, they tossed their burning cigarettes onto the street.

THE TOWERS
(LATE 1980S)

He wondered how they could fail to see it, the kids from the towers, and Yoel, and Shimon and Bentz and David Tzivony, and his parents, and even his big brother in New York—how could they not see that the sky in the wadi was crumpling toward the earth and sharp little needles were dangling dangerously above them all? How could they not hear that the whistles of the wind were twisting into a scream, that the gusts were carrying waves of sand and yellow dust, dry leaves, twigs and branches from the wadi to their buildings, that a sandy dome was gradually forming above their world and the sandy dust was clumping in the air, penetrating their nostrils, crawling on their skin, scraping their breath. Children walked down the streets unable to see a thing beyond their own bodies—how could anyone fail to see the certainty of disaster?

During recess he stayed at his desk in the back row and filled his notebook with a jumble of possible routes for the trench. They had dug too close to the military factory's electric fence, and now the trench had to make a sharp left turn to circumvent the factory and meander through an area they had never gone near before, in order to lead them to the back of the towers. Someone must have called his name and he hadn't heard, because a hand was placed on his notebook, and when he looked up he saw that they were standing too close to his desk. It was a group of boys from his class. Their cheeks were flushed, and he could smell wool, mothballs, baby oil and laundry softener. A thin stripe of toothpaste slunk over the lower lip of a boy standing on a skateboard.

"Get your hand off," Yonatan said.

The boy slid his hand off the notebook, slowly enough to crumple the illustrated pages as if by accident. Then he said there was going to be a class discussion in an hour about what he'd done: the insults, the curses, the hitting. To allow the other kids to speak openly, they said, he would have to leave the class during the discussion.

Yonatan eyed them and wondered if he saw a shadow of fear flashing in their eyes. Then they hardened their expressions. He realized they must have been plotting their revenge for a long time, uniting forces. But he didn't have time for their nonsense, he had to devote his shrewdness to a more urgent front. He briefly considered an angry outburst, but he was too tired to tease them and his whole body was burning.

Yesterday he and Yoel had dug until 7 p.m. When they'd begun, in the morning, they'd been in a great mood and competed over who could stick the shovel deeper into the earth. When they took a break, Yonatan described the day when they would finish the trench and walk through it upright without anyone seeing them, and Yoel talked about how the bums could sleep there on winter nights. But toward the end of the day the winds kicked up and they felt their skin peeling away until all that was left were bones, and when they could no longer bear the stinging, they fled from the gusts that chased them down and slapped their bodies.

"Are you listening?" the boy said loudly, his hand now drumming on the scratched desk. Another boy let out a snort of laughter. Yonatan looked down at his black Air Jordans and his eyes narrowed into two thin hexagons—they used to make fun of him for having eyes like Optimus Prime's. His brother had sent him the sneakers last week, after a few girls had made fun of his old ones, a brand no one had ever heard of. When he'd gone home that day, according to his mother, he'd "raged and terrorized them" until they said Shaul would buy him a pair of Air Jordans in New York.

He'd learned the method from Shaul. On his brother's annual visits, Yonatan always insisted on dragging his mattress into Shaul's room, and for those two weeks he waited impatiently from the moment he woke up for the hours to go by and darken the sky so he could lie next to his brother, stifling every yawn and worrying about Shaul's, because at night the room was engulfed in a mysterious grandeur from faraway lands. His brother recounted episodes of *Columbo* and let him solve the mysteries, and invented characters with strange super-powers, like Clarisse Deph, who could touch a person's chest and know when they were going to die.

But most of all he looked forward to hearing stories about their family before he was born. For example, about how one day, around 1972, Shaul was walking on Jaffa Street with their mother, and they stopped to look at fur coats and wool scarves draped on tall, beautiful women whom he did not immediately recognize as mannequins, in the display window of an upscale shop called Epstein & Feldheim. Their mother confidently strides into the store, where men in light striped suits start dancing around her, scurrying back and forth to show her dresses, skirts and belts, singing her praises is if she were not standing right there. "So elegant, the lady!" one enthuses. "Just stepped out of the opera house in Vienna!" his bespectacled, sharp-chinned colleague squawks. A third claps his hands and asks where her parents were born. "Guess," she replies with a tentative smile.

"Vienna? Berlin? Hamburg?" they call out. "Please, don't say you're from Warsaw." She informs them her parents were born in Israel and does not say another word. Shaul, who was about nine at the time, knew that his grandfather Albert was born in Aden, Yemen. Sometimes Shaul's parents took him to the old neighborhood of Nachalat Shiva, where Grandpa Albert would sit with his elderly mother, who knew roughly twenty words in Hebrew and whose friends knew her by the Arabic moniker Um Aziz. They would wax nostalgic with her in Arabic about Aden (translating for Shaul every so often), comparing it with miserable Jerusalem, which Albert viewed as a paradise for talentless provincial crooks, and that was why he'd left his wife and moved to Haifa.

The salesclerk with glasses turns to Shaul. "Do you know how many times we've begged your mother to let us photograph her in a dress and put the picture up in our display window? We've promised to give her anything her heart desires from the shop in return."

Their mother laughs and waves her hand dismissively, and tells them to stop sweet-talking her. But her face glows and she twirls around on her tiptoes, holding her dress, and the clerks applaud, put their hands over their hearts and swear they will call the photographer right then and there. She curtsies graciously.

"Did she end up getting the pictures taken?" he asked Shaul when they woke up the next morning.

"The pictures?" Shaul repeated.

"For that clothing store," he said, and it occurred to him that Shaul had made up the story.

"How should I know?" Shaul said. "Mom, getting her picture taken? You know her, don't you?"

Another day his brother told him that as a young boy his parents hadn't given him money for the snack bar near his high school, and every recess when his friends crowded around to buy food, he would find an excuse to disappear, and the kids made fun of him for being cheap. Then his brother said something that was engraved on Yonatan's memory: "All Mom and Dad understand is force."

His arms itched. He touched them, followed the scratch lines, then focused on his adversaries. They were looking at the ceiling and at the window while stealing glances at him, and he realized he had to keep his gaze steady; anything he did, even if it was only to touch his hair, might be interpreted as weakness. He accepted their proposal without complaining and even suggested that he not come to class at all.

"Don't you want to hear what goes on?" one of them asked.

"I do, but I'm afraid I'll get bored," he replied scornfully.

They were surprised by his tone but ignored it. They seemed to have been expecting him to get angry. They insisted that he come to class and leave before the discussion started. At first he was afraid they wanted to humiliate him, but they kept dancing around him to make sure they weren't doing him an injustice. He realized that even their cruelest deeds, like the way they'd bullied Vered Saragusti until she'd left the school, came packaged in a language of justice and morality, castigating the victim so that he would mend his ways. That was something they'd learned from their parents, some of whom hung around the schoolyard, the shopping center and the park, scolding everyone they came across, reminding people about the values of the decent world—the one that no longer existed—"which are being crushed and pulverized under the boot of the corrupt times we live in," as Yoav Gordon's father once said. They really did believe that one day the masses would understand that only a life lived by these values could be considered worthy.

In fourth period, Tomer Shoshani and Yoav Gordon stood before the class. Yonatan watched his enemies preparing for their big moment, exchanging looks and notes. Clutching his notebook, now full of sketches of the trench, he stood up to leave the classroom. The homeroom teacher realized that a plan had been hatched behind her back, and she stopped him by the door. "Such chutzpah," she said, with a hint of a smile. "Sixth grade children do not get to decide what will happen in class." As he stood there with all his classmates watching him, he imagined thousands of fingers scratching his skin, and wondered if they could see the cuts on his legs and arms through his clothes.

He frantically scanned the room until he found Yoel, who sat in the fourth row next to the window. Yoel had turned his back on the class, propped his notebook against the windowpane and was scribbling in it. Yonatan squinted, but Yoel moved the notebook and shielded it with his body, and he stayed in that peculiar position while his right hand moved his pen over the page. It was clear that Yoel knew Yonatan's eyes were stabbing him from behind, and that if Yonatan were to confront him about his behavior later, he would deny it. He was more skilled at playing innocent than anyone Yonatan knew, sticking to his lies even when they were exposed. He never admitted that he'd lied, just as he never admitted defeat or that he'd wronged another kid, and that might have been the biggest difference between them. Yoel did not walk the streets of Beit HaKerem like a sinner; he genuinely believed he was a virtuous boy who deserved to be liked.

Yonatan remembered that yesterday, when they'd been digging in the wadi, Yoel had asked if he believed their revenge would change things. "That's not the point," Yonatan had answered. "If we don't finish the trench before the fight we'll get beaten up at Rivka's kindergarten, right? Without the trench we won't survive this winter." But Yoel insisted that he answer the question. Yonatan became worried: had Yoel told anyone about the trench? His big brother Noam? Yoel swore he hadn't.

He told Yoel about a picture their chess club teacher had shown them once, something that happened after a duel between a famous Russian poet and some other deadbeat. The picture showed two people holding this guy back while they watched a horse-drawn carriage cart the poet's body away, covered with a fur, down a snowy track. The chess teacher explained the picture to them by discussing a Japanese tenet of warfare, which they copied into their notebooks. The avenger, according to this tenet, does not celebrate and is not happy, perhaps even the opposite: he's just doing his duty. "And that's the story here: we're going to teach the tower kids a lesson, so that you never go home to your parents covered with blood and thistles again, and we will have done our duty."

"That teacher you worship got kicked out because he turned up at the chess club wearing a woman's fur coat, screaming about how no one in this neighborhood was afraid of death, only of crazy people, and said he was going to burn down the clubhouse," Yoel remarked.

"Okay, whatever, but that happened later."

Every time he mentioned the chess teacher, Yoel's face clouded over. Most people—kids and grown-ups alike—were more fond of Yoel than of Yonatan, but the chess teacher liked him and was often belligerent with Yoel, who did not admit that he was hurt by this, and insisted there was nothing unusual about the way the teacher treated him. It was as if he couldn't acknowledge the existence of someone who disliked everything about him, and it wasn't until their last club meeting that Yoel had an outburst. The teacher reached for Yoel's knight and told him for the umpteenth time that there was nothing consistent in the way he played, nothing authentic, that his game wasn't improving because he kept imitating different players.

Yoel grabbed his hand. "Get your filthy hands off that," he hissed. He stood up, put on his coat and wool hat, stared straight at the teacher and left the room.

Yonatan heard a shout, the turmoil in the class surged, and he realized the teacher had told him to go back to his seat. She explained that she wasn't proposing they cancel the discussion, just that they allow him to make his case. How could she not realize that was far worse? He sat down at his desk in the back row and listened to the boys; none of the girls participated. One after the other, they put their hands up and proceeded to complain about his behavior.

One said he'd called him a "fucking Dutchman" (he interrupted to point out that it was actually "Dutch trash"), another said he'd threatened to stick thumbtacks in his eyes. He'd kicked a ball in someone's face on purpose ("But it's impossible to aim"—that was his second interruption), and they all said he was always cursing and that the curses were contagious: no one used to say "son of a thousand whores" until he started to, and even the counselors in the youth movement said there was a difference between a whore and a son of a thousand whores. And why, every time a kid kicked the ball over the goal, did he call him "You Arab"? The counselors were even more shocked by this, and said it was what happened to kids who dropped out of the youth movements, and besides, "Arab" wasn't a bad word.

Later, out in the yard, when he walked past Yoel who was flying a paper airplane, he felt his muscles contract and the sweat drip down his face. He was afraid he would resent Yoel for the way he'd sat hunched over his notebook without looking up even once, and that he would be unable to suppress his anger at him. How had he ended up needing the trench more than Yoel did? Hadn't this whole thing started because they'd rolled that whiner Yoel around in the wadi, in mud and thistles, until his whole face was covered with blood?

Yonatan walked away from Yoel, whose paper plane had crumpled, and headed to the school gate. His forehead and neck were still burning. His undershirt and pants were clinging to his skin. He walked to the park and sat down on the damp ground on the lower lawn. The earth was covered with leaves that had changed to dark brown, which he crumbled between his fingers. Green threads still wove their way through some of the leaves, and he felt them over and over again, struggling to understand why he felt so weak. Perhaps that flourishing remnant alluded to a departed era, as with their soccer matches, when even in the throes of a big win he was already mourning its passing. He dug among the branches until he found what he wanted. A few mothers were sitting on benches with their babies. He smiled and blew kisses, and wondered if he envied them.

A few minutes later he heard the voices. There were two of them, on the other side of the lawn. He stood up. They walked toward him, speaking too loudly and bursting into laughter every so often. Their carefree ease annoyed him less than the way they kept touching each other's shoulders, reaching out to fake-strangle each other. During his flashes of honesty, when his contempt for the neighborhood kids could no longer disguise what he really wanted, he had to admit that he found them and their families enviable.

When they rounded the path they spotted him, and they all

recognized their inevitable movement toward the same point. They fell silent, moved slightly away from each other, looked at him, at the stick he had found among the branches, at the mothers on the benches, at the sky above the park, which a flock of birds was cutting across. Even if they'd wanted to, they could not stop now. He moved closer to them, tapping the stick on the rough asphalt. One of them reached into his bag and rummaged around, and his face fell; the other zipped up his coat. Perhaps they were still trying to believe they'd run into him by chance, that they could walk past him and go their own way. They slowed down. He also measured his pace: no one wanted to be the first to reach the steps.

He stopped, they paused and scanned the park again, eyeing the mothers on the benches. Then they took off and sprinted to the steps, and he ran after them, whacking his stick on the path. The babies behind him started crying and the mothers cursed him. They ran down the path, he chased them, and when they had no choice but to turn and face him, he was already at their side. They looked taller than he'd expected but he was still bigger. "Watch out," one of them said, "haven't you had enough in class today?"

He moved the stick from one hand to the other. He felt encouraged by the distance that had opened up between the two boys—how easily he had dissolved their union. They dropped their backpacks to the ground. He swung the stick with his right hand, but as he did so they fell on him. "I told you to watch out!" the first one yelled, grabbing his wrist and digging his fingernails into his flesh. It was too late to swing again, but he still struggled to hold onto the stick while the other boy grabbed it, panting. The boy blinked, looked sideways, and Yonatan remembered that once, in the rain, this boy had offered to share his umbrella on the walk home.

He suddenly couldn't understand how he'd even wanted to hit him with a stick. Sometimes his inability to un-remember things was maddening. It weakened him, the way even long-past days were never completely flushed out of his body but lay dormant until his memory shone a ray of warmth on them, like a laser, and they heated up again—not as warm as they once were, but enough to undermine the equations of the present so that he could not truly hate anyone he had once liked.

They might have sensed his nagging doubts. "Watch out!" the first one yelled, and the freckles on his face looked like blood cells from the illustrations in biology class. Yonatan was surprised by their lack of fear. They used to be afraid, but something had changed. Perhaps they'd grown stronger and taller when he wasn't paying attention. The mothers by the benches shouted: "Stop it, you thugs!" and one of them started marching over to them. He was ashamed to feel relieved.

All three of them took off down the steps. They turned right, he turned left, and he breathed in the smell of burnt pine needles. He could see that one of the boys was clutching his waist, even though Yonatan hadn't hit him, and the other hugged his shoulder. For a moment he wanted them to touch him too, with the same affection and concern, and was overcome by a desire to run after them and fall on them, to make the taste of defeat disappear. His fury had evaporated, and now he tried to fight off his sense of regret.

"Regret for real, or because you were scared?" Yoel would ask, if Yonatan ever talked to him again after the way he'd ignored him in class today.

On the way home the world turned yellow, the sights became blurry and muddied, and he could no longer gauge the distance between himself and the cars parked beside the road. He heard shouts, thunder, engines, and had no idea where the sounds were coming from. Near his building he saw two shadows moving in the wadi with that swift, self-assured movement that only those who knew all of the terrain's secrets could pull off. He thought it was Yoel and Tali, but the idea was preposterous. Maybe it was the kids from the towers spying on them.

The phone rang as soon as he took off his coat. He knew it was his mother. How was your day? she'd ask, bothering him with questions to which she didn't really want to know the answers. She couldn't help him, and neither could Dad, and anyway she'd been in a good mood yesterday and he didn't want to make her sad. He lit the kerosene heater with a match. He wasn't allowed to touch it when he was home alone. In the middle of the heater there were five rectangles burning in purple-white, orange-pink, and pink-blue. The colors kept changing, and he liked to look at them until his eyes teared up. Through the glass balcony door he looked at the other side of the street, at Yoel's window, but a bubble of yellow fog was hovering between them.

Something in the familiar order of things had come loose. He saw the living room without walls, high up in the sky and very cold—Shaul said the air outside an airplane was so cold that it would kill you in five minutes—and the wind propelled the living room into the yellow fog. He saw a street with two stripes of mud running all along it and nothing else, not even earth or asphalt, only translucent-blue tree trunks like the pillars of light you sometimes see after the rain, towering up from the ground to the sky. He'd always wanted to find out if you could touch something in them or if it was just a specter, a trick of the light like a rainbow in a cloud: you couldn't believe anything until you touched it. People were suspended in mid-air above the street, and two ugly boys, their faces smeared with golden paint yet their pockmarks still visible, told everyone that there used to be a street there, with people and cars and kids and all of that. Yes, they swear there was once a street here.

———

The girls didn't hate Yonatan and they didn't mock him: they were simply oblivious to his existence. He wasn't one of the good-looking and funny kids they danced around, or one of the well-mannered ones like Ran Horesh—who was known by some mothers, including Yonatan's, as 'the gentleman'—or even one of the weak smart-asses, whose witticisms they laughed at even as they pitied them.

To them he was just one of the regular kids, a strong, sweaty boy who yelled a lot. He believed that if they saw him playing soccer they'd think more highly of him, but they never did. Except that now, after the class discussion, the girls realized they'd made a mistake by positioning him on an uninteresting rung down the social ladder, because most of the boys loathed him, including the ones on his soccer team. The girls started trying to cheer him up, they said he was "a poor boy" and decided the whole episode was dumb, and that it was all because of their crazy teacher with the puffy red cheeks. But the girls from HaShomer HaTzair—who took their socialist youth movement's values to heart and always had a bad word for the kids who guzzled hamburgers at MacDavid or soft-serve American-style ice-cream at Caravel or spat out gum on the floor—remained wary of him. As he and Yoel always said, "HaShomer HaTzair kids aren't as dumb as the ones in the Scouts, but they're believers, so actually they're dumber."

Perhaps that was why Alona Mishor stopped him in the hallway one day and invited him to her birthday party the following Friday evening at seven, and pinned her green eyes on him until he swore he would be there. He worshipped Alona, who was considered a wild girl with eccentric outfits ("her mother is a California-sixties type artist," the other girls whispered, parroting their own mothers) that included baggy sweaters with rainbows and various Sanskrit symbols, faded jeans ripped at the knee like the girls downtown wore, and silver chains with big pendants shaped like shells or swords. A few of the parents had called Alona's mother to ask that she "not wear the sword pendant, which might encourage violence." Seven was considered late—birthdays were always held in the afternoons—yet not late enough to arouse suspicion. And there was some excitement among the girls, who whispered among themselves a lot and kept their distance from the boys; it was clear they were plotting something.

In recent days the girls had let Yonatan straggle after them on the way home from school. They walked in a gang, and when they got to the wide path between Beit HaKerem Street and HaHalutz Street, which was surrounded by trees and fences with signs warning against barking dogs and poisonous mushrooms, they used to take a red tape deck out of one of the backpacks and shriek along with the singers, laughing out loud, accusing each other of being out of tune, and mangling the English lyrics. They listened to Madonna, Cyndi Lauper, and someone called Tiffany, whom they claimed girls in the United States were crazy about. Alona and her friend Michal, who meandered on the outskirts of the group, played "Time After Time" on their walkmans, and also listened to "Touch Me," which many parents forbade their children to hear. When it wasn't raining, they would stop in the middle of the path, try on each other's sunglasses and big, gold-plated earrings, exchange barrettes and hair ties, shake their hair out and slather it with gel to make it stand up in a puffy mane. Alona was accused of being slutty because she'd stolen her mom's red lipstick (the girls wiped it off her lips with the hem of her shirt), and Michal of being a whore because she dyed a strip of her blonde hair black. On that pathway, hidden from the world, they were different, as if they'd escaped the borders of Beit HaKerem and entered a vortex of uninhibited, screechy delight. As soon as they emerged back on HaHalutz Street, they looked just as they did in school. Watching them always raised his spirits. They projected a power that would one day disrupt the old order of the neighborhood; he had no doubt that it was already happening.

On the evening of the party he showered and combed his hair for a long time, then put on white pants and a mauve sweater that said 'Oxford.' The pants were too tight around his waist, but he didn't have anything nicer. He didn't like his face, especially not his bulging eyes.

"You look wonderful," said his mother, who was going dancing with Kaufman, as she sometimes did when his father was away. Kaufman, who until recently had worked at the communications office with Yonatan's mother and had since got rich from various business dealings with Frenchmen, used to turn up at their house in a smart suit, bright tie, elegant wool coat and shiny boots with pointy toes. He once heard his mother say to a girlfriend: "He's not like all those men who wear Israeli brands." He had a silver wristwatch with three little inset watches, and he always used to say, "Name a place and I'll tell you what time it is there." Kaufman's presence cheered Yonatan up. The apartment seemed to wake up and fill with glimmering lights when he was there, only to fold back into silent darkness when he left.

They drove off in Kaufman's black car, which smelled of cigars and aftershave. It was raining lightly. The yellow dust lifted from the road and stuck to the stone walls, the fences, the curbs. He wanted to ask his mother if she could see it. Next to the Reich Hotel he saw Yoel walking up HaGuy Street, wearing his brother's shiny jacket and a scarf Yonatan had never seen. The colored lights on the hotel balcony tinted his hair with red and blue sparks. Yoel was dragging his feet from side to side, perhaps wanting to prolong his walk to the party. They hadn't talked since the class discussion. And Yoel, just as he'd expected, hadn't apologized. Nor had he gone anywhere near their trench.

"Isn't that Yoel?" his mother asked, and motioned for Kaufman to stop the car. They waited for Yonatan to get out—Yoel looked lonely out there, alone in the rain, rubbing his scarf against his cheeks—but he knew his own tendency to exaggerate the unhappiness of anyone he'd had a fight with, especially his mother and Yoel, so that he could justify his desire to please them. This time he decided that pleasing Yoel would only make it harder to truly forgive him, and it would pollute the arteries of their friendship. The two of them always had the capacity to make up stories and lie to everyone else, but at the foundation of their friendship stood a shared recognition—free of illusions and affectionate chatter—that no lie would ever come between them.

"It's Tamir," he said.

His mother turned around. "Who's Tamir?"

"Just a kid I hate from the other class."

Kaufman sped up and Yoel disappeared from their view.

"Did you have a fight again?" his mother asked.

"I told you, it wasn't Yoel!" he snapped.

"If the boy says it's not Yoel, it's not Yoel," Kaufman summed up cheerfully, though he'd never met Yoel.

The two of them fell silent and Kaufman turned on the radio and they listened to an upbeat song in Spanish. Kaufman hummed along, and every so often said something in a foreign language his mother said was French, and they laughed. They were getting on Yonatan's nerves. It was clear from their exuberance that they were looking forward to their evening of dancing, while he was fearing the moment when he would knock on Alona's door. Lots of bad things could happen at this party. Most of the boys probably wouldn't understand how he had the gall to show up, and if he and Yoel hadn't fought they'd probably be doing something else tonight.

He got out of the car next to the round synagogue, where in a year he would have his bar mitzvah, and took the narrow alley between Beit HaKerem and HaHalutz streets, where kids who were scared of getting bullied by the girls on the nearby path sometimes hid. It was, essentially, the nerds' alley. And it was where he expected Yoel to appear. But maybe he'd missed him.

In Alona's living room, which was smaller than he'd expected, balloons hung from the ceiling on colorful ribbons and there was a string of lights wrapped in bright cellophane. A birthday sign made by the girls said "For Beautiful Alona!" The walls were bare and there were lots of nails protruding from them. Alona and her mother must have removed all the pictures before the party. He thought that looked phony. Now that he saw where she lived, he realized that, after she walked down the path with the girls every day, she must go back up to her house through the nerds' alley. Was she really such a rebel? Could it be that all the boys and girls wanted the same things, and the only difference was how they disguised their desire?

The boys sat in a semicircle on the right side of the living room, near the wall. Behind them were two white sculptures of hook-nosed eagles. Stripes of light from the colorful bulbs ran over the floor, across the boys' bodies, and brushed the sculptures. He followed the movement of the light—he had always taken pleasure in the way light moved across a set course. A few girls huddled near the hallway, next to a large tape deck hooked up to speakers on either side of the room, and he heard "Touch Me" at a birthday party for the first time. Instead of the usual bowls of chips, pretzel sticks, and half pitas with humus, there were only bottles of Coke and Sprite, and something that looked like slightly set grape juice. He walked over to the boys.

"Where's Yoel?" one of the girls asked teasingly.

"How should I know?" he said and thought he heard her laugh, but the loud music made him uncertain.

He sat down next to the boys. A few said hello indifferently, and some smiled. One of them looked at his clothes and asked, "You getting married today?" Two boys were discussing a picture that Maor Feldman's grandfather had shown them when he came to talk to the class. It showed a prison yard in some European city after all the Jews had died. Everything suddenly looked so stupid. The huge tension that had engulfed him all day was gone, his body softened and his muscles felt light, and even his pants felt a little looser. His whole day had been a nightmare because of this party, but no one cared if he was here or not. Perhaps he was no longer capable of seeing things as they were.

Alona and a few other girls stood before the boys with secretive looks. Now he noticed they were all wearing black and white dresses or skirts, apart from Alona, who sported a blue dress with gold stars and long black socks, and Michal, who had on a pink dress that was shorter than the other girls' and a thin gold chain around her neck. Her eyes looked odd, slanted. Most of the girls wore long thin socks in various colors and black shoes, but Hila had on boots. They all had different hairstyles than they wore to school, and then he realized: they looked like they did on the pathway.

One of the girls turned the lights off, and Alona, who was holding a white candle, said, "Today we're going to do something different. Today we're dancing." A song that he didn't know came on, and everyone froze: the girls in their fancy dresses and the boys in jeans or faded corduroys or sweatpants, with the same shirts they wore to school, and muddy sneakers. He was overcome by an inexplicable desire to soak up the vitality radiating from the girls and their excitement about a new era approaching; perhaps he even longed to be a girl like them. For a while his mind suspended this newly elucidated yearning, which left a shadow inside him, faded evidence of an idea he was already ashamed of. Then the boys started shouting and whistling, and he shouted too, and a couple of them got up, and danced together in the living room, crashing into the group of girls over and over again.

The commotion soon died down. The girls stood in the middle of the room ignoring the boys, whose jollity was gone. They blinked a lot, touched their faces, ran their fingers through their hair, and looked miserable. He wondered if he looked like that, because he was actually feeling better. It was a simple equation: when they grew weaker, he grew stronger. He noticed Ran Horesh, in a black button-down shirt and white pants, standing next to Alona's mom, who was smoking a cigarette and holding a bottle of wine. They whispered and laughed, and the girls grew more excited. They pushed each other toward Ran, and finally Alona broke away from the group and stood close to him. Yonatan noticed that his clammy hands were clutched together, and he knew that of all the girls, she was the one he'd feared might break away.

Ran Horesh ceremoniously took Alona's hand, while her mother winked at them and blew smoke in their faces, and they walked back toward the girls, who scattered in every direction. Their linked hands swung up and down, and from Alona's look, which had changed from festive to surprised, it was clear that she had forgotten that when Ran Horesh walked he actually bounced slightly. All the boys who said they liked him—because being fond of someone like Ran meant that you were virtuous—secretly hated him, and often mimicked his billy-goat gait. Finally they stopped. Alona put her hands on Ran's shoulders, and he reached his out to her waist, though at times they seemed to be holding onto thin air. The boys stared at the two of them in gloomy silence, as if seeing a landscape they'd never looked at before. He looked at the wall clock: it was eight-thirty. He'd been here for more than an hour, and Yoel still hadn't turned up.

When Hila came over to him there were five couples dancing, and the rest were busy negotiating. Messengers ran back and forth between the girls and the boys, made a match, suggested another, earned contempt or amazement or excitement or silence, and went back to update their group. There had to be a certain logic behind every new couple: they both had a dog, or a library card, or an annoying big brother.

He got up and walked after Hila. They passed Alona and Ran Horesh, who giggled with their bodies pressed together. Ran's hands curved around Alona's waist. A red bubble of light isolated them from the other couples, and to him they seemed sublime. Hila stopped too close to Ran and Alona, and Yonatan stood opposite her. She suddenly looked pretty. When she placed his hands on her waist, his heart pounded and his legs shook, and he prayed the palms of his hands were not burning her skin through her dress. They danced at some distance from one another, but every so often she pressed up against him, perhaps by accident, and his stomach rubbed against her chest. The touch of her fingers on his shoulder was delicate and slightly cool, and he breathed in the smell of her curly hair, which reminded him of sweet lemon, if there is such a thing. Then her hand touched his cheek and tilted his head toward her, and she asked if he was embarrassed. He said he wasn't, but she declared: "You are embarrassed." He admitted that he was, a little, and found he couldn't look into her eyes. "But you're not a bad dancer," she commented.

Feeling buoyed, he told her that his mother and Kaufman were dancing at the Moriah Hotel, and maybe they would dance there one day. She looked around at the other dancers and asked who Kaufman was—his mother's secret boyfriend? Hila always spoke succinctly, and her questions were assertions: if you agreed with them, it was a sign you'd understood, and if you didn't, perhaps you'd understand one day. He said Kaufman was his parents' friend. She asked if it didn't bother his dad, and he said of course it didn't, Kaufman was his dad's friend. She asked if his parents danced at Moriah Hotel together too, and he said no, and she laughed and said it was cute the way he didn't understand anything. He wanted to tell her things: that the warmth of her body was invading his body and now both of their warmths were merging inside him. That he was afraid the next few days would swallow up this night and he didn't know how to ensure that something of all this would still be there tomorrow. But every sentence he thought of saying sounded more excitable and exaggerated than the last. Whenever he shared a moment of intimacy with someone, he tended to express too much affection and turn them off, so he kept quiet.

Hila asked if his head was spinning. He said, "Vertigo," and asked if she'd seen the film. "What film?" she asked, and he explained that it was by a director called Hitchcock, who his father said was the only genius other than some Russian dictator, and she said, "Great," with a lack of interest, and complained that her head was spinning because Alona's mom had let them sip wine.

"Really?" he asked and wondered if she was hinting that she'd rather stop dancing.

"Have you ever had wine?" she asked.

"Of course," he lied, and said that at home they drank lots of wine from some region in France.

She seemed satisfied by his answer: "Then you're not so boring," she said.

He rummaged through his memory, desperate to recall a time when something inside him had burned for Hila—this couldn't all be happening only now.

Sometimes he theorized that there were a number of different children inside him, each with different qualities: some were restrained and polite, some were cheerful and charming and universally liked, some genuinely liked being lonely. Under certain circumstances, any of these kids could steal his body. Perhaps it was no coincidence that this moment seemed too dreamy, and it was simply happening to one of the children inside him, who was slightly him yet different. If this was how things might be from now on, he would gladly give that child his body.

Hila shut her eyes and her face looked serene, and he realized deep down that anything she did would seem magical to him. For a moment he panicked that he was really disappearing, so he commanded his mind to conjure up pictures from his life: Yoel and him waiting in his room for evening to fall, then lying on his bed rearranging the map of Beit HaKerem that was projected on the ceiling by streetlights and headlights: "Beit HaKerem of the Night," they called it, and they would whisk away entire streets and make all their residents vanish; walking with Mom and Dad at night with the Old City walls towering above, the wind blowing away their umbrella and Mom's hat, her hair flying as they ran to the car, and his face burning in the wind but he doesn't want it to stop because his parents look young and strong; his big brother disappearing up the stairs to the departure lounge at the airport again, and the last mornings of summer, always in shades of concrete, crashing down on him when he wakes up at 6 a.m. in an empty room facing the bed where his brother had slept for two weeks, now piled with clothes, new sneakers, monopoly and chess boards. But all the pictures blurred, like crumbling postcards of the trivial things that had preoccupied him before this storm surged in his body.

Later, shortly before midnight, in Alona's dark bedroom, Hila sat on the bed and he stood facing her, looking at the floor, which was piled with photographs and pictures in black frames. In the drawing at the edge of the pile he saw a row of little children in red uniforms and tall pointy blue hats, and they knelt on the grass aiming rifles at a woman whose black hair hid her face. Her arms hugged the tree trunks around her, and only by straining his eyes did he realize that the tree leaves were made of her hair. He rubbed his arms. He was cold, mostly in his chest, and he couldn't remember where he'd left his coat.

Hila said maybe they could be boyfriend and girlfriend. He asked why. She replied that she liked Ran Horesh and he liked Alona—he was about to deny it, but he realized from her expression that there was no point, and for a moment he felt close to her, because she'd taken the trouble to find out his secrets and made sure he knew that his lies would do no good—but Alona and Ran were dancing together, so they couldn't get what they really wanted, but that didn't mean they had to suffer and be jealous: they could be a couple, at least for now.

He stammered a little when he asked if they weren't supposed to like each other, and Hila smiled and said he was a romantic boy, even though he didn't look it, and that maybe his parents should buy him a button-down shirt. She thought they could be a couple for now and sometimes do things together: after all, they both liked movies. Her businesslike tone, as if she'd already planned everything out, angered him. Perhaps girls like her didn't understand what it was like to have an unshakable passion for something and be unable to relinquish it, even though you know it will never happen, and for your imagination to keep recreating it in minute detail. He pictured himself pushing away the other children inside him and returning fully to his own body.

She asked if he was afraid of Yoel's reaction and gave him a piercing look, as if expecting him to tell her the truth. The idea amused him: one kid meets another, and within two hours demands the truth. She asked what was the real reason he and Yoel spent so much time together in that wadi. He looked at the crumbs of chocolate on the straps of her white dress and said that he and Yoel lived in the same world. She straightened up on the bed and looked thoughtful, as if she were trying to understand, then said that everyone lived in the same world. He rubbed his arms and knees, trying in vain to warm them. How could it be that only five minutes ago he'd still believed his life was just background noise for this evening?

"You *are* afraid!" she said, and before he could respond she added there was no reason for him to be scared, and how come Yoel hadn't come to the party? He said he didn't know, he'd seen him walking up HaGuy Street but he must have changed his mind. She laughed and said Yoel had turned around and gone back down HaGuy, because a few days ago he'd asked Tali, their neighbor, to be his girlfriend—it was a secret, but all the girls knew. Yoel must have told his parents and everyone else that he'd be at the party, but in fact he was watching a movie at Tali's. Hila asked if he hadn't suspected anything—she seemed disappointed that he was so surprised. He touched the cold fabric of a pile of clothes on Alona's desk and said it couldn't be true.

MEXICO

Every morning he wakes up at almost four, flings the sheets off his
sweaty body, and lies in bed looking through the glass door at the dark
path down the lawn—figures occasionally pass by, he hears whispers,
sees flashlight beams flickering on the walls—and then at pictures of
Shira and Itamar on his phone from that morning in Tel Aviv. Finally
he yields to a different scene: he and Shira tell Itamar that Daddy is
going on an airplane to a faraway place called Mexico for a few days,
and the boy walks over to the suitcase and holds onto it, giving him
an enigmatic smile. The memory makes his mind shudder, arousing
the revulsion he feels every time his eyes stop on the reflection of his
own body in the ceiling mirror.

At five forty-five he takes a shower, puts on the same clothes—black
sweats, white undershirt, light gray hoodie with the string tied around
his neck—leaves the room and walks along the blue carpeting of the
poorly lit hallway. He turns right to the empty lobby, where a uniformed
employee says hello, and takes a short flight of stairs down to the

breakfast room. A sharp white light blinds him and his face burns.

Apart from the waiters in stripy green shirts and black pants—he recognizes most of them by now—leaning idly on the counters, there is usually no one else there this early. But being in the breakfast room tempers his loneliness and lifts his spirits. He jokes around with the waiters in Spanglish, and tips more than twenty percent so they will welcome him the next day, too. The acts of a lonely man, he muses: one of those people who exude the scent of loneliness on their breath, and whose every gesture is designed to tempt someone to ease their solitude if only for an instant. Or perhaps he is intentionally adopting the gestures of a lonely person, precisely because he has a home port to return to. Then again, the gestures might have preceded his recognition of the doubt that has begun to gnaw at him regarding his place in that port, to which he was supposed to have returned five days ago.

He always sits at a table on the side of the room, drinks coffee, eats fruit, or an omelet with bacon, or toast with butter and jam, and sometimes all of that together. He puts his earbuds in and listens to songs he likes, or watches a basketball game from the nineties on the tiny screen—Chicago Bulls vs. New York Knicks, which he and his father used to wake up in the middle of the night to watch together. Through the windows he sees the rising dawn. The weather changes every day, sometimes a few times a day, blue skies giving way to thick cloud, caressing spring breezes swirling into harsh winds and pelting rain. In Tel Aviv summer has arrived—he can see it in Shira and Itamar's clothes, and in their pictures from the beach. Before he turns off his phone he checks the temperature in Jerusalem.

By the time he leaves the breakfast room, the tables are full, and he starts his regular morning beat around the block. He walks down the boulevard at the front of the hotel, with tall trees and manicured lawns, sometimes squeezes past a bus stop full of people huddled in their coats, then turns left onto Leibnitz Street, ducks among puddles and broken bricks, a fine cloud of dust towering above him. Behind a row of iron posts reminiscent of his and Yoel's drawings from the wadi wars, and their kingdom, he sees the side of the hotel. From that angle he always discovers something new about the building, a turret or a railed-in staircase or solar panels.

He was becoming attached to the hotel: the ballroom level, where he dragged his feet over the laminate wood floors to one of the three tall iron doors; the shadowy hallways, each of which was named after a state or region (his room was in Santiago); the fountain at the front cascading into a large marble basin where waves frothed night and day. When he stood near the hotel doormen—whose blue uniforms and hats looked like the ones Yoel used to wear when he worked as a doorman at the Hilton after his army service, and Yonatan used to visit him late at night and they would stand by the revolving door and plan their trip to London—he sometimes imagined what he would look like in ten years, when he was approaching fifty, and he would visit a hotel without anyone meeting him at the airport, and there would be no festivals and no publishing team welcoming him—warmly or coolly, depending on how his books were selling.

Perhaps he wouldn't even have books anymore: it had been more than two years since he'd written anything, because there was only one story roiling in his mind and it was one he could not write. Defeat had always been waiting in the wings, but it had become a certainty in the past two years, once the forces he'd always enlisted to repel it had waned, and he found it more difficult to cover his face with the customary mask.

Here too, during the festival, after he'd spent ten hours in bed, he would get up twenty minutes before an interview or a reading, shower in cold water, get dressed, then sit facing the interviewer or the audience and smile, crack jokes, speak fluidly, and as soon as it was over he'd hurry back to his room, take his clothes off the second he shut the door, and lie down in bed until he had to get up again.

In the past, he'd liked these trips: he'd enjoyed meeting new people, hearing stories from different worlds, learning of books he'd never heard of, impressing the crowds, getting drunk with brand-new acquaintances. But now the mask he wore for public events testified to a region in his soul that had frozen: it faked excitement about people and reading their books, and it sent out flashes of personal charm.

At every reception or festival he'd been to in the past few years, there'd been a moment when he'd imagined Yoel walking around there instead of him, or had simply borrowed Yoel's body for that refined dance between writers, editors, journalists and hangers-on. He had no doubt that Yoel, at least on his good days, would have easily circulated from group to group, rebuffed any implied insult with a kind remark or a dismissive smile, and found himself maneuvering among throngs of followers by the end of the evening.

Up until two years ago, he hadn't imagined that Yoel had paid a price for his contact with people, that the expectation for him to excel and entertain his crowd placed a heavy burden on him, and that perhaps he no longer recognized the voice that had been making his arguments, telling his stories. Yoel's crowd was still looking for him. Yonatan often received Facebook messages, emails, phone calls, questions on the street or at the airport or in the playground, from men, women, former lovers, friends' mothers, employers, army buddies, fellow Sinai travelers, all wanting to know where Yoel had disappeared to, all claiming that Yoel was one of their closest friends, that they'd made all kinds of plans together, that they loved him. Most of them were people Yonatan had never heard of.

When he approaches the intersection of Leibnitz and Victor Hugo streets, the dust around him clears. He turns left and walks down a wide street where pedestrians hurry past office buildings still shuttered with iron grates and chains. From here the hotel looks rather meager: three large cubes, old windows, dusty curtains, flaking yellow walls stained with soot.

Every day there were events at the hotel. He would find himself squeezing past young men and women in suits who'd arrived from all over the country for the annual convention of some corporation; scruffy students in jeans and undershirts or dresses and tennis shoes, celebrating graduation; women in ball gowns and heels alongside men in tuxes clutching envelopes and gifts. As the days went by he began to surrender to this hubbub, amused by his impersonation of a host inspecting new guests as he walked the hallways, wandering around wedding receptions, sitting down next to young salespeople at a convention and applauding at the end of a video presentation lauding the company's achievements. Within the hour or the night they would all disappear, but the next day the place was abuzz with new people, new events flashing on the digital display in the lobby, as if nothing in the hotel ever ended, the blood in its arteries drained out and flowed back in constantly.

The fourth street is narrower than all the others, a sort of snaking alleyway, and from here he sees three rows of yellowed, dusty air vents and filthy air-conditioning pumps on the hotel wall. There is something ugly and industrial about this final wall, and he doesn't like to look at it.

He usually completes his morning round in twenty minutes or so, then goes back to the hotel, where every hour brings him closer to the airport, to the plane, to the certainty of disaster.

———

Between the end of winter in sixth grade and the first week of ninth grade, Yonatan and Yoel barely spoke. Even when Yoel's sister was born, Yonatan didn't congratulate him. Yoel became friendly with Michael, a new boy in class. Yoel had an interest in science, but Michael was a real science whiz, who sat in his room building machines that chopped cucumbers or measured the speed of wind, and, inspired by Yoel, he also constructed a plastic Geiger counter that was supposed to make the uranium deposits in the wadi glow.

On Saturdays, Michael's American parents had him present his inventions to their religious expat friends, who walked all the way to their neighborhood from Rehavia. This irked the other parents in Beit HaKerem—where there was little tolerance for kids with extraordinary talents, even less for kids who flaunted them, and none at all for parents who boasted about them—because it threatened to disrupt the camaraderie of the neighborhood, and smacked of indulgent American individualism. As Yonatan was told by one of the fathers after he cheered his own goal in a soccer match: "If you did well, keep quiet. If you did really well, keep even quieter."

During the period when Michael and Yoel became friends, Yonatan started hanging around with a group of boys from the nearby neighborhood of Yefeh Nof, who often gathered at the shopping center in the evenings. Like them, he wore faded flared jeans and a black leather belt with a shiny silver buckle, stripy Crocker shirts and baseball caps, and black or white (never colored) Chuck Taylors. Like them, he stiffened his forelock with hair gel and kept the back cut short in a flat-top known as an 'ashtray.' On Saturday nights they went downtown, where Yonatan discovered a noisy new world of boys who smoked cigarettes, rolled joints and played pool for money, and girls in tight pants and crop tops who tapped around in high heels and left traces of pink lipstick on their cigarettes.

Of all the boys who used to gather at the shopping center, there was only one, Eyal Salman, whom Yonatan really befriended. Sometimes, on Saturdays, Salman's father would drive them out to the Judean Desert in his Ford Cortina. The warm wind mussed their hair and dried their faces, its roar competing with the seventies hits that blared from the speakers. They would stick their heads out the windows, close their eyes and scream the lyrics to "Got to Be Real" or "Dancing in the Moonlight" at the barren hills, and the sand would fill their nostrils and cake their tongues while the car lurched from pothole to pothole, got stuck in the sand, rattled, spluttered, and screeched its brakes. Sometimes Salman's father—who favored short-sleeved button-down Reyn Spooner shirts pulled too tight over his belly, their patterns bursting with colorful palm trees, beaches, suntanning girls—let them drive the car for a stretch. At the end of the day they always went back to Tracy Chapman's "For My Lover," which "slashes our hearts open," as Salman said, and aroused an unsettling feeling they did not fully understand. It seemed to hint at feelings that might, when they were older, become clear. The exuberance of those Saturdays surprised Yonatan, who had never imagined that spending time with someone's parents could be so free of prohibitions. When he was with Salman and his father, he realized that a veil of dejection lay upon his own family even when they were taking trips and having fun.

One evening the kids were playing poker at the shopping center, when someone yelled that a man had been stabbed downtown, and one of the Yefeh Nof boys, Pretty Matti, stood on the steps and bragged about a new game he'd made up, called "How to get back at the Arabs." The little cliques made a twisting snake around him when he proclaimed that he would find out which village the terrorist had come from and burn down the next-door village.

"But why the next-door one?" they all wanted to know.

"To show them how crazy we are!" he yelled.

Redhead Burman supported the idea, and told everyone something secret that Ofer Alon had told his big brother at his army discharge party: every night in Gaza, Israeli soldiers would burst into houses and wake everyone up, and there'd be babies screaming, and women shouting and wailing, and they'd make the men whitewash graffiti off the walls. He said all the Arabs kept a bucket of whitewash and a paintbrush ready to go by the door. Ofer Alon had started a custom of smashing the TV in every fourth house. "Why every fourth?" someone demanded. "How the fuck should I know?" Burman snapped, "Maybe 'cause of the four horsemen." Anyway, sometimes when Ofer Alon really flipped out, he threw a TV out the window and woke up the whole street. TVs make a lot of noise when they shatter.

"You have to be unpredictable with the Arabs," Ofer Alon had explained, "to make them understand that no matter how screwed up and sick in the head they are, we're even worse. That's the idea."

As he watched the boys getting riled up, Yonatan remembered something Yoel had told him in one of their toxic exchanges, when they'd run into each other on the street some time back. Nothing but hatred could explain the shift between their years of friendship and those days when they acted like utter strangers, and so, even if there were different emotions flooding them, they had to stick to the hatred.

"It's funny how your friends play at being wild kids even when they really are wild kids," Yoel had observed.

A long-haired boy ran across the square diagonally and yelled that everyone was going down to the Bayit VaGan main road because they'd caught some Arabs there. "The fuckers are hiding! Our guys are surrounding them, and there are more Arabs in the area, too, 'cause they sleep in the buildings where they work construction!"

Yonatan assumed Shimon, Bentz and Tzivony were there too. At first everyone ignored the long-haired kid, as if they couldn't understand how this information was relevant to them, but then a few of them started cheering on the older kids in Bayit VaGan.

"They can't hear you from here!" the long-haired kid shouted. "I thought I was coming to find real men!"

No one listened to Eyal Salman and Yonatan when they said you couldn't just beat up innocent Arabs because one Arab had stabbed someone. Pretty Matti walked over to them, combing his oiled hair. "So let me understand—are you saying you like Arabs?"

Yonatan felt the fear pierce his body, and he heard a high-pitched buzz in his head as he desperately tried to come up with a response that would placate Matti. "Are you crazy?" he and Salman stuttered almost in unison.

"Forget about those losers!" shouted Burman, and then Yonatan knew they were safe, because Burman was considered crazier than Matti. He realized that, of all the boys, only Burman could possibly be convinced to call this whole thing off. He always seemed somewhat capricious, sometimes taking pity on the unpopular kids and propping them up for a while. Even though he did some horrible things, there was always a glint of irony in his bright eyes, as though he knew it was all a game and he was simply playing his part, contemptuous of his own followers.

They took off in a sprint, and when they got to the first intersection they split up: the older kids charged down Herzl Boulevard, while Yonatan and Salman went with Burman's group. As they charged through Esrim Park, he noticed their numbers had shrunk from ten to six or seven. They ran down paths and passageways, they ran over grass and asphalt and through ditches alongside the park, trampling pine needles and eucalyptus leaves. Shouts, calls and whistles echoed around the park. They met at the steps, then spread back out through the park, and consolidated into a sort of rolling arrow. When they dispersed the air felt cooler and when they united it warmed. He was intoxicated by their power, but also saw the boys through different eyes, frightened ones, those of the local residents who retreated into yards and houses and peered out at the storm brewing in their neighborhood: even though they recognized the limbs of this rolling arrow, the sum of the parts was strange and frightening. When they ran down the middle of HaHalutz Street and cars stopped or swerved, he realized Salman wasn't there anymore, but he didn't care. For the first time in his life he imagined he had defeated Beit HaKerem, that complacent neighborhood with all its tired old people who lounged on their balconies at siesta time and scolded anyone who was too noisy, and the couples strolling along shady streets, as tranquil as the dead, and the children in Scouts uniforms singing—which had suddenly become a ghost town.

He hoped the running would never end. He'd noticed recently that he liked to be in between places, cherishing the moments before you reached your destination and all the expectations you'd pinned on it were shattered. Light from the streetlamps fell on the sidewalks, painting them with shadows of treetops and fences. When he looked up he saw two figures walking toward them.

They emerged from the shadows and one of them raised his hand and mussed the other's hair. The streetlamps blended with car headlights and poured a golden-orange hue onto them. Now he could see the pockmarks on Yoel's face.

He expected Yoel to understand what was going on and shove Michael aside, but Michael stood in the middle of the street and grinned at them, uncomprehending. Yoel's eyes met Yonatan's, and he turned to look at the starry sky. Michael asked where they were going, and Burman replied with an affability that surprised them all that they were heading to the Bayit VaGan road to beat up Arabs.

Michael laughed. "Seriously, where are you going?"

"To the Bayit VaGan road, to beat up Arabs," Burman repeated.

Yonatan prayed Michael wouldn't jump into the trap. The creases of Michael's smile vanished from his face, and Yoel tugged at his shirt.

"But those Arabs didn't do anything to you," Michael said, puzzled, and shook off Yoel's hand. He said if they weren't joking he would call the police. Yonatan remembered how much he loathed Michael, with his black ratty eyes and broad forehead, and his lazy voice, which still had traces of an American accent. He'd never understood what Yoel saw in this boy. Michael stood there eyeing them with contempt, and everyone attempted to translate his response into the language spoken in their world: was it possible that he had tough friends?

"Get out of here before I kick your head in!" Burman yelled.

Yonatan looked at Yoel and saw that his eyes were wide open, as they always were when he got scared, and his hands were constantly fingering his shirt. Yoel licked his lips, and when their eyes met he realized Yoel was expecting him to get them out of there. How could he not see it was too late?

When everyone rushed at Michael, he let out a sort of snarl and put up both hands to protect his face. Yonatan stared at Yoel, who was screaming at them. The boys screamed, too, and maybe some of the neighbors shouted from their balconies. One single scene burned in his mind: the boys jumping on Yoel and knocking him to the ground. Michael rocked from side to side while two boys hung on him. He flung one of them off and slammed him to the ground. There was a dull thud, and Yonatan realized that Michael was very strong, which only increased the danger he was in.

The air grew steamy and close with the smell of pine needles, sweat and bitter saliva. Burman and one of his friends, who let go of Michael for a moment, turned to Yoel, who was yelling and trying to reach the cluster of boys attacking his friend. Yonatan stood between Yoel and the others. Burman picked something up off the street—perhaps a stone—and gave him a sideways glance. The orange light made the bottom half of his face glow and his freckles looked enormous, but his eyes and forehead were obscured. The other boys' faces changed color too, turning gray and then orange-gold, and when the headlights cast dark and light stripes on them they looked like chessboards.

His heart pounded, he was dripping with sweat, bolstered only by the certainty that nothing could make him budge. Burman, perhaps recognizing this, did not get any closer to Yoel. Yonatan pressed his back against Yoel's chest and tried to push him back, but Yoel stood his ground. Then the boys were gone and the street was silent. Michael, still upright, put his hand on his head, let out a huge roar, and looked around with a crazed stare. He saw Michael's hand coming toward him covered in bright red, and he looked down and saw black drops pooling on the asphalt, and he smelled Michael's breath and the blood. Just as he turned to leave, the hand clapped his back and seemed to stick to him.

Yoel watched with a vacant expression, then bent over to pick up Michael's wallet and keys and his English books. They turned and walked away, and Yoel put his arm around Michael's shoulders. Yonatan ran in the opposite direction, and when he looked back they'd disappeared.

He caught up with the other boys where HaHalutz Street curved around toward the last two buildings—that was where the neighborhood ended and the thorny field opened up. Beyond that was the community center and their gray soccer pitch. Burman looked at him and his shirt in silence. The other boys stared at his shirt too. He took it off: five red fingers were imprinted on it.

"Look what he did to your shirt!" someone said with a laugh.

"Shut up or I'll kill you," Burman hissed.

Yonatan had the fleeting recognition that Burman hadn't wanted to reach the Arabs in Bayit VaGan at all, that he'd used Michael to thwart their mad rush. No one said anything. Everyone looked at the stained shirt, and they didn't even make fun of his chubby body. He heard gasps, whispers and coughs, and the breeze overhead. He saw sand and thistles blowing around, and particles of mist caught in the beams from the headlights that were once again sliding down the street. He saw Yoel and him walking home from the local library at age seven…nine…eleven…Clutching copies of *The Paul Street Boys*, *Flowers in the Attic*, *Five Weeks in a Balloon*, *The Courts of Chaos*, *The Famous Five*, and later, *The Rise and Fall of the Third Reich*, which they never returned and both lied about having read. Out on the thistle field, they used to kick at the dirt, put the books on the ground, grab handfuls of sand, scrunch their eyes shut and fling it up, jumping back so it wouldn't hit them.

Then he saw two people emerge from the last building and walk down the street arm in arm, as though Beit HaKerem had been restored to its ordinary evening rhythm. How could he ever have imagined it was defeated?

FINAL YEAR
(MID-1990S)

The rain stopped and the sky arched over him. He could see the horizon brightening over the edge of the hills. When the darkness tore open the earth and the sky separated, the wadi's stark borders—to the east the first trees of the wood near his school, in the center the square building of the Academy of Music, and to the west the fences surrounding the military factory—became visible. A pain sliced his back. He slid his right hand under his body and felt a sharp stone. With some effort he pulled it out of the ground. The weight of his wet clothes was oppressive. As long as he lay without moving a single limb, his body did not hurt, but when he shifted his hand or foot, his flesh burned.

How many hours had he been lying there? He glanced to the right and recognized the two white rocks with tops that looked like chicken combs, the bushes colored gray by the dust in summer, which they used to kick thick clouds out of, and the swath of velvety mud where they'd dug the trench in the winter of sixth grade. He strained his memory, expecting the black screen to tear open and reveal when he'd arrived in that spot. He knew it must have been in the past few hours that he'd crossed the dirt lot between their street and the wadi. But he was beset by a muddle of habitual scenes devoid of chronology: he locks the front door, he talks on the phone with his father in New York, he starts the car.

He coughed, and the cold tightened around his feet as if they were covered with ice. He struggled to move them. He knew he had to get up and leave immediately.

He rolled onto his stomach and his shoulder spasmed in pain. He saw little stones, weeds, smooth mounds of mud. He put his hands on the earth, pushed his body up into a kneeling position, stifling a yelp, though he could have screamed as much as he wanted and no one would have heard. He stood up, examined his muddy palms and black fingernails, then ran his fingers over his stomach and thighs, pinching and rubbing the flesh to warm up. He was pleased now—he had managed to will himself off the ground, and even if he could not remember the events that had led him there, shreds of memory would soon form.

He heard a distant engine, a baby wailing, a door slamming. The darkness of night had not yet left the sky, and he estimated it was about six o'clock. What day was it? Did he have school? The morning noises prodded him to turn around and walk to the meeting point between the wadi and the dirt lot, exactly where he'd been standing when Shaul had shouted at him during a soccer game to let Noam score the goal and not rush at him; the next thing he knew, his face was bloodied, and Shaul was carrying him to their front yard, where everyone stood around while Shaul washed his face with a hose and stroked his hair and screamed that he'd said *not* to rush, and begged him not to tell Mom and Dad.

When he got closer to the dirt lot he saw his car parked there, its front wheels deep in the mud. His black shoes were also covered with mud. He looked at his clothes: the gray wool pants he often wore in the evenings were covered with thick brown stains, the back of the wool coat he wore over a blue striped sweater was the color of the earth. He was dressed for a night out, maybe in one of the pubs at the Russian Compound downtown. Maybe he'd had too much to drink or smoke, and when he'd come home, instead of parking in the lot and going upstairs, he'd left the car at the edge of the wadi and lain down. He searched his coat pockets for the car keys but couldn't find them. He wondered if he should go back to the wadi, until he remembered something: he sped up, and through the car window he saw the keys on the driver's seat.

He sat down at the wheel and started the engine, then angled the rearview mirror toward the seat next to him, afraid to look at his face.

He turned the car around, and spotted Yoel walking toward him. Yoel's hands were in his pockets, he wore a wool hat, with a few shiny wet curls clinging to his forehead. He had on one of the checkered sweater vests people said he borrowed from his father, and no coat. Yonatan blinked; the Yoel he saw seemed as dreamlike as those kids around the table. The sweater vest was too familiar: the Yoel of his dreams always wore it. Pictures from the past—dreams, hallucinations—had started piling up inside him. Perhaps this was what madness was: opening your eyes in the middle of the street and seeing past, present and future all at once.

Yoel stood in the middle of the dirt lot. The branches of the last tree on the street swayed, and its trampled leaves, blackened by winter, fluttered on the ground around him. His doubts vanished and he drove toward Yoel. He could still swerve to the right or left and drive around him. Yoel glanced to either side, then looked at Yonatan as if to warn him: you wouldn't do something so pathetic, would you?

He stopped the car. Yoel placed his hands on the engine hood. A breeze whipped up his hair, and Yonatan saw black leaves soaring to the balconies, the roofs and the treetops. The dirt lot looked small, at the mercy of the towers and giant trees surrounding it.

Yoel got into the passenger seat and sat down next to him, wiped his eyes, which were tearing up from the wind, and starting fiddling with the air-conditioning controls, as he always did. Hot air blew at them. "Is it reaching you?" Yoel asked and held his hand out, then lowered it to Yonatan's knees and briefly fluttered over his pants, which were caked with hardened mud. Yoel's touch reminded Yonatan of the pain that now sharpened again, hitting his bones. Yoel was freshly shaved and his skin smelled of aftershave, probably Jazz. His sideburns were cut exactly at the line of his ears and they curved onto his cheeks. Yonatan stared at his filthy hands and looked around for something to wipe them on.

"Going somewhere?" Yoel asked.

He remembered that he was going to visit Yaara today. "Yes, somewhere."

"Looking like Mudman?"

"Yes."

"Where?"

"What are you doing here, Yoel?" he pressed. "It's six a.m. isn't it?"

"Quarter to six," Yoel replied. Neither of them ever wore a watch. "I haven't seen you at school for three days, you don't answer the phone, you even missed the soldiers who came to tell us about the Armored Corps."

"It's funny that you would talk about disappearing," Yonatan responded. "You're the one who goes missing for three days sometimes."

"That hardly ever happens anymore," Yoel said.

"It happened two months ago."

"Forget about that, my dear," Yoel said with a giggle. "A guy has trouble sleeping and rests in his room for a while, thinking things over, as they say, and you make a big fuss."

"Okay, but what are you doing here now?"

"Sometimes you wake up early," Yoel said, and a glimmer flashed in his eyes as he savored the obvious lie. Yonatan realized that Yoel had seen him sleeping in the trench. It was strange that he hadn't woken him and taken him home. He must have been watching from his living room balcony and waiting for Yonatan to wake up. He wondered if Tali had also seen him asleep in the wadi.

Yoel rubbed his hands together and grumbled about the car's heating. Yonatan thought: Yoel moves too much, it's annoying.

"So where are we going?" Yoel asked cheerfully.

"*We* aren't going anywhere," he snapped.

"Because you want to be alone with your new girlfriend?"

"Maybe."

"The new girlfriend from Herzliya?"

"Tel Aviv."

"The lovely Yaara."

"Correct."

"*My children: believe in youth!*" Yoel sang out. They both knew the line; he'd written it on one of the kingdom notes, when the Army Minister had asked him to cheer up the young soldiers freezing on their behalf in the Land of Twelve Skeletons.

"Stop fucking around, okay," Yonatan said. It irritated him that Yoel used their notes like that, stripping them of their glory. He was too proud to admit that he lamented the kingdom and thought they shouldn't have abandoned it to lie frozen and silenced.

"Interesting how she never comes to visit you in Jerusalem."

"I'm afraid she'll see you and fall in love."

"Have you fucked yet?"

He didn't answer. Yoel had taken to talking freely about sex, chatting about blowjobs and fucking and how he liked to go down on a girl and lick her to make her climax. He'd asked Yonatan how he made Lior cum. Yonatan tried to answer naturally, but it was clear to both of them that he was embarrassed and that Yoel enjoyed teasing him. He once waved a popsicle at Yonatan and said, "Show me how you lick her," and Yonatan sounded like an idiot when he hissed, "That's none of your business."

The other boys didn't talk like Yoel, at least not with him, and Yoel said everyone at school was horribly puritanical, that they fucked like their Polish parents, and he'd bet there wasn't a single guy who knew how to lick a girl properly, except maybe some of the unpopular kids, who had no image to maintain and nothing to lose. "It's just a theory," he added with a smile.

Yoel's crack about the puritans was clearly also aimed at Yonatan, which was another sign of how he'd changed. Sometime in their junior year Yoel had started sharing his personal charm with the world. He did it capriciously, like a superhero who has yet to discover his power, or like Balzac's young protagonists, whom they learned about in literature class: characters who have no idea why peopled lavish them with favors. At recess, more and more boys and girls surrounded Yoel, either to amuse him or to draw out his wit and turn it into common property. Yoel could make anyone believe that they had at least one unique trait. He instilled a sense of self-worth in people, even as he showered them with hollow compliments whose implicit irony no one stopped to consider before mindlessly repeating them: "Everyone's in your court," or "There's no question that you interest people." Yonatan started hearing Yoel's lines in the school hallways, parroted by kids he didn't know. The ground was laid for Yoel's great leap to the summit, at least among those kids that he and Yoel jokingly referred to as "the working class"—the majority of kids in the middle who were neither particularly popular nor unpopular. He knew that Yoel would soon understand everything, and then his charm would burst out with nightmarish force.

Sometimes he felt that each time they met, he was encountering a slightly different character. Yoel was always trying out a new gesture or imitating a style of speech he liked, constantly refining. Whereas Yonatan only posed as someone else, while deep down he clung to the same old insights that, although never explicitly questioned by Yoel, were challenged by the changes in his conduct. Lior said that Yoel wasn't really changing that much, it was just that Yonatan saw it and it scared him, because their world at the end of the block was running out of time. "Another girl already said that six years ago," he answered.

Two cars drove out of his building's parking lot and sailed up the street. A few people emerged into their front yards.

"You don't have a girlfriend in Herzliya, and I'll bet a hundred shekels you don't have one in Tel Aviv either," Yoel said.

Ratzon Dahari from downstairs walked out with his little girl, who was talking loudly and waving her hands around, and Yonatan marveled at them. In his enfeebled state, all these morning scenes struck him as tremendous, just as, when he'd been a child lying in bed with a fever, the ceiling had grown enormous and dome-like, and every time he looked at it the distance between him and it had shrunk. Yoel got out of the car but Yonatan stayed glued to his seat, still focused on finding a retort to hurl at him and prove Yaara's existence. But the bitter, sober taste was already in his mouth: there was no longer any point in the grandiose denial he was plotting. He wondered if Lior knew too. Maybe when she'd asked him on the phone if he'd seen Yaara, she already knew there was no Yaara.

He remembered the last time they'd sat in the car on an empty street, last summer: they'd taken the road leading to the Knesset and then to the Israel Museum. The drumbeat from "Rocket Queen" thudded in the rear speakers, and a wild current warmed his body the way it always did when he heard that song. Intoxicating stabs of dream fragments flashed through his mind, and the looming months of desolate boredom looked so predictable, so dead. They talked about the trips they might take together, and Yoel said it was very possible that, thanks to the peace progress, a few years from now boys like them—in the summer between their junior and senior years—would drive to Jordan and Syria, maybe even Lebanon. They could leave in the morning and be in Damascus or Beirut by afternoon, and they'd spend the evening clubbing or hang out at Turkish baths. It would be just like in the US, where you could get in your car and drive across an endless expanse and no one ever stopped you. "Only then will we understand how suffocated we were before," Yoel said, "how everything was small and closing in on us and we couldn't do anything."

After the Guns N' Roses and Metallica shows at Yarkon Park in Tel Aviv, they started enthusing about the nineties. It seemed to them that the provincial Israel they'd grown up in, surrounded by adults who were seduced by the brightly colored enticements of New York,

London and California, yet convinced of the West's fundamental corruption and the moral supremacy of their own socialist values—was ripped to shreds. The Beit HaKerem parents were mostly civil servants, professors, politicians, teachers, doctors, journalists, as well as two lawyers and one therapist. There was something about them that was faded, with their Israeli-made clothes, "billowy floral blouses in the colors of winter, or Gypsy dresses," as his mother said. They all avoided the type of attention that might attract gossip. These were the people who had fashioned Beit HaKerem of the eighties—with its sing-alongs, its poppies and sunflowers, its nature hikes, it youth movements, its socialist role models, its disdain of anyone who was showy or garrulous, and its underlying guilt about not living on a kibbutz.

At their high school, where there were kids from all over Jerusalem, they'd met the sons and daughters of businessmen and entrepreneurs, partners in big law or accounting firms, importers of cars, clothes and jewelry, engineers and architects in the private sector. These people wore expensive suits and drove Mercedes and popped over to Europe for winter vacations, they bought buildings and hotels and restaurants, they read books by successful businessmen, and they even lived in houses with pools.

Yoel said that in Beit HaKerem there were people whose power was unrelated to money, while at school they met people who were wealthy, but didn't really influence anything. And it was the latter who set the tone for the nineties, when everything seemed to be happening all at once: at the mall they saw signs for McDonalds; in the papers they read about international hotel chains and clothing stores opening branches in Israel; they heard of Jerusalem businessmen sealing all sorts of deals around the world; two kids from their class left when their parents got jobs in Geneva and Rome. Things seemed possible.

Yoel and Yonatan maintained that until the early nineties, Israelis' yen for the West had been accompanied by a recognition of their remoteness, whereas now everyone believed that, thanks to their improved relations with the Arab world, they now had a seat in the world—albeit at a side table. There had always been in-the-know kids who read stories in American magazines about bands or movie stars or WWF wrestlers, or just made them up, and who could inform everyone that Axl Rose had shot his dog while Guns N' Roses were on tour with Metallica, or that the Undertaker had hired an assassin to murder Mister Perfect. But these mediators were no longer needed, since now everyone could watch MTV and get the same information.

As they discussed the trips they could have taken if only history had come slightly sooner, and looked up at the night sky above the museum, Yonatan backed up at a traffic light and broke the headlight of the car behind them. They got out and the driver, a woman of around thirty-five, asked to see his license. When he told her he'd left it at home, she said, "You don't have a license, do you?" She looked around—he was relieved there was no pay phone—and said she was going to call the police. At home in his sock drawer, Yonatan had $250 that his brother had left him on his last visit, and he offered her the money. He wasn't scared of his parents but he did fear the police, because if they got involved he wouldn't be able to get his coveted license for years.

Yoel asked how many kids she had, and she answered begrudgingly, "Two." When he asked what their names were, she said it was none of his business. Then he heard Yoel say, "My friend would never tell you this, but his mother is very ill. It would be a shame to add to his sorrows." His boyish tone was tinged with a deep, sober bass, the kind used by grown-ups who really knew the world and said things like "May you know no more sorrow" to mourners.

Yonatan wanted to see the expression on Yoel's face, but he did not look at him. He couldn't remember when they'd discussed his mother's illness. Yoel knew he didn't talk about it, and he'd stopped asking questions.

"Is that true?" she asked Yonatan.

"Yes, it's true."

She followed them to Beit HaKerem, and they did not say a word the whole way. The road curved, and the cars hurtling toward them from the opposite direction looked too close, and the sky too dark. He had trouble keeping the car steady. They pulled over, and he got out and ran up home. When he came back with the cash, he found Yoel and the woman leaning against the hood sharing a cigarette, while Yoel told her his favorite story. It was about a Moorish ruler setting sail from Grenada, after losing the last Muslim stronghold in a battle on the Iberian Peninsula. As he sat there crying inconsolably, his mother scolded: "Don't wail like a woman over the place you did not protect like a man."

Then Yoel asked the woman if she thought he should go out with Tali—he'd apparently been talking about her—and she said she thought he should, it sounded like he loved her. Yoel, sounding utterly cheerless, said he'd wasted too much time making up his mind, and now Tali was dating a paratrooper.

"Don't worry," the woman said tenderly, "when you really want it, you'll get the chance."

Yoel rubbed his hands together. "It'll be too late then. It's already too late."

The woman laughed. "You're not even eighteen yet, nothing's too late."

Yoel straightened and said, "I can't sleep. I toss and turn with these questions like some miserable obsessive. I make a decision at dawn and then it starts all over again. Know what I mean?"

The woman said nothing, as though she'd suddenly decided this was not just another youthful escapade. Yonatan couldn't see Yoel's expression; he wondered why he hadn't told him about his sleepless nights. But then again, he didn't tell Yoel much either.

They stood silently for a while, until Yoel assumed the character of a pestering old man, and shouted: "Lady, such applause they're giving you!" Then he added, "It's a good thing my clumsy friend broke your headlight, 'cause you've been pretty helpful, to be honest."

She laughed, sounding relieved, and patted Yoel's arm and said he was cute.

Yonatan was not surprised by this exchange. It was not the first time Yoel had asked complete strangers, usually older ones, for advice on a troubling situation—his relationship with Tali, or his army service, even his future vocation. Sometimes he urged them to make a decision for him, and a month or two later he'd ask a different stranger the exact same question.

Yoel walked around the car and opened the driver's door and asked Yonatan to get out. He obeyed, and Yoel linked arms with him and walked him to the edge of the dirt lot, where their warm breath turned to vapor as they stood looking out onto the wadi.

"Where are your parents?" Yoel asked.

"New York."

"Is your mom getting treatment?"

"Yes."

"How's she doing?"

"They're taking care of her," he answered grudgingly.

"They've been gone for a long time."

"Three weeks."

"I can imagine what the house looks like."

"Want to see?"

"I don't know, I'm on the blacklist for your place. I haven't been there in a million years."

"Since Yom Kippur."

When his mom got sick, she didn't want his friends hanging around at home, especially not Yoel, whom she'd never liked—a fact she no longer tried to hide—and Yonatan didn't insist on having anyone visit except Lior, who slept over in his room every so often. His mother accepted her presence reluctantly, and complained that she had to calculate her every move when Lior was there because she didn't want a strange girl seeing her in a weakened state and hearing all sorts of things. But she made an effort to welcome her.

Once, after Lior witnessed a tense exchange between Yonatan and his parents, he told her about some things his mother sometimes blurted out when they fought. A few months later, when he mentioned that his father was demanding that he "adapt to the new situation already,"

Lior said she couldn't understand how they expected a young boy who'd been told by his mother he had the eyes of a Gestapo officer to start behaving properly. She got the words out quickly, before she could change her mind, and he stared at her as she walked onto the balcony for a cigarette, having realized the gravity of what she'd said.

"But that's just what she says when we fight," he said, hurrying after her. "I say terrible things too, you know." He carelessly listed a few of his sins, but Lior's words rang in his ears as he spoke. He felt despicable for giving her the idea that the order of things was different than it really was, or that he was the one who'd been wronged.

Yoel spat in a perfect arc at a rock about fifteen feet away. From the east they saw a figure walking on the narrow path between their school and the woods. They'd recently started paving a new road there, to connect the school with what was going to be the tallest building in the neighborhood: at least a dozen stories, they said, with smooth white siding instead of the customary rough Jerusalem stone. "Remember when they rolled me in the mud and thistles?" Yoel asked, pointing at the distant figure. "In a few years there'll be cars driving there."

Fascinated, Yonatan gazed at Yoel's hand. It wasn't up where he was pointing that they'd rolled him in the mud, but right here, near where they stood, a few yards from the trench. But Yoel's outstretched hand still pointed far up, maybe even at the horizon over the woods. Yonatan felt like pushing that hand down to the earth. Yoel exhaled, hugged his body, and rubbed his arms. "It really is cold, goddammit," he mumbled. Two girls climbed up the hill across the way, skipping from rock to rock to avoid the mud.

Yoel opened his eyes wide. They were both shivering now. "Everyone lies sometimes," he said.

Yonatan turned to look back at the wadi, now engulfed in a lethargy that dulled everything. A voice inside him told him to go to sleep, promising that if he lay down in his parents' bed with the space heater on, he would remember nothing of this morning tomorrow. Or perhaps he would drag it into a dream burrow. It was possible: there were no barriers between things that happened and things that were dreamed or invented, in the end they all blended together in the mind's swamp. It was only Yoel who demanded separation, interrogating him about Yaara, seeking truth and lies. Was there any way for them to even know?

"Do you want to go?" he heard Yoel say.

"Yes," he replied.

He felt Yoel's arm around his shoulder, and when he turned he saw that Yoel's face and sweater were also streaked with mud. He was surprised that Yoel hadn't complained. A piercing look flashed in Yoel's eyes again. "We'll go wherever you want," he said.

———

After the last houses of French Hill, the landscape slowly folded in until everything around them was brushed with tar-black paint. They made their way along a narrow, dark street, at times imagining they were suspended in mid-air surrounded by an abyss, and when the headlights illuminated the desert around them, with cliffs and hills and rocks, they felt relieved because the car seemed to tighten its grip on the ground. On previous trips the sky had felt high, with a multitude of twinkling stars, and jets of light that burst forth and exploded into radiant little spheres. For some reason they'd assumed it would always look like that when they drove out here at night. But now they saw no stars, only dark swaths of clouds that got closer to the earth as they drove on. Yoel, who was driving, said that if something didn't change, the sky would soon crush the road.

The rings of smoke from their cigarettes hung in the car. Yonatan rolled down the window and a cold breeze hit them. He rolled it back up and lit another cigarette, then examined his face in the lighter's flame: he was wearing four silver earrings, two chains with pendants of swords and a cross, and two rings. He looked to his left as if he couldn't remember: Yoel wore no jewelry.

Earlier, at home, after Yoel threw his muddy pants in the trash and said he was better off never seeing them again, Yonatan took a scalding hot shower and scrubbed his entire body to wipe off any sign of the wadi. He asked Yoel to stay in the bathroom with him, and they shouted at each other through the curtain. He was amazed at how calm he felt knowing that Yoel was there.

Then they sat on the living room couch, swept all the trash off the glass-top table with their bare feet, and drank vodka out of Styrofoam cups that Yoel found in the cabinet because he refused to go near the kitchen sink. Yonatan assumed Yoel was disgusted by the mess, since his home was always clean, and even if he pretended not to be influenced by his parents, he had trouble hiding his aversion to dirty dishes or the pita they used to bake in a forest clearing on school trips, with pine needles clumped to it.

It was noon, and it started raining again. He remembered Yaara and his visit. Yoel hadn't mentioned her again, but everyone would soon find out his lie. His body felt tense, the exuberance was gone, and something in his mind shuddered again, shaken by the terror of the abundance, of the noise, of everything that seethed and simmered and ignited inside it.

They finished drinking, catapulted their cups at the empty vase on the wooden cabinet, and moved to his parents' room. As they lay there watching music videos on MTV, waiting to catch Alicia Silverstone in "Cryin'", Yoel said maybe they should take a nap, since it probably hadn't been great to sleep on the mud in the wadi. His tone of voice, implying that they had all the time in the world, made Yonatan's fears disappear. But he still did not have the courage to tell Yoel what he felt: You won't leave, will you?

Yoel drove off the road and stopped the car. Yonatan looked out and his gaze was swallowed up in an all-embracing darkness; he had no idea where they were. The headlights shone on a cliff with a sharpened peak and large, reddish rocks on either side, which looked like three rock faces—a father and his twins. To the south, far beyond the road, distant lights glimmered, perhaps from the outskirts of Jericho. He felt weighed down, and had trouble calming his breath. All day long his spirits had been rising and falling in a frenetic whirlwind. Perhaps all his efforts to get through these days were pointless, as they were only a gateway to more days that would bring worse news.

Protected by the twilight in between decisions, he admitted that he feared the moment when his parents would come back from New York and he would have to look at his mother. He'd seen the years since her diagnosis as a hallway that led to only one end, yet in his core there was still a glimmer of hope—to which he sometimes surrendered, savoring its warmth—that things that happened to other people would not happen to them. That they would be saved. So he was in no hurry to urge his mother to tell him the secrets she had sworn she would reveal when he grew up. He never painted the picture after her death. Even when he decided he had to examine it, that he had no choice but to prepare, it looked very blurry. He believed they still had time.

"Are you okay?" Yoel asked softly.

Yonatan found his tone infuriating. As though he were speaking to a patient. "I don't know," he whispered.

"You're not going to do something extreme, are you?" Yoel asked.

"That's what you're worried about?" He let out a laugh.

"Partly."

"Then don't be."

"End of story."

"Have you seen Lior recently?" he couldn't resist asking.

"Where would I see her, you ass," Yoel exclaimed with a truncated laugh.

"With Tali's friends. You hang out with them."

"I hang out with Tali."

"Are you fucking her?"

"Where did that come from?"

"I saw her leaving your building early in the morning once."

"That…" Yoel stuck his tongue out. "I'm just comforting our Tali a little because her parents are splitting up."

"How are you comforting her?"

"We're fucking," Yoel laughed, "but forget that, you rascal, you don't understand Tali—that chick has more hobbies than Laura Palmer."

"Are you together or not?"

"You know how it goes, you told me once I was the champion of undefined relationships."

"But do you want to be her boyfriend?"

"It's unclear."

"It's been unclear for two years."

"At least four," Yoel said glumly. "It's driving me crazy, I'm scratching the walls with my fingernails."

There was a silence.

"So you are hanging out with her and her friends?"

"Most of the time we're with other people," Yoel insisted.

"What other people?"

"You don't know them."

"It's hard to be popular."

"Less than you think."

They both laughed.

Yonatan was formulating the question that would trap Yoel, but he hoped Yoel would get away—it was what he hadn't dared ask him in two months. "Is Lior seeing someone?"

"Stop going crazy."

"Don't lie. Not now."

"Remember, my friends: when you wear the right mask, every lie is the truth."

"Stop quoting!" Yonatan lost his temper again at the way Yoel glibly mouthed their kingdom notes.

"Because?" Yoel grumbled.

"You've turned into a collection of quotes, you're always imitating someone."

"Okay, okay," Yoel said with a joyless giggle, "I've heard this one before. A month ago you told me my soul was hollow because the beginning of 'Fade to Black' doesn't do anything for me."

"Is she seeing someone, yes or no?" he pressed.

"I heard she was going around with someone for a while," Yoel answered stingily.

"From where?"

"The arts school."

A gust rocked the car slightly. Yoel put both hands on the windshield and wiped off the steam.

"Did she sleep with him?" He hoped Yoel would evade the question.

"Probably not."

"How much exactly did they do?"

"Does it matter?"

"Yes."

"I don't know, I heard he's a kid, a junior, like Lior and Tali. Some tortured soul who wears all black and plays guitar ballads. You know the genre."

"Just tell me everything already!" Yonatan yelled. Something passed between the beams of light, far away, between the three cliff faces. It might have been a gazelle, but he couldn't see clearly. He turned off the lights, pushed the door open and got out. The wind attacked him and he couldn't hear anything as he walked over stones, tripping in his rush to where he thought the cliff faces were. It occurred to him that he could disappear tonight, vanish into the great darkness— he was already hidden between its wings. The picture cheered him up even as it frightened him. He heard the car door slam shut and Yoel's footsteps came closer, then there was the sound of someone panting behind him, or perhaps it was the wind—since when had Yoel got so fast? He sped up, no longer noticing the stones, but Yoel grabbed his shoulder and shouted something. He stopped. Yoel spun him around to face him.

They stood on a sandy hill. He had trouble making out the outline of Yoel's body, which kept fading in and out of the darkness. For the first time that night, he saw a few faded stars between the clouds.

They stood there silently for some time. He couldn't see the car, didn't even know exactly where the road was.

"Was Lior happy with you?" Yoel suddenly asked.

"How should I know?" Now he suspected Yoel knew something else.

"Did you ever think about it?"

"Did she tell you she wasn't?"

"No, I swear," Yoel answered, "I saw her once, not long ago, we were both too drunk to remember what year it was."

A car approached and they both moved out of the headlight beams. It seemed to be slowing down. Then it lurched forward with a screech, zoomed past them and disappeared. "They were as scared of us as we were of them," Yonatan laughed. Not long ago, some Israelis had been killed by a car bomb nearby.

"I had no idea you were still so worked up about her," Yoel said.

"Of course you didn't, you thought I was just making up the story about Yaara."

"I assumed you'd had a thing with her."

"We held hands on the kibbutz." He kicked the clumpy earth.

"That's not nothing. How come you didn't do anything afterwards?"

"I wanted to, but she'd already gone back to her boyfriend."

"So you just embellished," Yoel said.

"Why would I do that?" he asked indignantly.

"Are you seriously asking?"

"Yes," he said. He wanted to hear Yoel say it.

"Because it's what we always did." Obviously Yoel could not understand why Yonatan was forcing him to state the obvious. Yonatan felt relieved that he could not see Yoel's expression. There was something stunned in his voice, as though it were the first time he had discovered the chasm that had opened up between them. Yoel coughed, and he lit a cigarette. The flame lit up his flushed face. He coughed again and spat on the sand. His coat and pants were wet. It must have rained.

"There's nothing to embellish," Yonatan said, "the whole thing was made up, and everything's a lie anyway, or isn't it anymore for you? You're done with the lies, you've retired to your estate, the war is over."

He heard Yoel's footsteps circling him. "You can still talk to a friend in this world," Yoel said.

"Remember the rules: you don't dig around in the pain. When the world doesn't give you what you want, you fake a new world."

"That was once," Yoel said.

"That is always."

"We're not twelve anymore," Yoel hissed, as if the last line had aggravated an old anger that he couldn't rein in, not even now.

"You don't really believe that, do you, Yoel?" Yonatan laughed and wiped his nose on his sleeve. "Are you telling me you've left all that behind?"

"I'm not going to wallow in that trench forever," Yoel said, "and neither are you."

"Since when is it up to us?"

"Stop this bullshit already."

"So it's not us against everyone else anymore? Then tell me if she's seeing someone. Tell me if she even loved me."

Suddenly Yoel was very close to him, hugging him with both arms. His warm hands seemed to quiet Yonatan's pounding heart. "That is forever," Yoel whispered, "you won't be alone."

He became convinced that these words were merely adorning the moment, and that there would soon be another moment. That is what their words always were: flighty reflections of the moment, devoted to it, their severity fading as the days went by. They knew it only too well: words create a world and then it collapses, or is declared boring, and another world is created. That is what they had chosen to be: men of temporary loyalties. Of course he wanted to believe Yoel, but he knew that tomorrow or the next day this moment would dissolve into the routine of loneliness, and perhaps it would have been better if they hadn't met at all today, because when the illusion is over you are slammed back into the bottom of the abyss, and it's a deeper one.

Yoel gripped his shoulder with one hand, and mussed his hair with the other. It felt familiar. *You,* he wanted to tell Yoel, *you're different now, so stop being so familiar.* He feared the strip of light in the sky—the nights were getting shorter—that would signal the approaching dawn, because he didn't want them ever to leave this night. It was something of a phantom night, present both here and in all of their other times, because every meeting between them was a melding of all their times together into one burgeoning moment—a thousand past-screams against a feeble present whimper—and he himself, alone, was no longer enough.

PART TWO

MEXICO

He called Shira and explained that something was stirring after a long period of not writing—a year and a half, he told people, but it was more than two—and said he had to cultivate the seed before it withered, as all the previous seeds had, and only return to Tel Aviv "when something is really taking shape." He wasn't sure if he was telling the truth or playing the last card that could keep him in Mexico City for a few more days, but after that call he felt obliged to dust off his keyboard and run a cloth over the filthy screen. Also—to turn on the computer.

After breakfast he sat down at the desk in his room. The chair was too high for the desk, so he perched his laptop on some folded towels, but he still had to hunch. In the late morning he moved to a wooden table by the pool, where he sipped an espresso, smoked a cigarette, and ordered a beer as soon as the clock showed noon. When the noise around the pool became too loud, he relocated to a stone bench by the bubbling fountain in front of the hotel, where he focused on the screen and listened to car engines, people conversing in various languages, and suitcase wheels rolling on the asphalt.

He summoned up patches of ideas, characters and scenes that had flittered around his mind for the past two years. When nothing came into focus, he searched his notes and computer files, even little memos he'd saved on his phone. He found some raw ideas, but when he tried to write them, they aroused nothing. He knew that it's often possible to write something that is actually dead, and you only become aware of it later, when it fails to stimulate you or whip up your imagination, when it does not flood you with contemplations and insights, does not erupt in your mind.

The next morning he sat down at his desk again, and for hours nothing happened, but when he moved to the pool he started writing a short story that did excite him, perhaps because it branched off from the childhood dream about the boy with a plank lodged in his throat. He worked on the story all day, and some parts even amused him, but back in his room that night, when he read over what he'd written, he found that many sentences were similar to passages in his previous books. A few were identical, others just using the same ending—like different tunnels that all lead to the same room. It was as though he were trapped in language and imagery from the past, unable to find a voice that would not echo something he'd already written. There was a sort of drabness engulfing him, in which he lacked the power to create a new world.

On the third day, in the early morning, he was still revising the story, but after a couple of hours he deleted the file. He looked at the white screen, awaiting clarity but not really expecting it. As the hours went by he grew weary and disgusted with the feel of his fingers on the sticky keyboard. At three in the afternoon he sat down at the bar, savoring its darkness, drank a vodka tonic and a tequila, stared at the screen, and eventually found himself playing memory games, something his father had taught him. To protect his memory from aging, calcifying, dissolving into a porridge of fragments, every night before bed his father listed the names of the soccer players who had lined up for

Maccabi Petah Tikva against Maccabi Tel Aviv in 1952, he listed all the Oscar winners throughout the sixties, all the kids who'd been in first grade with him.

"The game isn't about pivotal memories," his father explained, "but simple things. The point is just to flex the muscle."

There were some things his father did not remember: what his mother had said about Yonatan when she was ill. Whenever he asked, his father measured his words and said nothing Yonatan didn't know or couldn't have guessed, and always slid, as if by accident, into the years before Yonatan was born. At first he'd assumed his father was avoiding memories he thought neither of them really wanted to pick at because they would only stir up old tensions and drive a wedge between them. They'd spent years learning to maneuver among the embers that had only to be accidentally touched for the atmosphere to heat up. Recently he'd realized that his mother must not have talked about him much, and that his father was trying to protect him from learning this.

He sat at the bar playing the game. Community center soccer game scores: 5-6 against Beit Nehemiah, 2-2 against Nikanor, 1-6 loss to Beit Pomerantz in an away game, a match Shaul had watched. There was sewage leaking all over the field. Purim costumes from first to sixth grade: cowboy, cowboy, cowboy, ninja, ninja or pirate, cowboy, pirate or ninja.

At his thirty-fifth birthday dinner, he'd decided he'd had enough of all the vague talk. He said he'd been thinking about things, and it was pretty clear to him that his mother had exaggerated when she used to describe him as a wild boy, a mean one even, who tormented her. After all, if you looked at the overall picture, he might have been annoying and rude and all that, but he was also pretty ordinary. His father listened with open discomfort, and finally interrupted to say that Yonatan had been a non-functional kid: he'd never stuck with anything, he was always cursing people, and it wasn't just Mom who'd said so, his teachers had too, and they'd even tried to kick him out of summer camp in Ein Karem. Yonatan was surprised to learn that, although his father had avoided the topic for years, when he was prodded into talking candidly, he turned out to be committed to the picture his mother had painted.

Yoel, who was sitting next to Yonatan's father that evening, stood up, picked up his knife, clanged his wineglass and said that, if he might be permitted to interfere, their positions were not mutually exclusive. He declared that it was admirable for a father and son to be able to talk honestly—even if some might argue that this was not exactly the ideal time—because, as the Talmudic saying goes, a knife is only sharpened on another knife. In his family, he said, this sort of discussion would never happen, and in fact he was somewhat envious of it. Or perhaps horrified...Everyone smiled, and the tension at the table dissipated. It was hard to resist Yoel's charm, and he was somehow even more appealing when he said things he didn't believe in, speaking with an overwrought gravity that sent a message to everyone: we are playing a game here, juggling words, not meanings. Then he delivered a lengthy speech in honor of Yonatan's birthday and waxed nostalgic, as if he were trying to bore everyone, and finished off with a quote from one of their kingdom notes: "This world is a game, it's pointless to search for truth or lies in it, so just play and quit whining."

That was the last time he'd seen Yoel before "the lost months," as his close friends called the period between when each of them last saw him and when he moved in with his parents. He saw almost no one during those months. He quit his job, told some people he was going away for a while, and others that he had another job or was on vacation. He told Tali, mostly in writing, that he was a little depressed and was planning his next move. And then he simply disappeared, shaking everyone off. No one knew exactly how he spent those days, but he seemed to have mostly been lying in bed in his Tel Aviv apartment, and he made one solo trip to the desert. His parents and sister began visiting him every day, and finally they took him home to Jerusalem.

Every time Yoel's friends talked, they returned to those lost months, even now, two years later. They searched for clues they'd missed that summer, when they were still seeing him, they analyzed messages he'd sent, ambiguous words he'd said on the phone, strange things he'd done (like sending a Facebook message to Alona, whom he hadn't talked to since the end of elementary school, and asking if they'd ever been to a movie together, just the two of them). Someone had seen him on Rothschild Boulevard looking bedraggled, a co-worker reported that he'd been distant from everyone at work even before quitting, a few people remembered thinking he seemed down. He'd written to friends saying that he'd missed all the boats, that it was time for a reckoning. Others remembered cheerful messages, in which he'd reminisced about funny things and asked them to travel to all kinds of places with him. The truth was that until the day Yoel's sister Rachel phoned Tali, even though Yoel had forbidden her to talk to his friends, and Yonatan and Tali went to see him at his parents' house, it hadn't occurred to them that something might really happen to him.

He looked around. The people who'd been at the bar earlier were gone. He opened and shut his eyes, struggling to stay upright, leaned over the bar, propped himself on his hands, ordered another beer and resumed his game. All the summer camps he and Yoel had done since first grade: Ziv community center, Ministry of Commerce and Industry, YMCA, Hebrew University, Ein Karem. Names of kids at elementary school. *Five on a Treasure Island, Five Run Away Together, Five Get into a Fix.*

Evening must have fallen, though it was impossible to tell from his spot at the bar, where there were no windows. He tracked the bluish light, which seemed to be swallowed up in a faint golden hue that trembled on the armchairs and tables. A young bearded man in a suit sat down next to him. He ordered a tequila and gave Yonatan and his laptop one of those fleeting friendly looks, the kind Yonatan recognized from his other evenings at the bar, which seemed to say: we're both bored, why don't we chat or do something interesting? He nodded at the man, looked him over, and wondered if he had any coke; he'd be up for doing a few lines—the man constantly moved his hands, drummed on the bar, stroked his beard—but decided he didn't and that he was probably also looking for some.

In his first week at the hotel, Yonatan hadn't talked to anyone except the waiters, but for the past few nights—perhaps because he was tired of the loneliness and afraid it would settle into his soul and something in him would be changed when he went home—he'd started chatting a little at the bar. He kept his distance from men and women like him, who preferred to listen rather than talk, and approached the ones who talked about their work—investment banking, teaching literacy, running an illegal casino in Sonora—and not about their marriages, their parents or their kids, because those topics aroused fears and comparisons in him. If anyone asked what he did, he would say he sold military equipment for a company affiliated with the Israeli Mossad or he was a former soccer player in the Israeli league who now worked as a sports agent, he was a ghostwriter for Klaus Barbie's daughter (it was precisely his Israeli background that allowed him to understand her; how did you write a character like Klaus Barbie? How did you write at all? You had to put every character's mask on your own face, and then believe in it).

He looked up. "You almost fell asleep," said the bearded man in Spanish-accented English. Yonatan whipped his head around: there was no one else in the bar.

"Are you staying at the hotel?" the man asked.

"Yes," he nodded. He wanted a drink of water and put his hand up for the barman but realized there was no one there.

"They've shut down," the man said with a little smile. "They know you here, so I signed your name, I hope that's okay."

Yonatan looked at his computer, annoyed to see something still flickering on the screen, and slammed it shut.

"Will you be able to get back to your room alone?" the man asked, leaning his elbow on the bar and his cheek on his hand. His eyes were red.

Why was he still here, this man? Yonatan wondered suspiciously. Does he want money, drugs, connections? Is he lonely? Is he from a cartel? They kidnap people here, and if you're lucky they drive you to an ATM and empty your bank account, but if you're not, like the magazine publisher, they shove you in a cellar. He wanted to leave the bar but had trouble moving, like in those dreams.

"I'll walk you back," the man said warmly and took a last sip of his drink.

Yonatan was sweating. He opened his eyes and something blinded him, and he saw tiny objects. He was too foggy and wouldn't be able to protect himself if this man did something to him. He stood up and started walking away.

"Señor," he heard the man say behind him. He considered not even turning around, but the motion seemed to precede his resolve. The man was holding his laptop: "You probably need this." He walked to the reception area and the man followed, his footsteps sounding light, as though he were floating on air. Yonatan struggled to remember the man's body—was there room for a pistol there? He may never see Itamar and Shira again; he had trouble breathing. He saw the front desk and sped up, and when he got close to the receptionist he felt a sensation of freedom, almost joy. The man stood next to him. "The gentleman has had a little too much to drink. Please help him get to his room, and make sure his computer gets there too," he said to the young clerk and put the laptop on the counter. "Writers need a computer," he said, "but some things are too serious to write stories about."

"That is true, Señor Hernandez," said the clerk.

"I wish you the best of luck," Hernandez said to him and walked away. "Don't be late getting back to your lovely boy."

"Thank you very much, Señor Hernandez," he mumbled, struggling to recall if he'd told him anything about Itamar, until he realized: his screensaver was a picture of them together.

"Do you know him?" he asked the clerk.

"Señor Hernandez is a poet," the clerk whispered. "He's been coming here every week for ten years to write his magazine column."

"Which magazine?" Yonatan asked, trying to remember the name on the issues in the publisher's office. Had he told the poet to talk to

Yonatan? Could they have found the young woman with glasses?

"A minor poetry magazine," the clerk replied, "Señor Hernandez owns it."

For a moment Yonatan was embarrassed: here he was, another coward with an overactive imagination, like all those westerners Carlos had made fun of. It was just like his and Yoel's games in the wadi when they'd pinned a conspiracy on anyone who walked by. He tapped his fingers on the counter and smiled at the clerk. The sense of relief was more exciting and crushing than all the anxieties. Warm currents whirled in his body. "You know something," he told the clerk, "it's starting to feel like home, this hotel of yours." He suddenly felt like singing.

———

"Care for a victory lap of your childhood haunts?" Yoel asked when he sat down in the car. Moments before, he'd been standing outside the supermarket, wearing black pants and a blue button-down shirt. He was freshly shaved, and his frizzy hair with its side part was glistening with gel. He put down his black leather bag, took a pack of cigarettes out of his pocket, lit one and blew smoke at the blue sky. His suntanned face acquired a contemplative expression. He seemed like his relaxed old self, in the elegant clothes he'd taken to wearing since finishing law school and starting his residency at a law firm in Jerusalem, but his head looked outsized, like those butterfly or turtle costumes their summer camp counselors used to wear, as though his outfit needed a different head to complete the picture. It took a few moments for Yonatan to notice that Yoel's brown wallet was sticking out of his pants pocket and his hems were crumpled. Yoel was sweating, as Yonatan was, and he noticed sweat stains on his blue shirt under the arms and above his stomach; perhaps that was why they didn't hug or shake hands.

The smell of cigarettes and sweat mingled with a sharper odor in the car, something like old onions. Outside the supermarket, rotting vegetables were strewn about among torn cardboard boxes. "It's hot in here," Yoel grumbled and started fiddling with the air conditioning while he prattled about his twenty-sixth birthday and the dinner his roommates in Nachlaot were insisting on. If Tali could come all the way from Haifa, he noted, Yonatan could make the effort to come from Tel Aviv.

"I'll be there," Yonatan replied, and did not ask why he'd been hearing for three years that Tali was coming to these birthdays and she never made it.

"I hope you're not disappointed," Yoel said with a pout, "but we're not like your brilliant Tel Avivi singles and intellectuals doing their BA for all eternity and finding everything terribly provincial." It was a line they both knew, and he recited the words wearily.

"Okay, let's not get into Jerusalem vs. Tel Aviv again," Yonatan said, blowing warm air on Yoel's face. "I'd rather kill myself."

He put in the first CD he saw on the floor, without even recognizing the name of the band; some British trash he'd picked up in London when he used to frequent cellar concert venues and brag about knowing bands no one else had heard of. Yoel listened to the music and grimaced. A few years ago, after they both got out of the army and were living in Jerusalem, they liked to listen to the political talk shows on the car radio and discuss them. He couldn't remember when they'd stopped that. At the time, Yoel had always claimed there was one answer to every question: the 2001 Intifada. Until that was over, he insisted, nothing would change.

In the shopping center up the street from the supermarket, there was nothing going on. At Café Neeman, an old man leaned on a filthy table while an umbrella with the chain's logo rolled around by his feet. The man ambled past shop windows, all bare apart from Play & Learn, which displayed cans of paint and paintbrushes scattered around two paint-stained ladders. Yonatan remembered seeing the same display last time he'd been there, a few years ago—they must be getting ready for something big, he decided, and examined his bitter smile in the rearview mirror. He disliked the way it made his lips look crooked.

Pictures from those shop windows at a different time—say, 1985—scroll through his mind: he walks past the hamburger joint, the newsstand, the café. Outside Play & Learn, he spins the rack of musical greeting cards: "To My Favorite Teacher," "To the Best Mom in the World," and even, "I Love my Dog." Unsatisfied, he buys some white paper, sits down in the alcove between the patio and the video rental library, and writes, "I'm sorry, Mom." He draws a house and black grass. It looks pathetic, so he adds a hat and a flower.

Overcome by exhaustion, he rubbed his heavy eyelids, scalded by the sun blazing through the car windows. Didn't there use to be more trees here? he wondered. The sky seemed to have shrunk, too: if he stretched his arm up high it would disappear into the clouds.

"Did they change the streets?" he asked Yoel.

"Yeah, it's no big deal," Yoel answered languidly, "just turn left." Yoel was clearly also dejected; Yonatan knew the quick dives his mood could take. It didn't happen frequently, but when it did he spoke in monosyllables, all the vibrancy drained from his voice. Even when he emitted a purr of laughter, not a single muscle moved, and nothing could cheer him up. And then he would vanish, the way he did when they lived in London after the army, but a day or two later he'd come back, cheerful as ever, showering his charm on everyone.

Yonatan had been postponing this visit to Jerusalem for months, until his father told him there'd been a fire at the storage facility in Givat Shaul. He didn't know any details and couldn't even remember which floor their storage unit was on, but Yoel somehow found the information "in five minutes." Concerned that they might clear out the unit and everything would be lost, his father suggested they go together, but Yonatan didn't want that. He'd never forgiven him for moving all their stuff into storage, and was even less forgiving of himself for never going there once in recent years, not even to retrieve the photo albums.

He thought back to his first weekend in Tel Aviv. Before that, he went home to Jerusalem every Friday morning and stayed with his father; sometimes Yoel slept over. But after he'd been living in Tel Aviv for almost a year, his father announced that he'd sold the Jerusalem apartment. At first Yonatan wasn't bothered about clearing out his childhood home, but one evening, when he found himself alone in the Tel Aviv apartment, he realized that he'd never viewed it as his home, and that he'd lived there protected by the knowledge that he had somewhere he could always go back to, a place where his movements followed a familiar rhythm. Perhaps the fact that he went back to his childhood home every weekend, wandered among the rooms, made noise and played music, preserved an ember of the vitality that had once been there.

He'd spent the whole weekend roaming the apartment, disgusted by the shabby rooms, his restlessness protecting him from the onslaught of scenes from family Sabbaths: eating breakfast with his mother, watching Hitchcock films in the living room, his father and Shaul competing over who could name more Oscar-winning films, playing ball on the balcony. It was as if the loss of the family home was the only way for him to acknowledge the end of their history in Jerusalem.

He turned right. Yoel was on a work call, mostly listening with a bored expression and occasionally giving a curt response. "They're laying people off everywhere right now," he said before hanging up. "We're in a crazy recession, my friend, but don't worry, you'll beat them all in the end." He tossed his phone into the glove compartment, slammed it shut, and murmured, "They restate the obvious as obsessively as an old sex addict in Thailand. They twist your soul, these characters, they shove their dreariness down your throat like medicine."

The car zigzagged down to Givat Shaul, past the gas station where he and Tomer Shoshani had washed windows in the summer of sixth grade. They used to exchange jabs and jokes with the Palestinian shift manager and his fifteen-year-old son, and sometimes they sprayed soapy water at each other. But a week after being hired they got into a fight with the son, and that Friday night they marched over there, smashed the warehouse padlock with a hammer, filched a few cans of engine oil and emptied them out on the field behind the station.

When Yonatan's father took them to work on Sunday morning, the manager asked to talk to him, and the two men walked around the gas pumps together while the manager's son sat on an empty crate and looked at them. Yonatan breathed in the gasoline smell he'd learned to like. Tomer Shoshani muttered that they didn't have to confess to anything because no one was going to believe an Arab.

Yonatan's father came back to the car with a blank expression and did not say a word. They didn't speak either. After dropping off Tomer Shoshani at home, he turned around to look at Yonatan and said, "I've never been as ashamed as I am today."

"That's only because you're clueless," he snapped back. His whole body was prickling and the hair on his arms stood on end.

A mocking smile came to his father's lips, but he was not a man to make faces or smirk. A shadow of fragility passed through his green eyes; the skin around them had gone ashen and saggy.

His father got out of the car, and Yonatan watched him walk to the steps with his shoulders hunched and his head bowed, and was afraid he was going to collapse. He got out and followed him, so he could catch him if he fell—ashamed of obeying his fear but unable to do otherwise. He was battered by visions of his father falling, or being beaten by strangers, or crashing his car into a wall. He remembered that, a couple of years earlier, his father had complained of chest pain for a couple of months and slept in the living room on a mattress on a wooden board. Every day after school, Yonatan would pick out a movie at the video library: *Death Wish 1, 2* and *3*, all four *Dirty Harry* films, and anything with Chuck Norris, Alain Delon or Jean-Paul Belmondo. They would eat lunch together, which in those days was a hot meal of rice and chicken breast, or schnitzel, and his father would tell him stories about the New York Knicks and characters in old Jerusalem or in Damon Runyon books. Then they'd sit in the living room with their arms around each other and watch a movie. When Yonatan imitated Chuck Norris, kicking and punching at the air, his father taught him how to do an uppercut and a cross punch. Sometimes he'd count how many times Yonatan could dribble a ball, impressed by his talent. Those were hours of happiness, free of castigation and guilt, when his short-tempered father treated him patiently. But when his mother came home from work, their camaraderie evaporated, and his father went back to playing—at times clumsily—the father figure.

To this day, his father sometimes said, "That was a good time, wasn't it?" And Yonatan would answer, "It was a good time."

"I didn't really do anything bad," he called after his father. A tremor of tenderness ran through him, and he wanted to hug him.

But his father barked, "We'll talk about it this evening," and it was clear that he was in a hurry to get to work.

A week later they got into another fight in the car, and his father said he and his mother had discussed sending him to a kibbutz for a while, so that he could acquire some better habits and learn how to function in society. He enumerated all the things Yonatan had started and abandoned: boxing, organ lessons, running team, computer club, chess club, karate class.

"Don't forget folk dancing, Dad."

"Be that as it may," his father said, clearing his throat. He explained that his mother had been feeling unwell, and her blood sedimentation rate was low. They could no longer tolerate the way he tormented her and didn't help out around the house. It wasn't just his mother: he'd even been rude to Ratzon from downstairs, and now Ratzon wasn't talking to him.

When he was little, he used to sleep over at Ratzon's every Thursday when his parents went to Tel Aviv, and whenever they went overseas. He would wake up early in the morning, jump out of bed, and walk barefoot down the hallway wrapped in a blanket, hoping he wasn't too late to catch Ratzon putting on tefillin. He usually found Ratzon standing in the living room with the black leather straps bound around his forearm. Ratzon would whisper hello, and Yonatan would also whisper, so as not to disturb the ritual. Sometimes Ratzon agreed to wrap the strap, still warm and sticky from his skin, around Yonatan's arm. And they would stand together by the window facing the large trees, with the wadi looking like a black swollen hat to their left, and the dark skies above them. Ratzon would hold the prayer book and read from it, and Yonatan would join in for the few lines he'd memorized: *And from thy wisdom, O most high God, thou shall reserve for me; and from thy understanding thou shalt give me understanding; and with thy loving-kindness thou shalt do great things for me; and with thy might thou shalt destroy my enemies and my adversaries.*

He wanted to apologize to Ratzon, but he kept putting it off. After all, things one has said to another person have already made inroads in their soul, and no apology can pull them out or wipe their traces away. A poisoned piece of consciousness, like burnt earth, can never again be as it was, and Ratzon would never again see his good virtues.

"That's a good idea," he said to his father in a matter-of-fact voice. "Why don't you send me to live on a kibbutz?"

His father replied angrily, "Suddenly you want to live there?" His father had clearly expected him to be frightened by the idea and try to please them by promising to improve his behavior.

He wasn't sure if he was faking courage or if he was really willing to leave. And perhaps this was the solution that would save everyone. He could no longer tolerate the gloomy mornings; he never got out of bed until his father yanked the covers off, and even if things were not as bad as he perceived them, it didn't matter: there were days when he woke up anticipating change and making new plays, but by midday he slumped home feeling dejected, and in the evenings he watched TV or disappeared into an adventure book and wished he could forget everything. He realized, for the first time, that perhaps his mother would be happier and stronger if he lived somewhere else. Maybe that light-hearted, secretive smile he saw on her face in old pictures would come back, and they could meet on weekends and have meals together and laugh a lot, like Tali and her parents.

But these weekend scenes soon began to look stupid, clumsily borrowed from other families—any minute now he'd be imagining them riding horses in the desert. Still, if he were somewhere else he could start over, having learned from his Beit HaKerem days. He positioned his alter ego in every different setting he visited—his parents' friends' house, a kibbutz they'd stayed at on a school trip—and outfitted him with new customs, friends and hobbies. Sometimes this other version of him, who lived on a kibbutz or in Rehovot or Beersheba, emerged again after being forgotten.

The kibbutz idea soon faded, though, and when he asked about it, his father acted as if they'd never seriously considered it. When he asked again, his mother cut him off and said it would never happen, he wasn't going anywhere. Her resolve surprised him, as did the warm currents in his limbs. He wondered if in fact he'd been afraid of the idea, and if all the imaginary scenes of a new life were merely part of a plot he'd hatched to outsmart the fear. Had such hopes truly existed?

They parked outside the storage facility and stepped out in the parking lot adjacent to the main road. Trucks roared past, people loaded wooden joists into a shipping container, they heard hammering and drilling, and a yellow crane towered above. The back of Yonatan's neck burned under the sun and his hands felt hot, probably from the steering wheel that was always sticky in summer. Yoel leaned against a wall next to a man in overalls who was sharpening knives. He did not say a word, but he was obviously impatient.

"Are you in a hurry?" he asked Yoel coolly. All this looked too familiar. At some point in their childhood Yoel's schedule had become perpetually full, and it took years for Yonatan to understand that Yoel needed an escape route from every event.

"Not at all," Yoel replied, smoothing out his wrinkled shirt and lighting a cigarette, and they both grimaced. "It's too hot for this."

Yonatan watched the sun playing tricks on the warehouse buildings: half the margosa tree was shaded, the other flooded with light that turned its leaves and branches golden, and the tree was reflected in the windows. A strange glimmer bounced off the car bumpers, spraying blinding light everywhere.

When they climbed up the steps, Yoel proceeded to recount cases he'd recently worked on, most of which involved real estate developers being sued for contract breaches. Yonatan already knew these stories from Yoel's visits to his bachelor pad in Tel Aviv. He would arrive late at night, light a cigarette, strip down and leave his clothes in a pile by the door, pick out a pair of shorts and a T-shirt from Yonatan's closet, and walk around barefoot, not even slightly embarrassed by his overgrown toenails. He mimicked the witnesses, the prosecutors and the judge, boasted about the droll questions he'd prepared for the senior attorney to "demolish the plaintiff," and denigrated his own law firm.

The stories were always fascinating, but Yoel's take on his own deeds never changed: he was the young Jerusalemite who had to serve the rich barons with a disgust posing as delight or a delight posing as disgust, depending on whom he was talking to and what sort of mood he was in. The only thing that did change was Yoel's loathing of his colleagues. He mocked the interns' rat-like ambition and the way they worshipped the partners—in contrast to his own self-professed "perfect flattery arising from perfect contempt." Mostly, he mocked the partners, with their bald heads and potbellies, their tedious political pronouncements after yet another terrorist attack, analyzing the failure of the Camp David peace talks or the Second Intifada, which they said "screwed up wonderful initiatives like the 'Gaza Riviera.'" He mocked their lifestyle, their vapid existence, but it also somehow aroused panic in him, and he described it obsessively, in great detail, searching for evidence of something similar in his and Yonatan's lives. At times he seemed to believe that no matter what they did, they would end up drifting to the same place, to that "faded old man in diapers" whom he mentioned often. His face would turn ashen and he would sit on the couch rubbing his hands together, staring into space or repeatedly insisting that he should have quit his job, he hadn't made a single good decision since high school, he'd missed opportunities and done nothing that really interested him, nothing that was "part of the body, like you and your writing." Sometimes he asked Yonatan, only half-jokingly, why he hadn't pressured him to make the right decisions. But then he would snap out of his state of dread and screech with laughter.

Yoel mocked the partners in his firm and joked about them ("I just want to shake that rat-faced loser and scream at him: 'You're a flaccid, bald, rich old man—how can you sit here every day just to make a buck off some hardworking people? Go to India! Go to Lapland! Live a little!'"). But Yonatan knew that Yoel's professed loathing was complicated, and that any time he admitted to hating someone, he risked exposing the stitches in the bright robe he wore when he went out into the world and charmed all the people who thronged after him and competed for his attention. In fact the only people he consistently talked about with avid hatred were their old enemies from the Beit HaKerem days.

"The master of empty gestures," Yonatan sometimes teased Yoel, claiming he showered affection on everyone because he didn't genuinely love or hate anyone, and that no one really made a dent in him. Yoel used to quote these observations admiringly, and said it was all slander: he might wear a mask with most people, certainly in a professional setting, but he also had a genuine face for the people he liked. "I'm a cheerful, affectionate person who doesn't walk around the world feeling disgruntled and spraying venom, like the artist and intellectual types you hang out with!" he said with a wink. Yoel found these characters so amusing that sometimes, when he was bored, he would tell Yonatan, "Go on, call up one of your pale-faced weirdo friends from the literature department and ask him over to talk about Lacan and the occupation."

As they got closer to the warehouse, Yonatan became more disgusted by his damp shirt, his clingy hair, and the acrid smell of cigarettes on his breath. They stopped at the sliding door and pushed it open together, mocking each other's weak muscles, and Yoel started reminiscing about a joke they'd played on their science teacher.

"Forget about that now," Yonatan interrupted.

The storage unit was dark apart from a few triangles of light dancing on the walls. He couldn't see anything. Maybe everything really did burn, he thought. A few strips of light clung to the old orange-yellow lampshade from their living room, which seemed to emerge from the shadows. He turned around and shut the door. They were left in total darkness, and he felt relieved. He found the light switch, and before flipping it his muscles tensed. Yoel asked: "Did you find it?" and he said, "Yes," and struggled to steady his breath, still not flipping the switch. Yoel did not say a word to rush him.

He switched the light on. Bright light from a dusty bulb painted the wall, and he caught sight of smeared blood, squashed mosquitos and flies. He turned when he heard Yoel's yelp of surprise, and found himself looking at their old living room, arranged exactly as it used to be on HaGuy Street. It was as if someone had replicated it here. The orange three-seat sofa was alongside the wall, the smaller couch was near it, and in the gap between them and the wall stood the grooved black table. On it was the lamp that filtered the light in a way he always liked, and in front of that was the square glass-top table, its chrome legs marred by white scratches. On the floor was the rug in shades of black, gray and purple, though it looked smaller than he remembered, and next to the big window looking out on the street was the rocking chair. Beside it was the two-tiered black lacquered wooden cart—its wheels were painted red because his mother had decided one day that the living room needed brightening up—and on it a vase they always kept pens and coins in. Opposite the large sofa were the black dressers, and to its left the white porcelain bowl, but without the gold-rimmed spoon it used to hold, and a few silver knives and forks scattered next to it. He remembered there being more of those.

A thick layer of dust coated the furniture, and cobwebs stretched between the ceiling and the small couch. There was a dank smell in the room, as there was in his building's basement. Scanning the layout, he began to notice that some things were missing, broken, scratched, spaced too far apart. He couldn't understand why he was doing it, but he couldn't stop.

Yoel leaned on the wall and rubbed his cheeks, while Yonatan ducked under the cobwebs and sat down on the large sofa. His body sank into it and he became aware of every single limb, as though he were examining how each of them clung to the sofa. Threads of gray dust hovered in the light, cohering into ships, arrows, ladders. He brushed them away, coughed, wiped his dusty hands on his pants before he remembered that they were filthy too, leaned his head back and closed his eyes. He remembered the weeks he'd spent sleeping on this sofa, after Lior left him and he wouldn't go near the bed in his room, where they'd slept together and where every indentation marked a trace of her body. Yoel came over and sat down next to him so gingerly that he wasn't willing to swear he'd actually put his bottom on the sofa.

Yonatan put his feet up on the glass-top table. After some hesitation, Yoel did too. He lit a cigarette and passed it to Yonatan, who inhaled and flicked ash on the table, while Yoel emptied out his cigarette box to use as an ashtray. Yonatan couldn't help laughing at Yoel's insistence on hygiene. As if it really made any difference now.

The mimetic pretense of the setup annoyed him—how could anyone have thought it would do any good? Even if they'd burned all the furniture to a cinder, it wouldn't have made any difference. He grabbed the cigarette from Yoel, who resisted, perhaps guessing at Yonatan's intention, and sparks fell on the sofa between them. He flicked the cigarette onto the middle of the rug and they sat there for a few minutes, waiting for something to happen.

He got up and walked over to the chest of drawers from his room, past a pile of labeled cardboard boxes: pots, books, pictures, jewelry, miscellaneous. Instead of clothes, the drawers contained bills, envelopes, and thin blue sheets of paper covered with his mother's large handwriting: "My dears, I know I've been lazy about writing letters recently, but I believe it's a condition that not only applies to writing, but invades everyday life too. And that is unlike me..." Next to her signature she'd added, in a different colored ink: "July 10, 1971." There were also his mother's military discharge papers, and folded inside them, a death notice clipped from the newspaper, with condolences to his mother from the Minister and Ministry of Communications, for the death of her mother ("May you be comforted among the mourners of Zion and Jerusalem"). There were driver's licenses, a musical mug he'd bought her, prescriptions for medication, and the blue cassette tape Shaul had sent him for Hila's dance party at the end of sixth grade.

Digging through the items, he found a few black-and-white photos bundled together with a rubber band, in the largest of which his mother stood before a dark wall or a black screen dotted with butterflies of light. She wore a tight gray dress that accentuated her breasts, with a white lace collar, a gold bracelet on her wrist and a cigarette between her fingers. Her right leg was folded behind her, with her foot on the screen. Her curls, longer than they were in the other pictures, fell over her forehead, and in her black eyes, gazing slightly upward, there was a dreamy expression he did not recognize. He was amazed by her natural expression. There was no doubt in his heart that this was the Epstein & Feldheim photograph, and he wished they'd seen it together when she was alive. He recalled that when he'd asked her about the picture, she'd poked fun at his big brother's overactive imagination, but now he wondered if that exchange had really happened. Tiny specks of mist separated the memory from ones he was more certain about. He had already found that sometimes, hiding between the memories, were events that had never happened, little apparitions that had first emerged in childhood and continued to permeate his mind, camouflaged as memories.

He held the picture, debating whether or not to put it back, and was revisited by a notion he'd seldom thought of lately, perhaps because it frightened him: when she used to talk about the things they'd missed out on, his mother was not only grieving those childhood years when he'd loved her so deeply, but lamenting the fact that he hadn't known her in the years before he was born. By the time he was growing up, her strength had waned and she was disillusioned, and the persona he remembered, the one who was present in his home, captured only a small part of her and committed an injustice to the woman she really was. He remembered Yaara's stories about his mother sitting in their home drinking wine and entertaining them, and he reconstructed

Yaara's sardonic expression, which seemed to be implying that he did not understand his mother at all.

He shut the drawers, sat back down on the sofa and held the photograph against his thigh.

"I still remember every minute of that morning, after you called," Yoel said.

"I called you? When?"

"At four a.m."

"I don't remember that," he murmured, surprised by Yoel's boldness. "You've said so many things over the years."

Yoel sat silently looking at his shoes, then said in a subdued voice: "Maybe those are the things I wanted to see."

For a moment he hoped Yoel might tell him again how much his mother had loved him and how close they actually were. He had the illusion that, if he said those things, then not everything was signed and sealed, and there was still a chance that Yoel was seeing something he himself could not. But Yoel said nothing, and he knew that it was because Yoel had read things he'd written. Yonatan sat up straight. "Let's get out of here."

"But we haven't found the photo albums," Yoel said.

"We'll come another time."

"I can keep them at my house," Yoel suggested, answering a question that had not been asked. He did not say what was obvious to them both: they were never coming back.

"I don't need them now," he told Yoel, sounding almost pleading.

"I'll keep them at my house," Yoel insisted. "Go out for some fresh air."

He had trouble disconnecting from the touch of the sofa, but eventually he stood up and walked away. He hurried down the corridor, holding the photograph close to his body, being careful not to get it dirty. He skipped down the steps and glanced at his reflection in a mirror: he was dusty gray, and his neck looked grimy where the sweat had mingled with dust. The sight of his thick gray eyebrows amused him. He stepped away from the mirror and dashed outside into a blazing sphere of light under a sky blotted with a grayish-yellow hue. Unable to stop his momentum, he marched to the car, sat down in the driver's seat, put the photo in the glove compartment, wiped the sweat off his face, gripped the burning hot wheel with both hands and drove away.

THE TOWERS
(LATE 1980S)

It was Saturday, the day after Alona's party, and they turned up at the
school gates during a soccer match. For an instant nothing else moved,
not even the birds on the lampposts, while everyone stared at them.
The rays of sun that had emerged after a few gray days illuminated
their muscular arms, the black stubble on their faces, their friendship
bracelets, and the shiny rifles slung over their shoulders on colorful
straps. They seemed to be bathed in a golden halo of light, while the
rest of the schoolyard was drowned in the dreariness of a Beit HaKerem
winter. Despite the cold weather, they wore surfer shorts with white
tank tops and sneakers. One of them was barefoot. And suddenly their
ebullience ran through the yard like an electrical current and rattled
the older boys, who crowded around them, touching their arms,
shoving each other aside to stroke their rifles.

Yonatan saw Shimon, David Tzivony and Bentz slapping the
soldiers' backs, competing for their attention. He'd never imagined

that the boys who lorded over the block could look so tiny.

Then they stood in the middle of the yard and everyone kicked the balls to them. They launched a couple of balls over the gate toward the school windows, but lost interest and sat down on the benches smoking cigarettes. Some younger kids hung on the fence outside looking in at them.

Everyone whispered that they were home on leave after a couple of months in the West Bank and Gaza, where they were handling the Arabs who'd been rioting for a long time. They didn't talk about it, wouldn't answer any questions, and said they weren't allowed to say anything. But the kids spread the facts around in whispers: they were serving in a unit full of tough guys who would stop at nothing; even the other soldiers were afraid to talk to them; they beat the crap out of the Arabs with batons and chains, they cracked their asses open with rifle stocks; it was said they'd grabbed a few kids in Gaza who'd thrown stones and made them run naked in the fields and hit their legs with chains and forced them to eat dirt; they could pass right through Molotov cocktail fire because they had special fireproof uniforms; at nights they painted their faces with charcoal and no one could see them. They were crazy and everyone knew it, they got drunk at the clubs in Tel Aviv and slept with girls in cars and on the beach and sometimes videotaped everything, and whenever an Arab caught sight of them he'd run and hide in a sewage trench or in a baby stroller.

Fat Gideon, who called himself a Zionist punk and liked bands no one else had heard of, like Killing Joke, and was always quoting things famous people had said when they were young, said that in fifty years they'd appreciate what great things these soldiers had done, and he asked how he could join their unit. David Tzivony said Gideon was too fat, and everyone laughed but the laughter was swallowed up in a whistle of wind that shook the treetops, and suddenly there were menacing faces everywhere, with rows of big teeth, and each kid's smile was twisted in a different way as the whole yard laughed. Gideon turned red and looked around. Finally, he picked up a large stone and threw it on the asphalt between David Tzivony's feet.

Tzivony dodged the stone and almost fell. Everyone clapped and yelled: "Don't let him get away with it!" He had no choice but to attack Fat Gideon, who stood there staring at the stone and then at Tzivony as if he didn't remember throwing it. They fell to the ground and punched each other, while the four soldiers sat on the benches with their legs splayed, blowing rings of smoke. When Gideon and Tzivony stood up—their shirts were ripped, their faces and necks were zigzagged with bloody scratches, and Tzivony's cheek was swollen like a balloon—and Tzivony reached for the stone, the barefoot soldier stood up. "No stones!" he shouted. Tzivony didn't stop, and the barefoot one yelled, "I said no stones!" The yard went silent again.

There was an air of recklessness in the crowded yard, and Yonatan wanted to get out, but he was afraid to draw attention to himself, and decided it was better to stay put and do nothing. It was only the night before, at Alona's party, that he'd felt mature because he'd slow-danced with Hila and she pressed up against him and looked into his eyes. But in fact he didn't understand anything, because the real grown-ups dealt with very different things that were occurring in places he'd never seen, far beyond the neighborhood's borders—downtown, and in Jenin or Gaza, and in all those nightclubs.

Suddenly the barefoot soldier glared at Yonatan as if he'd guessed what was going through his mind, and barked: "Kid, get over here." Yonatan stared back, convinced he was imagining things—the nightmare couldn't be coming true so quickly. But the dull pain in his stomach and the tremor in his body slammed him back to the asphalt. He grasped at the hope that perhaps he'd misunderstood and the soldier was talking to another kid standing behind him. But then he realized: he was the only boy left in the yard.

"I said get over here," he repeated, and Yonatan took a few small steps toward him, with his head bowed and his eyes scrutinizing the little stones and leaves and the white stripes bordering the soccer court. He stood before the barefoot soldier, who held his burly arm up to his eyes because the sun was blinding him, and his forearm muscles ballooned into a mountain. Yonatan could smell the sharp sweat from the soldier's armpits, and the damp circles on his white tank top widened. He asked Yonatan who his brother was, but he didn't immediately respond, fearing the answer might get him into trouble. Finally he said, "Shaul," and the barefoot guy mussed his hair with a hand that smelled of cigarettes and hair gel, and gave him an affectionate slap on the cheek. "Say hi to him from Ofer Alon. I used to play ping pong with him and Gavriel Mansour in your basement."

"I will."

"Bullet with my name on it," Ofer added, in English, "tell him that. We were crazy about that song." And his thick lips curled into a smile though it left no other mark on his expressionless face. "We used to make the whole basement shake until your neighbor, the religious guy—what's his name?"

"Ratzon."

"Yeah, Ratzon, until he lost his shit. Now all the Arabs in Gaza know that song."

A strange warmth prickled Yonatan's stomach and climbed all the way up to his forehead. He considered a series of brazen answers—in moments of elation he tended to lose his inhibition—but he pressed his tongue against his lower teeth and forced himself to be silent.

The soldier put his rifle up to Yonatan's face and the strong smell—he wasn't sure how to describe it; a sort of acidic metal—filled his nostrils. He held his breath and moved his face away slightly and ran both hands over the smooth and incredibly shiny handle, the only part of the rifle that had no holes or apertures that his fingers might get stuck in. The soldier laughed: "Pull the trigger, don't be scared." He was afraid his fingers would get cut on something; he'd always avoided the heavy machinery in shop class, unable to understand how it worked and convinced he would lacerate himself. But he put his finger on the trigger. The soldier put his large hand on Yonatan's and pressed their fingers together, and his dry, rough skin enfolded Yonatan's hand and it felt as if a dry leaf was touching him. To his surprise it was a pleasant feeling, igniting a warming recognition of something he dimly recalled from his distant past: that he was protected, perhaps even invincible.

The soldier loosened his grip and moved his hand away, and all at once Yonatan was on the cold, wet asphalt alone. Having no choice, he pressed the trigger but it didn't budge, and he quickly moved his hand off the rifle. The soldier gave him a surprised look and swung the rifle around his back. "If anyone messes with you, just let me know," he said as he walked away.

"Thank you very much," Yonatan said, sounding too obsequious. He turned back to look at Tzivony, Shimon and Bentz, who were staring at him with astonishment mixed with fear. The spectacle had clearly been so peculiar that they still hadn't fully grasped the implied threat. He felt dizzied by his newfound power: he had only to point in their direction, and they'd be sorry for all the times they'd bullied him and Yoel. Over summer vacation they'd caught him and Yoel playing poker in the wadi and threatened to tell their parents, and in return they'd demanded to know whether they jerked off to girls from class, their friends' sisters, Scouts counselors, girls from *Playboy*, or imaginary girls. Every time he and Yoel refused to answer or gave a feeble reply, they kicked them and forced them to write "Bentz & Tzivony & King Shimon" on the hot sand with their fingers, and they kept wiping the letters away with their shoes and making them write it again. If they hadn't been in a hurry to get home to call into the pop music quiz show on the radio, there was no telling how it might have ended. But he wasn't stupid enough to talk now; it was clear that the threat hanging in the air was more powerful than anything the barefoot soldier might really do to them, and that they would appreciate his not taking advantage of the moment to turn them in. Besides, that soldier seemed like too heavy a punishment. And even without all these considerations—Yonatan was no snitch.

It also dawned on him that they could be useful.

He caught up with them in Esrim Park. They were standing by the benches at the edge of the park, lighting matches and flicking them. Whenever smoke started curling up from the lawn or the dry leaves, one of them would get up and smother it with his shoe. They talked about the soldiers and the secret devices they supposedly used, each trying to come up with something more exciting than the other: Tzivony described gloves that delivered electric shocks to any Arab they touched; Shimon hyped the special goggles that you could look through in the middle of the night in pitch-black Gaza and see sunny blue skies like on the beach in Eilat; Bentz yelled that there was no such thing—maybe Shimon had read about them in *Penthouse*. They seemed agitated and kept shoving each other, kicking trash cans, accusing each other of lying, but they eventually agreed on two things: paratroopers had much better rifles than the barefoot soldier and his friends, and fuck if the story about the fireproof uniforms was true. Everyone was always exaggerating in the schoolyard, they grumbled. There was a brief silence, and they fell into the ominous boredom that lurked at the end of every bout of high spirits and drove them to keep the crowd happy by finding a new victim; that was when people like him had to make themselves scarce.

Shimon turned to David Tzivony and said something about the stone he hadn't picked up because the barefoot soldier had told him not to. "You were shaking," he jeered. "I could smell your wet boxers from thirty fucking feet away." Bentz backed him up: "And then Gideon beat the crap out of you and walked away without a scratch. Look at you—it's like half your face got thrown in a frying pan."

Tzivony, who did have an enormous blue-pink bruise puffing up on his cheek, hissed, "That fat fuck is gonna pay for that. But what was I supposed to do? Step up to Ofer Alon? Do you know what kind of things they do over there? The guy's a murderer."

They sat down on a bench and he watched them through the trees. Shimon and Bentz drummed on a broken stool and sang softly: *"Honey, spread your legs, for seven oppressed men, seven Palestinians. Twenty years of occupation—we're done waiting! Here we come with our hard-ons, to free Palestine!"*

"Enough, you fucking Arabs, you're making me crazy with that song," Tzivony snapped.

Yonatan knew all the songs from the underground musical, *Mami*, because Noam had played it for Yoel, after making him swear he wouldn't tell their parents; he said the clubs downtown played it every night.

He'd already changed his mind and decided to leave and talk to them another time, but he was flooded with pictures from Alona's party and the hours following it. He'd stood there like an idiot while Hila told him things about Yoel and Tali that all the girls already knew, and then he'd hurried home but instead of going upstairs he'd walked back and forth between Yoel's and Tali's apartment buildings, which were both opposite his own, secretly hoping to catch Yoel coming home from some other place, which would mean the whole story was a lie, just a trick Hila and the other girls had played on him. When he gave up and walked into his building, he looked back, and for the first time in his life the street was divided up differently: no longer their two buildings at the edge against all the others up the street, but Yoel and Tali's on one side, versus his on the other.

In the morning he walked to the wadi and loitered near the trench, waiting for Yoel or even Tali to come down, because he had no doubt that they were watching him from their windows. But there was no sign of them. Then he had an even worse thought: they weren't here, they'd gone for a walk together in some park in town, or worse—to one of his and Yoel's places, like the indoor pool at the Ramada Hotel. All day long he tortured himself with doubts, seeking evidence to verify or disprove the story: they were together or perhaps apart, in his home or perhaps hers, where he'd never been but he imagined it bursting with paintings and bookshelves, with brightly lit rooms.

He made up his mind: he had to do it. He walked straight up to Tzivony, Bentz and Shimon. It was a dangerous maneuver, but it was his only chance to restore things to their previous state, to reunite with Yoel and get rid of Tali.

They weren't surprised to see him, probably still picturing him with the barefoot soldier. "Look, it's Ofer Alon's new buddy," Shimon jabbed. Bentz flashed a crafty smile and whistled an old folk song, and when David Tzivony looked at him there were blood vessels visible in the whites of his eyes. Tzivony frightened him. He knew they couldn't touch him now, and they knew it too, but in a couple of months things would be back to normal: in their world, the last thing that happened was all that matters.

"Remember we arranged a fight with the kids from the towers because they beat up Yoel?" he said, talking quickly before he could change his mind. He smelled burned leaves, fresh grass. Shimon flicked a lit cigarette a few feet over Yonatan's head. He didn't duck, didn't even flinch. That surprised them.

"We did?" Shimon asked, and he did not seem to be teasing; he really didn't remember.

Yoel had accused Yonatan of secretly liking Shimon, like everyone did, and said he failed to understand that this was exactly what made him the most dangerous of the three. Yoel was immune to feeling any affection for their enemies, intent on their total downfall. Yonatan would have preferred to be like him.

"We agreed that me and Yoel would fight them," Yonatan said, "in the sandbox at Rivka's kindergarten."

"You must be kidding," Bentz said. "You think we have time for your games? We never talked about that."

"Don't you remember?" he insisted. "It was in our basement, we talked about it, you said you'd arrange a fight, and then Tali and her friend came."

There was a silence. Shimon squinted furiously at the sky, Tzivony trampled more dry leaves under his shoes, and Bentz arched his neck and spat at the trees behind him.

"We told you not to talk about that, didn't we?" Shimon said finally with a twinkle. His grin was captivating—his lips, eyes, dimples.

"I haven't said anything to anyone yet," Yonatan declared, "I'm talking about taking revenge on the towers. They beat up Yoel, ten against one, and you said that wasn't allowed. You said there was still justice in the world."

"There isn't," Tzivony muttered.

"But you said there was," he insisted.

"We asked if there was," Shimon corrected him.

From the spark in Shimon's eyes it was obvious that he remembered everything now. "Yes," he murmured ponderously, and combed his fingers through his crest of hair. "We talked to them about it afterwards, with the towers, but they said they didn't know who you guys were or something like that. They had no idea what we were talking about."

"They're fucking with you, they know exactly who we are," Yonatan argued. "They must have been scared of you so they lied. They grabbed Yoel in the wadi and rolled him around in mud and thorns, and we said we'd get back at them, and nothing's happened yet."

"Don't get so worked up," Shimon said, his voice softening.

"Why don't you talk to your friend Ofer Alon about it?" Tzivony grumbled.

Shimon gave Tzivony a menacing look, and Tzivony tried to laugh it off, but his cheek swelled and turned darker.

It was almost evening, and Yonatan didn't want to be in the park with them in the dark. "I can talk to him about it," he lied. "He wants Shaul's phone number in New York, he might go work for him after he gets out of the army."

"But he's only just started his service—"

"Well, the guy's a visionary, he's planning ahead," Bentz interrupted. "But what the fuck does that have to do with anything?"

"Nothing, I know." He was suddenly overcome with weakness. He felt hot and cold.

"How come you're suddenly into the fight?" Shimon seemed sincerely interested, but people were always in the fog when it came to Yonatan, whose expressions were often unrelated to the things he did. "You acted like a little girl that day in the basement. Even Yoel wasn't as scared as you. You put your finger on a rifle and now you're a man?"

"That doesn't matter either," Bentz snapped. "The kid wants a fight with the towers, we'll get him a fight with the towers!"

Shimon nodded.

"Just don't come crying to me if they slaughter you," Tzivony added, lighting a match and staring at it until he seemed to be holding the flame between his fingers. He looked completely deranged.

"You were right," Yonatan said, reciting the answer he'd prepared in the schoolyard, although it was probably unnecessary now. "We have to settle the score with those fuckers, and there isn't much time left."

When his fever climbed, his mother took him in a taxi to see Dr. Tzitzianov, who treated all the neighborhood children. Dr. Tzitzianov's face was centered around the most enormous, lumpy nose he'd ever seen, and she always pinched his cheeks and whispered that he should take care of his mother, whose blood sediment levels were too high and who wasn't as strong as she used to be. Every time he walked into her office, he was struck by his memory of that day in fourth grade, when his parents had rushed him to the clinic early in the morning and she'd listened to his lungs and pronounced: "Get to the hospital immediately, the boy has pneumonia."

His parents looked at each other and their faces turned pale as quickly as his had reddened. His father, half asserting, half asking, said, "But everything will be all right?" in the loud, throaty voice he sometimes used for political arguments at Yonatan's grandmother's house on Friday nights, and he looked like a scolded child. The doctor said everything would be fine, he was a strong boy, but they had to take him immediately. She waved them out of the office, leaving Yonatan to secretly celebrate when he realized he wouldn't have to go to school for several days.

He listened to his father panting as he carried him down the steps, and saw beads of sweat on his forehead. He put his cheek closer to his father's face and it stuck to his skin, and he became aware of something he usually did not notice: his father was not as young as most of his friends' fathers, and he was obviously feeling guilty about not bringing him to the doctor sooner, so he wasn't going to complain. But he had trouble tolerating his father's weakness and insisted on walking to the car. His mother and father supported him on either side, and he looked around and amused himself with the idea that he was seeing the skies of Beit HaKerem—always glimpsed through the green manes of trees—for the very last time.

His father honked and cursed and swerved from one lane to the next, and his mother said they should have called an ambulance. She reminded his father of something David Ben Gurion said to his driver: "Drive slowly, I'm in a hurry."

"May he be buried a thousand times," his father hissed, "that midget bastard."

They looked pathetic and funny, and Yonatan wanted to reassure them, because their tone frightened him more than his own frail body. Now that the mask of parenthood had fallen from their faces, he realized he preferred it to this startled expression. "Stop going crazy," he considered scolding them, "you're scaring me." Their extreme concern surprised him, and he was intoxicated by the recognition that he was loved after all, and that he was the center of their being. He considered repaying them in kind but was too tired.

He spent two weeks in hospital, with a needle in his arm attached to "a balloon where the water keeps running out." His father slept in his room, and bought him chocolates and cookies and told him stories about his childhood adventures, but when Yonatan told his father about his own exploits, his eyes roamed to the newspapers and books and the nurses' shoes as they patrolled the hallway, and so he condensed his stories so much that they lost all their sting. He resented his father for this, but decided they could get along fine if he listened to his father and took an interest in his stories, because his father answered questions patiently and their nights were pleasant—at least as long as he didn't get too close to the bed. His father was so clumsy that he was liable to cause damage: squeeze the balloon, dislodge the tube, press on Yonatan's shoulder. Once he got tangled up with the tube and the needle came out and blood spurted from Yonatan's arm, and his father dashed to the corridor in his undershirt and screeched: "Nurse! Quick, nurse!" Yonatan groaned with pain and laughter as the sheet around him grew bloodier, and two nurses leapt into action. Peeking behind them was his father's head, with drops of Yonatan's blood on his chin.

His mother said something in English to Dr. Tzitzianov, and he prayed that she would once again diagnose pneumonia or something just as serious, and they would drive back to the hospital and he would spend a few days there. He could not be at school and see Yoel and Tali acting as if nothing was going on between them, lying for no one. Because the whole class knew. For the past two days, instead of going to school he'd walked down to the wadi, hid in the trench and looked out at the towers. As soon as his mother left for work, he went back to the empty home and lay in bed until midday watching the rain through the window. Once he saw Yoel and Tali walking down the street together after school. Shimon and Tzivony, sitting on the curb, called out, "What a pair of lovebirds! Are you holding hands yet?" When his mother called to ask how school was, he simply said everything was fine. But he assumed his teacher would call them soon.

Dr. Tzitzianov said it was just a cold and he could go back to school tomorrow. She offered him candy, as usual, and he felt like hurling the bowl at the wall. He was about to describe his stomach pains when he was hit by exhaustion, and when he stood up, feeling furious, the ceiling gleamed with a blinding whiteness that stung his eyes, and his whole body ached—how lucky, he thought cheerfully, it really is something serious. Or was he actually faking it now? How would he know? His chest and back were sweating, he felt cold, and a strange pain crawled along his forehead. In the mirror he saw a miniature, doll-like shadow that looked like him but with the long hair of a girl, or like Shaul in his teenaged photos.

They put him on the exam table, his mother wiped his sweat with the cuffs of her white shirt. Her curls looked large, made of brown sewing thread, and her black eyes were too button-like. He turned away from her face, which seemed less and less familiar by the moment, but still gripped her arm. His eyes relaxed on the white wall and he saw pictures from soccer matches that failed to capture the stunning perfection of the game, in which he was the only thing that existed and all his aches and troubles had vanished—that was how it felt when they'd beaten Beit Nehemiah last month. He asked Dr. Tzitzianov if he was going to die, and she laughed: he would live for a long time and go to law school and compensate his mother for all the tough years. Her voice echoed from all over the room, and he asked if he would play soccer again and she said yes, and he murmured that there was an important fight with the tower kids soon. Dr. Tzitzianov, who wasn't listening properly by now, agreed that it would be best if he stayed home for a few days—they didn't learn much in seventh grade anyway. "He's in sixth grade," his mother corrected her.

He lay in bed looking at the white ceiling. When his body sweated he felt better, and when his skin turned rigid and bumpy he was overcome by nausea, then panic, because his limbs felt unfamiliar, as if he'd been wrapped in an old man's skin. People kept appearing, saying something and disappearing. Mom and Dad and Ratzon, they took things and brought them back, shoved, pushed, opened and closed. The closet drawers creaked all day and night, raindrops glistened on the door mirrors. Everyone looked tall, their hair touching the ceiling, even Mom's. "You! I know you all!" he called out. "Stop looking different!"

Sometimes he warned them that the ceiling was about to crush their heads and they told him to go to sleep. Every time his fever rose, he felt the existence of a scheming entity that moved around him and devoured things, especially when he slept and had delirious visions. Usually it was the ceiling, or something on the ceiling, and sometimes he saw a hint of eyes, a facial feature or a mask, or the woods. But no single clue could be isolated, and all he knew was that the entity was devouring his space. When there were other people there, it stopped moving or slowed down, plotting its next attack.

In his bedroom closet there were a sewing kit, jackets, coats, dresses, umbrellas, hats, an iron and a pile of old uniforms. People kept sliding the doors open and he could see Shaul's old army uniform. He had begun to suspect that Shaul was tired of the family, which seemed to be evidence of something. But now he realized he was wrong: he pictured Shaul walking slowly through Rivka's kindergarten, tall and handsome, even the kindergarten teachers said so, and the other kids froze while Yonatan leapt out of the circle and threw his arms around his brother. They were going to have an adventure: they would go downtown to catch a movie at Edison Cinema—where they'd seen

Raiders of the Lost Ark five times—then eat blintzes drowning in chocolate sauce and ice cream, and flip through LPs in the department store.

In his heart he believed that his mother's repeated complaints about his behavior had made Shaul turn his back on him on his last visit. She strongly objected to him sleeping in Shaul's room this time, and on some nights his brother sided with her, but on others he gave in to Yonatan's pleas. Their father feigned ignorance of the conflict and hovered around the apartment with his typical ability to be both guest and resident. "What are you whispering about in there all night?" his mother grumbled. He couldn't reconcile her behavior with her insistence that she wanted her sons to be close. Yoel couldn't understand it either, and asked Yonatan if he'd done anything to annoy his brother— maybe he was blaming his mother because it was easier? But when he told Hila about his mother's contradictory behavior at Alona's party that night, she cut him off halfway through: "It's so obvious, you idiot. Of course it's contradictory: she doesn't really want you two to be friends."

He wanted to hurl this at his mother, to offload his anger when she fed him hot chicken soup with rice, dabbed his feverish body with a towel full of ice cubes, drew him a bath with foamy bubbles, read to him from *East End Boys* and supported him when he begged to go out onto the balcony for some fresh air—he held onto her with one hand and ran the other over the wet, rusty railing. She listened when he pointed to the wadi and said, "The yellow dust is coming back. It was here but then it vanished, and now it's coming back!" He was excited, knowing she didn't understand and that when she did it would be too late. "This time it's coming up from the wadi like mist. That's a good sign, we need a huge disaster to rearrange everything."

At dusk, when his fever broke and there was talk of him going back to school, he lay on his stomach and closed his eyes, and when he opened them the sky had turned black and the streetlamp outside his window looked like a snake spewing luminance. His mother touched his shoulder. He turned to her. A spot of light trembled on her forehead when she said he had a visitor waiting in the living room. He hoped it was Hila, but the tone his mother used implied that it was someone she knew.

He asked his mother to tell Tali to wait, and he pulled on an undershirt, sweater, pants and socks. He breathed in the familiar sweaty odor from Shaul's uniform in the closet, shoved it into a large bag and pushed it deeper into the closet. Then he tiptoed to the bathroom and listened to his mother's ringing laughter from the living room and the praises she heaped on Tali, who must have been telling her about the books she'd read recently. His mother said that Yonatan only read "books about soccer, and adventures and fantasies," and he noticed how beautiful her voice was. Tali said all the boys were like that, she should be happy he read anything at all, and that you could tell by his vocabulary that he was a reader. He thought he detected a slight note of reproof in her voice, as if she found his mother's criticism distasteful. He remembered something Shaul had once told him: their mother was wonderful to her friends, who made pilgrimages to seek her advice and confess things to her, cherishing her bright face, her curiosity, and the tenderness with which she accepted their transgressions. But when she talked about her own life she often complained about her children and gloried in everyone else's.

The living room went quiet. He battled his surge of warmth for Tali, as well as his concern at being forced to acknowledge his adversary's advantages: she did not sound like the little snitch he used to know. He wondered if his mother was treating Tali with genuine affection or just doing a good job of hiding her loathing of the Meltzers. She urged Tali to eat a piece of coconut cake and drink her tea, and there was the sound of spoons and dishes clinking. They laughed and he heard his mother say, "It's hard to believe you're a year younger than the boys, only in fifth grade." Their voices grew softer, the way it sounds when you play the piano all the way from the high notes to the "dead ones," as he called them. He wasn't surprised at the intimacy; after all, his mother always claimed she wished she had a daughter to share her secrets with and see the world the way she did.

In the poorly lit bathroom, he washed his face, brushed his teeth, wet and combed his hair, then walked to the living room. Tali was sitting erect on the couch opposite him, with her legs pressed together and her white shoes shining. She wore a blue wool skirt and a striped black turtleneck sweater, and his mother was leaning over as if trying to please her. Tali looked straight at him, and he did not avert his eyes. He took two steps toward them. His mother stretched, and Tali brushed imaginary crumbs off her sweater. His mother got up and said she would leave them to talk, and then she read their looks and realized this was not a courtesy visit and that Tali was not bringing good tidings. She said goodbye in a dry voice and stopped to stroke his hair and kiss him on the cheek.

Standing close to her, he was flooded with affection: as long as she was in the living room, he was protected. He thought back to a day when he was six, waiting with her for the elevator in the Klal Building downtown: he'd jumped in excitedly while she lingered for a moment and the doors began to slide shut, and he stared at her horrified face but could not hear what she was saying, and suddenly it went dark. Then a few strong young men picked him up and carried him up the steps, and the time until he was in her arms stretched out eternally, and when they were united she sat down on the filthy floor in her black leather pants and hugged him tightly and there was nothing else he needed. He saw his face in her eyes, and he knew that they would only be apart if the world ceased to exist. She still yearned desperately, if sometimes hatefully, for those early childhood years. This past week, when she'd danced around him while he was sick, granting his every wish, he'd been filled with gratitude and had wondered if, just as they were digging a trench in the earth, one could dig into someone's soul, or body, because surely everything that throbbed in him with such power must leave a mark? It was not the memory he was looking for, but the kernel of love itself, which might be able to warm him up and breathe life into him. And then he wondered: Could she? Which love exactly was she grieving—his or hers?

He sat down on the couch, in the indentation left by his mother's body, and Tali said she'd heard he was sick. She drummed on the glass-top table with her fingers and her eyes darted around until they focused on the chest of drawers with the white china bowl and the gold-rimmed ladle, and the pewter forks and knifes. Finally he decided to talk. "There was no point in you coming here. I already know."

"I know you do," Tali replied, "Yoel knows too."

"So you just wanted to see if I was okay?"

"Yoel and I have been a couple for more than two weeks," Tali said, hardening her tone. "It's true, and you can't change it, but that doesn't mean you and him aren't friends anymore."

"How do you know what it does or doesn't mean?"

"I know."

"How?"

"He told me things."

"What kind of things?"

"Stop asking dumb questions," she grumbled. It did seem as though she'd planned to treat him warmly, but she couldn't keep it up. "I don't want to fight, and you're sick. I want you to know that Yoel talks about you a lot, even if he doesn't mean to. Do you understand?"

"Yes," he said submissively, "I understand."

"And this whole thing is dumb, the two of you are dumb." She smoothed out creases in her skirt with a supposedly absentminded movement. "You're fighting because Yoel has a girlfriend?"

"Not just that, it's also because in class that day…"

"Were you Yoel's girlfriend?"

"Yeah, right. Don't be an idiot." He had the urge to kick her leg, already measuring the distance with his eyes.

"Do you want to be Yoel's girlfriend?"

"Of course not." He suspected she'd been practicing the last two questions.

"Then what do you want?"

"For you to not be here."

"I can go," she said.

"I don't mean here, now," he explained, so she'd know it would never occur to him to kick her out, "I mean in general."

"That'll happen in your dreams," she declared. With her black hair combed to one side and pinned back with two colorful barrettes, the black glint in her large eyes which people called "owlish," her smooth cheeks tinged with a slight winter flush, and her round, vivacious face—she looked enchanting, even beautiful. "Maybe something changed and you weren't paying attention," she said.

"You've known Yoel for two weeks and you already know?" He felt cold, and considered covering himself with the woolen blanket folded on the chair opposite him.

"But this is what I wanted to tell you. It's not over, it'll just be a little different." Her relaxed tone reminded him of her father when he'd sat there in the living room a few months ago. It was as if she were quoting him.

"With you around?" Their honesty was waking him, and he no longer felt cold. He wondered if they might both be slightly terrified; they'd never spoken alone before.

"Get this into your head: Yoel and I are a couple now, even though we're not in the same grade." Tali crossed her legs lazily and put her hands on her lap, and she seemed to be celebrating her victory over all the years when they'd viewed her as a nuisance and insulted her. "We meet every couple of days. Yesterday we went to the library together."

"And after that you went for pizza?"

"Yes."

"Great, I hope you're having fun. There've already been all kinds, and then they were gone."

"There've been all kinds where?" she asked, and then she understood. "Do you know that the way you talk about each other is totally crazy? But I'm telling you," she said, leaning on the couch arm closest to him, and her voice softened, "and I'm not saying this to make you sad, but things are changing with Yoel. Everyone can see that, and you can change too."

"Where is Yoel? Wasn't he ashamed to send you here alone?" He wondered if he'd managed to wipe the traces of hurt pride from his voice.

"He doesn't know I'm here."

He believed her.

"You could ask Hila to be your girlfriend," she said, scanning him as if to gauge his chances. "If she says yes we can double-date sometimes. We'll do stuff together, we can go downtown to see movies. They'll let us if it's the four of us."

"I'm not interested in that, and neither is he."

"Because you're busy with your big plans." Her laughter sounded forced, yet he found himself liking it a little.

It occurred to him that Yoel hadn't told her about the towers and the trench and the upcoming fight, and he felt encouraged—maybe nothing was over. Had Yoel heard from Shimon, Bentz and Tzivony about the date for the fight? Had the fuckers done anything about it since that day in the park?

"If you had your own friends, maybe you wouldn't keep poking your nose in our business," he said.

"You and your business, it's more funny than stupid."

"Then laugh."

She smiled, leaned back and looked up, and he smiled too and looked at the lamp on the table. Since they were smiling together, even though it wasn't at each other, they must have needed a slight reprieve from the tension.

"You're only sixth graders."

"You figured that out all by yourself?"

"If I tell you that Yoel's been happy since we've been together, will that make any difference?"

"That's impossible," he said with a huff. His palms were itchy and they stung, and he kept rubbing them on the cold cup of tea his mother had left on the table.

"You can be sure it's true."

"Well, if he's happy and you're even happier, then what difference does it make if I care or not?" He immediately regretted his words—he sounded too bitter.

"It doesn't make any difference to me. If you want to know the truth, then I'd also like you not to be here." She seemed lost between a victor's desire to be magnanimous, and her urge to gloat. "But Yoel misses you, and I'm not like you—that does matter to me."

"That's not true, it matters to me."

"Then here you go: Yoel does like to go downtown, see movies, listen to cassette tapes. He wants to do things other than your games, interesting things, not just in his imagination. Ever since we got here you've been stuck in that dumb wadi. You're not third graders anymore."

"It's all interesting until something suddenly happens."

"What something?" She bit her lower lip and glanced toward Yoel's building through the glass balcony doors. Maybe she'd finally noticed that the world out there was yellow and devious. Maybe she was rattled by the idea that something might be hidden from her but visible to others.

"Things," he said, searching her face for a sign that she knew about the towers after all. "Things that once existed and might exist again. Can't you see that the air is turning yellow?"

A smile made her cheeks swell, and he was certain: she didn't know anything.

They both got up at the same time and stood facing each other. He measured her with his eyes: he was taller and broader than her, while Yoel was about her height. He liked the way she stood—she raised her left heel slightly and shifted her weight to her right foot—and found it provocative, and her body looked so supple. He remembered that she did ballet or folk dancing, and sometimes they saw her practicing on her balcony. She'd always been there, determined to break into their world—how had he failed to see that?

"If you need homework," she said, "call Yoel." She brushed a few strands of brown hair back with her fingers and adjusted her barrette. He was afraid that after this meeting he would no longer be able to fuel the hatred he needed to defeat her. He realized with anger that he now found her beautiful, and he couldn't afford to be so impressionable—just because Yoel had decided she was pretty, was she now pretty? But perhaps it made sense because, after all, their minds merged in so many places. That was what Tali did not understand: there were things that could not be separated.

"And get as much rest as you can."

"Thanks," he said, annoyed to realize that he'd hoped to hear a more supportive tone. She touched his shoulder politely, nodded and left the living room.

He stayed there until he heard the front door shut. Then he glued his face to the glass balcony door and watched her cross the street, surprised to discover how fearful he was of seeing her going into Yoel's building. But, to his relief, she went into her own. When he went back to his room, his head was spinning and he felt exhausted. He caught sight of his mother lying in bed. "She's a little haughty, Miss Meltzer," she said, inviting him to talk.

"She is," he said, "but she's also more honest than anyone else around here."

FINAL YEAR
(MID-1990S)

He'd taken to padding up and down the dark hallways at home and stopping outside his parents' room. Bending over to squint through the keyhole, he could see his mother's slight body huddled on the right side of the bed beneath heavy covers, her head disappearing among them.

In the weeks since they'd returned from the treatments in New York, his mother had said very little to them. She talked to her dead mother, addressed questions to the shadows that edged along the walls and whispered her life story, and repeatedly squabbled with fate, demanding explanations. "I've never harmed a soul," she claimed, and quoted the Psalm they always recited at the annual memorial service for her mother: *Princes have persecuted me without a cause.*

On a bright, hot morning in early May, they wandered around the cemetery looking for Grandma Sarah's grave. Every year they had to search for it again. "Plot C, Row 4," claimed his father, whose memory was his greatest pride. "No, it's up there, next to the black tombstone," his curly-haired uncle Yitzhak mumbled as he dabbed the sweat from his face with the hem of his damp shirt and asked Yonatan for a cigarette. Yitzhak was the youngest son, and often turned up at the memorials wearing clothes that reeked of sweat and chlorine, breathing whiskey and cigarettes on everyone. When they gave up searching, everyone turned to Shaul, who had come from New York allegedly for a two-week visit even though everyone knew he didn't have a return ticket. Shaul was famous for his flawless memory that safeguarded the family's history. If someone were to ask him when Mom had thrown up on the front desk at the hotel in Netanya, or what happened at the dress rehearsal for the play, when Yonatan threatened not to perform if they made him kiss the girl who was playing his mother—he would usually be able to. But this time Shaul was tongue-tied, since in fact he was hopeless at remembering places and was always getting lost when he drove around Jerusalem.

At last they found her grave, and they gathered around for the memorial. As usual, it was presided over by Shlomo Margalit, who'd met Sarah when he was a cantor at Nahalat Yaakov synagogue, where she'd embroidered a curtain for the holy ark. He'd later worked at the postal service, which in the early seventies had been rebranded as the Ministry of Communications, together with Yonatan's mother until she'd become ill, and he was one of the only people permitted to visit her at home since that Friday when she'd found out she had cancer and would undergo surgery. Two days after that, she'd come to the little office where she'd spent the past fifteen years, and packed up all her belongings. There were pictures from the late sixties, in which she was surrounded by men in suits and ties or short-sleeved white shirts, taller and straighter than most of them, wearing long or knee-length dresses in white or cream and high heels.

In some she was smoking a cigarette, not smiling but not looking stern either; she seemed to be enjoying her presence there, with a sort of secretive satisfaction in her eyes that even Yonatan had missed when he'd first looked at the pictures. There were also gifts, letters, commemorative wooden and glass plaques, and drawings by artists she'd commissioned works from. Many of her colleagues had been incensed when this Assistant to the Spokesman had taken it upon herself to redesign post offices all over Israel, despite having no training in the field. Undeterred by the disdainful comments, she drove from one branch to the next, talked to managers and employees, and many of her proposals were ultimately accepted.

In the three years since leaving work, she had complained with increasing frequency about the colleagues who took no interest in her well-being, who bothered her with questions and stories about their own relatives who had diseases, or who came to visit unannounced— she grumbled about all of them except Shlomo Margalit, who had a sacrosanct status as mediator between her family and anything to do with God and religion. He had made decisions about Yonatan's bar mitzvah, he conducted the memorial services, and no one dared question him.

Margalit recited the prayers, and everyone accompanied him with muttered amens. Yonatan's father stood with his arm around his mother's shoulders, and no one else looked at her. Their eyes roamed in every direction: they examined other graves, a dry patch of grass, gilded high heels and the surrounding cypress trees. His mother was hunched, with a pale blue scarf covering her gaunt head and her thin body in a black dress. How she had shriveled since those black-and-white photographs from the late sixties. He saw both women now, and tried in vain to remove the image from his mind. But the shadow that had writhed on the walls of his consciousness all day grew larger: an unspoken recognition that the fates of mother and daughter would be one and the same, and that was the sum of it.

Toward the end of the ceremony his mother took a step away from his father, who insisted on holding her hand until she sharply broke free. When he took two steps to accompany her, she turned to him with a reproachful look, and his father stood in place with his brow furrowed, while she approached the grave and ran her hand over it again and again. Everyone busied themselves with the earthy little stones they had picked up. "Don't worry, Mom, I'll be there soon, too," she said, in a tone that for a moment sounded cheerful. Then she turned to them with a supercilious smile.

No one would go near the grave. His father looked up at the sun and squinted; he looked as weak as he had sounded on the phone that day. Yitzhak started cleaning off the clods of earth from the stone he held, and the others followed suit, all except Shaul, who pinned his eyes on their mother. Yonatan wondered how Shaul was able to remember everything: was he busy recording each event while it unfolded?

He decided to move—perhaps they were expecting him to be the first to do something, and since he'd been cast as the wild kid, he might as well play the role when it was of some use. He went over to the grave, stood next to his mother and looked at her dusty hands, so alien to her body. He did not remember ever having seen dust or dirt on her skin. He placed the stone next to the letter *S*. Everyone else followed suit, walking around his mother on either side and placing their stones on the grave. His mother moved away, on her own, and the three of them trudged after her. When they reached the parking lot their faces were ashen and sweaty, but she looked cheerful.

On the drive home, Shaul sat next to him in the back seat and barely said a word. He began to feel envious of his big brother, who was the only one of them all who preserved the hours and the days, whose memory could keep things in chronological order, and who would remember her gestures and movements and the subtleties of her expressions better than any of them would. Their mother sat in the front seat, singing an old folk song, then plunged into silence and rejected his father's suggestion to stop at a restaurant. When he parked outside their house, she said, "I started learning death when I was little. It never stopped buzzing around me." She looked from one to the other and added, "Time and conscience knock, especially at night." They all said nothing, only their breathing disturbing the silence.

It was stiflingly hot after his father turned off the engine, but no one dared get out before his mother. Finally she stepped out, and Shaul and his father hurried after her, while he stayed in the car because he was supposed to go to school, even though very few of his classmates still showed up—most of them were studying for their matriculation exams in groups at each other's houses.

He drove quickly to Emek Refaim, to Lior's house, swerving between lanes, honking constantly, his front license plate lapping at the bumpers in front of him, and pulled up outside her building. He couldn't remember where her window was, and didn't care if she saw him, and he remembered how on that night, after Lior had criticized his mother for saying he had "Gestapo eyes," and after he'd enumerated all the ways he'd wronged his mother, she'd hugged him and told him to stop wearing her out with all his talk, and said that even if his mother was sick and his father didn't understand much, and even if he'd done terrible things, she wouldn't let them deny his right to exist the way he was—well, more or less the way he was.

He wanted to bark at her: Who's denying my right to exist, you psycho? Or to laugh at her dramatic tone. But it was too late for that. Her words were like a strong wind raging in his mind, churning sadness with shame and joy, until a peculiar warmth spread through his limbs, the kind that bubbles in your body when another person sees the world through your eyes, melting away your strangest fears precisely because he has recognized their power and their truth. Lior asked if he was happy, the way she sometimes used to do so that she could tease him for not being able to say it, and he was disgusted by her delight at meeting his needs. At the end of the night they lay naked and sweaty in bed, and Lior was asleep with her breasts pressed against his chest and her face buried in his neck, and he stared out at the sky, hoping dawn would not come, and realized that it was strange how nothing frightened him more than losing her.

He sat in the car for almost an hour before deciding she wasn't home and there was no point waiting: before, when he'd needed her embrace with desperate urgency, all he'd been able to see was the moment when she would gather him in and he would bury his face in her neck and kiss her skin and smell her hair and his stomach would be touching hers. Whereas now he saw the moment after: her arms would move away from his body and she would stand facing him, with all the sweaty estrangement of this summer between them, and the certainty would prevail once again: she would not be there when everything collapsed.

At night, when everyone was in bed, Yonatan sat down with a yellow notebook and began to write his impressions of the day. Shaul's capacity to remember everything worried him. Each time he looked at his brother, he imagined his endless abundance of memories, organized like books on a shelf, and it seemed as if since he'd landed in Israel—a sort of parasite that hadn't been here at all in the hard years and was now acting like someone who'd never left—he was robbing them, stealing their days, grabbing each event as soon as it ended and fleeing. Ever since he was a child, he'd admired the stunning wholeness of how Shaul spoke about the past, aware of the most minute details of color and sound, in a way that seemed to breathe new life into events. Perhaps he was coming to believe that Shaul knew the secret that could dull the reality of loss.

The diary he began writing, which for now he called "A Brief History of Death" (a name he borrowed from a secret meeting between the king and Warshovsky to debate wiping his subjects' memories of the many casualties from the twenty-three-year war), was supposed to be his written response to Shaul's memory. Sometimes when he lay in bed at night, he wondered if each of the people around him might possess a secret or a talent that allowed them to look directly at death.

He'd never really written before, apart from those five pages in the ninth grade which he burned on the balcony, and the ones where he described Yaara's father's death and its effect on their love, which he only wrote so he wouldn't get caught contradicting himself. As a child he'd liked adventure books, then he'd stopped reading, until one day, shortly before his fourteenth birthday, his mother had informed him mysteriously that it was time "for you to know the books." No one read books in the group of boys he hung around with. At nights they played poker on the empty store level of the shopping center, drank vodka, played pool in clubs downtown, talked about girls and fights—though they knew little about the former—and vented their bitterness by declaring the horrible things they would do to anyone who dared mess with them, even if at the moment of truth they avoided actual fights. Sometimes they went to small clubs on Jaffa Street because they were too young for the discos they really yearned for, and they danced in a circle of boys—Pretty Matti and Eyal Salman were the only ones who really kissed girls or at least managed to press up against their breasts when they played a slow song—and knew they were pathetic. And now his mother expected him to sit in her room reading her beloved Russian classics, probably under the influence of Chana Sternberg: Tolstoy, Gogol, Turgenev, Dostoyevsky.

She would lie in bed reading aloud while he stood near the door, or sprawled on the floor, or sulked on a stool, or examined his face in the winged mirror and combed his hair. He knew he didn't have to sit through it, but he stayed, as if there were some unspoken reason for him to do as she asked. He clearly remembered the point at which he began to listen. He liked Gogol's "The Overcoat" from the first page, but there was a moment when he became aware of the narrator's ignorance: "My memory begins to grow weak, and the innumerable streets and houses of St. Petersburg go round so confusedly in my head that I have difficulty finding my way about them." He liked that line, the words fired his imagination and elevated his spirits, and in class he rewrote them in his notebook. After a while, in the summer between grades eight and nine, they stopped reading together, perhaps because of her diagnosis. At dinners they talked about how one day, soon, they would read together again.

On the first night of writing, he discovered that he could not stop lying. The cemetery visit occurred on a stormy night; Shaul had a machine inside his body that stole everyone's memories; Yoel could see other people's dreams. The main character in his story was an amalgamation of his mother and his grandmother Sarah. As he wrote, he wanted to erect a wall between the two women and remain faithful to his mother, but Sarah kept invading the story, perhaps because his mother had taken to speaking of her as a woman who'd known nothing but suffering, the victim of other people's malice and treachery. Had he been asked to find one sentence to define his grandmother, whom he'd never known, he would have immediately said: "Princes have persecuted me without cause." And his mother claimed that she, much like Sarah, had been subjected to the bile of those who exploited her kindness, envied her, and sought her downfall.

Every day he lied and agonized: he summoned a horrible plague that afflicted all the residents of the block, and gave each of the family's acquaintances some satanic trait. He wrote dreams, too: he dreamed the botanic gardens, and little children in red shirts attacking a man in a suit, knocking him into a lake and tearing off pieces of flesh with their teeth; he dreamed a water tower like they had on kibbutzim, which changed colors above a pigsty, and the tower said it had demolished lots of people in its village and so it had been transferred here as punishment; he dreamed that he was dancing with Hila at that party and Tali was standing by Ran Horesh at age twelve, while she was her current age, about seventeen, and she wore a white tank top and lots of rings on her fingers, and Ran Horesh knelt down before her and held up her tank top and licked her breasts and Hila told him: "Now you think she's pretty because Yoel thinks she's pretty? Retard."

Every night, as he watched his mother through the keyhole, he swore once again to stick to the truth, but whenever he had to describe something that had happened at home he grew bored and went back to the lies. He interpreted his infidelity to the truth as weakness, as betrayal; for once he was supposed to face reality without embellishing, and yet again, as had happened with Yaara and Lior, he couldn't do it. It was only cowards who always went too far.

His main effort in the diary was to comprehend death, to look at it from the perspective of she who approached it day by day. Its first lines were:

We studied death
Not the death that is not ours
In that we have no interest
We are not philosophers.

Much as he tried to write death from the perspective of this woman, his mother-grandmother, he realized that it was like tossing a ball against the wall: his gaze at her imminent death always came back to him blindly, humiliated by a lack of knowledge. Because all those who surrounded his mother—Shaul and himself and his father, her sisters and friends—could not share in the experience of this woman who knew that soon she would no longer exist. Whether they wanted to or not, they were already contemplating life without her, envisioning the year after her death. Did she understand, he sometimes wondered, that in the future they saw—she was gone? He imagined her constantly moving farther away from them, sensing the widening chasm between them and her. The closer they tried to get to her, the more she retreated, already gliding in that hazy expanse between life and death where none of them could accompany her. They were, compared to her, so alive.

As his story progressed, its failures multiplied: since there was no truth in it, it could not compete with Shaul's memory, and it got no closer to his mother's death. By the end of May he had despaired of the twenty pages he'd amassed in the yellow notebook, but he did not have the courage to abandon them. He believed he had to keep his protagonist alive. Countless times he led her to the brink of death, to the end of the story, only to yank her back into the land of the living at the last minute.

On the last day of May he tore the first five pages out of his notebook and placed them on his mother's side of his parents' bed. He stayed out all day. He drove to Jerusalem Forest and careened back and forth along the winding roads, took the highway leading to French Hill and from there down toward Jericho, searching for the three cliff faces from that night with Yoel. He couldn't find them, perhaps he'd passed them, and in any case his spirits fell and the idea no longer excited him. He pulled over on the side of the road and looked around. The smooth black sand he remembered from that night had been replaced by wasteland: old fuel tanks, burnt logs, tattered coats and shirts and army uniforms, two front seats from a car. He turned around and went back to Jerusalem. When he got to their street he saw a light on in the living room and assumed Shaul was sitting there listening to old albums. He rang Yoel's doorbell but his mother said he was out, probably with Tali, and he thought she said her name resentfully.

At 10 p.m. he carefully pushed the front door open, bracing for a glimmer of accusatory lights from the living room and his parents' worried voices. But the house was dark and silent, apart from a soft tune coming from the old record player in Shaul's room. When he sat down on his bed he found the first page of "A Brief History of Death" on his pillow. The bottom half was tucked into the woolen blanket, covered like a little child. There were about a dozen proofreading marks in red ink. Here and there, a superfluous word was crossed out.

AWAKENING

He lay with Itamar on his stomach, cheek to chest, and stroked the baby's hair. Itamar's breathing was interrupted by grunts and wheezing, and every time he heard a sound he didn't like, he put his face closer to the baby and listened. At nights Itamar woke frequently, shouting and wailing, then sat up in bed and stared at them with large, glassy eyes, his lips trembling, with a pallor they did not recognize from his waking hours. It was as if he didn't know where he was and did not recognize them, pushing away their outstretched arms. Still stunned by the brutal awakening, they sensed a nagging doubt as to whether they knew this creature sitting before them. They had slid into sleep in an embrace, and awoken as three strangers.

Each time Itamar woke in the middle of the night and sat up, Yonatan had to rein in the signs of panic on his own face and maintain a steady voice so that Shira wouldn't notice. He imagined fragments of the baby's dreams, but behind the faces of the other children from daycare it was always the Beit HaKerem kids he saw. When he despaired of his imaginings, he began to devise a machine made of giant pipes, at the end of which was a magnet that joined one conscious-ness with another and enabled a person to infiltrate someone else's dreams. After jokingly describing the invention to Shira, she told him with a bitter smile that as far as she recalled it was Yoel, not him, who fabricated machines. He was surprised by the note of malice when she mentioned Yoel, whom they no longer discussed, and he knew what she really wanted to say: When our son wakes in a terror we cannot dispel, you can't tolerate being there, so you escape into your imagina-tion—but how do you know I can?

He looked through the balcony doors. He saw an airplane passing over two buildings with golden flecks of light sparking off its tail, perhaps from stars or some celestial reflection, and they trailed after it like a jet's contrail. His gaze wandered to the ceiling, where tiny shadows swirled, then to the piles of clothes, sheets, dirty diapers, towels, rattles and Shira's makeup, which she hadn't had time to tidy up before she went out.

Itamar mumbled something. It sounded as if he were saying 'more-more-more', his favorite new word. Yonatan wrapped his arms around the boy and breathed in the soapy smell of his skin, refraining from kissing him so as not to wake him up. He was careful not to rub his beard stubble on the boy's face, because it gave him little red spots. He could tell by the rhythm of Itamar's breathing that he'd fallen into a deeper sleep, and he felt deeply satisfied at having achieved this in Shira's absence. He began to gently tighten the red blanket around the boy, but stopped and wondered why he couldn't just leave him be.

He was overcome by exhaustion. He put his head on the pillow and closed his eyes, then opened them, feeling the heaviness of his eyelids before shutting them once again. He remembered Shaul's room at home in Jerusalem, late at night, perhaps midnight: orange bubbles dance on the ceiling from the streetlamps, milky strips stretch over the cobwebs on the bookshelves, half of which are empty, and a few snakes of light squirm around the hoop they used to shoot a foam ball into. He draws the curtain shut and the room is lost in darkness. He plays:

with light, without light. On the table is the small record player that folds up into a black case, with album covers and notebooks scattered around it. Shaul lies in bed while Yonatan moves around the room: he sits on the windowsill, leans on the chair, stands under the hoop and throws the ball in. Every so often he sits on the edge of Shaul's bed, and his brother tells him sleepily that it's time he went to bed in his own room, he's a big boy now. But he won't go near that room— even when the light is on, he sees things on the balcony, and hears tapping and creaking sounds from the roof and the bathroom, and sometimes the walls curve in and he knows there is an invisible entity eddying deep inside them, and unseen bodies slithering down the hallway. His room is far away from Shaul's. His parents' room is adjacent, but they're out, and when he's in his room and they're not there—even if Shaul is home—he is alone.

It's cold in Shaul's room, and he's tired. He sits on the narrow windowsill, which is opposite Yoel's window. He swings his feet and looks out, hoping to see his parents' car. Distant engines rattle up the street, arousing hope, and then headlights dance on the buildings and the trees, but most of the cars stop before they reach the last four buildings visible through the window. He cranes his neck and looks up the street, but the trees are in his way. He maneuvers his whole upper body out, holding onto the windowsill at the top and bottom. The cold air crawls over his face and down his neck to his chest, and a sharp stab chills his body. If the window frame breaks under his weight, he will fall. He is stunned to realize how easy it would be to plummet three stories down onto the lawn. Shaul would not be able to stop him. Perhaps Yoel would wake up and glance outside just in time to catch him hurtling through the air.

Most of his body is outside now. It would be a few years before the question that first flickered on those nights came into focus: At what age can no one stop you from killing yourself?

Shaul complains that he's cold and tells Yonatan to shut the window and go back to his room. Sometimes Shaul lets him lie in bed and wraps his arms around him and whispers that everything will be fine—that he won't really move out and leave Yonatan alone with them. "But you're not here like you used to be," Yonatan insists. Shaul's unavailability turns the world gray, and he doesn't know how to find the words to express how gloomy their home is without him. In any case, he knows it's a lost cause. There isn't really enough room in that bed for both of them, and so he lies there for another minute or two, then moves to the chair, or paces the room, silently cursing his parents. He asks the sleeping Shaul questions: about music, about the summer when he went to Chicago and came back with a Boston album with a colorful spaceship on its cover. "Let's listen to the first track," he suggests and drums the chorus in the air. The music plays in his mind, filling him with wild joy, and he is no longer frightened. Maybe he really will go back to his room, to the shadows and sounds and faces on the ceiling—he'll show them! But the flash of courage fades. "Let's listen to the track," he repeats. Shaul doesn't answer, he wants to sleep: he has to be at school in the morning, or maybe he's already in the army.

Itamar coughed. Yonatan noticed that his hand was wet and realized the boy had been drooling on him. He opened his eyes in a panic, already envisioning Itamar sitting up and staring at him with that strange look. But Itamar was fast asleep on his stomach. Yonatan's heart was pounding and he felt slightly dizzy. He rubbed his stinging eyes and focused on the living room lamp. He had an inexplicable need for light, blinking as if he'd lost control over his eyes, until his gaze fell on a lustrous spot with black butterflies flitting around it, and after a while he could no longer see anything else in the living room. He had to battle the barrage of memories: this was not the right time, he was in charge of Itamar. There is no room for illusions when it comes down to a single breath.

He was bewildered by the reappearance of that phrase, which had been absent for many years, and he galloped through several past realms attempting to pinpoint them until he encountered the creature. He'd never seen it whole—only a nebulous and ever-changing outline.

The rules were always the same: he stood at the top of the hill on HaGuy Street in the evening, night was deepening and the large treetops shading the street had turned black, and just then the creature rose from the depths of the earth, sounded a colossal screech and began loping toward him, crossing oceans and continents faster than light. Yonatan fled, charging wildly down the steep hill, the creature's breath already warm on his shirt, scorching his skin like a campfire burning too close.

He pressed his legs down hard against the mattress. Itamar slid down his chest and wheezed. He whispered a curse and pushed his legs ever harder. His muscles ached. Then he held Itamar and carefully tilted his head, but an involuntary motion made his limbs dance and disturbed the baby's sleep. Then the tiny body steadied, and Itamar's downy head felt heavy on his chest, perhaps on his heart, weighing down his breathing. But he did not dare move.

Itamar whimpered and seemed to be wriggling out of his grip, but then he lifted his head and let it fall back hard on Yonatan's chest. He heard a dim grumble and wondered if it had come from the baby's stomach or his own. He was afraid that Itamar would sit up and give him that look.

He heard a rustle from outside and looked at the eucalyptus branches that invaded their long, narrow balcony and wound their way around the rusty railing. He used to unravel them with his hands, getting covered with scratches, and ask his mother to see how he was setting them free. But that was not what he saw now: it was the double doors in his bedroom in Tel Aviv. A grating screech came from the balcony and he froze, listening—someone or something was moving a chair. He heard tapping from the other side of the wall, and another screech. Which balcony was he seeing?

He turned to look left, rubbing his chin on Itamar's fuzzy hair: in the living room only one black butterfly was still hovering between the strips of light. His fingers squeezed the sheet so tightly that he felt a sharp pain around his fingernails, as if they'd been cut with glass. He held up his hands to see if they were bleeding. They were sweaty. He must not touch Itamar. He decided he had to get up and turn on a light, but his hands and feet would not move. He wanted to believe that his body was disobeying him because Itamar was lying on him and not because he was afraid—now that he was thirty-seven years old—to go out into the noisy rooms, where all sorts of shapes were forming.

Itamar made a few whimpers and lifted his head. Yonatan avoided his eyes. He was afraid that a time from the depths of his memory was spreading through his Tel Aviv home, blending the rooms together.

Itamar put his stomach against Yonatan's torso and leaned his warm cheek on his chest again, but this closeness bothered him: he might infect the child with his fears, damage his soul, contaminate him. How can a father seat his child on a hornets' nest? At first he couldn't believe that this line—from a story by S. Yizhar, an author he so admired—was echoing in his mind now, betraying him. He tried to belittle the terror that gripped him, but it was too late. The idea was already imprinted, and even if he were to scorn it and mock its dramatic airs, it was inside him. *How can a father seat his child on a hornets' nest?*

He touched his skin, which felt rough and rigid, chilled. He swallowed, but his throat felt even dryer. His tongue was dry and its touch on the roof of his mouth disgusted him. He was afraid that if Itamar woke up now he would not be able to protect him, and they would stare at each other like two strangers. He made up his mind: he held Itamar on his left arm and, without breathing, lowered him onto his arm on the mattress—it was a move that frequently ended with the baby awakening. Itamar tensed and whimpered, Yonatan stroked his back until the little body was calm—he'd lost weight, which was worrying—and then slid his arm out. Now they were lying next to each other. He felt relieved to have the boy off his body.

He opened his eyes to see a silver dome glimmering above him, shut them again, and the sounds from around the house died down. For a moment he thought the storm had passed.

Shira came home at midnight. He heard her walking around the apartment, getting undressed in the bathroom, water running, and cursed her silently even though he knew how rarely she went out in the evenings and had in fact encouraged her to go out more, if only to cleanse his conscience. Finally she appeared in the room. He grinned, gave her a thumbs up, and got up before her gaze could linger on his face. She lay down next to Itamar, who woke up when he smelled her and immediately searched for her breast with his lips. Yonatan stood by the door and stared at him, cradled in her arms, and listened to the tranquil sucking sounds. It occurred to him that perhaps Itamar had not been asleep at all for those last few minutes, only waiting silently, as he had been, for Shira.

He filled Shira's water bottle at the kitchen sink and stuck his head under the faucet. He dried his face and hair, went back to the bedroom and placed the bottle on the bureau next to Shira. She ran her fingers over his shoulder gratefully, and her familiar touch saddened him because he was jarred, not for the first time, by a recognition that he was deceiving her, deceiving them both, hiding a secret that had only tonight become clear in his own mind: while Itamar was growing up—he was already one year old—Yonatan himself was receding. The walls that protected the present from the terrors of the past and allowed memories to filter through at a pace he could still tolerate had begun to crumble, and the past was a cloud floating toward him, firing a salvo of memory arrows that pierced his mind, shooting it through with pictures he begrudgingly accepted. The cloud would soon swallow him up. For part of each day he was sixteen, or eighteen. This had probably always been true, but the mask that had allowed him to function in the world had been disintegrating for some time. When he stood there watching them curled up peacefully, as if every strand of Itamar's body knew where to locate itself on Shira's, he had no doubt that there was no mask now, and that if Shira were to turn on the light there was no telling what face she would behold—he himself did not know.

Shira believed that everything was connected to Yoel, and that every time Yonatan went to visit him in Beit HaKerem—and they sprawled on the bed with a view of Shaul's old room, and the two of them shared secrets and memories (like the collapse of the pact between Shimon, Bentz and Tzivony after Shimon kissed Tzivony's older sister, or the war against the towers, which had ended in a disaster they'd never explicitly addressed), and arranged all of Yoel's notebooks in which he'd taped the crumpled old kingdom notes in chronological order, and enumerated their classmates' sins, because, as Yoel insisted, "there's not a single kid who didn't commit a crime," and from time to time they mocked their own devotion to those memories at the ripe old age of thirty-seven, and when Yoel's mother peered in they asked her, out of habit, if she could make meatballs for lunch, and only when Yoel stepped onto the balcony for a smoke did she grab Yonatan's arm with her sinewy hand and ask if he could help her son—she saw another crack open up in their family life in Tel Aviv. Perhaps that was why she'd encouraged him to go to Mexico for the festival that summer. "It'll be good for you, and for everyone," she said.

He didn't tell Shira that in those hours in Beit HaKerem—unlike the years when he and Yoel had dwelled on the past but also acknowledged the present, and sought each other's advice on work and life, and discussed politics and books and people—they were indifferent to the passage of time and tried to avoid alluding to it. Even when Yoel demanded to see a picture of Itamar, whom he'd only met once, it was obvious to them both that he was just going through the motions, simply taking a necessary step to rid their meeting of anything that might get in the way later.

On one occasion, when Yonatan was troubled, he decided to let Yoel in on what was bothering him. He told him about a novel he'd read, and the author's claim that, because of the birth of his children and the tribulations of daily life, the past had almost completely disappeared from his thoughts. "Only a small, pedantic personality would write something like that," Yoel retorted. But since his mother's death, Yonatan had not seen a single flash of her, not in his twenties or thirties, not when he published his books in Hebrew or in other languages, not when he'd experienced failure, not when he'd fallen in love with Shira, not when he'd been ill, not on birthdays. It was only after Itamar was born that he'd begun occasionally to see her knocking on their door, looking just as she had in her final days or perhaps slightly older (he never dared to picture her at seventy-five), and Itamar would run to her and she would swing him up in her arms. He realized that her expressions in these scenes must be cut from an old memory: he was about eight, and she and his father came home from a week in Rhodes, swung the door open and called out cheerfully: "We're here!" Then she stood there with her face glowing and held her hands up as if she were cheering someone on, and she was clearly thrilled to see him.

When he finished talking, Yoel sat there lost in thought, and every so often he looked up at Yonatan as if he was about to speak. He was obviously longing to tell Yonatan something comforting or distracting, but he could not find the words. That was enough for them to both understand how much everything had changed.

Finally, Yoel said in a weary voice, "I remember that when they were in Rhodes, you had dinner at our place one day and another day at Ratzon's." He looked disappointed at the triviality of his own remark.

"Yes, and Noam broke the table leg," Yonatan replied.

Relieved, Yoel went on, "Yeah, that was awesome."

Later, when they sat on the balcony looking at the spring sky, Yoel asked if Yonatan was doing anything over the sickeningly sticky summer that would soon arrive. He decided not to tell Yoel he was considering going to Mexico in early June, and said they had no plans.

Yoel spun the fingers of his right hand as if he were writing something in the air. "Last summer pretty much did me in."

"Well, every summer goes by in the end, Yoel."

"Every summer will go by. I won't." Yoel opened his eyes under the blinding sun. "Maybe you don't understand: I will not get through another summer like that. Not going to happen."

That might have been the day when Yonatan understood beyond a doubt that there was no longer any point in telling Yoel what was happening in his life, and that Yoel, from his hiding place, was trying to lure him back into a world he thought he'd left behind, unwilling or perhaps unable to speak in any other language. Together, they were restoring the colors and nuances that time had lost over the years.

He stopped encouraging Yoel to return to the life he'd had before moving back in with his parents, stopped talking to him about an apartment in Tel Aviv and a new job. Yoel had been living in Beit HaKerem for almost two years, and some of his friends said he was never coming back.

The only thing about Yonatan's life that still sometimes interested Yoel was the writing. He asked if he was working on anything, and when he said no, again, Yoel urged him to resume. It had only recently occurred to Yonatan that Yoel's keen interest in his writing stemmed not from the books he wrote, or the worlds he created, in which traces of their past always appeared, but from a stubborn core that Yoel had always seen in him and pegged as irreversible, "a part of your body." Everyone knew how tormented Yoel became when he faced a big decision. He would voice the same arguments over and over again, leaning in one direction and then in the opposite, arguing convincingly for both sides. Yoel himself was aware of the absurdity of this performance, able to make fun of himself, and perhaps that was why most people did not realize—nor did he—how anguished he really was. This was partly because Yoel expressed no disgruntlement or anger at anyone else. On the contrary: people liked to tell him about their accomplishments. Yonatan himself had always shared good news first with Yoel, whose responses were always warm and enthusiastic, who celebrated generously with him and insisted that Yonatan take pleasure in his accomplishments.

Ultimately, Yoel seemed to lack a certain force of instinct. All possibilities and all opportunities seemed the same to him because he did not have an existential sense of volition, of proclivity, and so even when he made a decision and proceeded to implement it, he wasn't genuinely committed to it. His mind would keep turning over the same arguments and doubts, not only about the present but about decisions made ten or fifteen years ago, which still tortured him. Perhaps what he was desperately seeking behind all the exhausting vacillations was his real drive—that thing that was "a part of your body."

Sometime before Yoel moved back in with his parents, Yonatan and Shira had gone to a party with him, and he'd dragged them to a table upstairs, where they'd sat for hours and listened to Yoel present exhaustive arguments for and against marrying his girlfriend. After a while his mood turned gloomy and he slumped on the sofa, constantly combing his fingers through his hair.

"Do you even love her?" Shira asked.

"Of course I do," Yoel replied, as if he couldn't understand what the question had to do with anything.

In Beit HaKerem, sitting on the bed, Yonatan reminded Yoel of that party and said he should have listened to Shira and made the commitment to his girlfriend, and perhaps then all this wouldn't have happened. After a pause, Yoel asked Yonatan why he hadn't pushed him—how could he have let him make so many terrible mistakes? Yonatan looked at him and he could hear Shira's voice. She'd recently reminded him, as if by chance, of something he'd told her years ago: that Yoel and he weren't really close friends anymore, that it was only the ethos of their friendship that dictated his answer when asked who his best friend was.

Every time he came home from Jerusalem, the sawing noise in his mind was so loud that it took a whole day of lying around doing nothing before he could face the tasks of the present. Fortunately, Shira saw him wake up and play with Itamar, feed him his yogurt and make him a sandwich with the crusts cut off, but she was at work by the time he came back from dropping Itamar at daycare and crawled back into bed and slept intermittently until 3 p.m., when he got dressed, had coffee, and washed his face with cold water.

When she came home with Itamar, he greeted them joyously, swung Itamar up and danced around with him, and the baby's ringing laughter was the only thing that gave him joy, although it, too, was tinged with little crashes of terror whenever he realized how precarious their existence in Tel Aviv was. The three of them sat close together, and he made up stories for Itamar, who sat on his lap, about every object the boy picked up—a car, a pacifier, a doll, a hat. Smiling mischievously, Itamar switched objects and said, "Daddy!" and sat on Shira as if to make her finish the story, and he shouted excitedly, but no matter where Yonatan turned to look, he saw shadows of the disaster.

Yonatan was sometimes plagued by the question of why he felt no irritation every time they polished those memories in Yoel's room. How was it possible that all that still excited him, that even his speech was frenetic and excitable like it used to be when he was twenty, and that sometimes they were so happy together that he didn't want to go back to Tel Aviv at all, and after he left Yoel's he wandered the streets of Jerusalem, now as confusing as a foreign city's, listening to songs he hadn't heard since the army, sometimes going near Lior's old street and feeling exhilarated just from being near her building. Were their reminiscences really more exciting than the things that were happening to him now in the life he had ostensibly chosen?

Perhaps it was no accident that Tali asked him—after he messaged her to suggest they visit Yoel together and she refused, because the three of them together was too much—if he was being careful: did he understand that he had to be careful? Unable to resist, he asked if she remembered the night they'd slow-danced at his high school gradua-tion party, which he sometimes thought was when he'd started wanting her. His body trembled as he saw her typing a reply. She said she remembered everything but she didn't want to talk about all that, especially not about what happened after the army. Not now. He realized he was disappointed, and that seemed so stupid that he let out a scorched and ugly laugh. Tali disappeared, and a few days later she wrote him a single line: You're getting sucked in, that's exactly what you need to be careful of.

THE TOWERS
(LATE 1980S)

He hadn't been to school for eight days. His mother said he was almost better, but then little Miss Meltzer came to visit and his fever went up again. "What did she want, that haughty girl?" his mother kept asking, and he mumbled something and fell back asleep, or something close to it: in the mornings he lay in bed half awake, seeing things.

At first, the forest was a forest and the earth was earth and the twigs were twigs. Noisy thunder plunges down on them as if the towers are crashing from the sky. They run and hold onto a rough tree trunk, a pair of arms is wrapped around him, he does not know whose they are. They look up at the treetops that have formed a dome with an ominous crack of gray sky. He strokes the trunk, runs his fingers through its etched grooves, joins the letters into words:

The forest has no time
There is no time in the forest

Fuck the world and Julis Base
Uri and Ofra forever

He recognizes the inscription from a different forest, a larger one: perhaps Jerusalem Forest on a field trip where they learned to identify flora, or a summer camp when they baked pitas, squares of gray concrete burning in the sun, green lawns that turned yellower with each passing day and by the end of summer looked like the thistles in the wadi and you couldn't walk barefoot anymore. He can't stop running his fingers over the inscription, touching its violent desperation, wondering where great loves are preserved after it's all over. They once talked about drinking an anti-memory potion, but Yoel didn't understand anything. Sometimes Yoel waxes nostalgic for something that happened to them two years ago, and Yonatan listens and turns melancholy and doesn't want to hear anymore. Perhaps he has already learned this: every soul is different. You can unite your gazes for a while, on certain matters, but in the end you drift alone into the kingdom of dreams.

Thunder crashes above them and the earth shakes. Pinecones fall, giant and silver. He hears a chilling yet familiar rustle and the tree trunk cleaves into two. He wants to let go of the tree that is about to fall, but finds his hands entangled in the thicket of branches. He pulls them back hard, his arms burn, and so much blood comes out that it frightens him. Unable to stop the momentum, he falls backward. He lies on a bed of twigs and grass, the tree's mane tears away from the trunk above him and sways from side to side, and two crows screech at the sky. It's too late to get up and run away, and he accepts his fate. He is relieved when the tree shatters onto the forest's western side. He hears shouts and thinks it's them—he was hoping the tree had fallen on them and buried them. But then suddenly he doesn't know who they are anymore. Helpless, he reconstructs the map of the forest that hangs on his wall of memory: in its center are a red spot and a steep slope. That that is where he heads.

———

They read *The Paul Street Boys* together in the wadi two years ago, while the grown-ups watched the World Cup soccer from Mexico every night. Yoel would read two pages in a pleasant, measured voice, then it was Yonatan's turn and he read fast, swallowing his words, until evening fell and they couldn't see anything. There were the Paul Street boys and their enemies from the Redshirts, and Geréb's betrayal—which Yoel never forgave, although Yonatan accepted his atonement—and the magnanimity of the Pásztor brothers from the Redshirts.

"People meet people, and things happen, and the dirt clings to them. Look at us, look at the two of us—haven't we done bad things?" he asks.

"Not really," Yoel says, "less than everyone else."

He laughs and doesn't bother answering. Every evening they would bury the book in a tin box and hide it in the wadi, covered with twigs, so that neither of them would be tempted to read on his own. When they stood by the box for the last time, his affection for Yoel broke through the pretending, the terror of rejection, and their customary restraint. It was the way he read with his finger tracing each word like an old man, and ran with an oddly crooked back, and finessed the truth so that they were never defeated, and was always impressed by the funny things and could blunt the sting of the hurtful ones, and insisted on telling Yonatan that his parents loved him even though he didn't really know them.

They walked home in silence, still not daring to discuss the death at the end of the book, predictable though it was. They saw headlights sliding down the street, and black-gray smoke curling up from the military factory's chimneys, and heard familiar stale ceremonial television voices, and saw men in white undershirts sitting on balconies, munching sunflower seeds or reaching into bowls of grapes and staring into space, and Yoel said they would go crazy or die in this place if they didn't have worthy enemies.

At first the forest was a forest, and now it had all flipped. He walks on lush greenery, past trees that look like giant mushrooms with parchment-branches protruding and pricking him all over his body, coarse as the sandpaper from shop class, which leaves interesting sores when you rub your skin with it. He looks around for the red spot, brushing away brunches emblazoned with the likenesses of Csapó, Boniek, Satrústegui and Andriy Bal from the 1982 World Cup.

In the last four buildings on the block, there were groups competing over who would be first to complete the set of soccer cards for the FIFA World Cup in Spain. There were four in their group: Yonatan and Yoel, and their big brothers. Shaul and Noam used to play ping pong in the basement together, and they were the ones who introduced their little brothers, whose only encounter had been at the beginning of that summer, when Yonatan accompanied his parents on a condolence visit to the Landaus, whose son was killed in the first days of the Lebanon war. Sitting outside in the unkempt yard, where no flowers or weeds grew, he whispered to the boy sitting next to him—whose face he recognized beneath his frizzy hair—that the building residents hated the Landaus because they were religious. The boy nodded but said nothing. He was staring at a woman with graying hair in a long braid, surrounded by her four little children: the boys wore white pants and white shirts, the girls black dresses, and their collars were torn in mourning. They gobbled down grapes and drank orange juice from large glasses full of ice cubes. The woman swayed back and forth in a rocking chair, her blue eyes fixed on the bowl of grapes, and every time someone came over to her she looked up for a moment and then back down at the bowl, and even when the sunlight danced on her face she did not move her gaze or shut her eyes.

Yonatan could not understand why the boy insisted on staring at the woman, who made him sad. He got up and went over to his parents, then squeezed between them on a bench. At home that evening, he asked his mother who the boy with the frizzy hair was. She asked his father, who was on the phone, for the name of the guy from No. 10 who worked at the Ministry of Commerce and Industry. His father didn't answer, but Shaul, who was sitting in the living room watching a soccer match, said he played ping pong with the boy's brother: his name was Yoel, and starting in September he'd be in first grade with Yonatan.

Their mother went over to stand between Shaul and the television and said she didn't want him to join the army. Shaul laughed and said he would join in a few months and by then the war in Lebanon would be over. She repeated in the same exact tone that she didn't want him to join the army, and Yonatan said he didn't want Shaul to go either, and he leaned on his brother and buried his face in his stubble and then in his long straw-like hair that smelled of cigarettes. Shaul tickled him and flashed his charming grin. "Everything will be fine," he said, and they both looked at their mother, who stood hugging her body and trembling. Shaul went over and put his arms around her, and she leaned her head on his chest and looked so small in his arms. "How will we manage without Shaul?" Yonatan asked. She said she didn't know, and Shaul said, "You'll take care of her, won't you?"

"He shouldn't be taking care of anyone, he's a little boy," his father said from behind them. He was leaning on the sliding door to the living room. That night, or another night years later, Yonatan heard his mother telling his father: "Everything will be fine, everything will be fine. That's the final lie we tell before we throw ourselves into the abyss."

Six years later, he and Yoel still rhapsodized about the summer of 1982, when they'd spent every evening arranging the soccer cards they'd traded that day, sometimes in the cherished company of Shaul and Noam, and the neighbors were out on the streets until late at night. They were intoxicated by the camaraderie forming between them and the attention from their big brothers. Those days came to an abrupt end when Shaul joined the army and Noam moved into his own room and stopped talking to them. The excitement on the block died down and they were surrounded by silence, and the ruins they saw all around them demanded that they construct a new world.

He stands in a forest clearing and from faraway, among the trees, something red flickers. He hurries down a path paved with dried leaves that crunch under his boots. He hears screams, sees blue shirts running through the woods, the faces above them hidden in the dark, and it makes him laugh—they look like HaShomer HaTzair shirts. He bumps into something and pain stabs his ribs. He strains his eyes: spades are arranged in a circle, stuck in the earth like they used to be next to the shed in the agricultural studies garden. He grabs one and pulls hard. It's lighter than he expected, like the plastic ninja sword he bought on Purim which broke in the first swordfight. His costumes were always duds.

He walks down a slippery incline, too fast, falls and rolls down, but for some reason it doesn't hurt at all and he surrenders to the motion. He feels like whistling. This rolling is wonderful, like the roller coaster at Disneyland last year, when his father scrunched his eyes tight but he kept his wide open, failing to understand how Dad could be afraid—as a force greater than them propelled them forward, twisting and dizzying them—when what Yonatan feared was decisions that depended on him.

Everything is suddenly lit up in a blinding light. The sky is blue and beautiful. He stands by a blue Subaru with one of the rear doors missing. Behind him, at the top of a steep hill, is the forest. Did I roll all the way down? he wonders. He kneels and looks at the car door floating on water near a small frothing waterfall. A figure rises from the depths, holding the door. The sun turns her black-brown hair golden, the light trembles on the water around her. She wears denim shorts with wet threads that cling to her thighs, and a white shirt stuck to her stomach. She sprawls on the car seat and clumsily stretches her legs. Her fleshy thighs, which have turned slightly red, touch the water, and around her neck is a chain with a shiny red ring—is that the red spot?

He longs to take off his shirt and jump into the water and swim to her, to touch her, but he can see his white chest and the fold of fat in his belly. He never takes off his shirt around other kids, always finding an excuse. "It's heaven here," says the cheerful voice of a boy from the lake, and he sees someone swimming over to the girl.

———

The kids from class went to the wadi to gather wood. They'd arranged to meet at the shopping center, but Yoel waited for them at the end of their block. He'd decided to take part in the Lag Ba'Omer campfire, and Yonatan said he could go ahead without him. He sat on the balcony watching the kids tumble down the street. When they saw Yoel, Tomer Shoshani made a face and said Yoel couldn't join them because he hadn't come to the shopping center at the appointed time. Yoel insisted that didn't matter. From his post on the balcony, Yonatan found it difficult to look at Yoel's perplexed expression as he tried to reason with them: it didn't matter if he'd gone to the shopping center or waited here, he argued, because they were going to the wadi, which was right here. It was as if he refused to understand.

Yonatan crawled into his room and sat on the floor, wishing he could take pleasure in having been right. Some time went by, and when he could no longer stand the silence, he peered out: Yoel was standing outside his building, watching the group walk away. He couldn't see Yoel's face but an ominous feeling came over him. He charged downstairs, and when he crossed the street he saw Yoel's mother leaning over him from behind with her arms wrapped around his stomach, pressing him against her as he kicked at the air. His face was twisted and his cheeks were puffy and flushed.

All Yonatan could hear was the monotonous sound of wheels on the asphalt. When Yoel's mother saw him, her eyes lit up, as if she expected him to save them. But then the street resumed its usual hum and Yoel was screaming, and his mother shouted: "Look who's here, honey!" They supported Yoel together and dragged him upstairs while he wailed and kicked and spit dribbled from his lips. In the living room, his mother started undressing him and shouted at Yonatan to stop standing there like a log and take Yoel's shirt off. He pulled Yoel's arms through the sleeves, and when Yoel resisted he pulled harder— alarmed at how hot his skin was—and they carried him in his underwear to the bath and rinsed him with cold water.

Yoel's mother stroked him and kissed his forehead and said, "It's okay, we'll fix everything." Her pleading tone annoyed Yonatan: how could she fail to understand that this was not what he needed to hear? He avoided looking at Yoel's face, because every time he met his tortured eyes, his body burned. Yoel's screeches slowly died down into soft mews, and he sat in the bathtub with his head between his knees. They wrapped him in a towel and laid him on the bed and his mother pulled a blanket over him, then signaled for Yonatan to sit next to him. She offered to make them chocolate milk, and when they didn't answer she left them alone. Yoel's arm trembled when Yonatan put his hand on it, and Yoel stared at him as if seeing him for the first time. He sighed, seemed to be smiling for a moment, but then gave Yonatan a hostile glare and turned to face the wall.

His mother came back with two glasses of chocolate milk on a tray. Close behind her was Noam, whose hair was ruffled and looked as though he'd just woken up. Yoel pretended to be asleep. Yonatan looked around wildly, got up, walked between Noam and his mother without saying a word, picked up Yoel's tennis racquet and ran out. He skipped down the stairs, taking a few at a time, and crossed the dirt lot. He heard someone panting behind him and quickened his steps, knowing Noam was a fast runner. He paused at the edge of the wadi and looked for the other kids: they were climbing up the western path near the military factory. He had a burning desire to confront them and slam the tennis racquet in Shoshani's face, and hit anyone who dared to intervene, but he was afraid his body would burst before he could catch up with them.

"The thing about revenge," their chess teacher had said, quoting a Japanese warrior, "is that it must be taken immediately, because the minute you start to ponder it too much you descend into fear. And so never be afraid to burst into your enemies' house alone, for there is no room for illusions when it comes down to a single breath."

Noam pounced on him from behind and knocked him to the ground, grabbed his arms and pinned him down, shouting: "It won't help Yoel if you beat them up, it'll help you!"

He lay there kicking up sand and listening to his own groans. There was sand in his face and eyes. They both coughed and spat. He was beginning to grasp the futility of violence, and his body slackened, as if a whole region inside him that had been seething and life-giving only a moment ago had emptied out. In his mind's eye he saw Yoel's hostile look, forcing him to acknowledge what he had denied: Yoel viewed the Lag Ba'Omer bonfire as a chance to extricate himself, if only temporarily, from their alliance, and to get close to the other kids. When it all fell through, it was Yonatan, of all people, whom Yoel had found sitting on his bed consoling him. Yonatan regretted going up there. Noam let go of his arms and sat down next to him, and he wiped the tears and sand from his eyes with his sleeve, which was also sandy, and Noam said there was no point in beating up those kids, everything would work out, they'd find a solution. Yonatan wanted to believe him.

The lake was dotted with a multitude of bodies and shirts and colorful bandanas, and the white froth of the water. The car engine roared suddenly—any minute now it would drive away and he would be exposed for all to see. He stood up and realized there was still a spade next to him, heavier than a plastic sword but lighter than a real spade. Like a tennis racquet.

The girl who'd been lying on the car door now sat on the shore drying out, her hands and feet buried in the sand. She turned her face up to the sun. She looked different, like a miniature replica of the girl he'd seen before, but still the same girl. He walked toward her and was pierced by the realization that he could have caught up with her back in the forest: he knew her.

He swung the spade and hot sweat stung his body, as if he'd been bathed in boiling water. He was close to her now, could see the drops of water on the back of her neck around a light birthmark. He wondered if she could hear his breath. As he looked at her back it still seemed possible, but he knew that if she turned to him and he saw her face and she really was Tali in every pore of her skin—he would not have the courage to strike her.

It all had to happen fast: he would do it, and Tali would not get in their way anymore. He stopped, straightened up, and looked at the picture-perfect blue sky. He breathed in the saltiness of the wind, delighting in the breeze, marveled at the beautiful lake glistening in the sunlight, then turned, allowed the spade to slip out of his hands, and trudged back to the forest.

That afternoon he called his mother into his room and told her he was going back to school.

FINAL YEAR
(MID-1990S)

He was aware of the flurry of events going on at school, although they seemed somewhat unreal, surrounded by a ghostly halo. Every morning he walked past classmates chattering about the end-of-year play, about parties and the yearbook, getting their pictures taken in excitable huddles on the lawn or the rooftop, with cigarettes between their lips and beers in their hands, talking secretively about night trips to the beach.

Outside the main building, cars stopped to unload ropes, sandbags, rocks and lighting poles, and boys in undershirts labored in the blazing hot sun to build the sets for the graduation party. Every so often they poured bottles of cold water over their heads. They looked like a commercial for Diet Coke, and Yoel commented that the teenage TV soaps had gone to their brains. At least their parents' generation had known who they were imitating, he said—Humphrey Bogart, for example—but now it was just a mishmash of gestures with no clear origin, or any origin at all.

He heard there was going to be a pool at the party, with two wooden bridges spanning its width and length, surrounded by deck chairs and strips of sand and umbrellas and a few surprises that only those in the know could discuss. Of course there would be hookahs, vodka and beer, and there was even talk of fireworks. The sleepy pace sped up and everything started happening at once: the front of the school looked like a construction site, instead of lolling around on the benches people dashed back and forth, and he couldn't understand why they were in such a hurry. A few had disappeared, and he assumed he'd never see them again. There were rumors of new couples who'd had sex, when he hadn't even known they knew each other. Yoel said a lot of kids were grasping that they were about to graduate high school as virgins and so there was a frantic rush to get laid.

But for Yonatan the days seemed merely to be prodding at his mind. As soon as he got near school every morning, he felt the tension: someone suggested an exciting idea, new alliances were forged, even the smell was different: there was a bold summer saltiness in the air, which some said came from the sandbags they'd filled on the beach in Tel Aviv. Even when he wanted to believe that these rituals were pointless and even stupid, he secretly envied the kids who dedicated themselves to them, and longed to be similarly swept up. At the very least, he wished he could be like Yoel, who misled everyone with vague commitments: sometimes he would carry out a task assiduously, but on other days he sat outside smoking, ignoring the preparations and speaking to no one. Kids who believed Yoel's eager promises about wanting to make sure "this graduation party will go down in history" would be brushed off the next day, and if they insisted, he looked at them as if he'd never seen them before and had no recollection of his promises.

Yonatan did want to take part in the work, and he enjoyed being out in the sun, feeling strangely light while he darted back and forth hauling ropes and sandbags. For a while he united with the main clique, absorbing the warmth it radiated and the sense of fraternity that bound it, but sometimes he was transported elsewhere, in the middle of carrying a deck chair or an inflatable doll. He had only to picture his parents, or Shaul smoking by his record player, to go limp and feel burdened by the slightest movement. Lurking at the end of every euphoria in that final year was the downfall. He'd begun to keep his distance from anything that might make him too happy, because the awakening was torture.

Still he forged ahead and took part in the preparations, though he frequently found himself on the margins and loathed this version of himself who could not look away from the popular kids. They radiated confidence; it was clear to them that their future depended only on their courage and talent, because they sensed no entity crawling through the depths of the earth threatening to crack it open beneath their feet and send them plunging into the abyss. Perhaps it was he, who had always posed as a fearless kid who did whatever he felt like, who was the greatest coward of them all. As long as he'd operated within clearly demarcated boundaries, he'd been able to deceive them, and he could not yet accept that this phase of life was over. For years he'd assumed that in high school something fundamental about him would change, some deeply held desire would emerge, or at least facets of his personality would be clarified and he would be ready for his army service and for adulthood. But none of this had happened, and perhaps that was why he expected his internal sense of time—an intersection of eras—to rip away the false chronology and reveal plenty of time left before high school ended.

When he tired of the commotion, he would go downstairs to the ground floor and wander the hallways looking for the chubby boy with thick, scratched thighs, an oversized face, and a pair of clear, green, thoughtful eyes whose beauty did not match his other features. He'd first seen him the year before, encircled by a gang of boys who were cursing and slapping him. The boy had backed up against a wall, his face and bruised arms turning red. He didn't shout, didn't even put up his hands in defense, just stood there with a surprised look. Yonatan stood between him and his tormenters and shooed them away, and that was when he noticed that the boy was dressed in dirty clothes, like a second grader rather than a middle schooler, as if no one cared what he looked like. He was furious at this kid's parents for letting him go to school dressed like that. The boy didn't thank him, only coughed, and put his hands to his cheeks, and walked away with spit dribbling down his chin. In the following weeks, without realizing it, Yonatan kept searching for him in the hallways, and when he spotted him chatting with other kids, he felt relieved.

Not long ago he went up to the boy—he couldn't resist it—and asked if anyone was bothering him. The boy, now wearing jeans and a silver chain around his neck, didn't answer, and it was doubtful he even remembered Yonatan. Before walking away, he turned and asked Yonatan if he had five shekels. He dug through his pockets, buying time, so that perhaps he could understand why this boy's tortured face kept flashing through his mind. It had occurred to him that the boy reminded him of Shaul in old photographs, but Yoel said that kid resembled Shaul like he resembled Yasser Arafat. "What's your story with that kid?" Yoel had asked. "It's starting to look really suspicious." He wasn't sure himself. Perhaps he was stirred by his realization that the boy was just beginning a track he himself was ending—that all these high school years were still ahead of him.

Yonatan gave the kid a five-shekel coin and told him he was graduating soon and wouldn't be there next year. The boy nodded and asked if he was going to get a short-barreled rifle when he joined the army, and Yonatan said, "Maybe." He waited for a response, a signal that the boy understood there was something oblique connecting them. He refused to believe that such a strong sense of kinship could have no outward signs. But the boy took the coin with a blank look and walked away.

More and more evidence of their school days coming to an end accumulated in the form of corrected yearbook proofs, loudspeakers set up around the pool, music and voices from the auditorium, where play rehearsals were being held. In his mind's eye he saw how the plenitude of their life at the school would now be packed up in a few final gestures that captured nothing of the pivotal events that had rocked them. Every morning he awoke with a dread that sharpened and dulled intermittently as the day went on. Sometimes he tried to translate the fear into specifics: perhaps he was afraid of the fog he was going out into, with no plan or enthusiasm or even curiosity, while other kids, including Yoel, who had been accepted into an intelligence unit, already knew where they would do their military service and had meticulous plans for the next few years.

When Yonatan wondered if he was the only high schooler who would have preferred things not to change, Yoel seemed surprised: "Don't you want to see other things, meet new people?"

"Of course I do," he replied, "in theory. But not now."

Yoel was enthusiastic about new people he met and always tried to find out if there was anything interesting about them. Yonatan, conversely, wanted to know if they liked him, which made his interactions with new acquaintances unnatural. He remembered something Lior had told him: he was simply afraid because the world he and Yoel had created had run out of time. In fact, although he'd never fully admitted it, that world had ended years ago, and there was nothing left of it but a few accidental gestures—like that morning when they drove to the outskirts of Jericho.

He was working alongside the other kids on the day they finished spreading sand around the pool, and in order to get even with Yoel— for what, he wasn't completely sure—he reminded them that Yoel had promised to help. Yoel laughed and slapped him on his back, and they both kneeled down to flatten out the sand into an even layer, sweating and itching and flinging sand at each other. They wrote their names in the sand, and Yoel wrote "Bentz & Tzivony," but he left out Shimon, who'd joined a paratroopers' unit, lost his mind, shut himself up in his room for a whole year, then disappeared in Nepal; his body was eventually found on Mount Everest. Before the funeral, Shimon's mother asked everyone to write something in his memory. Yonatan had come up with a few warm memories, while Yoel had ignored the request. Now Yoel had a malicious grin on his face, and Yonatan realized that Yoel was waiting for him to write out "Shimon the King" in celebration of their childhood victory, and he felt sickened. Maybe at the end of the day there was something mean about Yoel, he thought.

They went down to the water fountain and, almost out of habit, he asked Yoel if he'd seen Lior recently. Yoel said no, and Yonatan reminded him of their conversation when they'd driven toward Jericho that night. Yonatan had asked if Lior had said anything about him when Yoel had run into her, and Yoel had said, "You know, nothing special."

"What not-special things did she say?" he now pressed Yoel.

"Come on, I didn't engrave every word on my memory." When he realized Yonatan was not satisfied, Yoel said he hadn't wanted to anger him that night in the desert because he'd been very upset, and anyway when he'd seen Lior they'd both been drunk. But one thing she told him he did remember: that Yonatan used to talk too much about Tali.

"I talked a lot about Tali?" He was convinced Yoel was joking, and he looked up at the sun, which coated the asphalt around them with all the blue-gray splendor of summer. They washed their faces at the fountain, and the basin filled with murky water from their sweat.

"Well, it's okay," Yoel said laughingly, "everyone on our block is into Tali, right?"

Later, when they sat in their final social studies class and the teacher gave a farewell speech about the challenges ahead of them and the values they'd absorbed at school, including the experience of a meaningful military service, he got a note from Yoel:

> Honorable yet failing King,
> I have been made privy to a rumor that in District 1994 there is a gathering of the millions of honey-brained devils who have turned eighteen. With the technology they obtained where there is no sun and no rain and no sky, they are building the most enormous war machine in the shape of a swimming pool. Although I have retired to my

estate and live in peace, I cannot leave you alone in the battle, and, even if I wanted to, it is clear that without me you would suffer defeat. Between me and you, you're a total amateur who can't even read a map, and after they cut off your head they'll cut off my limbs. I therefore urge you to swallow your pride, which is incommensurate with your skills, and unite with me for the final battle of our lives.

Your last remaining ally,
Warshovsky.

After school, his clothes and skin still sandy, he got home and found the door to Shaul's room shut. He heard music playing softly, perhaps "Sultans of Swing," which his brother maintained included the greatest guitar solo in history, an assertion Yonatan used to quote often. When he was little, he and Shaul used to wait for their parents to go out and then shut all the windows and blinds and hold a competition: they each chose three songs, and Shaul handed out grades. When Shaul listened to music he loved, his eyes would glaze over, as if a passageway had opened up deep in his black-brown irises. Smiling, he would speak in quiet, cradling tones, almost a whisper. A melancholy film would glisten in his eyes. Yonatan wondered if the music made his brother think back to those early eighties days when he had long hair and wore flared jeans and colorful button-down shirts, with friends who sat around in his room chain-smoking and flipping albums on the record player at a dizzying pace. For years he'd wondered where those high school friends had disappeared and why Shaul never saw them when he visited Israel.

It saddened and slightly embarrassed him to acknowledge that, for most of his childhood, Shaul had been the person he'd loved more than anyone, the only one who cheered him up just by being himself. Tali and Yoel argued in vain that Shaul had never been around except on his annual visits, and that was why he'd always been (as Tali put it) "the shiny unobtainable house on the hilltop." But that view failed to even approximate the love Yonatan felt for him, which, even though they rarely spoke and some part of him had grown to loathe Shaul, still lived on in him every time he listened to their songs. It had recently occurred to him that might have been a burden to Shaul on those summer vacations in the late eighties, being so determined to implement all the fun plans he'd made for them. It was as if those visits fortified him for the coming year, carrying him aloft so that he could marvel at the possibilities of life. He had not paid attention to his brother's mood swings, to his troubles in work and marriage, and had made demands on his time even when he could see that Shaul was exhausted and sad. In short, he'd wanted a lot from Shaul and given nothing in return. This had obviously driven a wedge between them, perhaps even more than his mother's interferences had.

He heard a sound from the living room and saw his parents sitting next to each other watching a movie, his mother leaning her head on his father's shoulder and his father with his arm around her frail body. They both wore glasses. On the glass-top table in front of them stood a bottle of red wine and two full glasses, and a dish with slices of the coconut cake his mother sometimes baked and kept in the fridge. To his surprise, she was wearing the black curly wig that she only wore when she went out.

He waved at them as he walked by, but they acted as if they hadn't seen him. When Lior once saw his parents watching a movie, she said it felt as if they viewed the kids as a disturbance and would have gladly spent days on end without them. Her parents, on the other hand, like most of their friends' parents, communicated mostly through and about their kids. Since that conversation, Yonatan had made a point of not bothering them when they were alone together.

A chill shook his body, and black scarves wrapped themselves over his eyes and made the scene blurry, muddying the colors of the couches, the rug, his mother's blue nightgown and even the light filtering through the blinds. He leaned on the wall outside their field of vision and listened to his heart pounding. He saw the two of them on the couch through the years, then the empty living room in a year or two.

This would probably be one of the last times he saw them sitting together in that familiar position, and suddenly all the pictures scattered and only one streaked across his consciousness like a bird breaking away from its flock: he had come home from school a week earlier to find his mother and Ratzon sitting on the couch, softly singing a song he did not know: *A song of ascents, I will lift up mine eyes unto the mountains: from whence shall my help come? My help cometh from the Lord.*

As soon as they saw him, they stopped singing and there was an awkward silence. Ratzon stood up, and when he walked past Yonatan he hugged him hard, the way he used to when Yonatan was a little boy. That night his mother told him, although he had not asked: "Grandma Sarah used to love the Book of Psalms."

He examined the tracks left by his shoes in the hallway and assumed that if his parents saw them they would be angry. He walked to his room, wondered if he'd heard Christopher Walken's voice and if they were watching *The Deer Hunter* again, and replayed the information he'd recently heard about tests his mother was supposed to undergo—had there been one today? But all the tests were garbled in his mind, and he'd recently stopped asking his father questions and done his best to avoid him. He'd come home one evening and found his father sitting alone at the dining table with piles of paperwork. As he walked past, his father said, without looking up, "You know things are bad, right," with a note of reproach in his voice. Yonatan muttered, "I know," and hurried to his room, even though he assumed his father would have liked him to stay. But he was afraid of the moment when his father would tell him there was no hope left, and felt that if he spent one moment longer with him, that is what he would hear. In the world to which he clung with all his might, as long as he hadn't heard anything unequivocal from his father, even though the evidence was mounting—for example, Shaul's prolonged visit—he could still submerge their future in a fog. Even when he saw his mother's death, the picture was quickly covered over with scenes of her staying with them. Over the years he had learned to position himself between the wings of unknowing, in a place where things were vague and details could go either way, and from this position he saw without seeing, understood just a little but stopped understanding before too much could be deciphered. He had trained himself, unwittingly, to defuse his curiosity, the penchant he and Yoel shared for peeling away layers of camouflage and fakery to reach "the elemental core," as they called it—although, as Tali sardonically claimed, they did this "mostly about other people." When it came to his mother's disease, he was afraid of exactly that: a moment of absolute lucidity that could not be undermined even if it were papered with rumors, hopes, and stories of those who had defeated the illness.

He lay down on his bed fully clothed and kept very still, careful not to let the bedsprings creak. He'd been naive, he realized, to assume his mother was wearing the wig because she wanted to look her best: they'd been somewhere, probably at the doctor's, and then they'd come home. His father, who'd been very busy lately, had been planning to go to work but hadn't left because something major had happened. So they were sitting in the living room watching a movie, and had even put out a bottle of wine, because she was afraid to be alone at home. More than anything else, it pained him to see or imagine her lying in bed, alone or next to his father, when in fact she was lonely and scared.

He buried his face in the pillow, trying to silence the din of assumptions, and listened to the television. From the sounds, he concluded that they'd reached the Russian roulette scene in Saigon, or perhaps that scene was simply imprinted in his mind. Either way, as long as he could hear the movie, he was protected. The minutes ticked by. He hoped that when the film ended they would immediately start another one. He had a premonition that this evening it would all be over.

For three days he searched for an off-white trench coat like the one he'd seen on TV, but the only ones he could find were black or blue. Refusing to give up, he visited all the shops downtown, drove to the Malcha Mall and the one in Talpiot, and tried smaller stores in a couple of other neighborhoods. In a dimly lit warehouse in the orthodox neighborhood of Geula, he squeezed his way between racks of old coats reeking of mothballs, and finally found a thin, shiny cream-colored duster, with a different cut than the one he'd liked on the good-looking teenager on TV, but he tried it on, standing in front of a dusty mirror plastered with tattered bumper stickers emblazoned with right-wing slogans, and one that said, "Nobody loves us."

The watchful shopkeeper stroked his gray beard stubble and said in a bemused voice that it was a woman's coat. But seeing that Yonatan was determined to buy it, he rearranged the collar and used a little brush to remove some strands of wool, then helped him pull off the coat, which was too tight around his shoulders. He folded it into a fancy box covered with stars that looked completely out of place in the dusty shop. Then he told Yonatan to sit down, because he seemed short of breath and looked pale. He asked if he was all right, and Yonatan said he was having trouble swallowing. He touched his parched lips.

"Sit down, kid, sit, don't get up," the shopkeeper said, and poured some tea from a thermos into a little cup. The tea was sweet and had a slight whiff of whiskey. "Better?" he asked a couple of minutes later.

"Yes," Yonatan nodded.

"Sit here as long as you like, kid, I know your face from HaPoel soccer games at the YMCA. I used to be a fan, before I found the way," he said, pointing to his large black yarmulke.

Yonatan said, "That was ages ago." The man's generosity and the way he articulated the word "kid" made him choke up, which seemed to happen too frequently lately.

The shopkeeper laughed. "What do you mean, ages ago, buddy? You still have milk on your lips and your whole life ahead of you," he singsonged. "How old are you, twenty?"

He was surprised by how pleased he felt with the extra two years he'd been given. For the past few weeks he'd been astounded every time something that used to excite or interest him still did. His mother had shuffled from room to room one day, running her hand over the walls and pictures, touching the closet doors and the dining table and the books on her shelf and the musical mugs he'd given her. Shaul had supported her when she got tired and she'd sat down on the couch with her feet together, leaning forward with her hands on her lap, and the three of them had stood around in a silent watch, occasionally saying something to cheer her up. She did not answer them, only played with the chain around her neck and then removed her gold wristwatch, which showed the time in Jerusalem and in New York (so that she would always know where Shaul was), a watch Kaufman had bought her when they used to go dancing, and she let it fall to the couch and sat there until it was time to go to hospital, and no one spoke about when she would come home.

Since that day he'd expected that a new era would begin, and that everything that had preoccupied him in the past would come to a standstill in his mind, evidence of a vanished world. But in fact not everything changed. There were too many mornings when he awoke and pictured Lior, whom he hadn't seen for four months, and whose daily routine he still tracked in his imagination. These rituals of memory and fantasy had recently become rote, and at times it was not curiosity or yearning, nor pain, which summoned her image, but simply habit. Sometimes when he gave in to his lust for her or for one of the girls who worked at the bars downtown, or when he laughed at a joke or watched a movie all the way through—he felt that he was betraying his mother again.

He went to the hospital wearing the new coat and found Shaul sitting in his usual spot opposite their mother's bed. On the stool next to him was the blue plastic tray with lunch—chicken, mashed potatoes, salad—that his mother hadn't touched, and which, at the end of every day, someone would always end up gobbling and declaring it not that bad. He pressed his mother's hand but did not lean over to kiss her, because the coat smelled of cigarette smoke and he'd already been warned not to go near her after smoking. He stood in his regular place by the window, and his mother asked, "You bought a new coat?"

"Yes," he said.

"Very nice, good for you," she said in the sardonic-yet-impressed tone he knew well.

His aunt came in and hugged him, and Shaul pointed out the new coat, and she said, "Oh, it is nice." She touched the sleeve. "It looks great on you!" Shaul was clearly surprised by her warm response, and his mother's face turned dark. She asked if he was studying for his matriculation exams and when the next one was. He replied in English, and his mother said, "Shaul can help you," and Yonatan lied, "I know, he has already." Shaul nodded: "Ask me anything you want."

And then she said, "I want you two to always look after each other."

"We'll look after each other and we'll look after you," Shaul replied.

"Everything will be fine," Yonatan reiterated, "we just need to get you out of here."

Shaul added, "Soon you'll get out of here."

She gazed back and forth between her two sons, and he wasn't sure if she was trying to draw strength from their determination or worrying that they might actually believe in it. For weeks, every comment she'd made that alluded to a time when she would be gone was repelled with a denial that such a time could exist. Except once, a few months ago, when they'd had a bad argument and she'd said, "Don't worry, I'll be gone soon, and you'll be putting flowers on my grave." "Fine with me," Yonatan had shot back. He was not expecting her to forgive him, and he sometimes wondered if Shaul wanted forgiveness for things he'd hurled at her in New York two years ago, when he'd blamed her for his divorce.

She lifted her upper body. Shaul supported her waist and rearranged the pillows behind her back, and her headscarf slipped, exposing short tufts of hair. He felt a set of freezing cold fingernails digging at his stomach, and fought to silence a groan of pain. He leaned on the wall with his arms against his body, wanting to rush over and straighten her headscarf but at the same time needing to look at the window; for so many years he'd been haunted by the fear that something would happen—a draft blowing through the house—and her bald head would be exposed. He was overcome with shame at his miserable fears, just as he had been before her surgery, after the doctor explained that in some cases he could reconstruct the breast during the tumor-removal operation. Yonatan was very preoccupied by this information and frequently mentioned it, because he was afraid the others wouldn't remember, and he was disappointed to learn that the doctor had removed the entire breast. In the months after the operation, he kept asking his mother when she would have the reconstruction surgery, until his father snapped at him: That was the last thing on their minds now—hadn't he explained to Yonatan that the cancer had spread to twelve lymph nodes? How could he even talk about that?

He didn't really know, but he could not tolerate the notion that her body would always be damaged.

Shaul picked up the tray and sat down on the edge of the bed. He held a spoonful of mashed potatoes to her lips, and she moved her head toward the spoon and gave a slight grimace, without touching the food, and they both smiled. She pushed his hand away and for a moment she looked like a little girl, like Yoel's little sister when they gave her a dish she didn't like.

Eight months ago, on Yom Kippur Eve, they'd drunk vodka in his room, and Yoel, sprawled on his bed, asked why he spoke of his brother with such resentment. Lior, who was lying on the floor with her head on Yonatan's lap while he combed his fingers through her hair, said sleepily that maybe he was a little jealous. "Jealous of him being in New York?"

He pinched her gently, not understanding what she meant. Lior giggled and squirmed and said he was tickling her and she still couldn't believe his family fasted on Yom Kippur, and then she said tenderly, "Jealous of his relationship with your mom."

He was surprised to realize that he'd never considered that

possibility. Yoel, probably just to get on his nerves, exclaimed, "That makes sense—the kid is jealous!" Yonatan replied, "That's the last thing I want."

Lior shut her eyes and her hair fell over her face, and she put his hand on her stomach under her shirt, and he stroked her warm skin and looked forward to her lying on top of him when Yoel left. "It's just like you," Lior observed, "Both of you, but you especially. You hide all your passions under contempt, you're contemptuous of everything you don't want and also of everything you want so badly…"

Yoel laughed and said in a stammering but admiring tone that mimicked someone they could not identify: "Thank you for ag-ag-agreeing to t-t-talk with us, we are s-s-so p-p-pathetic and you are s-s-so s-s-smart."

"Do you have a hard-on, Yoel?" she asked, and then the three of them fell asleep.

His mother looked revived. She straightened up and sipped water from a bottle and signaled with her eyes to Shaul and her sister that she did not need their help. "Where is my husband?" she asked teasingly, and her sister said, "He'll be here soon." She squinted and said, "*You have no idea what a tired man I am. They're destroying me.*" Her impersonation of his father was far from perfect, but they all laughed.

Shaul, seeming cheered, passed him the tray: "Have you eaten anything today?" Yonatan felt like making fun of this unexpected concern, but realized that in this room he had no right to talk back to Shaul, who sat with their mother from early morning to evening, reading to her, putting cold washcloths on her forehead, making sure she got enough morphine, cutting visits short when some of her friends insisted on sharing their troubles with her. He'd heard his brother tell their father that in the hospital you could see, sometimes in the space of an hour, their worrying mother and their loyal mother and their bitter mother and their wise mother and their betrayed mother. Only in the evenings, when his father took over, did Shaul go home to sleep.

Yonatan knew that he could not have devoted himself to taking care of his mother the way Shaul had, and not only because of his youth; he did not possess Shaul's patient dedication. He knew, too, that he took after his father in this respect: neither of them was really willing to take care of someone else. Her impending death would hit Shaul harder; perhaps he was the only one of the three who would experience the loss in every tendon of his being. Because unlike his brother, Yonatan still found it hard to resist a call to lightheadedness, and as soon as evening fell he hunted for someone to join him on pub crawls in the Russian Compound. Yoel, who did not know that Yonatan's mother was in hospital, frequently accompanied him, and they'd hit on the redhead bartender, who showed them the ring her boyfriend had given her, but the fact that she conversed with them was considered major progress. When Yoel was busy, Yonatan asked Tali or someone else, it didn't matter who, and he no longer cared if he got a reputation as someone who would ask anyone to party with him.

His mother said she'd dreamed last night that she saw him here, or somewhere they once were, she couldn't remember. He detected a certain yearning in her eyes. Then she said that she often woke up and prayed for the night to be over, for morning to come. Her voice lacked the familiar cadence that had weakened but was not yet completely gone.

"I'm tired," she said. She looked tiny. Her face was still smooth and unwrinkled but smaller, and the veins on her thin hands protruded. Shaul and their aunt helped her lie down, and Yonatan remembered that he'd read that after death the voice of the dead was slowly erased from the memory of the living until it could no longer be heard. In a cracked voice, he said that he also dreamed about her a lot, and did not tell them that he sometimes visited this room around midnight. After he drank and partied downtown and prayed that every girl who looked back at him might ease his loneliness, and the place emptied out and they started playing end-of-night songs, he stopped hearing what was going on around him and every movement felt heavy, and he became convinced that tonight, while he sat there, his mother would die, or perhaps already had. Sometimes he cut the recognition down to size, but other times it filled his mind and was immutable, and then he would hurry out and speed to the hospital, take the elevator up and run to the oncology department, and wash his face and hands with soapy water in the bathroom. Then he would walk slowly to her bed and look at the screen monitoring her breath and make sure her chest was moving, and if he saw no movement he would touch her foot to make sure she was warm, and if the blanket had fallen off he would pull it up over her body. Then he would sit on Shaul's chair, staring at her and then at the night sky, and slip away before she woke up.

———

Showered and perfumed and sporting tailored pants and a black button-down shirt, Yoel good-naturedly mocked Yonatan's outfit: dark blue jeans, red button-down shirt with a colorful motif—"Gap style," he called it, and spat up at the sky.

They walked arm in arm through the dark fenced-in parking lot, at the edge of which was a rusty iron gate leading to the highest point in the wadi. From some distance they could smell the saltiness of the sand trucked in from Tel Aviv's beaches, and gunpowder, and fresh grass. They heard drumbeats reverberating from the speakers, and the thunder of cap guns, and shouts and whistles and wails of joy, all whirling together.

He'd expected to feel prickles of tension, but instead he was indifferent. It was Yoel who, after chattering in the car, now fell silent, smoothed down his clothes, and put his face in front of the car's rearview mirror to tidy his sideburns and curls in the starlight.

Yonatan kicked the mirror Yoel was looking at and had the feeling that a film of unreality was enveloping the night, and all the past nights, which had contained a numbing element, as had the stories he and Yoel used to make up as children. They had been passionate about those stories and loved to embellish them, but they had always been protected by the sense that they could cut off the plotline and return to normal life at any moment; that the Beit HaKerem of nighttime could be imposed on daytime too, with bayonet battles fought on snowy hilltops surrounded by a gaping chasm, because deep down they knew that they would not really die, they would not really be killed, that the calamity of their war against the towers, which had brought about a long estrangement between them, had occurred at a time when borders were being reshuffled anyway. A thin veil had blocked his view of the world, in which his mother now lay unconscious in hospital and no one was saying she was going to wake up again.

Earlier, at home, Shaul and his father had come back from the hospital with ashen faces. They sat in the living room watching the news, ate some cold roast chicken and left him a plate of food, then each retired to his room. He showered and dressed, and only when he was at the door did Shaul ask where he was going. He said it was his high school graduation party, and Shaul said, "You're out every single night." When he did not respond, Shaul asked: "Were you at the hospital today?"

"No, I'll go tomorrow."

"There may not be a tomorrow. Your mother is unconscious in hospital and you're partying every night."

"Fuck you," he shot back, "where have you been all this time?" He fought off the urge to remind Shaul of the accusations he'd leveled at their mother, and wondered if they might both be guilt-ridden, agonizing over their last sins toward her, each wanting to depict the other as the worse offender.

Then their father was standing at the end of the hallway, his hair disheveled and his white undershirt stained yellow. "Shut up already, both of you," he barked, as though he were playing the role of father with his last remaining strength, and what they saw was the familiar facade of home, with nothing behind it.

Their father walked away with small steps, and his hands probed the walls as if he were afraid to lose his balance. Yonatan wondered if his father was ailing. His grandfather had died very young of a heart attack, and the thought that had occasionally floated through his mind came into focus: if his father died too, if all his fears came to be, he would not remain in this world.

Shaul turned and collapsed into the black armchair next to the phone, and dialed a number without picking up the receiver. Yonatan suspected he'd been drinking. Perhaps the fear of an even greater disaster was the only thing that might reconcile them. But the idea almost made him laugh. He considered asking Shaul if he'd rather he stayed home, but he knew Shaul would say no, that his going out every night confirmed everything he already believed anyway, or, more accurately, everything their mother had said about him. He realized that what had always weakened him around Shaul was the remembrances. Not the details, because Shaul remembered those far better than he did, but the way memories could arouse affection and tenderness in him, even today, and that even at this moment his body could long for Shaul's familiar hug, for the stubble he loved to feel on his face. Whereas it was clear that in all of Shaul's memories from their times together, there was not even a single flutter of life.

Yoel and he let go of each other's arms near the school and walked into the glare of colorful lights. Traces of smoke from the cap guns still mingled with the fragrant air. Yoel disappeared to find them some vodka and Yonatan instantly felt cold. He noticed, for the first time, how chilly the nights were for July. He saw barefoot figures dancing on the sand and splashing around in the pool, girls in denim shorts or skirts and bras bobbing around in the water, surrounded by boys in jeans and tank tops, some shirtless. He saw a guy he didn't know with lots of rings on his fingers, putting his hands on Vered Weiss's belly—everyone had desired her at one time or another—and pressing up against her from behind. Next to them, a muscular chest with a patch of black frizzy hair pressed against a pair of breasts in a wet red bra, and the two fell into the water together. He couldn't help feeling drunk on the signs of pent-up lust on display: caresses, gazes, body against body, shrieks. Groups of boys and girls united into a hug or a dance, broke up, and reunited at a dizzying pace. He would have liked to jump into the chaos and ward off the pressure that had spread through his body the minute Yoel left.

Where was that fucker with the booze anyway?

He lit a cigarette and walked to the back row of deck chairs. A group of kids sat passing a hookah around. "What'll you give me if I touch those coals right now?" one of them called out.

"Don't you do that in your army training anyway?" a girl remarked in a lazy tone that seemed to delight in its own apathy.

"They only do that to Arabs," another kid intervened.

"Check out that faggot, he thinks he'll get into band, but he'll end up working the cafeteria," the first one quipped. Grains of sand glistened on the back of his bronzed neck, and he put his hand on the girl's back.

Yonatan recognized her, they'd talked on the phone a few times, just meaningless chatter, competing over who was more depressed, but they'd stopped talking recently, when she'd refused to go pub-crawling with him and gleefully grumbled about how busy she was. On the lawn beyond the square lit up with streetlamps, he spotted Yoel surrounded by friends, drinking vodka from a bottle. He clearly didn't remember he'd gone to get drinks for them both.

The lights went off and the square turned dark, everyone roared and whistled and wailed. "Do bad things now!" someone yelled. A figure approached him in the dark and he felt cold water dripping down his face. He licked it off and heard a peal of laughter that sounded familiar for an instant, and the figure disappeared into clouds of thick smoke from the hookah. The lights flashed a blinding neon-white, he saw shapes curving and squirming, and could no longer identify the body parts moving between light and shadow. Someone pressed something against his back and he was doused in freezing cold water. He spun around angrily and saw a water rifle with rainbow colors changing on its barrel. Behind him stood Lior.

When they moved away from the lights there was a dull popping sound behind them, and a cheer went up. A purple shard sparked in the sky and evaporated into a thin jet of smoke that curled above them. They turned right to the parking lot, which was now lit up in the golden beams of cars driving in and out. Far to their right, beyond the wadi, lights flickered from the first row of houses on HaShachar Street, and above them, with its head in the sky, the unfinished building loomed. He hadn't remembered it looking so black at night.

A breeze blew Lior's hair around and caressed his cheek, and he picked up a whiff of her familiar scent, which evaporated as he inhaled it. From the corner of his eye he saw a couple sitting on an engine hood with their arms around each other: the boy leaned over and kissed her tenderly, and the sight made him feel wistful. He didn't want to touch Lior before she touched him, but he couldn't resist any longer and so he interlaced his fingers with hers and felt for the three rings, pleased they were still there. They swung their arms back and forth, and he had the urge to lean his cheek on her neck and run his fingers through her hair. When he turned to the wadi so that she would not see his flushed face, his gaze became lost in the thick darkness. He let go of her hand in despair and immediately felt relief.

He turned to look at her: she wore a black dress he hadn't seen before, a thin belt loosely fastened around her waist, and gray high heels. There was glitter on her cheeks, silver and gold and purple, and her lips shone with an unfamiliar bright red. He had trouble reconciling the bright colors with the tension in her translucent face, where not a muscle was moving. He perceived a note of weakness in her appearance. It was strange how, all these months, he'd pictured her cool and confident, at least when it came to them. He hadn't believed she was tormented by their breakup, or that she sometimes lay in bed longing for his touch and wondering what he was doing. Perhaps she was putting on an act—the malicious idea stole into his heart—to justify joining Tali for this party that she had no reason to be at. But Tali wouldn't do that to him. If she'd invited Lior, she must have assumed something would happen, that perhaps they'd even get back together.

He pushed the creaky gate open, and they walked toward a mound of little stones, with a few shreds of canvas flapping above it. He held her hand and they made their way slowly. His shoes knew every stone and crease in the earth.

"Where to?" Lior asked.

"Don't know," he said, afraid she would want to go back to the party.

At the edge of the wadi, the moonlight brushed the hot-water heaters on his rooftop. His eyes focused on the only window visible from that spot, the one in his parents' bedroom. The window balled up into a blurry dot, and he imagined his father lying in bed, and Shaul in his old bedroom, and the two of them sliding into muddled, disturbed sleep. They met in the middle of the night, in the living room or the kitchen or the bathroom, and with each awakening the first thing that occurred to them was that the phone hadn't rung yet, and that it might happen as soon as they fell back asleep.

Four days had passed since his mother had lost consciousness, and the inevitability of the phone call haunted them at night. Had he possessed any shame, he would have been lying in his own bed now, or encountering them in their nocturnal roamings.

"Is your mom okay?" Lior asked.

"No. She's not."

"Aren't the treatments helping?"

"The treatments are done."

"Where is she now?" she asked with a creaking voice.

"Hospital."

He hadn't been planning to tell her, fearing she would pity him, but he was overcome by a strange desire to tell the truth. She cleared her throat as if to say something, and he was relieved she didn't ask when his mother was coming home. They walked silently for a while, and before the first descent into the wadi she stopped and held out both arms and pressed against his body. She touched his cheek. Her hand was as warm as he remembered it, and had the same fluttering touch. He listened to her breath and wondered why the closeness he'd longed for all this time seemed to be occurring outside his body, as if he were watching himself submit to the embrace and the sensations lacked the familiar rhythm. He felt no comfort.

The moon disappeared behind the clouds and his building vanished in the dark. He was filled with sadness—that she had only turned up now, when it was all over. He buried his face in the familiar hollow between her shoulder and neck, and she stroked his hair. Now he understood: as usual, he had underestimated those around him, even Yoel, always assuming that he himself was the only one who could deceive people with his stories. He had not stopped to consider what they might find out and which conclusions they would reach. Yoel had probably run into Shaul on the street, and even if they hadn't talked, as soon as Yoel knew Shaul was still in Beit HaKerem he would have been on alert and picked up the details: that Shaul drove off every morning, that their mother wasn't around, that Yonatan disappeared for hours and was desperate to go out drinking every night. Perhaps Ratzon and the other neighbors had gossiped. Everything was flipped now: it wasn't that Yoel had believed Yonatan's act, but that he himself hadn't understood the true motivation for Yoel's familiar gestures. Now he had no doubt that he hadn't been successfully hiding anything, that Yoel and Tali knew—perhaps everyone did—and that was why they'd invited Lior, because she was the only one who could help him.

They were still standing close but their embrace had slackened and their bodies carefully moved apart, as if they were afraid to hurt each other's feelings. His muscles felt rigid. He sat down on the ground, leaned his back on a big rock between two gray za'atar bushes, and lit a cigarette. Lior sat down next to him with her back against his chest, swung her legs playfully over his, and he wrapped her in his arms and held the cigarette to her lips. "What are you doing here?" he asked.

"I wanted to see you."

"Really?"

"And they said it was going to be an awesome party."

"Were they right?"

"Obviously: hookah, cap guns, you guys are out of control."

They both laughed, and he felt buoyed by this exchange, which echoed a familiar music in her voice, perhaps in his too. They heard calls from down the wadi. A soft flashlight beam jumped around the rocks, lit up a few charred logs, ran over their bodies and shuddered on the brown earth. There were still ashes from the Lag Ba'Omer bonfires on either side of the path. They tracked the beam of light, entranced. "It's the Scouts," he said, "they've been hanging out here at nights lately. It's the nineties, no one's scared of the wadi anymore."

"Even if we're not together now, that doesn't mean you don't mean a lot to me," she said, tightening her arms around her knees.

He felt like laughing—all this production to tell him something he already knew. "Whether or not we're together, that's the only thing that matters," he said.

She turned to him, and her sardonic expression, which he'd always liked and sometimes even admired, was gone. He realized he still loved her, and had he believed she wanted to get back together he would have agreed at once, but he also understood that his love had been growing duller. A gap had opened up between him and the person who had loved Lior and constantly pictured her. So many nights he'd prayed for the moment when he would stop constantly thinking about her, but now he was alarmed by the wasteland forming in his mind. When it was complete he would be able to stop loving her. Having believed for all these months that her absence from his life had cracked open a space inside him, he now considered the possibility that a much larger space had been created over these past few weeks. What would fill that space now? Perhaps he had naively failed to understand that it was his longing for Lior that had protected him all this time.

PART THREE

MEXICO

He saw black nettles, poppies, za'atar bushes, flashes of fire on the hills, and the outline of the mountain range that surrounds Mexico City, looming behind rows of crumbling stone houses and billboards along the road from the airport to Polanco. Stars littered the sky: not this sky, which disappeared behind the clouds, but a different one, perhaps the sky in Pokhara on his post-army trip. He was supposed to hike to Annapurna Base Camp, a beginners' trek by all accounts, on the morning of the fourth anniversary of his mother's death, but he woke before dawn, packed his gear, and left while everyone else was asleep. He sometimes still saw that sky when he awoke in the morning and wished he'd stayed and done the trek. In his stories about Nepal—he had.

He was standing on a rooftop and the cloud cover looked very close; if he jumped high enough, he would disappear into it. He put his hands on the railing and felt dizzied by the vast distance between him and the black Lego brick of a road down below. He took a step back and stood between Carlos and the young girl with glasses, whose name he had learned was Elizabeth. She was the daughter of religious fanatics and hadn't talked to her mother for eight years, although her father sometimes called. She ran a club night called "The Past Is Yet to Come" and was writing her dissertation in political philosophy at the Ibero-American University. Carlos had told him there had recently been several murders in her small hometown, and he'd gone there to write a report for a human rights organization. Carlos was also a writer, translator and poet, of course. He told Yonatan about the murders over breakfast at a cantina in Narvarte on his first morning in Mexico City, while groups of men sat in stony silence at the other tables: a gang had killed every man with the last name 'Garza' and buried them near the Texas border.

Yonatan put his arms out and held their hands. All three of them were sweating, which he found charming, and they swung their arms lazily. He felt protected between them, and loved. He marveled again at Carlos's good looks, his black hair falling on his forehead, a gray spark dancing in his slightly slanted green eyes, beneath thin brows, and smooth, tanned skin.

He looked at Elizabeth. He did not recall such a sharp chin, at odds with the cheeks in her dimples and her light brown eyes, first sincere and then bemused or perhaps skeptical. All the days he'd spent wanting to see her seemed clear now, not because of what he'd told her about his best friend who'd died, but thanks to the memory of her hands on his face when he'd rested his head on her lap that night, the imprint of her touch as she'd stroked him tenderly, as if she'd taken ownership of his body, perhaps his mind, whispering that he would get through that night and other nights. He'd believed her then, but now he wondered if some of her gestures had been ironic. For months the crater under his feet had been widening, cracking open right in front of him or to one side, and he'd had to maneuver his way in a cautious dance, sometimes avoiding all movement. At times it seemed he was frozen in place and the chasm was dancing around him. He knew that if he told Shira the truth it would scare her, destabilizing their lives even further. And even if he was wrong and she could help him, it was best not to confirm her fear that he would not survive the loss of Yoel—that even if he did, he would be a different man, not the father Itamar knew, the man he'd sworn to be out of a sense of duty even before the love. How could he reassure her when he didn't really know himself? He'd had a dream, here in Mexico, that he was late to pick up Itamar from daycare, but when he got there the entire building had vanished, as if he'd arrived into a faraway time, and the words Yoel had said to him in that dream kept screeching through his mind: "Maybe all this isn't really for us."

They sat on the top floor of a dark bar where a few dusty mattresses were laid out, drinking mezcal. He drank more and more and complained that it wasn't having any effect, or not enough. They stepped out into the night. It was raining and Elizabeth's glasses got wet. He wiped them with his sleeve and then took his coat off and held it over her head. They wandered around La Condesa, through narrow, dark alleyways and bright bustling streets. He was tired and thirsty, which reminded him that he was some years older than they were.

They stood on the gray concrete floor of a small outdoor club, and he bought beers for Elizabeth and Carlos and they all leaned on the wet wall. A few young men and women in shorts danced between the puddles. Carlos wandered away and came back with a bottle of water, which he passed around, and they all took swigs. "This is crazy shit, you'll see," Carlos said.

They took Carlos's car to the hotel, walked past the doormen and the reception clerks, and stood by the swimming pool kicking at the water. Then they lay down on the wet lawn and counted rainbows and their faces were wet from the light rain. Elizabeth said she'd read Shalamov's "The Snake Charmer," on Yonatan's recommendation: "It's a nice story, but that's about it." "You can't do anything with Shalamov's writing—it doesn't lead anywhere," Carlos opined, echoing Yonatan, who'd quoted Primo Levi when he'd been asked to recommend a book during the last event of the festival. There was a silence, and Yonatan said, "I've come to understand this here: every time you put pen to paper with a picture that has been attacking your consciousness for years—a memory, a fantasy, whatever—you kill it slightly. You kill its wildness and beauty, the potential it had before you wrote it. After that, it will never strike your mind with the same force again. Maybe that's why the pictures you aren't willing to lose—you do not write. And when you're not willing to lose anything, you don't write anything."

Then they were in his room, dancing to YouTube clips, and he crushed white rocks into lines on the glass table and told Carlos they might be too thick and Carlos laughed and said, "This time it's on you."

He saw a bamboo hut whose roof branched around pale red clouds, and behind it loomed a tower made of rough Jerusalem stone, and on the shelves seen from its windows there were black pieces of record albums, sharp and narrow as knives, and faded newspapers, and notes in his father's handwriting, and a space heater, and behind the tower there was nothing—the world ended. A chill ran down his spine. He fluttered in terror, the coke wasn't strong enough, it would all end, they would leave, he would be alone on the roof, were they even in the hotel anymore? But a new flood of warmth spread through his body. He sat down on the floor. Each movement seemed to happen twice, first in his mind and then in reality, as if he were watching his body from outside and then returning to it.

Elizabeth sat down and leaned on him. He put his arms around her, tightened them against her body and leaned his cheek on her shoulder. Her skin was warm, he lit a cigarette and they smoked together. He thought of those mornings in the hotel when he'd checked his cell phone as soon as he woke up: nothing had happened, no tempest. What news was he waiting to hear?

He saw a forest, and Burman hanging on Michael's stout body, and there was writing on his naked back in an old video-game font: "Sources report that his colleagues at the Holon Municipality knew him by his name, A. Burman, but in the firms where he advanced his private and allegedly illegal affairs, he went by 'Y. Man.'" The forest widened and he saw Salman observing them from between the trees. Salman seemed to be looking straight at him, and he wanted to hide from his gaze. Words flickered over Salman's body: "The effects of wastewater usage on the spread of bacteria-resistant antibiotics in water and soil. Ph.D. candidate Eyal Salman. Advisor: Dr. Azriel Sorokin." Searching for 'Hila Baron' on Google and Facebook gave multiple results, there were too many Hila Barons in the world.

The magazine publisher's black Chevrolet was waiting outside the hotel. The door was so heavy that he had trouble opening it, and there were bulletproof windows. He'd been in such cars here before. He sat down on the leather seat. He took a swig from the bottle of whiskey on the bar in front of him, and looked at the cloudy night sky: he didn't know where they were going and didn't ask. That morning the publisher had left him a message at the hotel: "I got what you asked for." Suspecting another prank—like when he'd made Yonatan wait for the girl in glasses until one a.m.—he was in no hurry to answer. He called back in the evening, after waking up on the lawn outside his room, blinded by the garden lights, with his heart pounding. He couldn't remember having gone out there at all. His last memory was of lying in bed watching a movie about two planes that crashed on the runway at the tiny airport in Tenerife, in 1977, the greatest aviation disaster in history.

He hurried to his room and washed blades of grass off his face and neck, took a Klonopin, and looked in the mirror: his forehead was the color of the grass and there were thick red lines snaking around the whites of his eyes. He lay down, stood up, sat on the couch, dialed Shira's number but changed his mind, called his father and hung up. He'd stopped calling Yoel long ago. In the past two years he'd frequently dialed his number distractedly—he could recite all Yoel's phone numbers from age eight—and stopped midway, until he finally broke the habit.

He had trouble breathing and he touched his chest as if to wake it up. Unable to be alone for a moment longer, he burst out of the room, charged down the hallway and sat in the well-lit lobby near a group of German tourists listening to a tour guide describe the Pyramid of the Sun at Teotihuacan, where they were going the next day. "I've been there, it's boring as hell. Even Frankfurt's more interesting," he whispered in English to an older couple sitting next to him.

He went back to his room and phoned the publisher, who told him he would be picked up in three hours and taken to the best mezcal bar in town, "where you will find your young lady with glasses, and another surprise..."

"It'll be nice to see you again," he told the publisher.

"Unfortunately we shall not meet. I'm very busy, and I only meet truly great writers twice."

He laughed, feeling for the first time that he liked the publisher, who also gave a little purr of laughter and hung up. He felt calmer, knowing that his loneliness would soon be tempered and he would be with people, and would touch them.

He saw Itamar running around the apartment with a ball. A breeze mussed his hair, and his thin arms looked too scrawny. Itamar kicked the ball to him, he kicked it back, and they ran together, yelling and laughing, toward the glass balcony door. Itamar touched the glass and turned to him with a victorious grin: "Again!" He looked around: Elizabeth and Carlos were leaning over him watching the video clip on his phone. The boy was very pretty, they said, very cute. Elizabeth wondered if he shouldn't go home to his boy: how long had he been here—two weeks? Twelve days, he corrected her; two weeks sounded excessive, almost cruel. "How come you didn't tell me you were still here?" Carlos said, putting his hand on Yonatan's shoulder, "I told you that you always have a friend in Mexico City." He said they would not see each other again after tonight.

Carlos put one foot up on the rooftop railing and said: "Did you notice that every drunken story by a Mexican writer ends with them going home and finding their girlfriend or boyfriend screwing their best friend?" A picture glimmered in Yonatan's mind: he comes home one day, shortly after moving in with Shira, and finds Shira and Yoel sitting beside each other on the couch, talking, looking at old photo albums, with beer bottles in their hands and a full ashtray between them. There was nothing unusual about the scene, yet it aroused in him a peculiar feeling—a shameful one, perhaps. He could not put his finger on it, but in the first look they gave him, before the welcoming smile and Yoel's shout of happiness, he imagined he saw a shadow, as if they were displeased with his return.

Then the three of them sat there and Yoel interrogated Shira about her trip to South America after her military service, and every time she mentioned a place he asked her to describe it in detail. Then Yoel said, in a low voice, that he hadn't gone anywhere after the army. "And your boyfriend"—he jerked a finger at Yonatan—"took a failed trip to the Far East, came home shamefaced after ten days in Nepal, and didn't call anyone so that people would think he was skipping over mountaintops." He explained that they'd gone to London together, but that was somewhere you could go even when you were a hundred years old.

Out of nowhere, Yoel suggested the four of them—Yonatan and Shira, with Yoel and his girlfriend Anat—go traveling around the US that summer, Kerouac-style. But as the hours went by the trip shrunk down to Europe, then Greece, then the Sinai Desert, and finally Yoel admitted that he and Anat weren't exactly together, they were considering their future, and that kind of trip might send the wrong message. Shira looked at Yoel in surprise and asked why he hadn't told them before. Yoel snorted, as did Yonatan, because they often made plans only for Yoel to back out when he remembered some detail about his work or his girlfriend or his parents. Every time it happened, he assumed that Yoel was excited about the plans, before doubts began to gnaw at him and he changed his mind.

For a while they said nothing, until Yoel asked how come they'd moved in together only a few months after they'd met. Shira laughed and said they'd moved in together because it was the most natural thing to do at the time, and that if things didn't work out they would stop living together. Yoel seemed unsatisfied with the casual answer, but he said the two of them were clearly meant for each other. When they said goodbye, Yonatan remembered something Tali had told him recently: Yoel thought that Yonatan needed a sense of home because his family had fallen apart after his mother's death, and that was why he'd hardly been alone since moving to Tel Aviv. The difference between them, Yoel had told Tali, was that Yonatan didn't always assume there was something better out there, and that he recognized that there were certain things he needed, and certain other things he was afraid of, and he made his choices accordingly. Tali had then told Yonatan that the problem with Yoel was that there was nothing he really needed.

Elizabeth kissed him on the lips and moved away.

He sees a downpour, and horses galloping over grass and mud, and he sees Yoel and himself sitting on chairs at the William Hill betting shop near the Baker Street tube. The counter is strewn with crumpled papers, red pens and cigarette butts, and when the horses near the finish line Yoel and Yonatan stand up with their arms around each other and yell, and everyone stares, and when their horse wins— like Rock'n'roll Boy, at 12/1—they tumble out into the street, sweaty and wild-haired, dancing and singing and waving their ten-pound notes, united by wild, unrestrained joy.

He sees a small kiddie pool full of thick cement, which a giant spoon is stirring. Every so often, images flicker inside the cement. On a snowy boulevard, a young man puts his arms around a bearded man with a muddy face and they fall to the snow. He sees fields and green lawns under a blue sky, where he and Shira walk on the grass with happy faces. *I remember that dream*, he wanted to tell Elizabeth and Carlos; he'd dreamt it shortly after meeting Shira. He sees a boy standing in the street, surrounded by people talking to him as he strokes the plank of wood sticking out of his throat and his gray eyes scan the crowd with an amused look. He sees HaHalutz Street in the evening, with a gang of kids jumping on a brawny boy who looks like Michael but with purple hair, and himself wearing a surfer shirt, hanging on Michael's back hitting his head over and over again with a water gun. He sees a park, stone paths, trees, a utility pole, clumps of brownish-yellow dust swirling in the air, and people walk past him and Yoel as if they weren't there, and beyond the houses a ball of sun floats into the park and stops right above him, and the whole world turns golden and his eyes sting and he cannot see anything.

He saw rays of light around the bleached mountain tops in the distance. Elizabeth and Carlos were lolling on the floor, leaning against the wall and staring into space. They weren't talking. For the first time he noticed that the roof smelled of rotting plants. He moved closer to them and knew they would leave in a few minutes—when it wears off you say goodbye, that's the rule. He had an urge to tell them a memory he'd never shared with anyone or dared to write. The intensity of emotion it aroused in him had always frightened him, and he knew that if he waited one more minute, the influence of everything he'd swallowed and snorted tonight would dissipate and he wouldn't have the courage to do it.

He sat close to them, his knee touching Carlos's, and linked his fingers with Elizabeth's. He told them that his mother was lying dead in her hospital room, and he was in the hallway with his father, who had already said goodbye to her body. He stood motionless, and finally dared to cross the threshold into the room, but he stopped at the edge, far from the bed. His brother was sitting there next to his ex-wife, and a sheet covered his mother's body up to her smooth, peaceful-looking face. She was still wearing the blue headscarf. He said his brother's name in a trembling voice, unsure exactly what he wanted, perhaps to sit next to him. His brother looked up at the ceiling and whispered something to his ex. Yonatan turned and left the room and stood outside, leaned on the wall, and knew that no matter how many years passed, even if he wanted to one day in the future, he would never forgive Shaul. And that every time he saw him, that picture would flicker in his memory. Through his tears—while some people recited the dawn prayers in the oncology ward at 4:30 a.m., and Ratzon and Yaara and Avigail's father whispered with his dad, and his aunt stood talking to him though he could not hear a word she said, and his mother's friend knelt on the floor with her face to the wall—he dimly saw Yoel at the end of the corridor. He hurried toward him, unable to bear the time until he could be close to him, and only when he was right there and could sense his body heat did he imagine that he did have a family after all.

THE TOWERS
(LATE 1980S)

"The yellow fog," they called it in the neighborhood, and it blew in from the desert or the mountains, or from Ramallah. The grown-ups finally noticed that the world had fogged over, that you could no longer see the hues of things like cyclamen petals or za'atar bushes, that the cars were caked with yellow blotches as if they'd come down with the chicken pox and you couldn't tell them apart, and they reacted as they did to every new phenomenon in the neighborhood: they made rules, bargained over punishments, and warned the children not to run into the road and to only walk in groups.

Some locals had a different interpretation of the affliction. Morris Sadowsky pointed fingers at the parents who were making good money on the stock exchange thanks to his free advice, but who had forced his son out of the HaShomer HaTzair due to his "conspicuous extravagance"—they were being punished, he maintained, for their cruelty. Then there were the cryptic slogans that someone put up on the notice board at the shopping center: "The children of Gaza remember every-thing—ask your soldier-sons at anti-occupation demonstrations! Those loyal to pure force, the establishment—set the masks free, death has no secrets from us." They said it was the chess teacher, still disgruntled about being fired. The most severe warning issued by the parents was about the wadi, which was cloaked in an impenetrable yellow cloud: they were forbidden to go anywhere near it.

Yonatan often looked out on the wadi from his balcony, searching in vain for a figure to emerge. Finally he plucked up the courage to cross the dirt lot, drunk on the knowledge that he was violating the rules and had broken free. He felt as if he'd fallen into another world. A blinding yellow refracted all around him, undermining his certainty that his feet were on the ground, and he remembered how fresh the earth had felt under their boots earlier that winter. He lost his sense of direction and began to panic. His eyes stung so badly that he was afraid he would not be able to keep them open. Hearing a whisper, he suspected the wind was playing tricks on him until he realized it was his own voice and that he did not know how to get out—he might be devoured by the wadi and no one would find him.

He stood motionless, trying to steady his breath the way the chess teacher had taught them, and reconstructed his steps. He turned right, and when he was back on the dirt lot and the world looked a little clearer, he felt proud of having kept his cool. He had to tell Yoel about this, even if Yoel didn't believe him, even if they weren't talking. The estrangement between them could not thwart the picture that emerged in his mind—of running to Yoel's house to tell him—and which preceded any sequence of events and any awareness.

At school they were not allowed out at recess. They played soccer in the hallways, and he was disappointed every time the bell rang. Since getting well and coming back to school, his relationships with his classmates had improved, perhaps because he'd been gone for ten days and there were rumors that he'd almost died, or perhaps they pitied him because he hadn't known about Yoel's relationship with Tali.

Yoel and Tali didn't spend much time together at school. They did walk home together, and Yonatan was careful to avoid them. But he wished he could see more of this Yoel who wore pressed jeans, an oversized plaid sweater and a wool scarf draped around his neck, with his hair combed like Ran Horesh's. He looked familiar yet different, and Yonatan was afraid that if he didn't monitor the changes, he would no longer recognize Yoel. A few times he considered going over to tell them it was all right and he wasn't exactly mad anymore, but he turned and went home alone.

From the day he returned to school he was consumed by an unfamiliar lassitude, as if he were not completely awake, perhaps because his former enemies had turned out to be pretty ordinary kids, who saw neither Yoel nor him as rebels and didn't take much of an interest. Their momentous plans were no longer needed, and perhaps never had been. Kids got up in the morning, zipped their coats, walked to school, came home. Sometimes he still hoped that behind everyone's expressions lay a dark underworld, but it became evident that he had already reached his enemies' headquarters and broken down the door, only to find nothing there. Now he could read books without marking passages and borrowing the protagonists' adventures for their world in the wadi. It was leisurely reading, less exciting but more enjoyable. Sometimes he thought that for years he and Yoel had run a secret workshop, which existed in their imaginations—and had reached its zenith when they'd dug the trench—where they spent hours upon hours scheming and planning. Without Yoel, he was left with only stumps of unimaginative ideas. When he shared some of these thoughts with Hila, she said, "I've known you for two weeks: your imagination doesn't depend on Yoel, you just think it does. You'll understand that when you're less of an idiot."

He still went down to the dirt lot sometimes and looked out onto the wadi, but he didn't dare cross the border again. Standing there one day, he realized he was waiting to see Yoel and Tali together, and he felt embarrassed and started running home, when he caught sight of an indistinct outline in the yellow fog. He went closer and recognized

Shimon, and he thought he could make out Bentz and Tzivony sitting on trash cans behind him. Shimon stood facing him, arranged his shirt collar and smoothed out the creases in his coat, and said, "Now you look like a man." The yellow fog had messed up their plans, he explained: the girls from Yefeh Nof wouldn't come anywhere near the neighborhood, and they weren't allowed to go visit them because Tzivony was mixed up in some bad business over there. Shimon folded his black wool hat and smoothed away the tuft of hair that clung to his forehead. "We heard you were sick."

"A little," he answered.

"We were so bored without you, you wouldn't believe it!" Shimon said with a laugh.

"It really is boring as all hell here."

"We were so bored," Shimon said, "that we decided to make your wish come true. From the bottom of our hearts, as they say."

"What wish?"

"What wish…" Shimon turned and shouted back to his friends. "The kid wants to know what wish!" They didn't answer, perhaps they weren't even there. "Didn't you make a little wish at the park or something?"

"Yeah," he said, as if he'd forgotten, "but that was ages ago, I've lost interest."

"*I've-lost-interest,*" Shimon mimicked, swallowing his words. "Here we are, slaving away, and the boring-as-all-hell young man has lost interest."

"You didn't do anything. You haven't done anything for weeks," he said, no longer able to hide his frustration, "and now it's too late."

"Are you talking back or is that just my wild imagination?"

"How should I know, you figure it out."

Shimon was surprised by the defiance. "Is everything okay?" he asked.

"Everything's great," he replied. If he told Shimon everything, maybe he would pity him and call off the fight, but he couldn't appeal to Shimon's pity.

"Do you know tomorrow?" Shimon asked.

He braced for a slap, but to his surprise Shimon's cold fingers pinched his cheek, and not very hard.

"Answer me, I'm not kidding around anymore. Do you know tomorrow?"

"Yeah, I know it."

"Well then after tomorrow comes the day after tomorrow, Friday, and at two o'clock you and your friend will be at Rivka's kindergarten. The towers will be there too, and we're expecting you to massacre them. Don't show up the block."

"But we're not talking," he blurted in desperation, hoping Shimon would pity him.

"So now you have a reason to talk," Shimon replied, twisting his hair around his finger. "We worked hard, we went up to the towers in the middle of the fog, just to make your wish come true." He dug his fingers into Yonatan's flesh, and the pain came after a slight delay. "Do you want to let us down?"

"No." There really was no other answer.

"Friday at two."

"In this fog we won't see them from a foot away."

"Then be smart. Use it."

"I will, but you guys let Yoel know."

"I saw your friend yesterday," Shimon said, "he came out of his building, and I swear he was about to charge into the wadi. So I yelled at him, 'Hey, you're not allowed near there, you dork!' So he turned around and went home, like some robot, didn't even look at me. He's fucked up, that kid."

"Maybe it was someone else."

"Anyway, I told you about Friday, and you tell him," Shimon summed up.

"I'm not telling him anything." Nothing they did to him could make him talk to Yoel first.

Shimon scrutinized him, taken aback by the stubbornness. "Okay," he agreed. He seemed to have lost interest. "We're respectable people:

we like to deliver good news. But be there, otherwise you know how it ends."

"I know."

"How?"

"You'll kill us."

"Don't get carried away."

"You'll massacre us."

"You're such an annoying little kid."

"You'll fuck us over."

"Exactly, no big deal." Shimon let go of his cheek. "I always liked you more than your skinny friend. But Tzivony, you know him, he hates everyone."

After Yoel came over on Thursday evening and they shut the door to his room and didn't mention Tali except once, when Yoel remarked that she didn't know anything, they covered the floor with papers, notebooks, markers and rulers, searched the drawers for notes and maps, examined their old plans and recollected favorite adventure books. Everything looked the way it used to, but there was no trace of the all-encompassing frenzy that had characterized their meetings in the past.

Late at night, when they heard the evening news coming from the living room, they hatched the only possible plan, divided it into four stages, and memorized them. At ten, after Yoel's mother called and he had to leave, Yoel asked Yonatan if he was scared, and he admitted he was. Yoel said he wasn't, Yonatan hissed, "Liar," and they grinned and said goodbye without touching each other.

After they turned up first at Rivka's and waited to the left of the sandbox, next to the merry-go-round, and watched Shimon, Bentz and Tzivony jump the fence and stand in the middle of the sandbox with inscrutable expressions, the tower kids appeared and surrounded them in a sort of trapezoid. When the formation broke up, two of the kids marched forward. They were almost a head taller than Yonatan.

Shimon disqualified them, saying they were too big, and the tower kids threatened to leave. Shimon yelled that in their fucking dreams it would be big kids against little kids, and there was a silence while he looked over the tower kids and selected two: one was thin and around their height, the other had a narrow rectangular head perched on a solid body, and short, thick arms, which he swung up and down while rotating his head like a wrestler on TV.

After he pressed Yoel's cold hand, and Yoel whispered that everything would be okay but had a furious, piercing look in his eyes, and Yonatan wondered if he might really be more scared than Yoel was, Shimon stood up in the middle of the sandbox and yelled *ten-nine-eight* and looked at Bentz and Tzivony and up at the sky and kicked sand in the air. When he got to *three*, they turned and ran over to a couple of chairs they'd hidden behind the bushes, and no one moved as they climbed up and jumped over the fence and ran down the street, and when they got past their buildings he glanced back and saw lots of boys covered with yellow flecks charging after them, and it surprised him that he couldn't hear anything except the wind.

They burst into the wadi—which seemed to be quivering, with tall pillars of sand swirling in its depths—and they dropped to the ground, and in the blinding smog they held hands, counted ten steps, turned around, stood close together and waited for the first of the tower kids to cross the threshold so they could drag him into the trench and take care of him, and then do the same to the others. They heard shouts and whistles and voices taunting, cursing, threatening, and they all blended into a chorus of hoarse roars, and all at once there was silence. They listened to Shimon, who swore he would kill them and told them to come out: it wasn't too late to do the right thing and be real men.

After more time had passed and, to their surprise, no one had appeared, and he whispered to Yoel that maybe they'd left and Yoel whispered that it was a trap, they both felt dejected because they'd really believed that the tower kids would fight them in the wadi just like they'd planned. He said he would go check if they were lurking outside, and Yoel snapped at him and grabbed his hand, and he shook

Yoel off and moved toward the edge of the wadi and suddenly a hand reached out at him from the other side and he felt a sharp pain, as if a fingernail had pierced his arm like a needle. He leapt back and kicked at the air, heard wild laughter and Yoel calling his name over and over, and he turned around and took ten steps in a straight line but he couldn't find Yoel. He called Yoel's name and spun around in a small circle and reached out in every direction and yelled that he was there. He thought he could hear voices from the edge of the wadi, mimicking him: *I'm-here-I'm-here*. But perhaps it was only the echo of his own voice in the wind.

He headed toward the trench, still calling for Yoel with no answer, but he didn't get to the trench. In fact he had no idea where he was. He was thirsty, his eyes stung, he was disoriented, and suddenly the earth sloped and his right foot slipped down a muddy incline and something heavy collapsed on it or the mud tightened around it like a deadbolt, and he let out a wail and tried to pull his leg up but it wouldn't move. After a while he lost sensation in his leg. Exhausted, he stopped moving.

Flashes of murky grit swirled in front of him, stained with dark blotches that sharpened into something that looked like charred tree skeletons shifting in the smog. Far up above, perhaps in the sky, a yellow-black glare exploded into shards, like fireworks on Independence Day. Mesmerized, he watched them falling, melting, vanishing into the wasteland, and he realized that as one moved deeper into the wadi, the yellow fog grew darker.

He thought he could feel his strength coming back to him and he pulled his leg hard and fell backwards, like in that forest dream. He realized he had to get out of the wadi, fast, and he wanted to believe that Yoel was already out. He walked carefully until he ran into an unfamiliar mound of stones. He turned again, south this time, or at least he hoped it was south, until a flash of light blinded him and he thought he was near the top edge of the wadi.

After wiping his watering eyes with his coat sleeve, and seeing a clump of buildings in a glassy glimmer, he assumed he was standing on the dirt lot. To his surprise, there was no one there. He ran to Yoel's and pounded on the door, and his brother Noam opened up, holding a candy bar, and grunted, "Are you crazy? It's Friday."

Yonatan asked where Yoel was and prayed Noam would send him to Yoel's room, but Noam looked at him gravely and said he had no idea.

"Yoel's in the wadi!" he yelled.

Noam grabbed him by the shoulders and shook him: "Where is he? Where is he?"

"Out there, outside," he stammered, and he remembered shaking Yoel's arm off as he'd headed to the edge of the wadi, and he hoped Noam would punch him in the face, but Noam let go, disappeared for a minute, then walked past him with their father. He stayed where he was until he saw Yoel's mother with the phone against her ear—when had they bought a cordless phone?—and the door slammed in his face.

He ran down the steps, crossed the street, went up to his apartment, lay in bed fully clothed and pulled the covers up. When he heard honking and shouting, he went out to the balcony and saw that evening had fallen and the dirt lot was bathed in bright white light and there were people everywhere, and blue lights flickered, and flashlights beamed, and someone shouted into a megaphone, and dogs barked, and a chain of people with their arms linked walked into the wadi. His mother came out and hugged his shoulders and led him to his room, where she took off his coat and shoes and pants, lay him in bed and covered him. "Where's Yoel?" he shouted, and she stroked his hair and said, "They'll find him, it'll be okay, Dad's gone out to search too."

After his father came into his room late at night, took off his coat and said, "They found Yoel, everything's all right," he asked, "Where?" and his father said, "The point is that they found him." "But where?" he yelled, and his father answered, "He was hiding in a little pit," and his mother corrected him: "He was *lying* in a little pit." "He was in the trench!" he shouted, and his father said, "Maybe it was a trench. He was wet and covered with mud, but the trench protected him from the wind. He'll be okay, I'm telling you he's going to be okay." He yelled, "But where is Yoel now?" and his parents exchanged looks and his father said, "He's in the hospital for some minor tests, but he'll be fine. I promise you, he's going to be fine."

After all that, he lay in bed with his mother sitting next to him stroking his hair. His father brought him a cup of tea and a few cubes of chocolate, and he realized he was coughing and his throat burned. He touched his bumpy, raw cheeks and smelled hardened snot on them. His father said that kids got into mischief, and things happened, and it wasn't his fault. He said that Yoel's parents would understand, because kids did things, it wasn't anyone's fault. "Turn off the light," Yonatan yelled, and he lay in the dark. His mother touched his forehead and said something in English to his father, and his father said he might not understand this now, but tomorrow morning everything would seem less terrible: sometimes you just had to get through the night. He raised his upper body and leaned on his elbow, and asked them if tomorrow morning he and Yoel would still be friends. His father said he didn't know, he hoped so, the future was determined in the future, and sometimes you just had to get through the night.

IRELAND

He dreamed that his father died. People said the funeral was going ahead despite the rain, and asked if there would be a shelter set up—a lot of people would be coming to pay their respects to his father, after all. But when he arrived at his father's house he found him sitting in the living room, coughing and convulsing, his face white. Every time he peeked into the living room his father was still there, and the color slowly returned to his face and he stopped coughing and sat watching a tennis match on TV. He called Yonatan over to sit with him, and he looked worried. Yonatan ran his hand over his father's arm and felt elated: "It's a great day!" he exclaimed. He'd always been pleased when good things happened, but this kind of wild exuberance only came when a disaster he'd predicted did not materialize. But his exhilaration was cut short when he noticed his father's friends sitting on white plastic chairs, set out around the room for the shiva, and they all looked despondent.

"How will we explain this to people?" one friend said, touching mustard-colored scars on his forehead.

"People's hearts are breaking, people ran bereavement notices, people wrote remembrances on Facebook," said a redheaded man.

"And now we're supposed to say: sorry, the deceased is watching the French Open," another giggled.

Yonatan thought how odd it was that these people, who had always treated his father respectfully, sometimes excessively so, were now discussing him as if he were not there.

You can't turn back the wheel, they decided. His father was dead: arrangements had been made, a funeral announced, eulogizers chosen, and now the events in this house had to keep pace. Otherwise, when his father really did die, people would not look upon it kindly, they'd hold a grudge, and he'd pass from the world unnoticed. You can't die twice. "In the good old days, you could still die…" someone commented.

His father sprawled on the couch, head leaning back, staring at a reflection of the tennis match on the ceiling. The yellow ball bounced back and forth between his eyes.

Then Yonatan was on a busy street, and he knew his father was going to kill himself so that he'd be dead in time for the funeral. He rushed over, ignoring passersby who consoled him, and reached a similar but not identical house. Its windows were broken and there was a freezing gale swirling around it. There were crows perched on the landscape paintings that hung in the living room, the way they used to sit on the tree outside Yoel's bedroom window. He knew he had to find his father before it was too late, and he saw his father's friends sitting around the balcony table drinking vodka.

"Show us a picture of your lovely pregnant wife!" one of them called. "Your first kid—that's no joke!" They all raised their glasses and toasted his late father. When he yelled that his father wasn't dead, they looked at him sympathetically. Their eyes sparked as they started to rhyme at him: You're not a boy, soon you'll have a boy, no one here is a boy. They told him to act like a man in his mid-thirties: Alexander the Great had conquered the world and had time to die by his age.

He grabbed the vodka bottle, smashed its neck on the table, and blood dripped from his hand onto his shoes. Everyone scattered.

"Where is he?" he yelled, but no one answered. He went up to the redhead and brandished the broken glass against his neck, and he realized he was going to have to do it, though he was sickened by the thought of cutting through the folds in that freckled skin; he remembered that the redhead man had always stood next to him at memorials, and had bought copies of his books for everyone he knew. The redhead pointed, and Yonatan skipped down the steps and pushed open a heavy metal door that looked like the basement door in their old building. Inside, he found his father lying on an old mattress. His entire body, from head to toe, was wrapped in layers of cling film the way a fragile gift might be wrapped. His body was still.

He stood staring, unable to move, but after a while he saw his father's hands shift under the plastic wrap. His father rolled his eyes and a pallor spread over his face, and Yonatan screamed and cursed at him and started tearing off the plastic, but it was too tightly wrapped, so he picked up the broken bottle and slashed at the layers. He fell back, out of breath, and wiped the sweat from his face with his bleeding hand. His father sat up, shreds of bloodied plastic clinging to his face, glared at him furiously and said, "Enough! Are you out of your mind? The fifth set is starting soon."

He put his back against the thin mattress. His body felt ossified by the cold room. His throat burned: he obviously had a cold. He pulled the thin wool blanket up over his body. He spotted a strip of sky hidden behind the curtains, which had begun flapping, their hems lapping at the damp logs in the fireplace. Fragmentary scenes from his father's living room moved farther away from the well-lit station of his dream. Desperately trying to snatch several dream trails, he chased too many and most of them combusted right before his eyes. He wondered whether he'd been thrown into another dream, but he sensed a presence behind him. Rolling onto his side, he saw a silhouette sitting on his bed. He rubbed his eyes hard, closed and opened them, until he recognized Yoel, with a lit cigarette between his fingers, staring straight at him.

How long had he been sitting here? he wondered with horror. Yoel did not take his eyes off him, just sat holding the now-extinguished cigarette as if he hadn't noticed that Yonatan was awake. He must not have been looking at Yonatan at all.

He buried his face in the pillow, feeling weak. He was thirsty again. He often woke up at night with a dreadful thirst, and he'd begun keeping a water bottle next to his bed. The doctor said he had to understand that he wasn't a young man anymore, his body had different needs, and besides, the stress ahead of the birth of his first child might be having an effect.

He replayed their day: he and Yoel had driven through western Ireland to County Clare, in a rented black BMW, listening to the same songs over and over again. The roads were narrow and winding, and the landscape—little villages, smoking chimneys, wooden fences, grassy meadows, sheep and cows—had a monotonous, replicating beauty. They marveled at something one moment, and the next moment saw its slightly less or slightly more beautiful double.

They started driving at 6 a.m. and did not stop even once, and for the first time since Shira had reached the thirtieth week of her pregnancy, he didn't call or text twice a day to ask how she was feeling. If their momentum were to slow and the music to go quiet, it seemed, the masks he and Yoel wore, which enabled them to take this trip and pose as the friends they used to be—would fall away. In the afternoon it became overcast, but a channel of blue sky still shone bright along the road they were on, which lifted Yonatan's spirits. "Look at the channel—isn't it strange?" he said, and Yoel murmured, "Yes, but it's closing up, can't you see?"

He couldn't. He stared at Yoel's hands on the wheel, marred by two deep, dry wounds, purplish gashes with a white coating. As they drove on, the gray clouds floated toward the channel, the light became murkier, the trees and wooden houses became so washed-out that one could not swear they were there. Finally the clouds swallowed up the channel of blue sky, and for the first time that day, juicy drops of rain fell like little leaves, the road was flooded with puddles, and they couldn't see a thing through the windshield. But Yoel did not slow down, enjoying the jets sprayed by the wheels, and drove recklessly through craters full of water.

He insisted on taking over the wheel: Shira would never forgive him, he told Yoel, if he died before their first child was born.

"They, too, shall learn to forgive," Yoel replied dismissively. There were creases of a smile on his forehead, below his receding hairline. Yoel said the visibility was low and they wouldn't be able to see the cliffs overlooking the sea, and Yonatan said there was no way to tell: it might brighten up. Yoel had always dreamed of seeing those cliffs, since back when he and Michael had planned to conduct some sort of Uranium Club ritual on them. When he and Yonatan had lived in London after the army, they'd planned to take the train to Ireland but something had come up, he couldn't remember what, and Yoel had gone back to Israel; maybe he'd invented a job offer or a lover.

The whole London episode was a failure they both acknowledged, and perhaps that was why they hadn't traveled together for so long. They'd dropped out of the English course at Paddington a minute before the millennium celebrations; hung around SoHo for nights on end, after playing blackjack at a casino and betting on the horses; and bought fake ecstasy twice. Most of the time, though, they were lonely and didn't meet anyone new. Even when Yaara's sister Avigail happened to be in town and slept over in their flat for a few days, things did not improve. They prattled about sex and got drunk every night, but nothing interesting happened.

Yonatan had hardly seen the sisters since his mother's death. In fact, all his parents' friends and their kids had disappeared from his life within two years of his mother dying. At first they still asked him and his father over sometimes, but it always felt forced. For some time after he joined the army, he kept coming to these meetings for his father's sake, until he realized his father was also unenthusiastic—and that perhaps he was doing it for Yonatan, so as not to interrupt the continuity of life. But it was his mother who had nurtured all those relationships, and it was her whom the friends had loved. After a while their meetings dwindled down to once a year: when they visited her grave for the memorial service.

At some point in their late twenties, Yonatan began to understand that Yoel didn't really know how to read people. He didn't pick up on hidden cues, perhaps because, contrary to what he professed and in fact believed, people did not really interest him. He knew how to probe their intentions and motives, he showed an interest in their stories and enjoyed the way human and political games were played out, but he was not capable of imagining—to the extent that anyone can—the way someone else might see the world, and he did not have the capacity to commiserate with them. This was the deceptive space in Yoel, and even Yonatan, who supposedly knew him better than anyone else, had taken years to decipher it and still doubted his own conclusions, especially since Yoel's charm was so crushing and he was so generous and affectionate, lacking any pettiness or jealousy.

Had he asked any of their acquaintances, most would have answered that they found Yoel easier to talk to than him. But Yoel packed whatever people told him into a tyrannical machine that embodied his worldview. If he met a married woman who was raising two kids and claimed to be satisfied with her life, he would describe her boring weekends with the annoying in-laws in the suburbs and point out how lucky he was to have free and flexible relationships instead of being trapped in that kind of marriage, because he did not really see her as a whole human being who was not merely designed to reflect his own choices.

Only rarely did he conclude that he'd wronged someone. After he went back to live with his parents in Beit HaKerem, he kept asking Yonatan if he'd felt supported by Yoel after his mother's death. Yonatan answered begrudgingly that those days were hazy in his mind, but that in every flash of memory he saw Tali and Lior and Yoel, which must mean that yes, Yoel had stood by him. Still, Yoel expressed remorse, intimating an intense dislike of the person he used to be. But his interest in that era wasn't really related to Yonatan's mother's death, but to the reckoning he claimed he was conducting.

Yoel lit another cigarette, and even though the thick smoke in the car was already making Yonatan nauseous, he did not complain. The sky grew even darker and no cliffs were visible on the horizon, which in any case was veiled behind dark clouds. Yonatan said it was time to stop for an early dinner, and Yoel nodded, but every time they approached a restaurant or a pub, Yoel went into great detail about how pathetic it was and wearily suggested driving on to find somewhere better. They were both hungry and Yonatan lost his patience: Yoel's tirades were exhausting and he felt as if they were driving around in circles.

They finally sat down in an ugly, drafty pub where they were served dried-out roast beef. They didn't touch the food. They walked out and stood under a shelter with balloons tied to it, and drank beer and smoked cigarettes until they felt nauseous. Just as they were about to leave, a red Range Rover pulled up and a group of kids in shiny jackets tumbled out. They coalesced into a bundle and made their way into the pub, constantly touching each other, pinching and hugging, mussing each other's hair, laughing. The air felt close and steamy as Yonatan and Yoel watched the kids. When they were gone, they crushed out their cigarettes and walked to the car.

They drove on in silence until it was time to find somewhere to spend the night near the cliffs, which they imagined they would catch sight of on the horizon, swaddled in thick gray clouds. But Yoel rejected every hotel they passed: one was a miserable barn run by drunk Irishmen, the other was as poorly lit as a kibbutz lodge, yet another reminded him of the army where he'd done his basic training. There was no reason to compromise, he insisted: they weren't in a hurry. Yonatan was tired, but he reminded himself that the purpose of this trip was to reinstate Yoel in the world he'd known before he quit his job and cut off ties with his friends and lay in bed in his Tel Aviv apartment until his mother, who went every day from Jerusalem to spend the night with him, convinced him to move back to Beit HaKerem.

When Yonatan was no longer able to restrain his anger, he remarked that all the places looked the same, they were all crappy little hotels. Yoel, as if he hadn't heard him, enumerated the drawbacks of yet another hotel they were approaching: the rooms were probably freezing and full of spiders, there was no hot water, it was like some impoverished Russian nobleman's dacha. His diatribes showed the occasional glimmer of his old volubility. Yonatan usually delighted in Yoel's rants, but he couldn't help feeling that Yoel was caught in an insatiable, feverish whirlwind, and that his seemingly coherent words were simply being tossed into the world like a net, catching whatever they may. Perhaps it was his own fault: he'd danced around Yoel all day, enticing him to talk the way he used to, and he'd got what he asked for, only to find that it made everything worse.

The brakes screeched as he pulled up outside a cluster of huts connected by gravel paths with droopy weeds on either side. Unlike everyone else who'd been with Yoel since he moved back home, Yonatan felt he had to resist Yoel's capricious desires and impose some limitations. In fact, this might be what everyone was expecting of him: to finally put an end to it all. "This is where we're staying," he declared.

"Look how pathetic those bored farmers are, with their fat red cheeks," Yoel said. "Even the darkness doesn't want to come down here. Let's just go to the next hotel."

"There's nowhere else out there, calm down!" Yonatan shouted.

"But you don't always have to give up, we can find somewhere better," Yoel shot back.

"How do you know?"

"It's obvious. You don't always have to compromise."

Now Yonatan was really angry, because he suspected that Yoel's last words were directed at something much larger. "We're sleeping in this fucking hotel," he spat, and got out of the car and slammed the door.

He sat up in bed and leaned against the wooden beams. Cool air flowed in between them and chilled the back of his neck. Even though he tried not to look at Yoel, he kept seeing him out of the corner of his eye, and he could not tolerate the thought of Yoel staring at him in the dark.

"Turn the light on," he said.

"I can't, the power's out," Yoel said.

He waited for the gloating, now that Yoel's opinion of the hotel had been confirmed, but there was none.

"How long have you been up?"

"I don't know."

"Did you even sleep at all?"

"I haven't slept in ages," Yoel said, and his voice sounded alien. He seemed annoyed by Yonatan's feigned ignorance. Yoel's mother had told him that sometimes Yoel lay in bed in the dark, from morning till evening, for seven or nine hours, staring at the ceiling. She asked Yonatan what her son was seeing up there, and the question had haunted him. He heard it rustle in the music he listened to, and in the wind's whispers, and blowing through words people said to him. Sometimes it simply screamed in his mind, especially on nights when he lay next to Shira and panicked that he himself was looking at the ceiling too much, and that, by asking the question, Yoel's mother had activated a virus that had always been in both of them, waiting to be set free.

A tremor crawled through his legs and up to his groin, and he struggled to describe the sensation: perhaps fear. Not of Yoel, of course, but perhaps of the burden he'd taken on. He regretted suggesting this trip. Yoel hadn't wanted to go anyway, he couldn't care less about the cliffs. (*"Wa'aish ana wa'ihom,"* he'd said with a laugh, and Yonatan had been surprised that Yoel remembered the Arabic line he'd given a character in his first book: "Doesn't matter where we go, my head is always in the same place.") But Yoel's family had seized on the idea, and Tali had also joined the lobbying effort. Even Shira had said that if he wanted to go to Ireland to save Yoel, this was his chance, before their baby was born and everything changed. The plan took on outsized proportions, as if people close to Yoel were already dividing time into 'before the trip' and 'after the trip'. Yonatan found the level of anticipation alarming, and secretly hoped Yoel would stick to his refusal. Whenever the two of them were alone, he mentioned other places they could go to, perhaps as a way to dissolve the whole notion: India, Brazil, the Virgin Islands—it was a big world out there.

A few weeks went by, and he invited Yoel to visit them in Tel Aviv on Purim. To his astonishment, Yoel turned up at their apartment wearing gray pressed trousers and a light blue button-down shirt, one of many identical ones which hung in his closet, or so his friends liked to tease him. He'd shaved, and his smooth face gave him a youthful look even though it had filled out. He'd combed his gray curls, replicating his old hairdo from law school days. He had a potbelly, probably because of the pills he took but never talked about. But he was obviously pleased with the way he looked, and when Shira complimented him, he impersonated a 1980s news anchor and exclaimed: "Still in the game! Don't claim I'm not, good people!" Then he let Shira make him up as a vampire from *Buffy*, which they used to watch in high school, and they went to a party: two vampires and one Cordelia.

At the party, Yoel stood with his back against the wall. He wore a blank expression. When someone he knew asked where he'd disappeared, or what he thought about the latest political developments, he smiled warmly—a faded replica of his old grin, which vanished as soon as the acquaintance walked away after waiting in vain for Yoel to entertain him or take an interest in him. Most of the time, Yoel and Yonatan stood by the wall without talking, as if nothing required comment, and sometimes they watched Shira dance with her friends. Determined to salvage the evening, Yonatan insisted that he and Yoel go back to his place, where he poured them some whiskey and snorted a few lines of coke left over from his birthday.

Yoel watched him. "Will it help if I do a line?" he asked.

"You're not supposed to."

"I know I'm not," Yoel grunted. He rolled up a bill and snorted one line. "I can't believe I waited till I was a wreck to do coke for the first time ever. What an ass."

Yonatan's mood was improving, and he put on some songs they

liked, and shouted out the lyrics. Yoel soon joined in and they drank almost the whole bottle and chain-smoked on the balcony—they were no longer allowed to smoke in the apartment—and when Shira came home they teased her for not being able to drink because of the pregnancy. Yonatan had never asked about that, and they had an unspoken agreement not to discuss it in his presence. They were both sweating and had taken off their shirts and were waving them around, singing. At 1 a.m. a neighbor knocked on the door to complain.

When he made the couch for Yoel to sleep on, Yoel said, "So, should we go? What do you say?"

"Of course we're going!" Yonatan replied. They hugged, and Yoel's skin felt warm.

"Let's get dressed and head to the cliffs. It's an hour's drive, right?" He tried to give his voice a note of positivity, even anticipation.

"I don't know, look at the map." Yoel's response had a crudeness that surprised him, because Yoel was one of the politest people he knew. Even after he moved back home, when he had visitors he didn't want to see, he still treated them kindly.

"Let's go, we'll figure it out," Yonatan said, "we can skip the breakfast at this place."

Yoel didn't laugh. "It's too early to leave," he said, seeming to take pleasure in Yonatan's distress.

Yonatan looked at the sky behind the curtains and prayed dawn was rising.

"It's four-thirty in the morning," Yoel whispered.

Yonatan felt suddenly bleak, and had no idea how they would spend the remaining hours until morning. He was about to suggest they go back to sleep, but realized how stupid and even cruel that would sound. They couldn't kill time in the shower because the water was freezing. Yoel was right: this hotel was a nightmare, and there was nowhere to go. As he contemplated a series of ways to get out of the room, something dawned on him. It was a fear they shared: that they would be trapped, with nowhere to escape to, and no amount of creative maneuvering would save them. In the past few years he'd come to understand that Yoel feared this more than he did, that he never set a clear course because he always coveted another space with another escape route—possibilities he found more alluring than his own life, in which everything seemed replaceable. Yoel naively believed that he could live his life without ever committing to anything, and that those close to him, even girlfriends, would accept it because otherwise they would lose him, and he knew that they did not want to lose him.

"Are you writing anything now?" Yoel asked.

"More or less, it's not entirely clear yet." That was the answer he gave people he didn't want to reveal anything to, mostly writerly types who were not on his side.

"Are there going to be things from our world in it? Good stuff, I hope."

"There's always a little, right? You know better than I do."

"It'll be the last book before you're a dad, and then you'll start writing about being tired and having quickies with the nanny," Yoel scoffed.

"Sounds pretty good," he replied.

"This thing where you have that world to live in," Yoel said, lighting a cigarette, "you said you'd go crazy without it?"

It wasn't really a question. "You know that's what I feel."

"Turning a demon into a story, you say. So you really believe in it, in that world, when you're writing?"

"Its totality draws me in, that's the thing, so it doesn't matter if I believe or not."

"So write about me after I die, and then I won't be completely dead for you."

"You're not going to die!" He moved closer to Yoel to add a sternness to his words. "Don't even bullshit about that."

"Maybe not." Yoel giggled dryly and spat into the ashtray. "We're just blabbering."

"Don't even blabber about it," he said. "Don't ever talk about it."

"But I really crashed, eh? So hard."

"You'll be back, that's obvious."

"Yeah, yeah," Yoel muttered, "what a drip you've turned into. Write about the tower kids, then. You only mentioned them a little."

"You're right, it wasn't enough. Those fuckers."

"Maybe they weren't that bad. We sucked them into our world, for the totality." Yoel sounded somewhat scornful.

"They did plenty to you in the wadi."

"Maybe they didn't do that much really."

"It was a lot."

"Never mind," Yoel said dismissively. "Actually, that was always what you liked to do. Writing, you say. Remember how when I was doing my clerkship you used to make fun of me for being an old man, with all those button-down shirts and the briefcase and the black shoes?"

"You didn't have to dress like an asshole lawyer," Yonatan teased.

"That's true. I was trying too hard. But you didn't do that. I used to look at you sometimes in the evenings and I couldn't figure out where you'd actually been all day. I was impressed."

"Only because you didn't understand." Yonatan knew that in their twenties Yoel had idealized his life, perceiving it as lawless and unscheduled, free of unfulfilled passions and capricious bosses. Mostly, Yoel had aggrandized the act of writing, transporting one's demons, dreams and memories to a different world.

"Sometimes it just wears you down," Yonatan said. "You start a book with a lot of hopes and ideas, but then it all narrows down and you only deliver on a few of them, and halfway through the book it stops being interesting and you get tempted by a million more exciting ideas, but you have to finish it. Maybe it's like a regular job."

"So in the end we were both a parody of grown-ups, you're saying," Yoel summed up.

"Were?"

"Yes. Were."

Neither of them said anything. Yonatan looked out the window, but not even a strip of dawn was visible. He got off the bed, walked to the bathroom in the dark, and splashed cold water on his face until he lost the feeling in his fingers. He was in a better mood and his body felt supple again. "We're getting out of here," he announced.

"Now?"

"Yes, right now." He used the flashlight on his phone to find the clothes strewn on the floor, packed both their bags and dragged them to the door. "Wash your face and let's get the hell out. We'll get to the cliffs by morning." He turned his back on Yoel and stood next to the bags, facing the door as if to clarify that there was no point discussing it any further. He was pleased when he heard Yoel's footsteps on the wooden floor, though he didn't hear the water running.

The cold air buffeted them as they trudged through the mud. He bowed his head to protect his face from the wind, but Yoel faced it brazenly, and held out his hand when they got to the car. Yonatan unwillingly handed him the car keys. They sat down on the leather seats and the engine thundered to a start. "Wake up, fat farmers!" Yoel cheered, and fiddled with the heating vents. Yonatan pushed his hand away and aimed the vents at himself, and they slapped each other's hands and he put his arm around Yoel's neck and strangled him, and Yoel laughed and pinched his stomach. The car started to warm up, and he felt as if his whole body was being caressed. With a cry of joy they remembered the two little whiskey bottles they'd left in the glove compartment. They drank and lit cigarettes and purred with pleasure, and Yoel turned on the radio and sped out of the parking lot.

"Do you know the way?" Yonatan asked.

"Pretty much. Fasten your seatbelt, it's dangerous here at night," Yoel whispered.

The sky was still dark, but on their left two clouds slumped over the hills, strewn with gray spots of dawn. The headlamps lit up the narrow road and he saw no cars, people, animals or houses, as if it were just the two of them left in all of County Clare. Something disquieting began to form inside him. Yoel, unbothered, put a CD in the player. It took him a few notes to recognize the song. "Where did you come up with that one?" he asked Yoel.

"Don't you like it?" Yoel asked.

"You know Dire Straits suck."

"So you're not a fan of 'Romeo and Juliet?'"

"I already told you, not really."

"Because I remember a young man, or rather a slightly chubby adolescent, let's say a high school senior, who listened to this song all the time!"

"I never listened to it even once. Maybe it was that fucking American neighbor," he said.

"Oh, the tormented teenager listened to it constantly," Yoel waxed poetic, "and so loudly that Tali and I learned all the words by heart from my room across the street."

"I never listened to it that much!" he argued, trying to stifle his laughter. It touched him that Yoel had burned the song and carefully laid the trap, waiting for the right moment. It was the kind of trick they used to play on each other.

Yoel pressed down on the gas pedal and took his hands off the wheel. "Admit that you listened to it constantly."

"When exactly?"

"Senior year, after Lior dumped you."

"I didn't."

"Like hell you didn't."

"I didn't listen to it!" he shouted. "Put your hands back!"

Yoel kept his hands in the air, and Yonatan realized this was not a game anymore. He reached for the wheel but pulled back at the last minute, fearing it would anger Yoel and he'd lose control of the car. Ominously dark clouds veiled the horizon. There'd been signs of dawn—or perhaps he'd just imagined them—but darkness now prevailed again. Was that possible?

"Admit that you listened to it?"

He heard Yoel's voice dimly, and then something screeched. Yonatan realized he had to say yes but he couldn't do it: not because of the song, or even because he'd always played the role of the reckless one who was the last to surrender. Perhaps he wanted to test Yoel, to bring everything to a head, to find out if he could still predict the behavior of this man sitting next to him.

The car veered sluggishly to the right, and he wondered if the wheels were misaligned or the road was crooked. He had trouble being fully present in the severity of the moment.

"Admit it," Yoel said in a raspy voice. Despite the car swerving, his hands were still off the wheel.

Yonatan hoped he'd heard a trace of fear. He watched the car slide onto a dirt path leading into a field. He'd seen large green shapes there before, trees or bushes, and he prayed the field wasn't fenced. Then he had an image of Shira lying awake in their bed. "I admit it!" he yelled.

Yoel let out a deep breath, grabbed the wheel and swung it wildly, but the car was already rolling down a dirt slope and he couldn't get it back onto the road. Yonatan heard muffled crunches, as if the under-carriage was grating against branches or bushes. "Stop!" he shouted and put his hand on the wheel in between Yoel's.

Yoel braked, the car rocked and bounced over a few stones, its nose dipped forward, and then they stopped with a thud. He remembered the muddy sheep they'd seen yesterday and the sheepdogs circling them, and imagined in the dark that he could see the yellow sparkling eyes of foxes. He hoped there was no creature bleeding under the car, because then he would do something to Yoel, he wouldn't be able to hold back.

He put both his hands on his sweaty chest and heard rhythmic panting, like he did when he ran, but he wasn't sure if it was coming from Yoel or from his own body. There was a cough or a burst of laughter, and he smelled grass and shit and sweat, and through the window he saw an orange flash—a flashlight beam or a flame—and imagined it was sheltered by a tiled roof. "I told you I didn't want to go away," Yoel said. When Yonatan looked to the right, he saw Yoel slumped forward with his chin on the wheel.

Yonatan had to tamp down a smile: maybe there was something amusing about the whole story—all those years—pooling into this stupid black field. He stared at the heating vent and his memory galloped through a horde of pictures, and suddenly he was filled with wonder: how, over all the years, despite all the clues, some of which Yoel must have left intentionally, had he never been suspicious, even for a second? The whole story about how Yoel had wandered around the wadi in his Sabbath clothes and run into the tower kids, maybe ten of them, and they'd knocked him down and rolled him in the mud and over stones and over thistles—it had never happened.

JERUSALEM

They walked down a manicured path paved with mauve stones—"The architect was Dutch, they say," Yoel remarked—lined by cypress and ash trees that cast striped shadows on the path and made it look like a railroad. The trees were interspersed with shrubs whose green leaves—their edges curled into pouty lips with a gap between them like a fish's mouth—turned golden when the sun broke through the gray clouds. The only sounds were a deep and familiar hum, the distant chirping of birds, and the crunch of leaves beneath their shoes. Swathes of grass on either side of the path were surrounded by bare earth dotted with weeds and stones, and between them, gray asphalt paths branched off under the occasional lamppost and purple-leaved plum tree that swayed in the barely perceptible breeze. He had never seen that variety in the neighborhood before. Yoel said if they turned left they'd be able to see some other monuments.

He'd cut his hair short, in a style reminiscent of their army days, with a little curled crest at the top. He had thick, black stubble on his cheeks, grayer around the chin and neck. The wounds and scabs on the back of his hands were gone, his nails were long and black. The whites of his eyes gleamed, gone was the redness, and his gaze was clearer, no longer darting back and forth or staring aimlessly. Or perhaps this was just Yonatan's wishful thinking; every time he visited he looked for signs of improvement, and, if there were none, he faked them.

Yonatan asked which monuments they could see.

"Like a memorial to a guy they say came up with the name 'Beit HaKerem.' Apparently he was proud that it wasn't built on the ruins of an Arab village."

"Impressive accomplishment," Yonatan observed.

"Turns out his granddaughter lives on our street," Yoel added. "Yoga teacher. She got cancer when she was forty-five and she teaches yoga—ironic, I guess. There are lots of them here, like Tzivony's dad. Ratzon's wife, too."

He knew this, his father had told him, and every time he visited Yoel he meant to go see Ratzon but he always put it off, lacking the courage to walk through the new gate to No. 7.

"They say it's because of the factory," Yoel continued. "A while ago there were lawyers here talking to people, and when I asked them if I could sue, they said: Sir, there is no correlation in the professional literature between your case and factory pollution."

"People have no imagination," he replied. For a moment he wondered if Yoel was insinuating something about his mother, if she'd even occurred to him, but he decided he wasn't.

"So left or right? Or we could go home—Mom made meatballs."

"We're not going back now." *And you are the guy who'll decide where to go.* He couldn't immediately peg the source of the line, which he did not say out loud, but then he remembered: a Dr. Seuss book he sometimes read to Itamar.

Yoel's last words nagged at him. They implied a resignation—no longer uttered with sorrow or shame, but with cheerful appetite—to his status: a grown man living at home, discussing his mother's cooking.

Sometimes he was racked with guilt for not insisting on drawing out Yoel's fears, for not trying to ease his pain on the rare occasions when he saw it, like when Yoel was in law school and got into a funk and began doubting himself, or when he was mourning a girlfriend who left him after they'd twice agreed to move in together but Yoel had got cold feet at the last minute. He used to call Yonatan at night and they'd talk until morning, and Yoel spoke softly, desolately, sometimes saying nothing at all, and he always sounded as if he'd just woken up. Every time Yoel seemed upbeat and vibrant again, they both acted as if nothing had happened.

That was always one of Yonatan's weaknesses: the pain, the failures, the fears and the helplessness of the few people he loved frightened him so much that he could not really help them, and so, perversely, he gave more help to those people who were less close to him when they were in need. He had failed to see this until Shira once told him about things she'd dreamed of doing and had given up on. As she spoke, he felt fingernails digging at his body, shoving their way into his chest, and he turned stone cold; his vision blurred and the room seemed to crumple, as if he were looking at the world through a funhouse mirror. He longed to make Shira's feeling go away at any cost, so he flooded her with suggestions and solutions, and when she rejected them he lost his temper. So he guarded himself against Yoel's fears, and, just like everyone else, he watched the Yoel Show from a distance, even as he belittled the other devoted viewers and imagined himself standing in the wings or onstage.

"Whatever you say," Yoel said.

Without knowing why, Yonatan insisted that they walk straight ahead, and once again, as he had done every day the past month, he reconstructed their last meeting. They'd arranged to look at an apartment in Tel Aviv, after Yoel had agreed to a new round of Yonatan's pleas that he move back to the city. In the elevator, Yoel gave the buttons a penetrating look and said, "If there was a button that would make me dead, I'd press it now." A picture flashed in Yonatan's mind: if Yoel reached for the buttons, he would grab his hand.

He knocked softly on the door, his legs still shaking, and hoped no one would hear him, but the landlady was already asking them in. Yoel walked past him, stood in the middle of the living room and exclaimed, "Such light! It bathes your soul." He walked around the rooms with the landlady and her sister, chatting about his job as a senior consultant in a non-profit that supported joint projects between Israeli and Asian companies, and how they had to flatter Israeli ministers and American donors while they mimed throat-slashing behind their backs. Would they like to hear his theory? The leftist elite, he believed, had been stripped of its political power in the past two decades and had essentially given up its power over the operational arms—state, government, ministries—and instead entrenched itself in the legal system and established a network of non-profits as its new sphere of power. Yoel effortlessly tied his stories to current events, and mentioned that he'd come to see the apartment on his lunch break.

When they returned to the living room, the landlady made Yoel an espresso, sat him down next to her, and told him about her artist daughter—to whom this apartment actually belonged—who made video art that featured radical confessions in sex clubs and was very political, though it was misunderstood in Israel, but maybe abroad they would appreciate it. Yoel immediately offered to "connect her with some EU people," and there was not a hint of impatience in his voice.

Then she showed him her daughter's Facebook friends so that he could meet one of them, and when he mentioned he was going through a rough spot, she put her hand on his shoulder and told him about an illness she'd had, and he listened with narrowed eyes and said, "I hear you," as if her words were making him see things in a new light.

All this time, Yonatan watched them without a word. He focused on the veins on the back of his hand, which stood out in a sickly shade of olive green, with new blemishes and little wrinkles. The texture of his skin looked uneven, and he was frightened to see that his fingers looked shorter than he remembered; his hands used to be something people complimented. He thought about his recent blood tests, which he'd been afraid to look at after he'd told his doctor there was something wrong and expected her to say the blood count was fine this time, but she didn't. He felt like vomiting, then shitting. The glare of blinding light from the porch was nauseating, scratching at his body, and the walls were boiling hot. He looked at Yoel, who sat next to the landlady as they ranked the women's pictures and posts and analyzed their compatibility with him. He knew he could no longer block out the certainty that spending time with Yoel was destabilizing for him. It was as if an invisible breeze emanated from Yoel's body and infiltrated his own.

They walked past apricot-colored iron benches that smelled of fresh paint. To their right, roughly where they'd dug the trench, with the military factory's pair of chimneys in the background, there were now brightly colored slides and swings. They lit cigarettes and blew smoke rings. A man pushing a stroller glared at them, then a thin girl with short brown hair and white earbuds hurried by, probably on her way to their old school. An older man in a blue shirt sat down on the bench behind them. His face was shiny and his white hair neatly combed— probably a doctor or journalist or lawyer, one of the 1980s parents commonly seen on the streets of Beit HaKerem—and he watched the young man with the stroller intently and wrung his hands.

"I'm going to Mexico," Yonatan said.

"When?"

Yoel did not seem especially interested—not that it mattered. After all, Yonatan hadn't visited him even once in the past month, and they rarely corresponded. Weeks could go by before Yoel read his messages.

"In two weeks. End of May."

"Mexico. Sounds good," Yoel said and stretched his arms. The short, wrinkled shirt, with nicotine and saliva stains on its collar, tightened over his belly, which had sprouted a bulge since their last meeting. "Festivals, parties, all that stuff."

"I don't have the schedule yet."

"Childhood memories sell books, and there are a lot of them in this one, aren't there?"

"More than usual. Didn't you say you thought they were missing in the last one?" Yonatan smiled, because Yoel's sister Rachel had told him that Yoel had started the book several times but hadn't been able to finish it: further evidence of his decline.

"I just said that for no reason." Yoel gazed at the slides as if he couldn't be bothered to look at Yonatan.

The path sloped upwards and they huffed as they climbed up to a bridge with red iron railings and gray panels on either side. Cars zoomed up and down a new multi-lane highway built far below the paths and trees.

They walked down a narrow staircase and stood on a newly paved road, the tar not yet completely hardened, blinking at the sunlight. They'd never reached this spot in the center of the wadi's upper border before, because it had abutted a wilderness of tall weeds, rocks and thistles. Yonatan remembered a fence, too, but Yoel said there hadn't been one.

They looked at the neighborhood spread out before them in a single perfect arc. In its center was the tall building above the shopping center, around it a ring of two-story houses amid clumps of green trees and other buildings whose rough stone was turning a grimy shade of yellow, and lots of red tiled roofs. The old towers melted into the background from this vantage point, dwarfed by far taller buildings. To their left, at one end of the arc, sat a group of terraced houses that formed the new neighborhood, a sort of extension of the original Beit HaKerem. It started at the thistle field, where nothing ever bloomed, and the smooth, white brick facade of these new buildings marked a clear border between the old and new neighborhoods. He looked for a trace of the wadi's yellow-brown soil, but found none. He could not identify even the most general outline of the place he used to know, and even the topography seemed altered. The distance from their house to the Music Academy was much shorter, the incline gentler, as if the wadi had been compressed like an old car in a scrap metal shredder. He could almost believe they were walking through a miniaturized model of the old wadi, and that deep beneath the ground they'd known all those years ago was now a bustling network of highways crisscrossing the town.

The sky was clear, but it was a light blue specked with gray, rather than the familiar summer glare. When they stopped outside a small cafeteria on the ground floor of the Music Academy, he realized he'd never been this close to the building.

"It's kind of a funny idea, writing about your past and presenting it at some festival on the other side of the world, isn't it?" Yoel observed.

Yonatan suspected he'd been holding onto the thread of their conversation exactly where it had left off, waiting to ask the question on the tip of his tongue. He considered changing the topic, but assumed Yoel would not let it go. "It is strange sometimes," he replied elusively. When Yoel had visited them last summer, the first and last time he'd seen Itamar, he'd hinted at something to do with Yonatan's writing that Yonatan had not completely understood. "All these festivals are getting too commercialized," he added, aware of how trivial he sounded, perhaps hoping to divert the discussion onto a take-down of the capitalist era and smother it with boredom.

"Commercialized," Yoel scoffed, and put his hand up to shelter his eyes from the sun. "You think I care about that? We're not twenty anymore, I've spent my whole life commercializing things that influence real people's lives. Literature is just like any other merchandise—I figured that out a long time ago."

"Well, you sounded a little naive before," Yonatan insisted. "At the end of the day, writers do the same thing everyone else does, except with various degrees of hypocrisy and whining. There's no choice, that's the world."

"Naive?" Yoel lowered his hand and looked at Yonatan and, essentially, into the sun. "You're the naive one. Do you really believe you can probe this world with a few plotlines, a few characters—that you've touched even a speck of what existed here?"

He said nothing, feeling a sort of dulled surprise. Yoel's tone was tinged with the mockery the two of them had always been accused of shooting at everyone else, but some part of him had probably been preparing for the moment when it would be turned against him. "Yes, I do believe that," he said finally, "otherwise I wouldn't write."

"Well, I'm telling you it's impossible. The only thing you can do is wrap it up, package it: kill it. And serve up a few stories with a dash of ruminations. You're not penetrating the core of anything, you're not resurrecting anything."

"Are you telling me you *can* resurrect something?" Yonatan blurted, ashamed of his irritable tone. He should know how to brush off insults like lint off a coat; Yoel always told him that.

"When I'm not crazed," Yoel said. "Or maybe when I'm there, I'm not crazed—you pick. And I know you can't really touch it unless you totally surrender, and not even then, actually. But that's the difference between us: you're already outside and you have a wife and a child."

Yonatan did not reply. Everything he'd said in the past hour had slid off Yoel, who was already somewhere else.

Yoel put his hands on the bridge's railing and kept twisting his fingers around it, leaning his whole body over. Yonatan considered pulling him back and standing in between him and the railing. How could he have become accustomed to having those thoughts?

"Maybe I'm the keeper of the seals, or whatever you call it," Yoel said with a snort, "at least as long as I'm still around, which isn't much longer. I've already told you, all of you—there's no chance I'll make it through another summer here."

"We want you to get out of here."

"I won't ever get out now." Yoel sounded more placatory, as if he really wanted to make Yonatan understand. "I mean, we know: I'll never go back to being the person I used to be. Best case scenario is I'd be a fraction, maybe fifty percent. I'd be your weird friend in Jerusalem. And that's not going to happen. Your mind—once you lose control of it and it lets loose on you—is not something you can ever repair again. You just can't. If you could spend even one hour seeing the things that go through my field of vision at night, you wouldn't be talking about me going back anywhere."

"There's no choice. You don't know where you'll be in a few months, and we said you wouldn't do that to your parents."

"They'll be all right," Yoel grunted, as if discussing an issue that had already been resolved and no longer concerned him. He gave Yonatan a tender look, perhaps regretting his insensitivity, and Yonatan imagined that Yoel had just woken him from a long slumber. Perhaps he'd been asleep for the whole past two years, believing they were speaking candidly all that time when in fact the polite Yoel, who never wanted to be a burden on anyone, had been protecting him and, apart from a few uncontrollable flashes, had not been talking truthfully, not with this sort of sobriety.

He climbed wearily up the new road that twisted its way to their school, sheltering in the shade cast by the Music Academy. The dusty air dried his nostrils, and for a moment he hoped Yoel might stay where he was and they would meet later, outside or at his place; they were always good at short goodbyes, when a hostility had flared up between them that could not be easily dissolved. But Yoel straggled a few feet behind him, dragging his feet loudly over the asphalt—the neighbors, especially Ratzon, always used to get mad when they did that. In front of the basketball court, there was a hill of dry earth with a few stones, thistles, and clumps of scorched weeds sticking out, looking completely dead. He stopped and Yoel stood next to him. Perhaps they both had the same thought: were they looking at a piece of the old wadi? But that was impossible—they were already above it.

They walked further up, and the shade quavered on the road behind them. It was getting hotter, the sun beating down on the Music Academy rooftop. He was sweaty and thirsty. He cursed, stripped off his sweater and tied it around his waist.

"You used to wear those plaid shirts tied around your jeans," Yoel said, "Seattle-Grunge style, right?"

"You called it Gap style."

"That was some other failed effort, later, in senior year."

As they always did when things turned sour, they exchanged harmless little jabs about laughable events from the past, each trying to get the last word in.

The road curved to the left and they walked past a fenced-in lot where two tractors were hauling wooden logs. He almost told Yoel about Itamar's love of tractors, but he stopped himself. "Would you want to stand under the shovel and have me press the button?" he said.

Yoel tilted his head and frowned in exaggerated astonishment. "Very funny. Good one." They were both quiet. Then Yoel giggled: "I can't believe you left me to die out here in that yellow fog."

"And it almost worked," Yonatan said with a smile.

"If you hadn't changed your mind and run crying to Noam it would have."

"Stop fucking around, it's not funny." He already regretted his last few remarks—could he be harming Yoel? Precipitating something? But who could really tell. Talking about death, not talking about death, acknowledging its possibility, not acknowledging it—he couldn't really imagine a world without Yoel.

Behind the tractors, beyond the trees and the weeds and another bridge, they caught sight of the back gate to their school. There were signs hanging on it: "Can science and religion coexist?" "Do we make decisions out of free will?"

"I see they're still going strong with their Beit HaKerem liberalism," Yonatan quipped, pouncing on the chance to unite their voices. "Everything in Israel was so great before the Six-Day War and all that crap. They never give up."

"Yeah, pretty nauseating, those guys," Yoel hissed. "I've never seen such pains in the ass." He looked up and spat in an arc at the highway, and the spit disappeared before it fell to the road.

They turned their backs on the gate and looked out at the neighborhood again. Everything was blooming in the wadi below; a medley of white and pink petals, enclaves of green grass with birds hopping around as lithely as rabbits, tall pine trees full of cones. A few white clouds freckled with gray roamed the blue sky. Yoel looked at them and said it would rain soon. Feeling relieved, Yonatan put two cigarettes in his mouth, lit them and handed one to Yoel. For a moment he saw those mornings in his childhood bed, awakening with a first glance at the sky over the wadi—gray and uniform on the surface, but then revealing several shades blending and swirling. He looked sideways at Yoel, who sat down wearily on the road, and realized that it was the hope of a rain shower that would wipe away the signs of the looming summer that had lifted his spirits. But how could Yoel be talking about rain: it was May.

"It's kind of funny," Yoel said, "that you assumed I cared about you using our world for your books and then selling them here or in Mexico or on Mars. That's the last thing I care about. I always wanted you to be happy."

"I know." He had trouble speaking. The tenderness in Yoel's voice choked him up. "I wanted that for you too." He felt desperate. Yoel was trapped in an impenetrable bubble, his face bore the subtle imprint of a turmoil that nothing could eradicate, and Yonatan felt defenseless in the face of Yoel's powers of persuasion, which stripped away all Yonatan's explanations and dim hopes, scab by scab, until he began to see that there really was no way out. "But that stuff you said about fifty percent of you being left, that's just desperate guessing," he said, determined to recover. "You never know, maybe you'll go back to a different place, a better one? I know lots of people that happened to."

"Except I could tell you always knew it didn't mean anything," Yoel said, without responding to what he'd said at all. "You know it's not really an exorcism or any crap like that, even if while you're writing you believe that it is, that it's some kind of séance, and when you don't hear an answer you just fake the voices of the dead. But I get it now: the innocence protects you. It's what enabled you to get out of here."

Shira had once told him: it wasn't really their memories that held them together but rather the way they had discovered the world and continued to write its rules together, and in that fundamental sense nothing much had changed. It was their memories themselves that changed constantly, even if they didn't notice, but she did, because she sometimes listened to them.

"Remember that thing you said on that night near Jericho?"

"That was a rough night." Yoel picked up a little stone off the asphalt and bounced it around in his hands. "We were too dramatic, especially you, and the same with all the wadi stuff. It's not like the things that happened to us didn't happen to lots of other people too."

"You said you weren't going to hang around in the trench forever."

"Well, obviously." Yoel stood up. "I didn't want to, but look around." He held his hand up and ran it over the arc of all of Beit HaKerem, from the spot that was once a forest all the way to the military factory. "To put matters simply, the truth is that you're the park, and I'm the wadi."

"You'll come back, that's totally obvious."

"Obvious to you?"

"To anyone who knows you."

"You swear?"

"Of course, I'm certain of it."

"Swear on your son?" Yoel gave him a mocking look and gripped his arm. Yonatan found the touch horrifying and it took all his powers of restraint to not shake him off. "I didn't mean that, forget it," Yoel said and his chin drooped; his stubble brushed Yonatan's shoulder, "Don't answer, don't say anything, we don't have to talk anymore."

As they walked down the path further into the park, the sky grew overcast and sunk lower, enfolding the top of HaGuy Street until it looked as if a dark gate would soon be shut on the street. It started to drizzle, drops of water pooled on the shrubs' leaves, and he ran his finger over them and touched his dry lips. The bright colors from the park—the swings, the trees, the mauve stones—seemed to be wrapped in a faded shell. Everything here turned ugly so fast, he thought, surprised at how this pleased him. Yoel hugged his bare arms and rubbed them with his hands. They walked faster. To their right, two young women in skin-tight workout clothes picked up their mats, ropes and boxing gloves. Yonatan said they were sexy, and Yoel nodded: "But too young for us." The tension between them had dissipated.

They left the park and stood by Yonatan's car. Yoel leaned on the window but quickly straightened again, planning to say goodbye, and

275

said something like, "Knock 'em dead in Mexico City"—he couldn't hear exactly because the wind kicked up at that moment. He could see the window of the room he used to sleep in at Ratzon's. Branches thudded on the windowpane; they hadn't been there when he was a child. He could hear the buzz of the fluorescent light in that room, without which he had trouble falling asleep. He heard his voice demanding to come over for Yoel's mother's meatballs, even though Yoel seemed exhausted, his eyelids so heavy it looked as if he might fall asleep.

He knew the tricks Yoel used when he wanted to get rid of someone. People had always demanded pieces of his time, lots of people, too many, and Yoel had juggled them all, disappearing for a while and reappearing later, skillfully neutralizing any insult or anger he provoked. Not long ago, Yonatan had sat at home feverishly reading through all the emails and text messages and Facebook messages they'd exchanged, desperate to pinpoint the moment when things had started to go wrong. To his surprise, he found long stretches of time when they had not corresponded at all. He'd written to Yoel in January and Yoel hadn't answered until late March. He also learned that roughly eighty percent of their meetings had been his initiative. Had it ever been different? Toward the end, he reread a confrontation that was more severe than he'd remembered. They'd arranged to meet at a café in Tel Aviv after not seeing each other for a few months, but Yoel hadn't turned up or answered his messages, and texted him the next day to say he was sorry, he'd forgotten, he wasn't in great shape. Yonatan had cursed him but later wrote something conciliatory and demanded compensation, as they always did. Yoel asked what he suggested, and he wrote back something about having a drink together one night. At first Yoel replied, "I'll only drink Jameson," but then he wrote angrily: "You want compensation, you asshole?" and accused Yonatan of disappearing whenever he felt like it, for years, ignoring arrangements they'd made, and now he had the gall to make demands? Yonatan was stunned, and reread the message looking for signs of humor, perhaps an imitation of someone. Finally he wrote back, "You've made your position clear," and Yoel replied, "Exactly. I wish you the best." Then there was no correspondence for a few months.

This happened about a year before Yoel secluded himself at home. It was obvious that Yoel's fury was not spontaneous but something he'd been amassing for a long time. Yet if Yonatan had been able to swallow his pride and understood that Yoel's response—which was highly unusual—indicated his imbalance, could he have helped him before things turned really bad? The picture of Yoel he'd always seen was so constant in his mind that even when he heard from Tali that something was wrong, that Yoel had moved back in with his parents and hardly got out of bed, he hadn't been able to envisage it. Only the shock when he and Tali went to visit him together—and Yoel looked at them with hollow and sometimes terrified eyes, speaking one moment in his familiar tone about books and politics and getting laid, and the next stuttering, with lots of silences, losing interest mid-sentence, chain-smoking, describing his disgust with summer in Jerusalem and the terrible mistakes he'd made, not listening to a word Yonatan said—undermined the picture of Yoel that had been frozen in his mind for all those years.

He moved away from Yoel and walked up to his building, and a moment later Yoel caught up and they turned on the light in the stairwell and walked upstairs together. Once Yoel had accepted that Yonatan was coming over, he told him not to worry, this time they'd give him a big serving—a reference to his age-old claim that they didn't provide enough food at Yoel's and you always had to ask for seconds. He remembered the non-kosher café downtown that used to serve fried eggs with bacon, where Yoel would ask for every dish he ordered, even soup, to come with a side of bacon, as a sort of youthful rebellion; unlike all the other kids, Yoel rarely fought with his parents.

Yoel's parents were sitting on the living room couch as if they'd been waiting for them. They welcomed Yonatan warmly and asked how Itamar and Shira were, and Yoel's mother wanted to see a picture, "but show me in a little while." Their faces were blank, without the hopefulness he'd seen in the early days—when they'd still viewed every visit as an opportunity, dim as it may be, for a return to the trajectory Yoel had abandoned. It always ended with bitter disappointment, a few hours or days later. Yonatan had disappointed them, and they did not bother to hide it. After the trip to Ireland, which hadn't changed a thing, they'd still pinned hopes on him, but those were eventually dashed, too, and now they were too exhausted to entertain guests who did not have the power to help their son.

Yoel put his arm around Yonatan's shoulder and he smelled oranges, cigarettes and sweat. "Give the kid some food, he's got no family," Yoel called out and they all laughed. Yoel's mother said, "He's always had a home here," and he remembered how, after his mother's death, he'd grown close to Yoel's mother, or rather, he'd spent a lot of time in their home with Yoel and Tali—the three of them had even slept in Yoel's room for the seven days of shiva. He must have wanted her closeness, although he hadn't admitted it because the desire seemed embarrassingly simple. Sometimes he and Yoel's mother talked alone, but he realized she wasn't interested in him except insofar as he was Yoel's friend, and that her attitude to him was merely a reflection of the relationship between him and Yoel in that particular week or month. She did not speak about his mother much, perhaps because his mother was one of the few people who did not find Yoel impressive, and this became more acute when she got ill. In the years after her death, Yoel insisted that he'd always liked Yonatan's mother, "but I guess there wasn't a connection." Once when they were drunk, Yonatan had told Yoel that he knew she hadn't liked him, and joked that perhaps it was because they were both Mizrahis in denial and his mother wanted him to be friends with the pure whites in the neighborhood, like Ran Horesh. Yoel's mother never said a bad word about Yonatan's mother, but it was clear that she hadn't forgiven her for the insult; she believed that only a flawed person could fail to respond to her son's charms.

They sat down in the living room, at a long wooden table that was covered with a white floral cloth. They were joined by Yoel's sister Rachel, who'd just earned her teaching certificate, and chatted with Yoel's parents about politics. Yonatan and Yoel's father did most of the talking, while Yoel exchanged whispers with his mother and made a few political comments meant, as usual, to bridge the gaps between Yonatan and his father and show that in fact they did not disagree on the big issues. The wind screeched against the living room door, but no one got up to shut it.

Rachel, with her black curly hair in a tight braid, did not touch the rice and meatballs, and stayed out of the political discussion. To everyone's annoyance, she insisted on hearing about their walk in the park, the apartment they'd looked at in Tel Aviv last month, and the job offer Yoel had expressed interest in not long ago. The conversation died down and for some time they all sat in silence.

Yoel was dimly aware that Yonatan and Rachel talked on the phone at least once a month, because she oversaw all his health issues and told Yonatan about the medications, the therapists, the psychiatrists, the diagnoses, the magnets, the electricity, all the things Yoel never mentioned. Yoel was angry when he first realized she was relaying details about his treatments to Yonatan, but he no longer cared. When Yonatan asked Yoel about the treatments, he snapped that it wasn't interesting and nothing was helping. Rachel had also told him about the things that preoccupied Yoel, like when he'd decided there was no atonement for the big mistakes of his life and conducted trials for all his friends, assessing their influence on the wrong paths he'd taken, presenting arguments for both the prosecution and the defense, and finally deciding on the severity—or leniency—of the sentence. There were some friends he refused to see after these trials, and some he acquitted or forgave over time. When Yonatan insisted that Rachel tell him about the trial Yoel had held for him, she confessed that he'd spoken of him harshly but had ultimately granted him a partial acquittal. And Tali? Yoel's sister laughed and said he hadn't held a trial for Tali; he said she wasn't to blame for anything, that she was the only one who could have saved him but now it was too late.

After dinner they went out to smoke on the balcony. Evening had fallen, and Yonatan stared across the street at his old window. A white curtain fluttered there, and behind it he saw a white wall, a clock and a picture. He hadn't checked his phone for hours: he must have missed calls from Shira. Itamar would be home from daycare, and he wasn't there to greet him. He thought about all the work he had to do. He needed to read books in English by the authors who were doing festival events with him, at least a few pages of each, and answer questionnaires from the Mexican press: Are you in touch with Palestinian writers? Which Mexican author do you admire? How many writers from the continent do you even know? Of course he would have to come up with somewhat sophisticated responses, not just list writers everyone knew like Carlos Fuentes, Juan Rulfo or Roberto Bolaño. A Mexican author had once advised him that it was best "to note a writer that even a lot of Mexican intellectuals have never heard of, someone who hasn't been translated into any language—hell, someone who isn't even published! That's the kind of thing they really appreciate here."

Yoel stubbed out his cigarette on the balcony railing and dropped it onto the lawn, and said in a secretive voice that he had a bottle of vodka hidden in his closet because he wasn't allowed to drink: "You up for it?" Yonatan put his hand on Yoel's shoulder: "Absolutely!" Arm in arm, they walked to his room past Rachel and their parents, who were staring at a muted show on the television. In the hallway, Yoel ran his fingers along the wall, and Yonatan ran his on the opposite wall, and he had no doubt that they were both remembering when Yoel's dad caught them playing poker for money in the ninth grade and threw the pack of cards out the window. When they pushed open his bedroom door, which always got stuck in the frame, Yoel said, "Here we are, naked, returning to ground zero."

SUMMER

Sometimes he wants to tell Itamar about the dead. Not exactly tell him—just make sure he knows these people once existed. Itamar sits on his lap, running his fingers over his arm while they look at pictures on the phone together—mom, dad, child—and he is tempted to skip to pictures of Yoel and his mother, so the boy will see their faces, even for an instant, in a medley of other faces. It seems illogical to him that his son will not know that these people were in the world. But at the last minute he always changes his mind. Once he and Itamar were walking, holding hands, down the hill near the yellow building where Yoel lived before he left Tel Aviv. He sang an Israeli rock song he used to like: *You might find something to write about,* and Itamar giggled the next lyrics: *Not something deep, something sweet, a love story.* He could have avoided the street, as he usually did, but something drove him there with Itamar. He looked up at the third floor, where Yoel had lived for years—the place where they'd spent days and nights, where Yoel had shattered, the place he'd left as a changed man to go back home—and tried to find something to say. The building somehow looked emptied, as if everything had been sucked out of it and it was now a mere replica of the life that once was, perfect and therefore so painful. The indifference of inanimate objects to the life that had been around them and inside them—he never really got used to that. Finally he said to Itamar, "Look how pretty that building is." A dull pain spread through his body when Itamar remarked, "Yellow house."

When they got home, Itamar told Shira: "Daddy, yellow house."

"Which house?" she asked.

"Daddy, yellow-yellow house," Itamar repeated.

Shira asked, "Did Daddy show you a yellow house?"

Yonatan stood looking at the two of them curled up on the couch, like a boy afraid he would get caught.

The seasons of the year, weekends, holidays, parties at kindergarten, vacations, rituals every day and every week, the division of labor, lists on the fridge—Itamar's schedule, and therefore theirs too, filled up with events and customs, and the passing of time once again took on the outline of the place they lived in, as if they'd gone back to listening to its rhythm, its ceremonies, its songs, as they'd done in childhood. On autumn and winter days he imagined the sunlight striking narrow, filthy streets with no trees, deterring any breeze, and how every morning he would reach Itamar's kindergarten drenched with sweat. He knew it took patience, moderation and fortitude to get through a Tel Aviv summer, and he was afraid he would not have the strength for it. But summer came and he grew accustomed to it.

In the mornings the sky is high and clear, glimmering in a bright purple-blue. He is impressed by its beauty, and teaches Itamar to be impressed. He learns the names of flowers and trees, learns species of butterflies and birds, learns about the tide—he never imagined how many simple things he did not know. They learn to love the lengthening daylight hours, when the leaves rustle on the trees around their house, a soft breeze blows into the room to whirl the dusty, sweaty air they breathe. They learn to love the graying, blurring sky that leans onto their rooftop and hides airplanes in its folds.

Itamar is aware of every aircraft, near or far. Sometimes he points and shouts, "Airplane!" and Yonatan spots something behind a cluster of clouds, but sometimes by the time he looks up the airplane is gone. Itamar's interest in airplanes is connected with Yonatan's travels—in the boy's world he has always just come home, even if he hasn't traveled for months. Itamar's perception confirms his own sense that his presence in the home is somehow unsteady. Not his physical presence, because he spends a lot of time with the boy, but even though at times he is fully there, playing and showering him with hugs and kisses and enticing him to talk, the next moment he'll be gone, pulled out of his own body to watch the events in his own home from the outside. He knows that Itamar notices these moments when his presence blurs, that he watches suspiciously as his father battles his way back into his body with exaggerated gestures of affection, feeble questions, half-hearted offers to play.

Shira says that she only understands these past few years when she reads his books. It happens to her with every new book: she looks back on many of their exchanges, which had seemed coincidental—why he asked certain questions, dwelled on certain topics, interrogated her about an experience or a choice of dress—and understands that he was not really present. What she doesn't say, although it's on the tip of her tongue, and his, is that when she reads his books she feels cheated, sometimes even betrayed. That his writing molds intimate moments from her memory into different, unfamiliar shapes and she can no longer cling to them, no longer draw strength from them, no longer find comfort in evidence of their intimacy on days when their love seems faded. He wonders if this is what he has learned: to slip away from a place while still being there. And that his and Yoel's fear of being trapped in a life from which no other possibilities branch off still lives in him, except that he has constructed a place he can always retreat into, while Yoel had no such place and, therefore, regarded Yonatan with both admiration and contempt.

Tali said that when Yoel and Yonatan were together, their fears were united, but when each of them returned to his own world, they split off. She also said that the things Shira supposedly discovered in his books could also lead to the opposite conclusion about their love: Shira was growing alienated from him, and she chose to see things— things that might be beautiful—in a different light because she did not believe she could help him.

One night Itamar had a high fever. He lay in bed convulsing and was unresponsive when they called his name, and they rushed him to the hospital. For weeks afterwards, Yonatan was afraid to retreat into his absences when he was at home. He was alert, prepared for any development, and examined every detail of his behavior that night— every minute wasted, every flash of panic, every error or inattention. He made sure he had the phone numbers of several taxi companies and the ambulance, examined the fastest routes from their house to Ichilov Hospital, and every night before they fell asleep he made sure both their cell phones were charged. When he was younger, his father once told him that he only paid attention to detail and demonstrated thoroughness when he was writing, and that no one who knew him could understand it. But now he doggedly transferred those calcula- tions—examining the minutiae of every plot twist, filling out every facet of his fictional world, handling all the little discrepancies—to his plans in case they had to rush Itamar to the hospital again. He let Shira in on only a small portion of these scenarios, because he was afraid of her reaction, but when he was leaving for a two-day trip to Jerusalem, he couldn't hold back and made her sit down with the notebook where he'd written everything. She sat on the couch as he went through it, page by page. Finally, she gave him an astonished look and said: "It's been four months since we were at the ER. What disaster are you really preparing for?"

Sometimes he opens his eyes in the morning and wants to scream.

He and Shira curl up on the couch one night, watching footage from the two-year memorial for his mother. The twentieth anniversary of her death is coming up, and he and his father are planning to gather friends and family to watch the old event together. Earlier in the week he digitized the dusty videotape Yoel found that day in the storage unit, and burned CDs to give out to the guests. On the computer screen they see a young man in a long black coat that is too big and makes his body look rectangular. His hair is long and tangled and his complexion pale. He drums his hands on the sides of the podium and does not look up at the audience even once, keeping his eyes on a yellow piece of paper. "Many daughters have done valiantly, but thou excellest them all," he concludes and steps off the stage. Yonatan doesn't remember using that quote from Proverbs: it sounds flowery, exaggerated, unrelated to his mother. A week before the memorial he'd gone to see a fellow soldier he knew, whose father ran a yeshiva in a settlement. (They'd already exchanged all the predictable barbs—You're Arab-lovers, you're murderers, you're giving away the land, you're robbing the land, you cried like babies after Rabin was assassinated, you danced like assholes.) He'd decided he needed a biblical quote to pull his eulogy together, an imitation of something, perhaps the floweriness of a Moshe Dayan speech that he and his father had once read. He had asked to speak at the memorial, although no one had expected him to, and he believed it was appropriate to quote from the scriptures: this was the first time anyone except his mother would hear something he'd written. Now he hates that soldier for not giving him a better verse.

When the screen goes dark and they hear a soft chorus singing 'U'netaneh Tokef,' a liturgical song his mother liked, Shira asks when he last watched the tape. He lies and says it was a few years ago, and does not tell her that what has haunted him and made him avoid ever watching it, the thing that he had trouble even contemplating, was that his mother would have preferred that he not get up to describe her and admit his weaknesses and ask forgiveness "from the woman I did not know how to talk to, and to whom I caused sorrow, but who was at the top of my priorities," or something like that.

He saw her face before his eyes on many mornings, and it was not any different with Yoel so far—in fact it was worse. For months, perhaps a year, the dead person's face was always there, and then there would be the occasional awakening when he would shake him off, and then he would wake up and not see him at all, and finally he would see him only rarely and would sometimes think of him without pain stabbing his chest. But then he would see the face again and the pain would strike as if it had only been a week since his death. There was no clear movement in one direction—getting further away from the death of a loved one—but rather loops, intersections, U-turns. And there was the wildness of memory.

———

When he woke up in the hotel in the early evening, a blurry newspaper clipping flickered on his phone screen. He held the phone closer—it was slippery and smelled of beer and sweat—took a deep breath and enlarged the picture: black-and-white squares with lots of words and numbers down the side. His eyes moistened and stung. Something floated in his right eye, a speck of glass or a crumb; he could follow it from right to left, as though he were looking into his own eye. Perhaps when he'd crashed into bed before dawn, after saying goodbye to Carlos and Elizabeth on the rooftop—he'd stayed there to watch them leave the hotel, two spots of tar, granted human features for a moment by the glimmer of dawn, until they disappeared among the trees—he hadn't noticed that there was still some powder on the pillow and sheets, and now it was in his eyes.

He picked up a bottle of water from the nightstand, tipped it onto his eyes and rinsed them. The water trickled down his chest. He felt better. He looked at the image again. It was a cryptic crossword, with one of the clues circled in red pen: "The boy who walked through fire sees no vineyard in the coastal city." He assumed his father had sent the picture and that the answer had something to do with his name or one of his book titles. He read the clue a few times but hadn't the faintest idea of the answer.

He was pleased to find no other messages. A lightness caressed his limbs, which seemed to still hold the memory of the warmth they'd been swaddled in last night on the rooftop. He played "The Rat" by The Walkmen on his laptop, and the guitar sounds lit up a wild spark in him—when had his mind turned into a fear machine, anyway? He looked at the picture again, then sent it to a Facebook group, to Tali and Shira, to two other friends, and finally to Yoel: it occurred to him that the clue had something to do with Beit HaKerem, because of the vineyard—*kerem*. He wasn't expecting Yoel to answer or even see the message; he'd sent him a few from Mexico and Yoel hadn't responded.

Then he smoked a cigarette by the pool. A group of young people drinking beer and champagne was taking up most of the tables. One of them was talking in a faint Russian accent to a girl in a white sundress who rolled a silver pipe between her fingers, about how his father was in prison because he'd shot two people at a party, like that rapper 50 Cent. He told her they didn't talk anymore, and that he wanted to be a professional golfer. She said she was going home to Houston to open a business, maybe a boutique hotel or a little restaurant. Her chestnut hair fluttered in the wind when they raised their champagne flutes, and after she'd had a few sips she tipped her head back, and took a puff from the pipe. A ribbon of colorful paper stuck out from her glass.

He went back to his room. The carpet was littered with miniature bottles, empty bags of chips, candy bar wrappings, a few cigarette butts, damp towels, a white hair ribbon. He shoved everything into the trash can. Then he sat down at the desk, pushed open the door to the garden with his foot, and savored the breeze.

Shira answered: It's easy, but you can solve it on your own.

Talia wrote: WTF.

Yoel wrote: So the boy doesn't see Beit HaKerem from Tel Aviv?

Stunned that Yoel had responded, he started writing messages only to erase them. He tried a friendly admonition, then loving words, then casual amusement. Finally, wrote: I don't know, we're bad at this stuff, aren't we?

Yoel: Maybe not so much anymore.

He sent Yoel a private message: So you've finally showed up. How are you?

Outside the hotel, waves were surging in the large sunken basin, spraying white foam. For the first time he also noticed that the basin itself was swaying back and forth slightly, and for some time he stood watching it, trying to decide if the dizzying movement of the waves was simulating the motion of the basin or if it really was moving. It was one of those things that never bothered him except when he was writing, and then he became aware of minute details everywhere and filled entire notebooks describing them.

The quiet in the hotel made him gloomy. He went back to his room and started packing, piling up dirty laundry, shoving it into plastic bags which he placed on the bottom of the suitcase, then books which he'd been given by writers at the festival.

When he heard the knocks he hoped he was dreaming. As they got louder, he assumed he was awake. He sat down on his bed in the dark and listened. Colorful moths flitted around the lamp outside, storming the light only to recoil. He focused on them while a faint voice whispered that he had one more blink of an eye, one final flutter in the disoriented seam between consciousness and unconsciousness, and then there would be resolution. He knew it already. The knocking grew louder still. He got up and threw a towel over his shoulders. As soon as his hand touched the door, the scene became fully coherent.

A hotel worker whose face he did not recognize pointed to the room phone and said something in Spanish. He looked around for his cell phone in the tangle of sheets. His fingers gripped the curtain when the hotel phone rang. He picked up the receiver and heard Shira's voice dimly, as if he'd been fished out of a dream. She said Rachel had called her because she couldn't get hold of him, and that it was the last thing she wanted to have to tell him.

He heard footsteps in the hallway, whispers, then a buzz. Sometimes in the middle of the night the hallway lights creaked and hummed, and in the morning everything was quiet again. Two big moths floated around the lamp in the garden, and then there were four.

"I have to call Rachel," he said.

Shira said she didn't want him to be alone, and he said yes, okay, and asked her not to be alone with Itamar, to call her parents: Talk to them now, he repeated, talk to them now. He hung up, kneeled on the floor and searched for his cell phone. He crawled around the bed between towels and sweaty shirts and underwear and rolled up bills of money, until he found it. He turned off the lamp, sat leaning on the wall, and called Rachel.

Yoel is gone, she said. Their father had found him at 4 a.m., unresponsive. He realized she'd already told lots of people: it was 10 a.m. in Israel. We've lost him, she said, and he murmured, Yes. Maybe we lost him a long time ago, she said. You did everything for him, he told her, you couldn't do anything more. He stared at the moths in the garden, making colorful loops and arcs in the beam of light, little whirlwinds of light dancing in the air. He did not ask any questions, though perhaps she was expecting him to, and he prayed she would not give any more details. They were quiet. Finally she said the funeral would be on Monday at midday. He heard chairs moving, voices talking. She said they'd see him at the funeral.

He looked at the screen again and reread Yoel's answer, sent exactly nine hours earlier. It was all planned by then, probably. "Write something nice about me," Yoel had told him in one of those conversations he'd always been in a hurry to cut off. "Give the whole thing a romantic, inspirational touch, don't be a dick." He lost all sensation in his body, as if he'd become an airy, weightless dream figure. He put his hands on the textured wall and rubbed them hard until his right wrist bled, and at once his body was slammed back to the ground. He remembered how he'd stood on his balcony and told a friend that one morning they would wake up and Yoel would be gone. But even when he'd said it clearly, declaring that this was how things were, still there was a part in the recess of his heart—unsteady, swelling and shrinking, but always there—that believed it would not really happen. And perhaps he'd said it to that friend to trick hope into revealing itself and making its argument.

Shira asked if he'd called anyone, and he lied and said yes, people were coming to see him soon. She said: You didn't call anyone, did you? He answered: No. She asked him to describe the hotel room. He turned on the light. He said he was standing at the foot of the bed and there was a desk with a lamp, and a textured white wall with a black-and-white photograph of children running to the sea, and on the carpet was a suitcase, and outside there were butterflies swirling around the light. She asked if he wanted to lie on the bed and talk. He didn't answer. She said he would get through this night and then they would be together again, the three of them. He said he would get through this night, and he stared at the shirts hanging in the closet, scrutinizing the creases around the collars.

He hurried down the hallway and walked out of the hotel. Cold gusts of air hit him, scratching his face with their fingernails as if the wind had split up into sharp gusts that dug into him from every direction. He felt lots of little fires burning on his skin. The top of the only tree in front of the hotel slammed against the wall. A bundle of leaves flew over him when he stopped next to the two doormen in black coats huddled in the wooden hut with a leaking roof. It was raining, he realized. He asked them for a light and one of them held out a lighter. He held it but his hand must have been shaking, because the doorman took it and lit his cigarette, then pointed to a bench: *Señor, sentarse en el banco.* He heard bells ringing and his voice asking, in Hebrew: Do you hear the bells? He stared at the stains and rips in their uniforms— like Yoel's uniform in that hotel he'd worked at. At first glance they always looked shiny and perfect, but if you looked closer you found frayed threads, stains, unmatched buttons. Yoel said: Some things in this world are only good for one look.

The water in the marble basin frothed. He noticed a rubbery taste in his mouth from the cigarette, which had gone out. Shiny black cars slid silently onto the driveway and they looked massive, the way objects in his room used to when he was feverish. A swarm of bronzed young men poured out of the cars, wearing tailored pants and button-down shirts, all carrying blazers folded over one arm and rolling black suitcases. They joked and laughed, anticipating the pleasures of the next few days. He watched them until they merged into one big ball of light rolling through the lobby. Perhaps he hadn't really understood all of Yoel's talk about summer, treating it as a noise he had to silence so that they could talk about the really important things—coming back to life, a hopeful future, an apartment in Tel Aviv, a job. He'd tried to use memories of the past to reignite Yoel's lust for life. "I've had thirty-five wonderful years in the world," Yoel had said, and he'd alluded to the summer and to his own death with gravity. He seemed to have wanted Yonatan's opinion, as if he believed Yonatan had access to something unseen, even asking him how he felt when he killed off a character he was attached to in his books. But Yonatan had insisted on diverting their conversation back to life and the possibilities it held, even on the day when they'd stood at the top of the park looking out on Beit HaKerem and had contemplated Yoel's death. It was exactly what everyone used to do to his mother in hospital: those who are close to death want to talk about it, but no one really listens to them. We purport to want to cheer up the dying and instill them with hope, but in fact we don't want to hear everything, preferring that death surprise us a little, even when we have all the evidence before us. And if Yonatan had truly listened to all that talk of death and the harsh summer? Everything would have been exactly the same, people would tell him. But he would never know.

In the end it was fairly simple: they wanted Yoel—even fifty percent of him—to stay at his parents' home, in his old room, even when he was lying in bed in the dark for days on end without talking to anyone, even when he no longer took an interest in them, when he frightened them, when he made them doubt the foundations of their lives, even when they knew Yoel didn't really care if they existed or vanished forever. They wanted him to be, and Yoel did not want to be, because in the end it was him lying on his childhood bed, looking at the ceiling and seeing the things he saw, and he did not want to see them anymore.

The chiming of bells had given way to the trickling of water in the basin. The pictures I'm seeing are too lucid, he thought, and so are the memories. It's supposed to be different, I'm supposed to be stunned. Or perhaps it only blurs in retrospect, and years later you say: we were in a blur, we didn't see anything, it was all glinting and graying and igniting and blackening. When in fact we were *too* clear-sighted when they died.

He stood up and his legs had fallen asleep and they hurt. In the lobby he looked at the digital bulletin board where upcoming events were displayed. It would be morning soon. He prayed it would come quick. He wandered from one wing to the next—California, St. Petersburg, he got lost in Cairo—until he was at his door. Inside, he sat down on the bed and looked around. Then he went to the closet and started folding clothes and placing them in the suitcase: pants, T-shirts, a scarf and sweaters, black shoes. He took the shirts off the hangers, folded them and put them on top of the pile, and when daylight broke and the last of the moths were gone, he fastened the suitcase shut and dragged it to the door.

———

In the afternoons of the final days of summer, before Itamar started kindergarten, they often went to the beach. At five they would leave home and stroll down Bograshov Street, switching from one sidewalk to the other in a set order; the floodlit sections and the shady ones always followed the same pattern. He talked constantly to Itamar in the stroller, asking him more and more questions, so that he could hear his voice when he could not see his face. They crossed at the big intersection, stayed close to the stone wall along the narrow street, walked down a staircase, and there was the sea. There was always something sudden in that moment of revelation, and the sight expanded his heart. He swung Itamar up and pointed to the sea, wondering if the boy felt something too.

A few times he imagined that there on the sand—with the wind in his face, the water lapping at his feet, as he held hands with Itamar in the waves—his body and soul were airing out, taking respite from the sweltering expanse whose borders were constantly being redrawn around him. He never felt so much a prisoner of his memories as he did at the end of summer. And it was not only memories: he was watching Itamar growing up, knowing that in a few years the boy would lose interest in Shira. Sometimes Shira, amused, said she knew it was going to happen, and he wanted to warn her that she was only laughing because she didn't understand; you cannot understand a thing like that until it happens. There, on the sand, a tremor ran through his body at the vision of eight-year-old Itamar's betrayal, even as he bounced the two-year-old boy in his arms. He wondered if it really was the future picture that worried him, because after all the foolish notion of a child betraying his mother was also a memory. "What do you call a memory that isn't exactly a memory?" he asked Itamar, and the boy kicked sand in the air and shrieked: "Memory!"

Sometimes when they walked away from the beach, before evening fell, and he was sweaty and tired and itchy, he thought he must look like that man who performs the tasks of life, fights the fights, talks the talk and worries the worries, and keeps the books: the man whom Yoel used to describe with such contempt, the man he had feared he would become—and now never would. Yonatan had sometimes feared it too. But ultimately, there are those who leave and those who stay, and the ones who stay not only have the years ahead of them, but also all the time that has gone, with its pictures that emerge sometimes, rising from the depths, as new in one's mind as the current experiences, changing one's perception of an entire era in the blink of an eye. When the gray glass sky sheltered the city, he pushed Itamar home in the stroller and the boy dozed, and he touched his neck to check his body temperature, then bent over and took his shoes off, shook the sand out, put them in a bag, drew the shelter over the stroller and walked up the street.

There were mosquitoes everywhere—on the walls, on the ceilings, on the pictures and the books—and they attacked them, killing them with a broom or a magazine, or with hands already bleeding, until, approaching midnight, they decided there was no choice but to sleep in the living room, where it was cooler because of the wind from the wadi, and they spread a sheet over the rug and lay down, the four of them—Mom, Dad, Shaul and him—and kept bumping into each other, hands, feet and arms squirming because there wasn't enough room, and Dad said, "Enough, it's time to sleep," but then he cleared his throat and Shaul said, "Quiet, we're sleeping as of…now!" and after a minute Dad started snoring and they laughed, and Mom said, "Everyone go to sleep now, no talking," in a clear bell of a voice—for the first time since she'd died he could hear the sound of her voice, in the middle of bustling Bograshov Street—and Shaul burped and laughed, and Mom grumbled that they were pushing her onto the balcony, and Dad moved his arm to make room and crushed him with his large body, and he let out a screech that made Shaul jump, and a soft breeze blew on their faces, and the warmth from Dad and Shaul flowed into his body from either side, and the shadows of the trees trembled on the walls in the light patches cast by the streetlamps, and he was moved by their beauty and even more so by the fact that there was no school tomorrow, that Shaul had just arrived and would stay for several weeks, and that all the summer he could imagine was still ahead.

Tel Aviv
2015–2018